D0926236

FIRESTORM

by CLAUDINE T. GRIGGS

FIRESTORM

A NOVEL

CLAUDINE T. GRIGGS

ANANKE PRESS

Firestorm
Published by Ananke Press
Copyright © 2022 by Claudine T. Griggs
All rights reserved

This is a work of fiction. Names, characters, businesses, places, events, locales, and incidents are either the products of the author's imagination or used in a fictitious manner. Any resemblance to actual persons, living or dead, or actual events is purely coincidental. All rights reserved, including the right to reproduce this book or portions thereof in any form without the express permission of the publisher.

Interior and cover design by Ananke Press

ISBN: 978-1-7341720-9-6 (paperback)

Ananke Press
178 Columbus Avenue, #230137, New York, NY 10023
anankepress.com
info@anankepress.com

Contents

Foreword

I'm very pleased with this Ananke Press collection of twenty-three of my speculative stories, and I am likewise pleased to have learned over the years that short-form fiction is much more meaningful to me than I would have otherwise imagined. I always thought, "Books are the mark of a real writer. Articles and stories are merely a prelude to the real." So, to paraphrase a scene from *The Matrix*, what is *real*? In partial answer to that question I've selected this grouping of stories. They matter to me; they examine qualities of the human condition; many were fun to write; some were exciting; a few were torture. And my fiction has offered me surprising success—via publication, reader response, and/or authorial satisfaction—in a genre that I admire and hold dear.

"Firestorm" was my first accepted science fiction (SF) story, which was published by *Zahir* in January 2011. It was not my first publication because I had written lots of nonfiction over the years, but the glory of scoring in my first-love genre offered me a thrill that few academic or journalistic publications could top. And having been a college writing instructor for so long, in a career field where speculative stories were terribly undervalued, "Firestorm" offered multiple levels of authorial satisfaction. Also, I really like this story about a critically burned woman who seems to hold her lost beauty above everything else in life.

If you enjoy time-travel speculation, try "Neverland through the Looking Glass," "The Self-Murder Solution," or "One Million Years in a Day." I've been fascinated (obsessed?) with time travel since I discovered H.G. Wells' *The Time Machine* in fifth grade, and I won't reveal how many times that I read that book or watched the 1960 George Pal movie…. "The Self-Murder Solution" describes a suicide crisis a few hundred years in the future from the point of view of a contemporary woman who tries to kill herself and, consequently, ends up in this new world. I'm not sure whether I like her or her data-based conclusions very much, but I do like this woman's uncompromising independence. And in "One Million Years in a Day," an up-close survey of the supermassive black hole at the center of our Milky Way Galaxy goes awry when a pilot erroneously crosses the event horizon and finds that the distorted space-time on the inside may offer her a way home. In "Neverland through the Looking Glass," just about everything that can go wrong does, and the culpable scientific and military people try to undo the damage within a narrow window of opportunity. (I'm an Air Force veteran who generally likes the discipline of uniformed services, but some of these characters are…, well, they're desperate, so maybe I can't blame them.)

There are also three trans-stories in the mix: "Informed Consent," "Yes, Dear, Breast Cancer can Kill a Trans Woman," and "The Gender Blender." I am a male-to-female transsexual, and these stories (all of which have been previously published) are drawn from my experience as an early transitioned (1974) trans woman. These were not good years for gender diversity, gender fluidity, or just surviving outside the stone-cold gender binaries of the 1960s and early 70s. "Informed Consent" is based on my desperate and failed attempts in 1974-77 to find a competent and ethical surgeon. "Cancer can Kill" follows, closely, my internal debates after I was diagnosed with breast cancer in 2011; part of me still wishes I had followed my protagonist's example. And "The Gender Blender" is a disturbing tale (even for me) of a trans woman and a trans man who both struggle to value themselves and to clone a genetically identical child that will be "normal."

Dystopian stories include "Ride the Snake," "Maiden Voyage of the Fearless," and "The Black Hole: A Tale for Men and Women Who Aren't Trying to Kill Feminism." "Ride the Snake" was written, almost scene for scene, from a dream I had in 2010 that describes a "golden" future that is a little bit more than tarnished. I scribbled a first draft the morning after the dream, which still gives me chills. And because I often struggle with depression and anxiety, "The Maiden Voyage" focuses on a miracle cure for anxieties of all kinds. I don't typically believe in miracles, but in this story, my protagonist is slipped the Magical Mickey Finn and begins to make wondrous gains that soon seem a little too wondrous. Many readers have said, "…." Oh, never mind what they said. Read the story and let's see what you think about medical miracles. And regarding the "Black Hole," I am a feminist, but I believe that women in western civilization might be a couple crises away from catastrophic oppression. I worry about the status of women in this world and our future world. And I really worry about the kind of people who would happily—nay, enthusiastically—denigrate that status.

If you like hard science fiction, try "The Cold Waters of Europa" (a recreational diving expedition goes wrong with the help of eco-terrorists), "Helping Hand" (a seriously tough stranded astronaut proves that she is seriously tough), or "Raptures of the Deep" (what could possibly turn sideways when exploring the Mariana Trench?). If you want a little humor and/or word play, there are "Growing Up Human" (cybernetic creatures try to be like people), "The Mimic" (one character accuses the other of being an alien and vice versa), or "Aliens Anonymous" (a quasi-twelve-step program to help people cope with their emotional distress after having been abducted). "Electro Genesis" is a novelette about a woman who survives an electric jolt to the brain and is dying at the same time her cognitive abilities are expanding. To me, the protagonist seems like Charlie Gordon blended with too much Norman Bates. And in "Center of the Universe," astronomers begin to worry when all the visible stars, except Sol, appear to be growing dimmer at a constant rate.

In "The Predator Trap," a quirky and unpopular entomology student solves a missing-person mystery without intending to, finds a new species during her field research, and ultimately…well, I don't want to go there. "Crime Warp" mixes science fiction and fantasy when a junior professor discovers that worldwide crime rates are falling dramatically; he also locates a lone Southern California woman who claims to have returned from the dead and to know why crime is on the slide. "Death After Dying" takes a look at the possibility of post-mortem brain waves and quasi-life-after-death experiences of the recently departed. And "The Final Launch" centers on a kick-ass Air Force Colonel who will stop at nothing to launch her missile after the orders come through, but her silo partner isn't so sure. And the most recently added story, "The Conservationist Hunter," is an adult fairy tale about big-game hunting on a lush planet in the Wolf 359 star system.

I write about many topics in this collection—time travel, science gone right and wrong, bad guys and good guys, gender identity, social ostracism, death, who we are, and where we might be headed. But almost every tale examines some aspect of the human condition. We are traveling day by day into the future. Technology will expand. People will live and die, but I trust that humans will be recognizably human regardless of the scientific and industrial marvels that they find in ten years or a million. I basically like our species and believe in them. And in the long run, I don't think social dystopias have a chance among humans. I think we're headed for a bountiful civilization where good people do good things in quantities that far exceed the abilities of "bad guys" to hold us down.

"Science fiction" and/or "speculative fiction" are genres of hope. And despite the many stories that describe darkness or downright destruction (which I often enjoy), this hope can help lead the world toward a progressively better future for an increasing number of people. Such fiction is the stuff of dreams—and dreams are conspicuously human.

— Claudine T. Griggs

FIRESTORM

Journal Entry #1:

Most bad accidents happen in routine moments that suddenly skew into disaster. To stub a toe and fall in the backyard is no big deal. Embarrassment, a few curses, and on with the day. Stub that same toe at the edge of the Grand Canyon and they pack your body out on a burro.

My stumble happened as I was fueling my Subaru Outback. The pump's automatic shutoff failed, the tank overflowed, and a splash of gasoline trickled on the ground. Bland, really. This would normally produce a foul smell, fuel evaporation, and some extra air pollution. Probably happens a hundred times a day, maybe thousands. In this instance, however, that minor bit of nothing was accompanied by a static spark, and Wham! I was up to my Wonder Bra in flames. But even that should have been relatively inconsequential—a vaporous mist, a small fire, and a madwoman dash out of harm's way. Then the fire department could clean up the after-burn, slap a few bandages, and cite the station owner for faulty equipment, environmental degradation, or unclean restrooms.

But accidents don't follow scripts. I was standing at the Canyon and didn't know it.

In an irreconcilable moment, I reflexively jerked the nozzle out of the filler duct, which not only fed the fire but provided air and access to the tank. It spilled its guts. I was engulfed by the Big Bang, lost my footing, and rolled to the asphalt with thirteen gallons of unleaded regular, where I apparently kicked and screamed until somebody pulled me out.

I remember trying to stand and run, but my feet skated on Brimstone Pond. The second time I went down, I choked on gasoline and blackness. As an ironic joke, the puddle seemed cool. When I came to, the only viable skin on my body was a small stretch of forearm that I had pressed against my eyes along with the corresponding face protected by the forearm. The rest smoldered like a roofer's mop. Somebody was crying hysterically, but it wasn't me.

I was transported to Rhode Island Hospital. The emergency room doctor said that they were airlifting me to the burn center in San Antonio, but I probably would not live long enough to get there. All they could do at the moment was ease the pain.

"I'm not in pain," I said.

"You will be," he said, and shot me with enough morphine to stop an asteroid. The doc told me again that I was critically burned, which was annoying because I heard him the first time. I figured he was exaggerating for reverse psychology, but he was a good old American realist who believed in fully informed patients. Bless him. He asked if I wanted a priest. I said, "No. Just tell my boyfriend I won't be able to make dinner tonight."

To tell you the truth, that would have been a good time to die. The double-dose morphine temporarily ended all my little problems, and life was pretty good in the haze. I quite suddenly had fond memories of San Antonio and the river walk when I visited an Air Force friend at Lackland AFB. I knew their hospital treated severe burns, which happens around jet fuel, although I thought treatment was reserved for military personnel and their families. Maybe they would bill my insurance company.

It was impossible, but I survived to Texas and beyond. That's not really the story, though. Not what's bothering me, and not why I'm keeping a diary, which is surprising. My response in sophomore English when Mrs.

Dettwelling extolled the benefits of journaling was several big yawns followed by a giggle. Personal writing was for humanities geeks who were too far gone to work their way up to losers. I was more interested in how to get out of fifth-period P.E. or who would ask me to the prom. But here I am. The new journal queen.

I won't bother with details about pigskin grafts, the years of cultivation and transplantation of dermal patches from my face and forearm, the repulsive goop immersions to deescalate the war against dehydration, or the blinding, screaming pain of multiple surgeries, infections, and recoveries followed by more surgery—month after month after month. The doctors and nurses said I was a living miracle, but they weren't the one in a rotating bed or eating through a tube. It's too bad the first doctor had not been right. That kind of faulty prognosis could make one lose confidence in the medical profession.

That's how I felt for many years. Quick death good; long recovery bad. But something happened to make me wonder.

I have told only one person. Junior Ryan Smythe, my best friend since fourth grade and my current boyfriend. Until recently, Junior was the egghead of our relationship; and for some strange reason, he continues to stand by me while we're trying to figure out how to manage my altered life. This is surprising because I won't be winning any modeling contracts. I have been cut and spliced more than Mary Shelley's monster. But the really weird part is the brainwaves.

JR, that's what I've called Junior since the second day we met, is a pretty fair biologist at the University of Rhode Island. He thinks my emerging intellect has something to do with five years of severe sensory deprivation. I told him from where I was sitting pain was pretty sensory. But according to JR, the pain functioned as corporeal white noise, isolating my brain from everything around me. As I'm sure you know, loss of sensory data can promote psychosis; people start to see and hear things that aren't there; lab rats might chew off body parts. So in sensory deprivation experiments, human subjects are limited to the "short-run" by ethical constraints. Mine was not. I couldn't feel through my skin. My eyes and what used to be my ears were bandaged for weeks at a time. My nose was ablated, and I couldn't eat or taste much for years (there's no such thing as a gourmet feeding tube). So the loss of sensory data combined with systemic pain suppressants set my brain adrift with nothing but three pounds of neurons as my whole reality.

JR says that people use 15-20 percent of their brain power. To survive, mine apparently went to 100 percent, which then generated extra capacity besides. JR called it a neuro-multiplier. I called it hell, but by unwillingly breaking experimentation limits, I developed a flaming IQ with kinetic abilities. Perhaps everyone has this potential.

JR wants to run controlled measurements when I am better. Me? I don't care. I'm smart enough to know I'd rather be beautiful. I miss slinking into a cocktail dress and showing off my young body on the dance floor. I liked to watch national beauty pageants and wonder how I might stack up against the competition. But my life went up in smoke, and I should have died with disco.

JR says I'll appreciate what's happened in a few more years, that I'm still growing and there's no telling where it will lead. I say to hell with JR, even if he is my boyfriend. Give me my former body and let's call it square.

Journal Entry #2 (Six Months Later):

I'm returning to Rhode Island permanently. No more extended visits to Texas, and hopefully no more reconstructive surgery or skin grafts. The surgeons say that I'm well enough for locals to take care of me. The risk of infection is about average. I've regained as much use of my hands as I'll probably ever have, which is almost nothing, though I can pinch a pencil between my right thumb stump and partial index finger. My left hand is basically a webbed lump. I can hobble with a cane for short distances, but I'm not strong enough for more than a few minutes. My arm gives out. JR promised to design a wrist-strap that will clamp onto a specially fitted walking stick to extend my distance. I had figured to rely on a wheelchair, but it's hard to sit for long periods. The skin on my thighs and back hurts, and there are circulatory issues. My legs tingle much of the time, and the pain gets worse if I'm in a chair more than a couple hours. This body is a mess, and walking for short distances is part of my physical therapy.

My eyes, protected by my arm in the fire, are in pretty good shape. If I wore a Hijab, I might be inconspicuous. Seriously, though, I couldn't handle blindness. That would be too much. I read a lot now, including the highbrow texts that JR brings. I used to laugh at his spending so much time with books, and before the accident, I couldn't make it past the titles of *Critique of Pure Reason* or *Popular Delusions and the Madness of Crowds* or *Human Action*. Book-learning just didn't click. Today I want everything. Physics, calculus, history, philosophy, rhetoric, psychology, paleontology, economics. And I'm skimming side-line languages like Chinese, Russian, Greek, German, Arabic. I gloriously failed Spanish in high school, but I now seem to remember everything that I didn't learn in Mrs. Espanola's class, or whatever her name was. I prefer reading texts in their original language when possible because translators often lie (so do authors for that matter), but reading helps pass the time. JR is sweet and goes out of his way to find what I request: Einstein, Balzac, Hugo, Tolstoy, Balzac, Camus, Stendhal, Kant, and Nietzsche. Quite suddenly, I'm into Edgar Rice Burroughs and Stephen King. A real kick.

Journal Entry #5:

I read Thoreau's *Walden* four times today, which helped me understand that JR might be telling the truth. He thinks I am beautiful. A week ago, I asked JR to take the short drive to Massachusetts to look at Walden Pond, which is now a state reservation. This was disappointing. The vehicle line getting in was longer than an amusement park ride. Then I realized how stupid I was. As if Thoreau would be found in the pond or cabin. I re-read *Walden* to confirm what I was thinking. JR does not see me as a deformed monster. He sees Thoreau's worn-out gloves that become more meaningful, more beautiful, with use and repair. A kind of existential utilitarian naturalism. In a similar way, I have become dearer to JR. We go back a long way. He cares.

That's when I start to consider time travel. Not the H. G. Wells' variety because Einstein convinced me that's impossible. Well, not precisely impossible, but requiring infinite energy, which is impossible. But I wondered about intellectual breaches along the continuum. If ideas have no mass, it might be possible to send them through time. Just a thought.

My lips still hurt when JR tries to kiss me, which I don't like anyway. The image is revolting. I sure as hell wouldn't kiss me.

Journal Entry #6:

I didn't mean to kill the man, but he deserved to die and I was mercifully quick.

JR took me out to dinner. I am getting better at solid food, and he decided we should go out for my birthday. When in public, I wear a polypropylene ski mask and gloves so as not to frighten small children. People in East Greenwich are used to me, so the facial covering is rarely a problem, but JR took me to the Federal Hill dining district in Providence. Some wise guy walked by and said something about only terrorists wear masks in July. JR was polite, but suggested that the guy should go about his business, so the jerk pushes JR aside and yanks off my mask.

Lon Chaney's phantom looks better than I do, and I swear what little nose I had left came off with the polypropylene. Felt like it anyway. I yelped and grabbed my face. JR, who cringes at harsh language, lit into Mister Bad Ass Wannabe without hesitation. The battle was over in two seconds. JR hit the ground. Mister Wannabe glanced my way and said, "With a face like yours, Babe, this dude's probably the best you can get, but Jeez-zus!"

JR staggered up to try again, but there was no need. Wannabe keeled over, and I asked JR to please take me home.

The next day we heard on the news that a man had dropped dead in Federal Hill. Medical examiners suspected a cerebral hemorrhage. When JR asked if the incident had anything to do with our birthday dinner, I told him the truth. Wannabe's brain felt like a wet sponge when I reached inside and squeezed his grey matter into scrambled eggs. JR is the only one who knows.

Journal Entry #7:

JR and I stopped at the same gas station where my accident occurred. The owner visited the hospital when I was recovering. Now he allows me to fill up for free and still cries when he sees me. JR doesn't like to accept the gifts, which makes him feel like a thief, but I told him that this makes the owner feel better. It does, too. I can sense emotions pretty good these days. The station agent is built with kindness from the ground up, and he carries a crippling remorse about my accident. So every month or two, we help him by accepting the free tank of gas. It's the right thing to do.

Journal Entry #8:

I tested my time-travel theory. Didn't work. Yet if I can levitate small objects in space, I might levitate my thoughts across time. Maybe I'm dreaming, but the difficulty seems to be with sensory perception. Without the body, how can I know when and where I've been? Or whether I've been at all? When I intellectually visit the past, I must somehow learn to "see" without the body's five senses. I'll study on it, of course, but nobody is researching in this area, nor does anyone else have my theoretical capacity.

I read mostly for pleasure these days, which is a bad habit. I went through the Encyclopedia Britannica, World Book, Oxford English Dictionary, and The Story of Civilization last week. I love old encyclopedias—learn a lot by examining standardized cultural viewpoints.

JR wanted to test my photographic recall and asked if I could remember phone numbers, like that savant movie, but I told him it would bore me to death. I suggested that he use the American Heritage Dictionary, which was on the kitchen counter and which I had already read. He gave me a page number, so I listed the headwords, described the "flipper" photo of a scuba diver, and mentioned a smudge at the entry for "flirtatious." JR doesn't bother with phonebook questions anymore.

Journal Entry #11:

I'm home from the hospital. Not the burn unit. The mental ward at Butler.

I flipped out. Started to hear voices and answer them. Started to fling pots and pans around my apartment—only I wasn't using my hands to do it.

JR got me calmed down enough that I wouldn't hurt anybody, or let on that I could throw things without touching them. We agreed that the government, if they found out, would probably lock me up as somebody's never-ending research project, but we also figured that a few days of observation with anti-psychotic medication might be good. Like chicken soup, it couldn't hurt.

What set me off? Somebody sent me a handsomely bound book entitled The Uncanny. When I opened the cover, there was a mirror inside. That broke me. I started screaming and making potholes in my kitchen.

The psychiatrist at Butler was pretty good. After a two-day observation, she said that I didn't warrant medication. I needed exercise and a strong dose of quit-feeling-sorry-for-yourself. "Face reality," she said. "Get out of the house, out of the books, and out of your head for a while. And quit wearing that damned ski mask! Let the world adjust to you. If they don't like it, they can check in here."

At first, I wanted to scramble her brains better than Mister Wannabe. Then, pretty soon, I wanted to give her a hundred years of extra life. (I wonder if that's possible.)

When JR brought me home from the hospital, I told him we could get married if he still had interest. Believe it or not, he pulled the engagement ring out of his pocket and slipped it over what's left of my right index finger, which is just long enough to sport a ring. Looks nice, too. If it weren't for uncanny books with mirrors in them, I might have felt beautiful.

Journal Entry #12 (For Your Eyes Only):

I scrutinized every physics, chemistry, and engineering manual that I could find via my on-line data access and HELIN multi-library consortium privileges. No help with brainwave time displacement. It's pretty clear that I'll have to write my own theory and tests à la the Wright Brothers. But I'll do it inside my head because I don't want the CIA to download whatever I come up with. Could be dangerous in the hands of fools.

JR dropped by my apartment two days ago (that hyperbolically wonderful nerd doesn't want to live together until after the wedding)—very excited because he devised an easy measure of my kinetic abilities with an old barbell set bought at the local flea market for three bucks. JR claims that practical teacher training should include a course called, "Lab Equipment on the Cheap," but anyway, my test would be to levitate the iron plates in increasing increments.

I smiled. JR was so proud hauling in that barbell set. I had been keeping secrets lately, but since we were to be married in four weeks, it was time let him in.

JR arranged a series of $2\frac{1}{2}$-, 5-, 10-, and 25-pound discs. He also took a can of refried beans from the cupboard in case the $2\frac{1}{2}$-pound plate was too heavy, but he was pretty sure after my flying-pots-and-pans that I could handle a couple pounds. I laughed and asked if he wanted me to lift the plates one at a time, all at once, or perhaps meld them into a single unit. He was puzzled, so I levitated the four discs off the floor, stacked them nicely in air, whistled the theme from Lost in Space, and melt-molded them into a single $42\frac{1}{2}$-pound tetrahedron. Simple, really, but you would have thought I had walked on water.

"That's impossible," said JR.

"Oh, I'm sorry," said I. "You should have told me sooner."

I reassured him that it wasn't as fancy as anybody might guess. I simply destabilize the atoms so they can slide together with a little push. Pretty easy with metals—almost like liquefaction without heat. Crystals don't work so well. I tried the diamond in my engagement ring, but the damned thing wouldn't meld at all. I reframed my theoretical underpinnings regarding quantum crystalline structures to no avail. Shape shifting won't work on a girl's best friend, but iron can be as malleable as Silly Putty.

Kinetic sidebar: I don't need a cane any more. My legs aren't any stronger, but I can make myself weigh less for short periods of time.

Journal Entry #13:

JR and I will be married tomorrow at the University of Rhode Island. Just a few friends with a minister. The bride and groom are both atheists, but so is the minister, so I suppose that's OK.

My dress is beautiful white-lace. It makes me sick to think what will be wearing it. I try to put those ideas out of my head, but they have a life of their own. Intermittent self-loathing is a beast.

JR really loves me. I know that. I try not to read his mind, which isn't fair, but sometimes there's no helping myself. His love is bottomless and warm and golden. He deserves better than he's getting. If I really loved him, I wouldn't allow this marriage. But I am a moral coward who wants to be a wife.

Three days ago, at the rehearsal, I went to the ladies room. While I was inside a cubicle, two students entered the room, washed their hands, and started talking about the woman they saw on campus.

"If I was toasted like that," said one, "I'd never go outside the house!"

The other offered, "I would have killed myself long ago. Don't see why she has to come around and gross-out the rest of us. Looks like barbequed peanut brittle."

The first woman suddenly turned generous. "Poor thing probably has no idea how bad she looks. Might be retarded."

I sat in the cubicle for fifteen minutes, crying and paralyzed with disgust until JR came to look for me. The sad part? Down deep, I agree with the students. It's hard to be ugly.

Journal Entry #15:

Morons! Morons! Morons! The world is filled with moronic morons who can't grasp the simplest equation! Everywhere I turn, morons magna cum laude. This frustrating discovery, however, has led me to understand fully Mrs. Dettwelling's infatuation with journals. When all else fails, hammering a few choice words into the computer with a tequila chaser can perk a girl right up. Murder in effigy. Vicarious vengeance. Jackass justice.

Feels great!

Journal Entry #16:

Ideas have no mass; therefore, theoretical limitations of spatial time travel do not apply. I should be able to send a thought back nine years, or any number of years, though this presents a fundamental untested glitch. Can a concept alter the past?

I had to take a break. Threw up again. Morning sickness is the pits. You'd think my towering intellect could do something about animalistic processes. It takes a lot of energy to grow a child, not to mention hormone jolts that make Red Bull compare as a sedative. And the mommy track cuts into contemplation of the fourth dimension, which is not a dimension at all. Time is time, not space, which is a key to my science project.

Had a routine ultrasound yesterday. The baby is a girl! I am excited but also worried. How could she love anything that looks like I do? Might be afraid of me.

Journal Entry #17:

DNA from a frog will not meld with the DNA of a rat. However, strands from a tadpole work fine. In conjunction with this discovery, I did a little experiment. Tried to go back in time two days and report to myself about the rat-frog failure to see if it could be avoided. But in avoiding the error, I didn't learn about the lethal genetic combination and repeated it. Too bad for the rodent. On the other hand, the recombined tad-rat is an interesting species. I will not try to breed it. Just an investigative trial while I considered splicing tadpole genes into stem cells to grow a new wrapper for my body. The process might actually work, but it's complex and requires lab equipment, testing and retesting, documentation, and a competent assistant to work with me and on me. Further, the skin-job would require years of effort.

JR offered to lend a hand. Sweet thing. But he's got his teaching job, and as much as I hate to say it, he might never grasp the theoretical foundations, some of which I managed to publish in respected scientific journals by ghostwriting under his name. JR was really pissed about this, but after he received an academic grant and was promoted to full professor for his work, he settled down. In JR's defense, I'm not sure anyone else can understand what I'm doing either. Some of the measurements and calibrations require extrasensory abilities like seeing molecular bonds, DNA sequences, or real-time cytological processes; nor do I fully understand how I do this, which is similar to watching a PBS video in my head. And I don't want to grow a new skin. I want to revoke the accident, reclaim the physical youth and passion, and remove a decade of pain and suffering. I want to be intellectually average and think I'm special.

Of course, the tad-rat was interesting.

Journal Entry #18:

Baby's due in two weeks. I'm scared to death but already love her. JR is all excitement. Me? I don't know. There were moments when abortion seemed best, so the child wouldn't have to meet its mother.

Journal Entry #21:

I did it! I mentally skipped back two months and told JR not to step off the curb. He is alive and well. JR hesitated just two seconds, and the car sped by harmlessly. The asshole driver also got a speeding ticket because I thoughtfully suggested to a cop that he might patrol the area at that moment.

JR doesn't remember being killed. When I explained the situation, he wanted me to visit the psychiatrist again. I don't care. The time paradox be damned! I know what happened. JR is alive and Susie's happy!

Further, suggestive time-thought-interface works—and surprisingly, the revised history didn't erase my memory of J's fatal match with a Camaro. It should have, and I still don't understand how I can remember something that, thanks to my intervention, never happened. Like a drug-induced flashback or a near-death hallucination, I seem to be the only person with knowledge of the dual realities.

Doesn't matter. I did it!

Susan and I aren't as close as we were. After her father died, she clung to me like she always clung to JR. And in the new space-time, she never told me that I was the prettiest Mommy. It's probably for the best, but I admit that a tiny part of me wanted to leave the accident untouched. Just for a second. I love JR, and he loves me and Susie. I can live with that lost mother-daughter moment.

But now there is the possibility of a game-winning score! A self-inflicted psychic time insertion. Maybe I don't have to remain bacon-crisp. Maybe I never have to be in the first place. Maybe I can reshape my universe.

Journal Entry #22:

I'm going back. If I changed history for JR, I should be able to do it for me. Time travel is difficult. First, it's hard to find my way to the right place and moment using only brainwaves. Second, I must plant an idea into a then living person. The concomitant precision and concentration are cryptic. Practice helps, but even my accelerating genius is barely up to task. The effort makes me dizzy.

During my research, I made a number of incidental discoveries, including a gene-splice inhibiter to prevent the HIV from breaching cellular walls or reproducing. It worked on me, anyway. (All those after-burn transfusions gave me AIDS, which I haven't mentioned because it seemed meaningless in light of the rest of me.) With a little more effort, I might find the on-off switch for cancer. Anyway, there's no time. I'm scrapping this work because I don't want anyone to interfere with my time sculpture. Call me weak, but I want my former life. I have a right to it.

Journal Entry #23:

This could be my last report. I retained memory after I fragmented JR's accident, but I'm not sure how things will play when I send ideas to myself ten years past. That young, healthy, unburned woman at the station. If I succeed, the station owner won't have to give me free gas.

I admit that my flash-life hasn't been all bad. I'm generally happy, and JR and Susan are very nice. The physical pain has lessened significantly in recent weeks, though I always seem to be thirsty and there's a high-pitched humming in my ears. I appreciate being smart and having the ability to crush bad people with a thought, but I am ready for the insertion. I cannot kill the desire to be normal; it's killing me instead.

It is possible to revisit that horrible day and to warn myself about the defective nozzle. I know because the accident made me very, very, very smart, and I've learned that being beautiful is better. I've practiced and calculated and cross-checked, but I must act soon. The complexity of time travel increases at a geometric rate the farther back I must go.

My real concern is that I will lose Susie in the process. Lovely little Susan. Even I can't recreate an entire human gene sequence, especially when I re-emerge as my C+ self. The consolation is that JR will be there. We can still be married and have children in the altered universe, and I know CVS won't discontinue my special shade of lipstick.

I should say goodbye—no, I won't wake her. Susie is the perfect fantasy daughter, and I shall look for her across space and time. It's all right, Honey. Don't be afraid. Mommy must leave, but you won't feel a thing. And someday, when the time is right, I'll tell Daddy all about the girl we left behind.

I'll just have a cool glass of water before I go. The firestorm is calling, and my thirst is unquenchable.

Modern understandings of relative gravitational and chronographic fluctuations are close enough for government work (i.e., to the 9th decimal), so pilots don't generally worry about miscalculations. And Unicom Mission Control wouldn't fund such trips unless the risks were minimal; plus, matter-antimatter intermix systems generate enough propulsion that most ships can skirt a white dwarf and still have reserve oomph to pull away—not that occupants would survive the G-forces. M-A muscle increases geometrically against the fuel, so 10 percent enrichment boosts thrust by 40, and on-board computers protect passengers from too much throttle by holding thrust to 20 Gs for short bursts unless certain emergency contingencies are met. Then the computer saves the ship. Simple math, really. Losing a crew is bad; losing a crew along with the vessel is worse. Machine logic chooses the lesser evil without regret or hesitation. Humans are less pure.

But the bottom line is that, after crossing the event horizon, I was alive and able to fly, so I pumped a little extra juice to the engines, trying to slow my spiral into darkness. Worth a try. Maybe I'd even pick up a few new bona fides about space-time in serious gravity wells, not that it would do civilization much good because nothing returns from a black hole. I realized that this may not be precisely true, but who wants to be emitted back into the universe as Hawking's radiation. Not high on my bucket list.

Strange. I'd been accelerating for 76 minutes according to instruments, which can't be fully trusted in this environment, and my downward spiral was not only slowing, it was slowing more than physics said was possible. Now, I believe in physics like some folks believe in the gods of old, yet my revised calculations suggest that in 2.4 hours, I'd achieve orbit around the singularity. Since even light can't do that (I think), these figures should be wrong, but what's a girl to do if she can't jibe instrumentation against her own math skills. Besides, pilots are hyper-confident about their abilities or none of us would ever survive the Mission Academy. Training is Heinlein tough, and I ranked among the best cadets in the past sesquicentennial. Modesty keeps me from admitting that I was the best.

The new orbital calculations are impossible, unless…. Let me reevaluate things after I've cruised through weird-space a bit longer and see what's to be seen. I'm saving full-throttle for something serious though I'm not sure what could be more serious than flying inside a BH event horizon.

Wow! Just, wow! It looked like S2 or S14 fell into Sagittarius A*. Such phenomena aren't visible outside the black hole, except for the accretion disk and gravitational effects, but from the inside, cosmic cataclysms are spectacular. Try to picture a disintegrating star as it bends and breaks and scatters into visible and invisible radiation like an elongated fusion pinwheel accelerating toward ultimate oblivion. If it weren't for my level-five shields, I would have been fried by the beauty. Swirling plasma rainbows fighting against darkness and gravity; spaghettified white hot nothing; silent mega-mega-explosions turning back on themselves; a B-class star swallowed by an infinite mass with no diameter. And after 55 minutes, the whole mosaic lightshow imploded into nothing. Did I say wow! I didn't expect to have quite as much fun when it was my turn to implode, but damn that was beautiful.

Instruments report that after four hours of 2.3-G acceleration, my ship achieved a stable orbit around the singularity. This should not be, but I remember an ancient mariner who said something like, "The impossible just takes a little longer." I see now he was right.

I couldn't confirm that my ship had reached orbital velocity in black-hole space—didn't really know what that speed would be anyhow—but I occasionally see falling objects and energy and streaks of light, so my relative station suggests I might be holding against the tide. Not that infinitely circling an invisible singularity is cause for unabridged jubilation, but longer life seems good. Anyway, I reduced accelerative power to 1-G and seemed to be maintaining orbit; also, I'm much more comfortable at 57 kilograms of mass instead of 130. Who wants to feel like an overweight slug in her own ship?

I crosschecked the instrumentation with pencil and paper because my ship's external and internal chronometers were contradictory—one faster and the other slower—which made it hard to figure velocity. Exterior time said I'd accelerated for 7 months; if so, I was approaching light speed. Yet my body agreed with the four-hour cabin reading; e.g., I'd peed once since entering the black hole.

Another peculiar issue? My gages reported that my matter-antimatter stockpiles had increased. Only one thing might account for this—speed.

Well, hell. I'd worn to the nub my number 2 pencil (still a perfect writing instrument for space), sharpened and resharpened, scribbled and rescribbled, and yet come up with the same bad news. Everybody I had ever known had been dead for upwards of three hundred thousand years, even with an average life expectancy of 182. Ship time was "relatively" slow because of the gravity well and my increasing speed, which should be near .96 C. And it was also pretty clear that the laws of physics outside black holes must be holding steady because no one had come to rescue me from a 300,000-year future. I assumed that people still existed, but I bet they didn't look like me. Evolution never stops.

Luckily, I stashed a pint of 100-proof bourbon shipside for a distressing day, so I flipped the autopilot to maintain 1-G acceleration, which actually demanded increasing energy, and enjoyed a tall drink—several, actually. My orbit was either steady or expanding by the diameter of a few molecules every five to ten minutes. Anyway, I kicked my feet up, put away all of the marvelously aged whiskey, and then slept for 10 hours to sober up. Tipsy is good, but sober is better when life is on the line. And since I apparently wasn't going anywhere soon, there would be time after my bourbon nap to double check calculations. But if my notepad scribbles were right, I might be able to break the death grip of Sagittarius A*.

The great drunk-a-log-sleep-off was agreeable, and I awakened to instruments and scribbles confirming data pretty much in line with what I expected. Relative time ran slower in the gravity well of a massive black hole. Combine that with my ship's velocity and together they created "Clash of the Diachronic Physics"; thus, I would soon exceed light speed in this gravitationally altered fun zone. I realized that nothing should affect absolute C in a vacuum, but Sagittarius A* didn't seem to care. My ship was at .987 C and accelerating, slowly, yes, but still gaining speed and mass. Pencil and paper suggest that if I increased acceleration for seven more hours at 2.0-Gs, I would reach 1.0001 C relative to "regular space"; two hours later, I'd be at 1.05 C. Then I'd attempt to break free and return to the Milky Way, which was more or less my plan before a ten-hour bourbon-infused nap.

Now, this maneuver wouldn't be as simple as pulling away from a white dwarf, and because escaping from a black hole had never been done before, my calculations might not be any better than pissing in a pot of soup to stretch the servings. But instruments suggested my orbit was increasing, so apparently the known laws physics were flying third-class on this trip.

I didn't know what would happen if actually I exceeded C, but if and when I did, the plan was simple enough. At 315,000 kilometers per second, attempt a course change, dip below my current orbit, pick-up a bit of gravitational sling, and aim for the event horizon at full survivable power. Once I was back outside, I figured my relative speed must drop below C. If it didn't, well, who knew? Flying a theoretically infinite mass was beyond my training. But again, C+ velocity was only possible because of the compounded gravity-time-speed differentials. My "real" velocity should not exceed light in "regular" space (I hate to use such words in the context of "relativity"), but collective scientific knowledge suggested that my ship must go sub-light outside the event horizon. If this didn't happen, I'd probably be

A million years after Commander Willia Clarke disappeared into a black hole, and despite all the scientific and technological advancements during that span, "humans" had lost none of their signature curiosity. And now that they saw that light speed had been surpassed, scientists set about analyzing the process. Their planned intergalactic explorations would be severely limited without C+ speeds, so they studied "The Sagittarius Expulsion" with the best methodologies available. Sooner or later answers would be revealed; and in this case, 316 years elapsed before an experimental Funnel Web Compression Drive was theorized, developed, and tested. It worked! and would soon open the universe to colonization, and Homo Superior could now dream of becoming Homo Omnipresent in its home galaxy and beyond.

The new compression/propulsion system, popularly called "Web-Drive," would be renamed several years later to honor Commander Willia Clarke.

The exploratory mission had not been planned as a rescue, but the new Funnel Web Compression Drive allowed scientists to overtake The Sagittarius Expulsion, which, unknown to them, was actually Commander Clarke's speeding vessel. Further, using a secondary Web-Drive, engineers felt sure they could reduce the Expulsion's velocity for capture and study. Just as space-time could be gravitationally compressed and allow an object to break the light barrier, space-time expansion could decelerate a C+ object to sub-light speeds.

Using a commercial vessel enhanced with Web-Drive, which proved almost as infallible as gravity itself, five scientists and three astronauts landed at the center of The Sagittarius Expulsion with the intention of using a secondary unit for deceleration. It was not clear whether the compact Web-Drive could be welded to a two-dimensional surface without damage, so they avoided the risk by using padded industrial magnets to affix the temporary funneling unit. And as space-time was gently stretched ahead of the "The Expulsion," it slowed to .8C and became immediately recognizable as an impossibly ancient spacecraft. Beautiful!

The Homo Superior's A.I. quickly connected with, reconfigured, and translated the Expulsion's anachronistic radio signal. The language was a very, very old Solarian English dialect.

"Mayday, mayday," said a strong female voice. "This is Commander Willia Clarke of the research vessel Curie. I just broke through the event horizon of Sagittarius A*. Does anyone read?"

The stunned group of astro-scientists and engineers in their own ship temporarily lost their collective voice, but after the message repeated three times, a cool-headed, gentle woman responded via the universal translator. "This is Citizen Vega Esperanza Alexander of Omicron Sigma Minor. We read you loud and clear, Commander. And we love you."

Vega paused and said, "Please allow a few seconds for our on-board computers to reconfigure communications. Modern language is part telepathic and part enunciative, but our A.I. can translate speech both ways once it formats the syntax and structure of your Solarian English. It's almost impossible for our race to communicate without some psychic bridging.... Please stand by."

"Hellfire and hello!" said Commander Clarke without hesitation. "I'll stand by until all the Kuiper Belts melt away. Just glad to hear a voice. Any voice!"

Four seconds passed. "OK, Commander.... Your transponder reports that the Curie launched in the 540th Century, and it's going to take a long time to figure out how many firsts you've achieved and how we should honor you. But I can't wait to meet you personally and sense your spirit."

"You sound human," said Clarke, "not that I really care at this point. By my calculations, I skipped across half a million years, though it seems like a day to me. Hope deep-space pilots haven't become obsolete. I was pretty good in my day."

"You've undoubtedly got some technical and social catching up to do," said Vega, "and I almost envy everything that you're going to learn. But mostly, you'll have to get used to being a galactic hero. Thanks to the development of Funnel Web Compression Drive that your ship has inspired, the entire galaxy will soon know your name. And we want every detail of how you emerged from Sagittarius A*…. By the way, you've bitten off just under a million years, not half."

"Oh, hell," said Clarke. "That means it will take me at least a week to catch up."

Vega laughed in translation, though Homo Superior did not typically vocalize joy. It was easier and more delightful to sense it. "I like your attitude, Commander."

"Call me Willia or Willie," responded Clarke, "and I look forward to recounting a sordid tale of How to Enter a Black Hole and Come Out Alive, which is harder than you might think."

"We want to hear all of it," thought-said Vega, who had been subliminally affirmed by her team to ease Commander Willia Clarke into the present. "But I need to report a few things myself, Willie. A million years brings changes to a species, and we now really are hairless apes, so to speak. A.I. confirms that our brains have slightly more capacity—logic, reason, memory—and there are other intellectual and nervous system developments that you don't have. Telepathy, for example, which is part of a rudimentary sixth sense. The good news is that there are implants available to compensate for your deficiencies if you wish. Oh, excuse me, Commander, I meant to think differences. We have assorted bio-technologies for citizens with varying cognitive abilities."

"Forget it," said Clarke. "I'm too happy about being alive for hurt feelings. Unless you're Morlocks planning to serve me as the main course, I expect we'll get along."

"That's an unpleasant concept," said Vega, not getting the joke, "and people rarely eat animal flesh these days." She changed the subject. "In addition to permanent enhancement implants, there are portable, temporary equipments used in first-education schools that can help with knowledge acquisition. We offer many choices."

"So," said Clarke, "there are options. Not sure what I'll do with them. I kind of like me the way I am."

"Understandable," replied Vega, rapidly absorbing transmissions, translations, and recommendations from the on-board A.I., "and so do we. Be advised, too, that we're about 20 centimeters taller than humans from your era, and our skin has a violet tinge due to increased adaptational blood volume along with fluid modifications derived from the horseshoe crab that have essentially eliminated cancers from our species. I hope you won't disparage our appearance. We're still human, and you are part of our direct lineage, our heritage."

"Fear not," said Clarke. "I have worked with some serious assholes from my own time, short and tall, and you seem a whole lot nicer. Smarter, too. Besides, I've always had a fondness for tall women with brains....I hope you still come in male and female models?"

Vega's computer translator now signaled a gentle laugh. "Of course! It would take more than a million years to disenfranchise that difference, and what would be the fun of asexual reproduction? However, as an aside," said Vega formally, "full human gestation now takes 11 months."

"Probably won't affect me...," said Clarke. "Now, not to seem rude, but I'm sort of anxious to get off this bucket and meet you. Yesterday, I thought I was gonna die. Today, I'm a million years in the future. Might as well start getting to know the new present." Clarke paused for effect. "But there's one thing I gotta know before committing myself."

"What's that?" asked Vega, wondering whether she had offended the Commander by speaking of gestation.

"Do you hairless blue giants still have Kentucky bourbon?"

"Are you kidding!" said Vega, realizing that the Commander had not been offended and seemed of stout, congenial composition. "Nation-state Kentucky was long ago relegated to once-upon-a-time land, but there's a multi-grain 100-proof Omicron blend worshipped across three solar systems, including Omicron Sigma Minor. And if you are willing to come aboard,

Dearest Willie, I'll buy the opening round, claiming the distinct privilege of being the first human to toast your homecoming. How's that for a heroic welcome back!"

"Sounds like a fair beginning," said Clarke. "Just keep three things in mind."

"Whatever you need, Commander," responded Vega.

"First, I've had a rough 24 hours and might be a bit grumpy. Second, I'll buy the subsequent rounds because somebody owes me one million years of back wages and flight pay. Third, as a short, hairy-headed, near-Neanderthal blast from the past, I can probably drink you and your entire crew under the table. And if Omicron whiskey is half as good as you claim, that's exactly where I plan to go."

RIDE THE SNAKE

The children were regimented from morning until night, as were their parents, for the governing elders discovered long ago that scripted routines diminished all varieties of excess and deficiency. Today, however, a citizen of the fourth grade at Huxley Academy would become singularly distinct during an encounter with one of thirteen remaining South American anacondas.

"Boys and girls," said the announcer, as the children entered the climate-controlled tropics around the center stage of an intimate auditorium, "please take your seats."

Forced hot air brushed the children's faces. Ancient continental birds and insects sang from hidden speakers. And the overall effect made one of the students think of a hellish fable from ancient literature.

"Listen to nature's discord," said the soft-spoken male announcer. "Notice the uncomfortable warmth and humidity. Imagine aboriginals plagued by disease, famine, and ethnic warfare. These early Amazonians—we can't really call them men and women—struggled for food and shelter, sometimes murdering others in the process. These early hominoids fared hardly better than domesticated animals."

The surround-sound suddenly wailed with New World primates, buzzed with wasps and mosquitoes, and growled with a South American jaguar. The children squirmed in their seats, but one precocious boy, age nine, bolder than the rest, whispered, "The Stone Age. Do not fear a dead past."

The announcer heard through his earpiece and responded. "Yes, boys and girls. Modern civilization has conquered nature and the baser impulses of its dominant species. Social unification has created security and abundance, and we no longer have with us the poor, the halt, and the blind. But today, this purposeful day, you shall witness a palpable demonstration of the modern versus the ancient."

The children shrieked with delight, and then, with side glances, internally questioned the propriety of such exuberance. However, they did not ponder this long or deeply, because the main event rolled onto the stage: a thirty-foot anaconda, sixteen inches in diameter at midsection, which lay in a glass enclosure lined with straw, a lavishly protected creature whose only hardship was boredom. The children oooh'd and aaah'd, knowing that they were safe now, but that seven hundred years ago, the Amazonians were not. How odd, and how glorious.

After waiting for the squeals and whispers to taper, the moderator swept his arm across the crowd of one hundred and one children. "And now," he proclaimed, "someone will be allowed a personal encounter with our reptilian guest. ONE of you shall revisit living antiquity. Do I have a volunteer?"

The credentialed orator, ten credentialed teachers, and ten credentialed assistants had to wait less than a second. Every child's hand shot into the air. "Me! Me! Me!" reverberated through the auditorium, small arms swaying for attention.

The moderator waited a prescribed length of time, pacing back and forth across the stage, smiling, gesturing toward the serpent, then the audience, and then the serpent once more. The excitement became thunderous.

"ME! ME! ME!"

Finally, he pointed to a girl, age seven, not quite as strong or pretty as the rest, but just as enthusiastic. She yelped and bounced toward the artificial meadow, glancing at her teacher to be assured the bounce was permissible.

A hidden directional microphone automatically swiveled toward the child, now standing twelve feet from the beast's enclosure. "And what's your name?" asked the announcer.

"Malika Oleander Principle," said the girl. "I stand for unity and abundance."

"Well, Malika," said the moderator, "are you ready for a unique experience? Something your classmates will admire?"

"Yes!" said Malika.

"Do you think you can handle it?"

"Oh, yes!" shouted Malika.

"Then," said the moderator to his audience, "let's watch bold Malika confront the ANA-CON-DA!"

This time, the children jumped and screeched without glancing at their teachers, and none was louder than Malika. She had been selected for special treatment. How odd, and how glorious.

"Are you ready!?" asked the announcer with carnival cadence.

"We are ready!" said Malika, shoulders back, as if society depended on her.

The anaconda began to test the enclosure, looking for an expected opening, and one hundred children vocalized their astonishment. It lived.

"Malika," said the announcer, "we recommend silence as you face the serpent." The command was unnecessary, because when a transparent panel slid away from the cage, Malika was paralyzed with a strange and distinctly unpleasant sensation. She had never experienced fear before.

Recognizing the child-scented air, the anaconda glided to the floor. It was much larger than the children imagined.

Malika stared motionless as a forked tongue flicked the air. At first, the serpent turned in the direction of the announcer, who flashed a corrective laser across its brow. The head then snapped toward the girl, followed by one hundred gasps of air.

"The anaconda is a mindless primitive," said the moderator. "Malika is not. What do you think will happen?"

Malika did not know the answer, but she was civilized, all right. She belonged to the One Society of a Golden Age.

The snake inched toward the child. Seven feet away. Then five. A spotlight focused between Malika and the anaconda, and then the creature laid eyes upon the girl.

With jungle quickness, the beast struck, sinking ancient teeth into the modern shoulder of a forty-five-pound child. Malika screamed as no one outside the auditorium had screamed in seven hundred years. The serpent coiled the child to center stage while Malika kicked and cried for help. The other children watched in obedient silence.

Malika began choking on half words, and the snake constricted as hard as the springs of an Auschwitz boxcar. Soon there was no sound, no breath, no heartbeat from the child. Then began a reptilian swallow that seemed to last for hours; and finally, as the last edge of Malika's left sole passed into the snake, the auditorium went dark for ten seconds. When the lights came up, the serpent, cage, and child were gone.

Speech slowly returned to the children, and the brave, precocious boy asked, "What happened to Malika?"

"She is with the anaconda," said the announcer.

"But she's all right?" suggested a girl, confused.

"Malika is dead," replied the announcer.

"That can't happen," said the boy. "This is some kind of trick!"

The other children nodded and began to giggle, suspecting an elaborate hoax.

"But where is Malika?" asked another, still unsure.

"I told you," said the announcer. "Malika died. Do you doubt your eyes?"

Now the children were distraught. What had they seen? They looked to their teachers, who offered no immediate clue about today's lesson.

"Impossible!" declared the courageous boy, standing.

"It is possible," replied the announcer, "for the good of the majority—and with consent of the martyr…and her parents. Surely you understand the concept of sacrifice. You studied it in first grade."

The boy looked skeptical. "I think you're lying, Mister!"

His teacher cast a sharp glance. "You may never speak that way to an Overseer!"

The boy did not back down. He liked Malika and felt a curious protectiveness toward her. "If he isn't a liar," said the boy, cocking his head with illicit independence, "why did Malika scream and fight?"

The teacher smiled, nodding at the announcer, who in turn smiled at the audience.

"Boys and girls," said the speaker. "Our Doubting Thomas apparently believes that Malika, a daughter of the Golden Age, was as primitive as the serpent, concerned merely for her own existence."

The audience was silent.

"Well?' asked the announcer. "Was she?"

"No," said several children unconvincingly.

Another asked, "But, sir, why did she cry? It was awful!"

The announcer gestured with outstretched palms covered in Malika's blood. "To offer a more realistic demonstration, that you might truly understand the benefits of our civilization. Boys and girls, Malika died for you. Each of you."

Sighs of relief filled the auditorium, followed by high-pitched giggles as the children began to understand. That was the lesson. To make them question the wisdom of their superiors. The notion was as preposterous as it was shaming, a fool's illusion generated by lack of faith in the One Society.

A girl laughed. "You played a trick!"

Another child smiled at her teacher. "This was the best field trip ever!"

"In the future," said the announcer, compassionately, "I hope you will doublethink before mistrusting our governors. And if you are ever confused, you might, at minimum, remember and honor the memory of Malika Oleander Principle, whose unselfish community spirit was demonstrated so compellingly this day."

The children broke into spontaneous applause, reinforced by the teachers. After a few moments, they began to chant. "Ma-lee-ka! Ma-lee-ka! We love Ma-lee-ka!"

The Overseer smiled. He bowed stage left, right, and center, repeating the cycle until the ovation began to diminish. Then he panned the audience, offering his applause to the children, who cheered themselves.

"We're the One! We're the One! We're the One!"

Beneath the auditorium, a resting serpent sensed the vibrations of a Golden Age. And in the audience, a very special young boy smoldered with revolutionary understanding.

THE COLD WATERS OF EUROPA

Scuba diving on Europa was supposed to be fun, a thrilling vacation for ten aquanauts who had reserved this trip five months in advance. They were rich enough to afford it and certified to swim beneath the ice. But now, nine were already dead or dying, trapped inside a sinking bell that had just disappeared on route toward the rocky mantle some 120 kilometers below. And I, too, would be dead in nine hours: Michelle Rainier Sterne, the lucky10th diver who had exited the capsule immediately before the cable snapped and the waterlock auto-sealed to "protect" the remaining occupants. Instead, it had closed the lid on a plummeting coffin that would implode 15 kilometers below ice-level.

My wife, Amelia, had been behind me as I left the portal with my research equipment. Now she's trapped with the others.

I am…was…the scientist in our relationship; she, the sports queen who'd ascended Everest, explored the Mariana Trench, spelunked the caves of Luna, wind-surfed the Martian polar caps, and done a dozen other crazy things that terrified me on her behalf. Amelia laughed gently at my concern but acknowledged that she would probably die on one of her trips. Neither of us imagined it would be on the comparatively tame Europa. Excursions below the ice had become almost routine, and much of the aquatic life had been catalogued by robotic submarines using organic attractors that native fish and gilled mammals found irresistible. Apparently, Wiggle-Bites tasted better than the plankton and shirpflies that anchor the food chain.

Europa's global ocean teemed with life, and almost every species in the benthic and abyssal zones used fluorescent light to make their way or to find a mate. The quasi-pelagic zone contained a mixture of small plant and animal life, but the low light made photosynthesis difficult though several deep-water seaweeds were adapted to feed on chemosynthetic bacteria near hydrothermal vents, providing another nutrient platform for smaller fish. In any case, the top carnivores sashayed through a neon smorgasbord of plenty.

This aquatic biome provided the sales pitch Amelia used to get me here. While I wasn't a stay-at-home wife, I was a stay-on-Earth marine biologist. But Amelia hit below the belt when she bragged how safe Europa had become and how I would find "new species by the hour." She was right, of course. Expeditions beneath the ice, while still expensive, had become almost a tourist trap. The nuclear-powered meltevators had operated for 13 years without a fatality. They were secure as secure could be on a Jovian moon where average equatorial surface temperatures hovered at minus 160 Celsius. The business wasn't quite ready to open its doors for couch potatoes, but with a perfect safety record and package prices falling, Tour Europa would probably offer college fieldtrips in a few years.

But this accident was no accident. A triple-strand titanium alloy cable doesn't just snap—cutting one is difficult enough, so it's almost certain that an improvised magnesium-laced heat wrap severed the line. And the first terrorist attack on Europa's research-tourist industry (a few nutcases wanted to "stop humans from destroying the environment") had cost me the love of my life, but I wouldn't have long to mourn under the ice: a launch-ready rescue capsule would take three hours to traverse the shaft, and who knew how long it would take to repair the cable and attach another pod?

Much longer than my life support.

After I floated under the ice for 15 minutes, I quit sulking and got mad. I needed to survive so I could kill the SOB who'd killed my wife. We'd been married 14 years. She was adventurous, confident, and stone-butch gorgeous; and except for those moments when I had wanted to strangle her, I loved her more than my life.

Any chance for my survival would require math, strategy, and luck to hold out until rescue. Actually, it would take a lot of luck, but Amelia's memory deserved an all-out effort on my part. Fortunately, the equations were relatively simple because math isn't my strong point. I'm competent but not dazzling.

It should take a minimum of 27 hours to retrieve and repair the bell cables, attach a backup pod, and melt through the crust. The elevator is constantly moving up and down, one roundtrip every six hours (with or without occupants), which keeps the ice from completely refreezing. Clearing a virgin shaft, even with 200-C nuclear hotplates fore and aft, takes a week to 10 days. But once the chute is breached a few times and enhanced with bio-safe crystal inhibitor, especially near the surface, the pathway remains slushy for several hours. Europa is minus 160 Celsius up top; right under the ice shelf, the salt water is a balmy minus 0.95 degree; and as one approaches the rocky mantel, temperatures range from comfortable to scalding, especially near thermal vents. Jupiter's gravitational tides help stir the mix, so I was much warmer under the ice than up top—if stranded on the surface, I'd already be stiff.

One genius had tried to develop a steel-lined shaft for faster elevators, but shifting ice continents (ranging in thickness from 3 to 17 kilometers) crumpled the tube before construction crews could say, "Houston, we have a problem." Heat, flexible cables, and regular use constituted the only practical ways to maintain a chute.

Still, my calculations were easy. Stay alive for 27, maybe 30 hours. I carried enough breathable hydro-heliox (configured to maximize body heat and minimize blood toxicity) for 9. My suit's heating units were good for 10 hours. The HHO mix contained 39.5% oxygen and was compressed into the latest 5000 psi tanks. I could capture most of my exhale bubble in an ice-clave, which would extend my breathing supply and allow the cold to get me before asphyxiation. Either way, basic arithmetic suggested that the bastard who killed the others had already killed me, too.

I decided that every hour I lived beyond my tank supply would be a success, so the first thing I did was position myself under an enclave near the shaft that would capture most of my exhale. The waste bubble still contains about 70% usable mix, and the holding area should add 10-12 hours of oxygen, breathing and re-breathing the blow out. CO_2 would accumulate, but by the time that became an issue, my heating units would turn cold (along with my 130-pound body). I lowered the suit thermostat to bare minimum, which should stretch my miserably cold existence 3 to 4 hours. Still, that could provide time to find another hour, and another, and maybe another.

Amelia was on my mind.

Waiting for an underwater bus. That's how I felt, floating beneath the ice shelf with nothing to do but watch bubbles accumulate while thinking, thinking, thinking. If I conserved every bit of O2 and heat (i.e., by freezing my ass off), I might live 14-15 hours total before turning solid. This was sort of good news. I'm phobic about suffocation, and from what I've heard, beyond a certain point, hypothermia is like falling asleep.

A thought suddenly occurred to me that folks up top might assume everybody died when the cable snapped, and they might take their sweet time about sending another pod. Interplanetary guidelines require "all possible speed" in searching for survivors and that "fatalities be confirmed" beyond a reasonable doubt before suspending rescue efforts. But these were just the rules, and there's a big motivational difference between people-need-help-now or everybody's-probably-dead-anyway. I didn't want the second part to become self-fulfilling.

I took off one of my belt weights and clicked an SOS against the ice shelf, though a floating planetary glacier generates so much internal cracking and crunching that no mortal could reasonably decipher my meager efforts. However, as I waited for the rescue pod that would likely arrive too late to save me, there wasn't much else to do but tap dots and dashes at the gods of technology. Some computer nerds owned a sixth sense about these things, and maybe the ground crew were faster than I calculated.

Damn, it's cold, and I'm only six hours into this mess. In another three, I'll need to open my face plate and breathe directly from the enclave, which is basically a dimly lit air pocket under a floating glacier. I figured to lie on my back until stiff. I even considered allowing my O2 to run dry and gradually go unconscious, but then I heard Amelia in the back of my mind.

"Quit whining!"

I protested that I couldn't be blamed for a no-win double-crap situation, but a stern voice replied, "Every hour of life is a victory and an opportunity. Get with it, Girl!"

I hated when she called me girl, and the woman's eternal optimism could drive me crazy even from the grave. Amelia saw the silver lining in everything but sloth, and in one of my want-to-strangle-her moments, I told her, "Michelle Rainier Sterne is going to plop in her lounge chair, enjoy a glass of wine, watch a worthless movie, and sit still for two hours straight. What do you think of that Miss Never-a-Dull-Moment?"

Amelia didn't even raise her voice. "All active minds and bodies need a break. Real apathy is not bothering to live in the first place. Besides, you've been spending so much time at the lab that you'll be asleep in 15 minutes."

She was right, too. I didn't even finish the wine....

I checked my suit regulators. Mixture fine; temperature tolerable. I tried to relax and slow my breathing.

Get with it, Girl. I didn't know what 'it' was, but thinking about Amelia made me feel better.

Far below, a light began to penetrate the darkness. It couldn't be artificial, so this suggested an animal unafraid to broadcast its presence while straight-line cruising. A predator—and a big one.

All Europan divers were supplied with bio-deterrents similar to old-style shark repellants that inked up the water, except these worked. Even the EurOrca, a one-ton gilled mammal that could polish off a woman in several love bites, would jackrabbit at full-speed after snorting Cousteau Skunkworks. Plus, our suits could ward off smaller species via an embedded electrified mesh if something bit through the polymers. This was especially effective for ankle biters. Still, the rising light was difficult to explain. Big appetites don't often patrol near the ice; their prey swim in darker, warmer waters. The grey shallows are typically the domain of shirpflies and plankton.

My heartbeat increased, and I removed a Skunkworks packet from the utility belt, ready to snap the seal. If Mr. or Ms. Badass tried to put the make on me, it would get a whiff of the foulest non-toxic toxicity ever invented. A guppy could fend off Jaws with one vial, and I was the guppy.

The light grew whiter as it rose slowly from the depths. "White" is almost always artificial on Europa because its bioluminescence leans toward blue or violet. So this was no EurOrca. Plus, straight lines are unnatural for vertebrates; the hex-jellyfish don't surface unless dead; and belly-up jellies are lightless.

Amelia said I'd find a new species, but I wasn't happy about it at the moment. I just hoped the thing was huggable or repellable. With today's luck, this might be the one galactic creature that enjoyed a little Skunkworks mustard with its Michelle Stern hotdog.

The light came from an empty wetsuit Amelia had somehow inflated and released through the diving bell's waterlock. Even so, the getup was barely buoyant, and when I discovered why, I broke down crying. Amelia had attached an extra 5000-psi tank along with a mini-guidance system to keep the ensemble from veering so far off course that I might never have found it.

How could she have managed this before implosion? It seemed impossible from everything I knew about pod construction, but I knew more about my wife. Also, there was no other explanation for the floating wetsuit. The diving bell must have been too deep for her to leave or she would have swum up with the rest of the survivors. Amelia was one of those leave-no-one-behind types—not on a mountain, in space, or underwater. Dead or alive, everyone comes home. But on this expedition, even if Amelia had somehow slowed their descent, I saw no other outcome but an unmarked grave with nine bodies at the bottom of the deepest known ocean. My soul would die with one of them.

The floating diving suit qualifies as luck even though Amelia sent it. Good fortune comes in surprising ways.

The arctic-grade diving suits are bulky and hard to maneuver, especially when cold, so donning one underwater would be impossible. Amelia must have assumed I could tap the resources—HHO and heat—to increase my odds of survival. She probably overestimated my abilities, though switching tank regulators would be easy enough. Also, the added bubble would give me plenty of ice-cave breathing room. Calculations still told me that the heat would last only 25 or 26 hours total—assuming I could jury-rig a connection. I needed 4 or 5 more unless the upside crew were really busting ass.

"Every extra hour is a victory and opportunity." Amelia was still banging around inside my head.

God, I'm stupid. The diving suits are basically plug-and-play, and all I had to do was remove the heating unit from the reserve outfit, discard mine, and insert the new battery pack. I figured I'd have to cut and splice to transfer energy from the extra suit. Next time I'll read the travel brochures more carefully.

Design engineers are sensible folks and aquatic units are apparently interchangeable, so I could count on 25 hours of low-range heat. I considered diving toward warmer waters, but that would leave my oxygen cave out of reach above me, not to mention that hydro-heliox isn't recommended below 200 meters. And at that depth, there wouldn't be much temperature rise. Plus, there's my suffocation phobia. I prefer to freeze.

I wish Amelia were here. She'd know how to stretch every oxygen molecule and every joule. I swear that woman could rub two icicles together and create fire. In fact, one of her most annoying features is that she's good at just about everything.

Twenty-two hours, and I'm shivering in my wetsuit. I've stored lots of air in the bubble cave, but my heating unit reports 3.2 hours of juice remaining, which gives me 3.3 hours to live.

I have an idea that would either make Amelia proud or want to confine me in a mental ward. Oh, what I would give for a nice, warm psychiatric hospital.

At first the waiting game seemed my only option, hoping that a rescue pod would emerge through the ice ahead of schedule. But no more. It's time to go EurOrca fishing! Time to meet one of the most ill-tempered and beautiful gilled mammals in creation, and there was an absolute surefire way to attract it from the depths. Blood. More irresistible than the glow of a Wiggle-Bite to any self-respecting predator.

All divers carry titanium utility knives. Won't rust or grow dull, and they have buoyancy compensators that keep them from sinking or floating away. Otherwise, with my shivering, I'd be afraid to pull it out of the sheath. Come on, strategy; come on, luck.

The plan is simple. Stick the knife through my wetsuit at mid-forearm just enough that I can let some EurOrca bait—half a pint of blood ought to make a nice cloud. Then, I'll gently pull out the blade and allow the suit seal the wound. My arm should stop bleeding quickly in this cold, and the blood's saline content will keep the stuff from freezing.

I also remove and extend the single bang-stick that's every diver's backup if Skunkworks doesn't scram a bad guy. But I don't mean to ward off my EurOrca. And while I understand that a ten-gauge charge on the end of a 75-centimeter rod is small stuff for this brute, I want the EurOrca to attack. I need him to attack.

The good news? If my scheme fails, I'll die quickly.

The knives are scalpel sharp, and I slowly press the point into the forearm of my wetsuit. There's an attention-getting electric jolt when the blade pierces the wire mesh. Now I understand why small fry don't bite divers. They learn as fast as I did.

I temporarily unplug the battery pack and reinsert the knife. The mesh is an aluminum-copper alloy that's no match for titanium. I slice to my skin and sink the tip about two centimeters. Blood; plenty much. But when I remove the blade, the suit pressure stops the bleeding as expected.

After five minutes, I'm too cold to know whether I'm also woozy, but I let out more blood until there's a red haze in the water. Then I re-plug the battery and hold my position. It could take a while for the scent to penetrate deep waters, so I hope an adult EurOrca is close enough to smell dinner. I dread this close encounter of the third kind, but it's necessary.

Waiting for the bus again. Waiting. In 20 minutes, release more blood. Probably the half a pint total I'd planned on.

Wait. Shiver. Breathe. Repeat.

There. Down below. A circling blue florescence. Please be a EurOrca!

Yes! A big male (distinctive dorsal fin). Surprisingly cautious. I suppose he's not used to the scent of human blood. Probably as afraid of me as I am of him, as they say, but he's prowling, all right, and death sometimes happens in pursuit of a full belly.

He's seen me! Enormous, penetrating eyes. The animal looks similar to an Arctic killer whale, but EurOrcas are solid black to blend with the darkness, though they can emit an array of blue-violet patterns. He's putting on a display for me like a sea leopard that can change its spots.

He dashes in my direction, turning abruptly at two meters, probably testing to be sure I don't have hidden fangs.

"Come on, sweetie!" I say. "Smell that luscious human blood? Want a bite?"

It's strange to see gills on a warm-blooded creature even though I've viewed lots of photos. And this bad boy is big, at least a metric ton. If I poke his flank with a bang-stick, it's just going to make him mad and I'll be chopped liver in the belly of a whale. Well, not actually a whale, but no difference to the chopped.

Another mock attack, but this time he turns at one meter, churning the water hard. I lose my grip on the bang-stick, which I kick upward with my fin just enough to grab it.

Ugh! The EurOrca clamps down on my left leg and shakes me like champagne after game 7 of the World Series. My only goal now is to hold onto that stick. Otherwise, I'm dead. I may be dead anyway.

It lets go abruptly, so I assume he received enough electricity from the mesh to scorch the inside of his mouth, which is where I planned to set off the 10-gauge. He's circling more cautiously, but his eyes are hard focused on me.

My chomped leg is bleeding badly and broken in several places. Only my suit is holding everything together and reducing the hemorrhage. If the animal waits 10 minutes, I'll be cold meat. So I open my regulator for a bubble surge, hoping this will signal distress and lure him in for the kill. One of us must die now!

The EurOrca charges with a maw that could chomp me in half. But this time, I'm ready. I shove the explosive charge, along with most of my right arm, deep inside its throat near the gills.

Bam and bananarama!

Blood gush. Death thralls. Not mine.

The beast reflexively holds onto my arm, quivering in uncontrolled spasms. I think the 10-gauge took out part of its brain and nervous system, and within 20 seconds, the EurOrca is still. He begins to sink, slowly, with my arm locked in its teeth.

These animals have inflatable bladders for buoyancy control, but my dead companion must have been planning to grab and dive because he isn't in float mode.

"Act fast," I think, "or the poor animal will have died for nothing."

I wedge the bang rod inside the mouth, using all the strength in my left arm to pry open the jaws a tiny bit. That doesn't help much, but it keeps the mouth from closing tighter. Then, I take my knife and start cutting around the five-centimeter teeth that are holding me.

I should've been a dentist. Tooth extraction with a titanium blade is almost easy (of course it helps when the patient is deceased). Once my mangled arm is free, I move underneath the carcass to the rectum. Taking a deep breath, I disconnect my breathing tube from the facemask and jam it inside as deep as possible, opening the pressure valve. The EurOrca bloats like a 10-month pregnancy and, with a few right-leg kicks on my part, we inch back toward the bubble enclave.

My breathing mixture tastes like feces when I reconnect the tube, but despite desperate injuries to my left leg and right arm, the plan has worked—so far. I remove a Fentanyl hypo from the med kit and take a shot to minimize the pain. I can't risk damaging the EurOrca's intestinal track and losing buoyancy, so I remove a few more of the larger teeth and begin to squirm my body feet first through the mouth. Now, I'm glad for the size of this beast, and the 10-gauge has broken his jaw hinge, which makes my progress a little easier.

My broken leg hurts bad even with the Fentanyl. I can feel it bend back on itself, but this isn't the time to worry. My heating units are nearly finished, and I need body warmth from the EurOrca. Its blubber should help retain heat, and with the combined insulation of a whale-equivalent and my wetsuit, I hope to stay alive until somebody finds this strange configuration.

After wriggling five minutes, I'm shoulder deep in the EurOrca's gullet and exhausted. We are floating inside the breathing enclave, but I can't keep my head above water much longer. I'm losing consciousness. Not to mention, the animal's too big to maneuver from my quasi-fetal position. All or nothing, I figure, and remove two inflatable dive-markers. I unplug the 70cm-long breathing tube from the tank (leaving my face mask in place), attach the two balloons to the free end, and activate the CO_2 inflators. With the tube now supported above the waterline, I exhale sharply to expel any water. I can only hope that the marker balloons keep the breathing end afloat and that my EurOrca won't have post-mortem flatulence. If he sinks, I'm sunk.

As I begin to fantasize about rescue, I fall into unconsciousness.

I awoke in the topside two-bed medical clinic; no doctor on staff, but an experienced paramedic in radio contact with an M.D. at the orbiting Jupiter lab and habitat. Amelia smiled and squeezed my hand gently, so I was pretty sure I was dead. People don't come back from the deep. I must have joined her.

"Hi, honey," she said. "You're in the worst shape of anybody from our group. I thought I'd lost you."

"Pretty sure you did," I said, feeling drugged, "because there's no way you're alive. I saw the capsule go down."

She grinned. "You think I can't handle no-hope situations. Besides, we had it easy compared with you. The pod was sinking pretty fast, and it took 15 minutes to bypass the safety protocols, but we sheared off our nuclear heating plates fore and aft using the explosive bolts. This makes the pod about as buoyant as a rectally inflated EurOrca. It took 40 hours to reach the surface. But we weren't in a hurry, and the engineers in our group, including me, didn't want to risk making the situation worse. With plenty of air and power, we relaxed and radioed topside for another bell; they double-humped and were waiting for us—after taking lots of photos of you in that 'cocoon.' Pretty weird."

The paramedic interjected. "At first, we figured you were dead."

"I'm still not convinced I'm not."

Amelia lightly thumped my broken leg, and I yelped.

"Sound alive," she said, still grinning. "Maybe this adventure stuff suits you. Of course, they had to pump a bit of water from your lungs, add two pints of blood, and punch 214 staples to close all the gashes. You also have a tinge of frostbite, and there's a very curious surgeon awaiting your presence at the station." She pointed. "What's left of that leg will need carbon implants. And the rest of your body looks like Muhammad Ali pounded it for a workout, but it's still the most beautiful piece of humanity I've ever seen."

I couldn't help but smile and then wince because my jaw also hurt. "My off-Earth days are over. I want a warm California lab with nothing larger than a clownfish. And if you thump my leg again, Wifey Dearest, I'll tell the police you're the one who broke it."

Amelia laughed. "The medic pulled two EurOrca teeth from your wetsuit, so I don't think the evidence will support the claim. Besides, I wanted your attention. I love you too much to let you think you're dead."

"I love you, too, but no more thumping!"

"Now," she said, "our friend here is going to add some pain meds to the I.V. Then we're shuttling to the Jovian hospital, and you're going to get well. Understand! Your survival story, or what little we know of it, is already spreading through the solar system."

"Oh, god," I said. "If I have to be some kind of celebrity, shove me back under the ice. I'd rather be chewed up by EurOrcas than the media."

Amelia smiled. "I'm the one who should worry. People love to love heroes. So just remember whose names are on our marriage certificate."

I cherished our bantering. "Whose name do you think kept me alive down there? Just get me warm and dry and back on Earth."

"Does that mean you're not coming with me next year to climb the largest known mountain in the solar system?"

I squeezed her hand gently. "The last I heard, Olympus Mons is not in California. But if you reserve a luxury suite at the Crater's Edge Hilton—with a hot tub in the room—I might be persuaded to meet you up top."

THE PREDATOR TRAP

"Have you seen Tehenna?" asked Jeremy Willard.

"Not since breakfast," said Mora Willard. "She's hiking."

"Might break a hundred today. Hope she took enough water."

"Of course she did!" said Mrs. Willard. "Tehenna was raised in Joshua Tree—and in case you haven't noticed, she's almost a grown woman."

"Going off to college isn't grown, and the desert's unforgiving about carelessness."

"She'll be fine. It takes brains to get into Berkeley, and our girl will practice law on Capitol Hill someday, not the local Tree House prosecuting shoplifters and barroom derelicts."

Mr. Willard broke a smile. "And what's wrong with thumping down drunk drivers?"

"Not a thing, Honey. You're a fabulous DA. Too bad you got tied down in the Mojave when you could have been fighting big-city crime."

Willard flashed a smile, embraced his wife, and kissed her on the cheek. "I like Joshua Tree, for your information, but I don't want T-Girl in law school. She can be a doctor."

"It's her decision."

Willard sighed. "True…, but if she's hiking without proper gear, good old Dad will prosecute her for reckless endangerment."

"Don't be ridiculous. She could walk the park blindfolded—and she loves the desert almost as much as you love her."

"You're a wise woman, Mrs. Willard, though prone to exaggeration."

Tehenna Willard's vehicle was eventually located near the trailhead for Lost Horse Mine. Her car was locked, the trunk contained half a case of bottled water, and Tehenna's backpack was missing. Despite an extended search, no trace of the girl was ever found.

"What's going on?" asked Professor Halverson.

"Cops are snooping around the department," said Professor Jackson. "Burt didn't show for start of classes. Nobody's heard from him."

"Christ," said Halverson. "I think he was digging in the Sierra Madre."

"You'd better tell the police," said Jackson.

"They ought to check with Burt's wife. She'd have more information."

"Joan hasn't heard from him either. Family's worried."

Halverson shook his head. "That can't be good. Burt's a big guy. Street smart, too." He whispered. "Always carries a gun in the backcountry. Practical and tough."

"Maybe not tough enough if he stumbled onto drug runners."

"Damn," said Halverson. "Hope we haven't lost one of our best anthropologists."

Manuel Joseph Rodriguez was twelve years old, an adventurous boy who hated school and loved the high plains of Arizona. Sometimes he would hop on his Yamaha dirt bike, ride to the forests along the north rim of the Grand Canyon, pitch a makeshift bivouac, and sleep under the stars.

Manuel's mother was native Anasazi. His father was a Mexican immigrant who met and married Manuel's mother and then abandoned her before Manuel could walk. Rumors suggested that, after making a fortune smuggling marijuana into the United States, he retired to a village south of Chihuahua. The boy had not seen his father in eleven years. He wouldn't recognize him if he did.

Manuel often escaped into the wilderness for two or three days without telling his mother. Upon his return, she never seemed to realize he'd been gone. Today, the clear April morning over the canyon was spectacular, and as Manuel watched the shifting colors, he wondered about his future. What would become of him? What did he want? Where would he live? He worried but never complained, and his visits to the rim country quieted his inner spirit.

At nine o'clock that morning, Manuel strapped his bedroll on the Yamaha and prepared for the ride home. Maybe his mother would make venison with gravy for dinner. Manuel often went without food during his excursions; after all, he was a boy and did not think about eating until his belly reminded him. It was talking now.

Manuel walked toward the woods to relieve himself before starting the rugged thirty-mile ride. As he stepped, the ground suddenly gave way, his skin crawled with a chemical fire, and endless darkness engulfed him.

"Listen," said Dr. Herbert Robertson, "I found an interesting specimen in Arizona. Who's that entomology whiz kid?"

"Sheila somebody," said Eldridge Wilder, the lab supervisor. "Other students call her 'The Brain' but don't seem to like her much."

"Track her down," said Robertson. "I want to know if my bug is special."

"I'll get her email from the secretary."

"Make it quick. I want to get somebody in the field if it's important."

Wilder looked puzzled. "You wouldn't go yourself?"

"Damned summer teaching plus a dissertation review. Dull as last year's tax code, but it looks like we'll send another Ph.D. into the world. He's not ambitious enough to do too much damage."

Wilder understood. If marginally competent students worked long enough and politely listened to their advisors, most would earn a degree, teach at a high school or community college, and never again research beyond their doctoral studies. "I know what you mean," said Wilder, "but Sheila's kind of a live wire. Possible makings of a real scientist."

Robertson nodded. He trusted Wilder's judgment in these matters. "I'll stop by the secretary's office myself. Thanks."

Sheila Hammond-Slatter was a home-stretch doctoral candidate with one more year as a Teaching Assistant before finishing her dissertation entitled "Insect Habitats in the Southwestern United States."   She argued that contemporary environmentalists were so focused on hydrocarbon emissions, global warming, or mammalian extinctions that they neglected insects, including the specialized Mojave bees, wasps, brine flies, ants, and beetles. To Slatter, however, desert insects were evolutionary survivalists that could eat next to anything and somehow thrive with next to nothing, including some ant varieties that dug down 30 feet in rocky alluvia to find water and comfort when the surface temperatures hovered at 120 degrees. And they had been doing it long before Homo sapiens crawled out of the muck and said, "Let's build condos."

"If we lose the insects," wrote Slatter, "we lose the plants. And if we lose the plants, we lose the planet." She also believed that insects were morally superior to humans. They killed only for survival.

Slatter had been summoned by Dr. Robertson, but she was cautious. The eminent professor rarely engaged directly with students, and she was an entomologist, not a paleontologist, so what could he want with her? Probably needed someone to teach a summer class; but then again, if this turned out to be some sexual harassment deal, she'd stuff a petrified pinecone up his ass.

Slatter knocked on the door, which was partially open. "Dr. Robertson?"
Sheila Slatter?" asked the professor.

"Yes."

"Please, sit down."

Slatter did as instructed.

"I don't have much time," said Robertson, reaching for a sealed plastic container. "I retrieved this little critter near the Virgin River Gorge in Arizona. What's your opinion?" He passed the vial to Slatter.

"An ant," she said, evaluating. "Almost certainly formicidae. Maybe camponotus. But not from Arizona."

Robertson was surprised. "Are you in the habit of conclusions at a glance?"

Slatter spoke with confidence. "A glance informed by experience. I studied insects long before college, and this is not a high-desert variety. Looks more tropical than arid."

Robertson had the right person. "I'll double-check my log, but the specimen came from Northern Arizona. I was there."

Slatter pulled a magnifying glass out of her faded jeans' back pocket and continued examining the insect, silently, and Robertson watched for several minutes. She seemed to have forgotten his presence.

Finally, Robertson skipped forward and asked, "What are you doing for summer?"

"Squatting in the library to finish my dissertation," said Slatter without looking up. Then she said slowly under her breath, "Beautiful!"

"Who's your advisor?"

"Bradbury."

"A good woman. With your permission, I'll talk with her." Robertson pointed at the vial. "I'd like you to search for more of these, and one summer of actual fieldwork is worth two years in the library."

She continued to examine the specimen. "Very strange.... Might be a new species."

"Well, if so, locate the colony, publish a paper about their behavior and habitat, and you'll hop-skip to your doctoral robing."

"Was this the only one you found?" asked Sheila.

"Yes, but I didn't really look. Wasn't sure it was special."

"Listen," said Slatter, "I need to compare samples. There are several hundred in my private collection, and I'll visit a friend at UC Riverside, but this is not an ant in the usual sense. Large eyes, streaks of albinism that hint of a subterranean habitat, while other portions have more typical surface pigmentation. Where you near any caverns?"

"Not that I know of….but don't all ants work underground?"

"Above and below," said Slatter, peering closely at the vial. "Could be both diurnal and nocturnal, and the color patterns are blended hymenoptera but, still, closely resemble wasps. Large mandibles. Body over an inch. Probably a soldier of some alpine-tropical hybrid, if that's possible. I need to get it under a microscope and to cross-check the known species and fossil catalogs." She paused and said again, "Beautiful!"

"How soon can you start?" asked Professor Robertson.

"Not for a while. I'm currently teaching Anthro 101. Three more weeks of class, another to grade final papers, and then I'm free."

"Forget it. Your lab partner will finish the course. You're now on a special research assignment. OK by you?"

Slatter exhaled with relief. "Better than OK, Professor! Glad I won't need a pinecone," and immediately regretted saying that.

"What?"

"Sorry," she stuttered. "I…I… just wasn't sure…exactly why you asked me here."

Robertson cracked a smile with a student for the first time in three years. "My dear Ms. Slatter, I'm not so naïve as to misjudge you in that way. Besides, your attire for this special meeting, especially considering I must sign off on your dissertation, tells me you probably don't care about much beyond your work. That's not all good, by the way—not that I should talk."

Sheila was already examining the ant again. "Magnificent. Just magnificent…."

Slatter pitched her camp east of the Virgin River Gorge on a solo expedition in search of what she believed was a new species—the kind of adventure she had dreamed of since her first bee sting at age six. This would be the summer of Sheila Slatter, hiking and digging with her six-legged friends.

The Anthropology Department maintained communal camping gear for fieldwork, but Sheila preferred her own, which was superior and familiar. She had a cast iron Dutch oven used directly over a campfire to prepare anything from basic stews to fresh bread. She had a dome tent, canned goods for two months, thirty gallons of water, and an old Jeep Wrangler that was held together mostly with prayers and bailing wire but climbed mountain roads like a bull market. She also carried her basic lab kit and microscope that were almost as battered and durable as her Jeep. And when she wanted a break from the grit and sand, which wasn't often, Sheila could drive to St. George to pick up cubed ice, fresh vegetables, cheese, or drinks, and find a campground coin operated shower to wash her body and hair.

All Slatter really needed to be happy was a magnifying glass and a specimen. She planned to spend two or three weeks searching the immediate area where Robertson found the first sample, which she dubbed as High Plains Bigfoot. If she didn't find the colony during the first survey, she'd move southwest toward the northern rim of the Grand Canyon; then, maybe she'd rent a canoe and rummage around the shores of Lake Mead. The whole desert was hers, and she was the desert.

"Did you hear about Miss Sheila Suck-up?" asked Megan, another graduate student back at the university.

"Yep," said Tyrone. "How come she rates an all-expense-paid vacation while the rest of us are locked down for final exams?"

"They let her off teaching, too," added Jennifer. "Dumped the course on her lab partner."

"Bitch," offered Tyrone, enjoying the sound. "Like she's so special."

Megan glanced around the cafeteria. "Don't say that I said so, but last week before she left, Sheila had a private meeting with old man Robertson…, if you know what I mean."

"Yeh," said Jennifer, "Closed doors. Open legs."

Megan grimaced. "Can you imagine having sex with that old fossil?!"

"No kidding?" asked Tyrone. "I always wondered how she kept that perfect GPA."

"There are probably more private meetings than we know," added Jennifer.

"Well, we should pity her," said Megan, turning generous. "Sheila's too weird to ever find a job. Dresses like a tramp. No social life. Cares about nothing but bugs…. And has she said more than ten words to anybody?"

"Not me."

"Me neither," said Tyrone. "Could be she doesn't know ten words, not counting slip off dem panties."

Megan laughed. "She's never heard of hairbrush or makeup, that's for sure. A pretty girl if she made an effort."

"By the way," asked Tyrone, "has anybody finished the final lab problem? Why are they throwing calculus at us?   Maybe Bradbury threw us a trick question."

"I don't get it, either," said Megan.

"Too bad Sheila's not here," said Jennifer. "She'd know the answer."

After six weeks, Sheila had found only desert typical fauna. This would normally have been enough, but she was desperate to locate another Bigfoot. The more she studied Robertson's specimen, the more she lamented over not having a live sample.

On June 21, Sheila relocated to a transitional zone of alpine forest and high chaparral at Grand Canyon's north rim. There, she spent nine or ten hours per day hiking, digging, and searching for a colony that might not exist. But Sheila's relentlessness said that a new species was waiting for her. She felt it as surely as the hot desert breeze through her hair.

After ten more days, Sheila had found nothing but an old, rusted Yamaha-80 dirt bike, apparently abandoned by some adolescent who couldn't afford a real motorcycle and didn't mind polluting the landscape with his broken-down mechanical garbage. She was annoyed but decided to retrieve her folding army shovel and bury the motorbike. The landscape was too beautiful to leave such an eyesore above ground.

Sheila dug in the 90-degree morning temperatures, rested when the thermometer hit 100, and drank lots and lots of water. It took her a day and a half to vanquish the motorcycle, and Sheila had two blisters to show for it. Afterward, returning to basecamp, she enjoyed hot lemon tea, raisin-heavy trail mix, and a late afternoon campfire. She was not a strict vegetarian but leaned toward an earth-friendly diet of grain and legume proteins because she didn't want to support cattle production or the dairy and beef products that accounted for nearly 25 percent of the country's methane emissions. Also, there was something disquieting about Americans feasting on slabs of grain-fed beef while half the world's population were undernourished. While she didn't have all the answers to such problems, she tried to live a conservationist lifestyle. She hoped to do more after finishing her studies; and by the grace of science, she would.

The peaceful, cloudless afternoon still hovered at 90 degrees with a gentle breeze, yet Slatter savored hot tea in all seasons. As she sat and drank and meditated, a small female deer walked from a pine thicket 40 yards away. The doe nibbled on a young Manzanita bush in the rocky soil, and it would occasionally raise its head to glance toward Sheila, twitch its tail, and resume grazing. Sheila watched and smiled and sipped the honeyed fragrant liquid. The doe took two cautious steps toward a leafier sprig and was suddenly swallowed by the earth in a silent cloud of dust.

Sheila Hammond-Slatter, a scientifically trained observer, believed her eyes. She approached the scene with extreme caution.

It was now the end of summer and two months since the foraging deer led Slatter to the High Plains Bigfoot colony. She had relocated her camp half a mile away to help prevent any random passerby from finding the site, which she knew was unlikely. Each morning she hiked from basecamp to the formicary, mapped its underground labyrinth as best she could with her portable seismic imaging equipment, and studied the ant behavior by snaking the tunnels with a remote camera. The flexible probe was too large for most insect burrows, but not the Bigfoot passages. Some measured three to four inches in diameter, and the central excavation trap was two and a half feet across and nearly five deep.

Slatter formally named the species formicidae apocretia because it resembled a wingless wasp as much as an ant. The social organization was more definitively camponotus, but in either family, Bigfoot was a bad-ass predator. When Slatter crept upon the fallen deer two months earlier, she found at least 100,000 ants storming over the carcass. The poor animal was already dead (or paralyzed) from stings, and later venom analysis revealed chemical neurotoxins resembling a wasp-ant amalgam. Each injected dose, though relatively small, was potent enough that three or four ants could bring down a mouse, ten could likely stop a lapdog, and two hundred would immobilize a human. But the colony's attack was calibrated in multiple degrees of overkill. Bigfoot had dug a death pit capped with a papery, secreted mulch, similar to a wasps' nest, and interlaced with twigs, pebbles, leaves, and other surface debris. The camouflaged, collapsible lid was strong enough to support a chipmunk, but a large adult rabbit could fall through, as would a deer, wolf, or human. And Bigfoot waited for its prey like a trained militia of trapdoor spiders.

The colony seemed reclusive—digging, eating, and reproducing underground—and were confirmed as primarily carnivorous. Worker ants seemed to venture onto the surface only to repair the trapdoor or to deposit earth from the tunnels. On close examination above ground, Slatter detected a faint, ringed excavation pattern surrounding the nest, which provided the sole hint of danger. And Slatter was astounded that within six hours of immobilizing the young deer, the ants had re-knitted the surface cover to an unblemished landscape. No trace of the doe or the deadly trap remained above ground.

Slatter discovered that Robertson's dead specimen was not one of the colony soldiers, which were larger, averaging 1.75 inches in length with an abdomen comparable to the southwestern spider wasp. Robertson's one-inch sample was a typical worker, suited for cutting and packing the harvested meat supply. The real soldiers kept order in the colony, scouted for external threats, and would single handedly confront a tarantula if threatened. Slatter once saw five ants drive off an armadillo that had ventured too near the trap (apparently leathery placental mammals weren't on the menu); and using the underground camera, Slatter recorded segments of "processing" the young deer, which might have weighed sixty pounds. In three weeks, the flesh and hide were stripped from the bones; in two more, the skeleton had been "mulched" by a dual process of gnawing and chemical degradation that she did not yet understand. And she had yet to find a Bigfoot queen or egg chamber. She wondered how deep these might be.

Regretfully, however, the summer expedition was coming to an end. During her last full day of fieldwork at the formicary, Slatter marked the site with her GPS locator and eliminated any signs of human presence. The next morning, she would pack all of her equipment and acquired specimens into her Jeep, drive four hours straight to the university, and report her findings to Dr. Robertson. Slatter worried that nonscientists and politicians would want to kill the new species, which could certainly be dangerous to humans, and she believed the renowned professor would know what to do. If not, she had already decided to never reveal the location of the Bigfoot colony to anyone.

A week later, the bedraggled Sheila Slatter arrived at the university. She was noticeably careworn.

"How was your summer?" asked Robertson, pretending to ignore her disheveled appearance. "Did you find anything noteworthy regarding our specimen?"

"Nothing, Sir," said Slatter. "But I'd like to go back during winter break for further investigation. Three months should be about right."

Robertson smiled. "Patience, my young scientist, though you're welcome to return in December. And who knows? Maybe soon you'll be working here as a colleague as the new Doctor Slatter."

"That would be wonderful," she said, but with less enthusiasm than the professor expected. Slatter seemed strangely distracted, wounded, and uncertain. Not the confident—almost arrogant—woman Robertson had met three months before.

"Sheila," said Robertson, awkwardly, "I hate to bring this up so soon after your return, but I received several calls from the Arizona State Police and the FBI while you were gone. They know we have researchers in the field, and I told them about you and your work."

Slatter raised an eyebrow. Her heart skipped a beat. "And?"

"Well…, a lone hiker was reported missing in your general area. Authorities found his vehicle and campsite, but not the man."

"What's that got to do with me?" asked Sheila, her pulse now racing.

"Ah…Yes. It's difficult for me to discuss this with a student, especially a young woman, but the police reportedly found a handwritten journal in that hiker's tent."

"So?"

"This might disturb you…, or even frighten you."

Slatter regained some confidence and stiffened. "I don't scare easily."

"No, I don't think you do. But one of the entries mentioned a young woman, a university researcher, working alone in the wilderness. The man ran into her. They talked and…." Professor Robertson faltered, "Oh, my, according to his journal notes, he planned to, ugh, you know, return during the night, force himself onto her, hold her for a while, and…eventually kill her. The descriptive details were rather lurid, I'm afraid. And if I had known your exact whereabouts, I would have asked the police to find you as a precaution. I admit to being worried. But that aside, according to the FBI psychologists, the diary could have simply been a disturbed, psychotic fantasy. People sometimes do that. Then, again, sometimes they are not fantasies. Serial killers do exist."

"Don't know anything about it," said Slatter, looking at the floor, her hand trembling slightly.

Robertson exhaled, again pretending not to notice her appearance and manner. "I'm relieved," he said. "In any case, the sadistic journal author has apparently disappeared, and authorities will want to know whether you might have encountered any vermin besides scorpions and rattlesnakes."

"Rattlesnakes aren't vermin!" said Slatter more certainly. She paused and added, "But, no, I met no one on the trail." She was an unpolished liar.

Dr. Robertson paused and said, "I admit to being apprehensive after the FBI called. Further, based on that diary, they are also investigating several previous missing person reports, including a young woman from Joshua Tree, California. Journal Man just might turn out to be a very bad fellow, indeed." He hesitated. "They also found rope and duct tape in his vehicle's trunk. Not too unusual, but still, after hearing about those diary notations, I am greatly relieved to see you here…in one piece and apparently unharmed."

"No need for concern," said Slatter, seeming to regain some confidence. "Aside from not washing my hair as much as I would like, the summer offered a routine expedition. And I'm never afraid in the desert. That's my turf. I know it better than the lice or cockroaches or human scum who might wander there."

"Well," said Dr. Robertson, "I am very glad you're OK." Something, however, suggested that she was not.

"Thank you, Sir. And if the FBI's Journal Man is guilty of anything beyond pornographic license, let's hope the Great Mojave executed its own system of justice. In the wilderness, the death of one can often sustain the lives of many."

The professor replied, "Not a pleasant way for someone to die, though, alone in the desert."

"Better than a damned psychopath might offer to his victims!" said Slatter with surprising stone cold bitterness. She winced a little and added, "Among desert appetites, the decaying flesh of a scoundrel is as nourishing as a saint."

Robertson felt a twinge of foreboding. "Are you certain you're all right, Ms. Slatter? You look fatigued…, and those bruises? I think a doctor should examine you, and why not take a couple days off before classes start?"

"Don't worry, Professor. I'll have the campus nurse practitioner check me to be sure. I've got a few scrapes and sore muscles, sure, and the last week of my expedition was rougher than expected. But I came out on top."

Robertson sensed that she was withholding information. "Listen, Sheila. Here's a business card for the Phoenix FBI office—Maureen Sullivan is the principal investigator. A nice woman and dedicated officer. If you remember anything that might help them, or if you would simply feel better talking with a woman than…me…, please call her."

"I appreciate it," said Slatter, taking the card and turning to leave. She looked back and added, "The Mojave Desert is a sacred cleanser of mind and, sometimes, murderous souls. And after a medical checkup, I think I'll start getting to know my fellow students a little better. Maybe, I can help some them through parts of the lab work—calculus doesn't come easily to everyone. I really haven't been too social during my time at the university. That's another thing I learned this summer."

"I'm pleased to hear this," said Dr. Robertson, still perplexed.

"Please don't worry, Professor. My fieldwork was righteously and scientifically fruitful. And while the great Mojave Desert may never reveal all of its secrets, in December, I plan to bring wondrous news back to you and this university."

MAIDEN VOYAGE OF THE FEARLESS

"Bite down hard," said the nurse.

Antoinette felt almost insulted. "I've done this before," she said, neither worried nor happy about the procedure. Despite her severe anxiety disorder, which was why she was here, the treatments were routine, and Antoinette liked routine. The nurse spread conductive gel on Antoinette's temples. The doctor positioned the electrode paddles. "Ready," he said, more out of habit than necessity, and stepped on the foot pedal to administer electroshock therapy to his patient.

Because the treatments were moderately helpful, Antoinette Rodriguez and her parents requested they be administered twice per year in addition to the usual medications for stress and depression. At age 34, Antoinette still lived with her parents, typically left her bedroom only for specially prepared meals, and almost never ventured outside the Rodriguez residence except to the hospital for biannual "electroconvulsive therapy."

ECT was rarely used because many medical practitioners considered it barbaric. The procedure certainly looked barbaric with its purposefully induced seizures by shooting electricity into the brain while restraining the patient on a table. The nurses, especially young women new to the profession, typically found it more distasteful than the doctors, but everyone who had worked with Antoinette during two decades of psychiatric care agreed. She needed these treatments. Pharmaceuticals, hypnosis, and counseling could do only so much, and even with enhanced anxiety medications, Antoinette was a curious case: acute agoraphobia compounded by depression, obsessive compulsive disorder, and other issues that could not be precisely labeled. Off the record, people said, "The woman's terrified of everything." Antoinette even worried about the day when her loving parents might abandon her, or die, or murder her and stuff the body into an industrial meat grinder to dispose of the evidence.

Antoinette understood that there were no rational bases for most of her fears, but by age 14 she had begun to have severe social difficulties. Too many people on campus. Too many at the shopping mall. Too many strangers. In fifth-period history class at Brookline High, Massachusetts, she started answering questions that had not been asked, and the teacher informed her parents. By age 15, with so many people "thinking bad thoughts," with so much danger everywhere, Antoinette refused to leave her bedroom.

To the relief of school authorities, the doctor transferred her to a psychiatric hospital in Belmont where she screamed hysterically about people trying to kill her, and then she cowered in a corner whenever left alone. Too many lab coats. Too much stimulation. Too much terror.

After four months of observation, medications, and electroconvulsive therapy, a psychiatric panel agreed that Antoinette Rodriguez was permanently disabled by mental illness. She would probably never be able to work, buy groceries, establish social relationships, or care for herself. She even had difficulty sleeping because dreams frightened her (insomnia added to the neurological troubles) and resisted exercise because she feared that the strain might induce a heart attack. Antoinette wondered whether even her shadow, which occasionally tried to console her, might turn malicious. A strong anti-anxiety and anti-depressant compound helped, but despite knowledgeable and compassionate doctors, Antoinette pleaded for the security of her own room.

"Like chicken soup," said Dr. William Crawford to her parents, "homecare couldn't hurt. And it might even help as we try different therapies."

So Antoinette returned to her familiar bedroom with a prescription, regular nursing visits, and bi-annual electroshock therapy. ECT worked better than anything else at temporarily calming the patient—enough, at least, so that Antoinette could function with in-house supervision of her parents. The insurance company supported the plan, as well, because it cost significantly less than inpatient hospital care.

Mr. and Mrs. Rodriguez worried what might happen to Antoinette should one or both of them die. They languished over grandchildren that would never be. They prayed that Antoinette would get better but, especially, not get worse. And the deeply religious Rodriguezes accepted God's purpose, whatever it may be, in the special care required of their daughter.

Thus, from age 15, Antoinette lived in her small bedroom with adjoining bath for the better part of 18 years, cleaning and sanitizing her living space every Wednesday and Saturday at 2:00 p.m. She had a desk, computer, and on-line access that included free library accounts and streaming via Netflix, Amazon, and HBO. There was no phone because Antoinette feared direct calls; thus, all communications from the doctors or would-be friends passed through Mr. and Mrs. Rodriguez, who talked through the door or passed notes under it. Antoinette generally accepted instructions from her mother or father as long as the messages were handwritten with a designated code number penned at the bottom. The code changed weekly. Her bedroom door remained locked at all times, though Mr. and Mrs. Rodriguez had a key, and Antoinette emerged for meals when summoned by the signal knock— dot, dot, dash, dash, dot, dot—followed by the words "Edgar's raven is not flitting." Antoinette trusted her parents as long as the codes and signals matched. Someone could impersonate them, and impersonators would be bad.

Mr. and Mrs. Rodriguez consented to all of Antoinette's requests. They had once considered corporeal punishment to pressure their daughter's socialization, which was strongly recommended by a family friend from Tennessee, but the Rodriguezes trusted in the therapeutic value of love.

Besides, the medications and electroconvulsive treatments seemed violent enough. What could coercion accomplish for Antoinette? And more to the point, Mr. and Mrs. Rodriguez absolutely cherished their daughter, and they would wait patiently for a medical miracle to come along—and they believed it would come.

God was good. God was merciful.

The miracle came. Pharmaceutical researchers developed what was informally called "courage in a bottle"; and the first-stage animal trials had remarkably decreased anxiety in some of the most timid creatures imaginable. A cat that cowered under the sofa when any stranger arrived suddenly became a lap kitty for all comers. A subordinate capuchin monkey turned calm, grew back its full body hair, and, when threatened, seemed almost anxious to fight other capuchins; further, the smaller (medicated) monkey did not become aggressive unless provoked. A mixed-breed shelter dog that had never lifted its tail from between its legs could suddenly trust humans, wag its whole body from tip to stern, tug on its leash to explore new territories, and appear ecstatic about everything it met. The previously abandoned animal was adopted by a research technician who noted that the Ferralyxis-infused pooch could sometimes be too happy to control.

Doctors and researchers quickly targeted Antoinette Rodriguez as a prime candidate for the human trials of Ferralyxis. She had spent 18 years in self-exile, essentially leaving home only for electroconvulsive therapy. Antoinette's parents were eager to test the medication on their daughter, hoping it might be the long-solicited miracle from heaven. Antoinette, however, resisted all persuasive efforts, for she long ago surrendered to the anxieties that were much stronger than she could ever be. She had grown comfortable in her protected life with a computer window to the external world.

"Happiness is a locked room," thought Antoinette. But while she sought security now and forever, her parents worried about a dark future where trees fell in the forest and made no sound because their daughter would never even attempt to hear them. After praying on the matter, Mr. and Mrs. Rodriguez signed consent forms to begin Antoinette's treatment with Ferralyxis.

Dr. Crawford (Antoinette's psychiatrist) and Dr. Kovack (pharmaceutical executive) visited Antoinette at home for the first therapeutic injection, which could not be administered because the patient barricaded her bedroom door when she heard their car pull into the driveway. This was not completely unexpected. Antoinette defended herself thusly against all intruders. Even Dr. Crawford, whom she trusted as much as she could anyone beyond her parents, failed to persuade her out of the bedroom for treatment. Irrational fear is its own defense, and since age 15, Antoinette's had been nearly insurmountable.

"It's all right, Antoinette," said Dr. Crawford through the door. "We won't force our way. I'll come back alone and talk with you another time."

The doctors both knew that Antoinette's regular ECT was set for 11:00 a.m. the following Thursday. They would simply administer the Ferralyxis then.

Antoinette always kept those appointments. She was afraid not to.

Antoinette's 32nd electroconvulsive therapy session proceeded much like all the others she had endured, almost enjoyed. They provided a degree of relaxation that could be counted on. Not a cure, but a change of pace, a different drummer. Combined with the sedative after Antoinette regained consciousness, ECT was similar to what other folks might feel when visiting a bar for whiskey and companionship. Something to do. Something to buzz the brain and body. But today, along with Antoinette's regular treatment, she unknowingly received a first dose of Ferralyxis before returning to the warm embrace of her bedroom.

Her parents had hope. Antoinette did not possess the knowledge to have hope.

The doctors provided Mr. and Mrs. Rodriguez with liquid Ferralyxis and instructed them to add five drops to Antoinette's lunchtime Kool-Aid, her favorite beverage, though she heated it to 182 degrees in a large coffee mug to destroy any lurking bacteria. At dinner, she preferred cherry flavored sparkling water straight from the bottle after washing the neck with disinfectant and then rinsing with distilled water, a ritual that had continued for 18 years. Antoinette's food was likewise scrutinized, and Mrs. Rodriguez had long ago learned to prepare nutritious meals that were satisfactory to her daughter, though Mrs. Rodriguez waited for a day when the meticulous routines might change.

That time, hopefully, had come. Medical professionals advised Mr. and Mrs. Rodriguez that Ferralyxis would probably require weeks or months to accumulate in Antoinette's brain with noticeable effects, but since she was the first human patient, precise effects could be neither predicted nor guaranteed. The initial dosage was minimal, based on animal tests, and would be gradually increased according to Antoinette's progress. The possibility remained that Ferralyxis would not benefit humans, so expectations should be curtailed until outcomes were confirmed and calibrated. Medical science worked this way.

Antoinette's parents did not care to think about failure. Their daughter presently clung to the bottom rung of Jacob's ladder.

"Nothing to lose," they agreed. "Everything to gain."

The first Ferralyxis Kool-Aid was repeated day by day, but for Mr. and Mrs. Rodriguez, that initial dose marked the beginning toward a new world. Similar optimism resided in the doctors and nurses, parents and friends, and pharmaceutical investors—everyone but Antoinette, who remained strategically unaware of the miracle drug pulsing through her body.

Antoinette responded quickly to treatment and within three weeks took her lunch beverage over ice. She likewise began to spend a few afternoons in the living room, watching TV and talking with her mother about places and things she had read about online. The fifth week, Antoinette greeted her father upon his return from work and hugged him, something she had not done since age 12—and this hug proved noticeably more convincing.

Mr. Rodriguez treasured the surprise embrace of his daughter but asked, "Aren't you afraid of germs?" immediately wishing he hadn't.

Antoinette giggled and squeezed him even tighter. "You're worth the risk, Papi."

After seven weeks, Antoinette visited a local park with both parents, climbed on a swing, and laughed out loud as she re-learned how to make it go. Later they all went to a burger restaurant for lunch. Antoinette ordered her sandwich well-done, which still seemed sensible, but used ketchup from the table on her fries. She also tasted beer for the first time in her life. Through years of reading she could describe hundreds of varieties, how they were brewed, differences in color and clarity and effervescence, but having missed the actual experience of taste, she could not know the bubbled flavor of 34-degree Budweiser from a frosted mug.

Antoinette grimaced on the first sip and pushed the pint toward her father. "I think this will be an acquired taste!"

She then ventured sparkling water with a squeeze of fresh lime. "Now that's good!" she said after downing half the bottle without sterilizing the neck. Tears began to flow as she added, "But the best part is where I am… out in the world with my parents…who always stood by me." She paused and kissed her father and mother on each cheek. "How could you love such a pathetic daughter all those years?"

Antoinette did not expect an answer, and her mother began to cry, too.

"How could we not?" said Mrs. Rodriguez.

Antoinette knew a lot about love and hardship and sacrifice. She'd read millions of words on many subjects. But like the taste of alcohol, there was no way to measure emotional flavors without relevant experience. How could she possibly grasp her parents' devotion? To Antoinette, heartfelt family bonds seemed as illogical as they were beautiful.

A year later Antoinette could not be contained. After 19 years of seclusion, she became a runner, backpacker, and climber. Her goals included visiting every U.S. National Park that she'd read about from her bedroom computer. After that, she'd explore South America, Europe, Asia, Australia, Africa, and the moon if it ever opened to tourism. Her ambitions became imperatives (a new kind of anxiety) because she'd missed almost half a lifetime through mental incapacitation. "Fear," she decided, "is a vampire on the human spirit." Antoinette would abide no more of that, and she would account for every drop of her embezzled lifeblood.

Fortunately, Mr. and Mrs. Rodriguez could afford Antoinette's adventures and willingly provided leeway in their daughter's extraordinary rehabilitative passions. However, they became moderately concerned 36 weeks into treatment when Antoinette, during a gymnasium workout, confronted a "bully" (Antoinette's term) who proved reluctant to share the free weights with women.

"It seems," said the 145-pound Antoinette to the man, "that you have a certain possessiveness about our workout space." She had limited social skills and sounded more hostile than intended.

"What's that to you?" asked the 210-pound, heavily muscled, 6-foot-2 Adonis wannabe.

Antoinette didn't get angry immediately. This seemed like a straightforward question. "Well," she responded, "everyone pays for membership and should qualify for equal access and all that."

"How about I give you equal access to mops and buckets to clean the bathrooms, Brown Sugar. Why don't you get at it?"

Even Antoinette recognized this slander to women and Hispanics. Still, she spoke calmly. "Instead, how about I shove the handle end of a mop up your ass. Or maybe turn the bucket upside your head."

The man slapped Antoinette hard across the jaw. Her face felt like it exploded, but she stood straight and smiled, a small trickle of blood leaking from the side of her lip.

"Thank you," she began with a slow, calculated pace. "No one has hit ever me. It's much more educational than reading about misogynistic violence on my computer."

The man pondered her response, suspected that Antoinette might be mentally deficient, and made a half-witted apology. "Maybe that'll learn you some manners, honey. I don't like hitting a woman even when she deserves it."

Antoinette glanced downward and turned sideways to relax the man's guard. Then she tore into his 210-pound frame without restraint. She knew every point of anatomy and slammed the side of her palm hard against his larynx. As he began to choke and reflexively clutched his throat with both hands, she squared her body and lifted a knee into his groin with a bountiful squish. Adonis went down and stayed down.

Paramedics barely saved the man's life with an on-site tracheotomy. Patrons defended Antoinette's actions as self-defense—no one much liked Adonis anyway—but her gym membership was revoked. She didn't care. There were many fitness centers, and the righteous warmth from crushing an aggressor agreed with her.

Dr. Crawford reduced Antoinette's Ferralyxis prescription in response to the incident. "Such is the nature of human trials," he told Mr. and Mrs. Rodriguez. "No one yet knows a therapeutic level from an overdose." He did not say that surplus courage with deficit fear could be dangerous. Besides, as Antoinette grew stronger and happier month by month, the medication seemed a modern miracle; and she now took it knowingly and with terrible resolve.

Antoinette began to march up Yosemite Falls trail at 6:05 a.m. sharp. Her goals included a conditioning climb to the upper falls, allowing 19 minutes for rest breaks and snacks. Then she would hike to the edge of El Capitan and ultimately retrace her steps to the valley floor before dark. Early October would offer gentle weather and only a small trickle from Yosemite Creek. And as luck would have it, the day's forecast was 72 degrees with scattered white clouds and a soft breeze. Perfect.

As usual, Antoinette hiked alone with a well-equipped daypack that included the 10 essentials in case of emergency. Solitary ventures suited her best. She could ascend and descend without delays inflicted by an out-of-shape or under-motivated partner. Further, the Yosemite trails were well traveled, and if needed, assistance would be available and cellphone service at the summit registered three bars. Antoinette worried more about her training and conditioning than injury.

She loved the national parks, especially Yosemite and Zion. Her rock climbing skills were improving, and today's trail trek preceded a planned assault on El Capitan's face in five months. This would require more technical practice and a likely partner, but the problem for Antoinette remained that most climbers were cowards who couldn't meet her rigid standards. The goal was everything. And she had already missed out on too much life to hold back on account of nervous fools.

Still, Antoinette watched for telltale signs of human courage and determination. If she had been cured with Ferralyxis, others would inevitably follow. Then she might find a worthy partner. In the meantime, she must tolerate weakling peasants.

Antoinette's quadriceps already burned from exertion-induced lactate. She increased the pace.

Antoinette Rodriguez conquered the trail in 7 hours and 48 minutes. Not as fast as she would have liked, but respectable.

She stood at the rim of El Capitan, her boots four inches from the edge, and looked across Yosemite Valley. A stiff breeze raced up the cliff and brought water to her eyes. She wondered how she had ever lived in a tiny bedroom, in her tiny mind, afraid of places and feelings such as these.

Antoinette checked her Marathon watch and set the chronometer. She would allow 21 minutes to enjoy the view, snack on a protein-and-carb trail mix, rehydrate, and begin retracing her route to the valley floor. That was the plan, anyway. But as she marveled at Yosemite with Ferralyxis enhanced emotion, a small earthquake rattled the ground along a minor slip-strike fault, as often happens in California. This was not a temblor that would make news beyond professional geologists—a 2.8 on the Richter scale, centered 3 miles north of El Capitan, and barely noticeable. But Antoinette noticed. A soft roll and a rumble.

Standing several feet away stood a rugged, handsome looking man with his German shepherd on a sturdy leather leash. The dog apparently also heard the temblor and growled toward nothing in particular. Antoinette disliked the throaty sound, and though a dog might be forgiven for primitive instincts and lack of human intelligence, she slipped the backpack from her shoulders and discretely removed a combat-ready Buck Knife. She opened the freshly honed blade and firmed her stance. Even as she consciously tried to calm her adrenaline response, she figured it couldn't hurt to be prepared.

Antoinette held silent for several seconds but finally said to the young man, "I'm sorry, but don't like threats, even from an animal. They make me edgy."

"Oh," said the kind-hearted man, "please forgive us. My dog's name is Questor, and we love hiking together. I'm sure the growl wasn't at you. He's loved everybody since he was a pup. Guess he's a little edgy, too." Trying to assure her further he added, "I'm actually surprised by this behavior. But don't worry. I've a firm grip on the leash."

However, as often happens after movement along a fault, there soon followed a mild aftershock just as Antoinette tried to calm herself in measure of the man's response. The time, the dog flinched and barked at the sky.

Antoinette vaulted toward Questor, grabbed his collar, and both went over the side of El Capitan. The young man followed because he tried to save his dog by holding onto the leather strap. He was strong, but not strong enough for the combined weight of a German shepherd and muscular woman propelled into thin air.

Antoinette had intended to jam her blade into Questor's ribs, but she immediately released the animal's collar as they plummeted.

"This is glorious!" she thought. "To free fall through space. To live without fear. To embrace every challenge." A spectacular moment in a spectacular life.

The valley floor approached very fast. The air burned Antoinette's skin and tore at her deep brown eyes, which remained strong and beautiful and unblinking. Questor's threat was now completely forgotten as a new enemy approached—just seconds away—an enemy that could not be defeated but could still be opposed.

Antoinette flashed a smile as she had done with the gymnasium Adonis. Her last bit of glory in a single instant of battle against the Earth. She prepared for a knife-trust into the ground. She would show no mercy.

The Boston Globe reported: "Antoinette Rodriguez of Brookline, Massachusetts, Jonathan Krieger of Thousand Oaks, California, and his beloved dog Questor slipped to their deaths yesterday from Yosemite's El Capitan.

"Sadly, according to witnesses, the dog became agitated after a small earthquake and may have pulled against his leash, causing Krieger to lose balance. It is believed that Antoinette Rodriguez tried to grab Questor in an attempt to prevent their fall. But unfortunately, all three tumbled over the edge.

"Doctors stated that Rodriguez had once suffered from extreme anxiety disorder, but treatment with a miraculous new drug enabled her to begin life as a vibrant and adventurous young woman. The clinical trials with Ferralyxis exceeded all expectations, and her recovery had been widely documented in leading medical journals. Unfortunately, as this new Wonder Woman stood on top of El Capitan, celebrating a vigorous morning hike, she lost her life trying to save others. This was a great tragedy not only for Rodriguez, Krieger, Questor, and their families, but for medical research as well. Still, doctors want to assure people suffering from acute anxiety that testing of Ferralyxis will continue and the miracle drug should soon be FDA approved for general psychiatric prescriptions.

"According to Dr. William Crawford, her treating physician, 'Antoinette Rodriguez did not live or die in vain because many others will someday replicate her triumph over mental illness.'"

NEVERLAND THROUGH THE LOOKING GLASS

"I told you time travel was dangerous," said Marsha Wellingly.

Robert Dee Forester, the chief project physicist, was his usual and practical self. "The damage is done. Let's figure how to fix it."

Dr. Pedro Manuel Principal shook his head. "That's gonna be tough because we can't run the machine on the lab generators alone, and there's not much above ground to fix, except a few beating hearts that won't last long."

Wellingly pointed at Forester. "If our resident genius had bothered to read a few science fiction stories, he'd have known better! Time travel is dangerous."

I seem to recall that the basic screw-up was yours!" said Forester. "But the biggest screw-up was including a sociologist on this project in the first place. Your whole field is pseudo-science cum laude."

Principal raised his hand, becoming the project manager once more. "You two stop bickering," he said. "Bob's right. We need to work the problem, and if the machine hasn't been damaged, there might be a chance."

"Without power," said Forester, too calmly, "it's about as useful as sociology."

Wellingly was still fuming. "Why not hang a plaque on the mainframe that says Relic to Galactic Stupidity. That way, future historians—if any— won't be confused about whose handiwork destroyed the planet."

"Calm down," said Principal while formulating a desperate plan. "Now listen. Our lab is still intact and our people are still alive. Don't know how or why, but take it as a gift, and if the hospital generator survived, or if it can be made to run, we might boost the electrical current enough to fire up the machine."

"Go topside?" asked Forester. "With enough rads to fry a cockroach?"

"Consider this," said Principal, gaining confidence as he spoke. "We're on the Pacific coast, and the onshore flow should soon clear enough dust for a quick recon. Then, if the main hospital generator is intact, we send Teller upstairs for the engineering. I'd go, myself, but I can't link two machines with varying capacities. And if we blow a circuit now there won't be any shipments from Radio Shack. Besides, whatever the topside radiation, whatever the cost, we must run the machine."

The conference room was silent for several seconds. Then Wellingly disjointedly blurted, "At least we know who's to blame!"

"I'm getting plenty sick of your I-told-you-so's," said Forester. "A good wallop across the chops might settle you down!"

Wellingly grinned. "Seems a bit early for Lord of the Flies. A preeminent scientist should take at least a week to degenerate into a savage."

Principal raised his palm. "Recriminations won't help. The world as we knew it is gone." He shrugged. "Looking back, it's a wonder civilization held out this long."

"I was just thinking," began Forester.

"Something you should have done beforehand." She was going to add, "I told you…," but changed her mind. Besides, Forester was right. The initial suggestion that led to the big fail had been hers.

"Hindsight is useless," said Principal. "Focus on the here and now."

"I was going to ask," said Forester, obviously still annoyed, "How do we even know the hospital generator exists? We altered the continuum in some catastrophic way. Maybe the university was never built in the new world. Maybe Berkeley was never built."

"If that were so," said Principal, "the displacement equipment would not have been built, either, and we wouldn't be having this conversation. So I think it's a good bet the University of California campus is there. Probably rubble, but it existed and supported our work. The only thing we know for sure is that bombs began to fall the instant Carruthers went back, which is strange. If we changed history, why did society almost mirror itself for 66 years and self-destruct yesterday?"

"You mean instead of 1959?" mused Forester, "or some other date?"

"Yes," said Principal.

"That is peculiar," said Wellingly.

"Anyway," continued Principal, "unless we repair the damage, the reasons won't make much difference. There's no way to survive more than a few months down here."

"I concur," said Forester as though they were in a regular Tuesday department meeting.

"And if we can power up the machine, one approach might be to intercept Carruthers, stop him from talking with Truman. Or better yet, stop us from sending him in the first place. I don't know how an altered universe works, but we must try something."

"Let's suppose," said Wellingly, sounding more dispassionate, "that we can start the time machine. We might make matters worse, create new problems."

Forester's jaw dropped. "Christ, woman! There is no worse."

Wellingly grimaced. "We should have gone into the future instead of interfering with the Enola Gay. A good deed obviously turned bad."

"But it didn't turn bad for 66 years," said Principal, "and that doesn't seem to make sense."

Forester pushed two volumes of the Encyclopedia Americana to the center of the small conference table. "My secretary brought these from the library's basement reading room, which is accessible from our first-level offices and is still protected from most of the radiation. The upstairs edition should be identical to the set in my laboratory residence. It isn't."

"But the library purchased both sets at the same time," said Wellingly. "One for their reference section and one for your office. Same edition; shipped in the same box. I know. I approved the order."

"I'm not trying to explain it," replied Forester. "But general history looks pretty much the same through the publication date, two years ago. And unless my memory has been scrambled along with these books, I don't see much difference. There's a Cuban Missile Crisis, Challenger explosion, World Trade Center attacks. The first moonwalk happens right on schedule—with Neil Armstrong, no less. So the big picture seems parallel, up until yesterday. Maybe different history happened between the publication date and now, and if we can get to the upper levels of the library to read newspapers and magazines, we might find additional information. Nonetheless, the library's encyclopedia suggests that Japan recovered more quickly after the war, developing an international economy 15 years ahead of schedule. Their population is bigger, too, probably as a direct effect of not dropping the two bombs at the end of World War Two."

"Carruthers succeeded!" said Principal.

"Yes," replied Forester, opening the volume to a marked page from the library's volume and sliding it toward Principal. "There's a photo of our man shaking hands with Truman. Another on the Missouri with MacArthur. And, according to the encyclopedia, the U.S. did not bomb Hiroshima or Nagasaki."

Principal glanced at the photos. It was Carruthers, all right. "We need to get Teller immediately," said Principal. "He must link the hospital generator with ours, repair it if necessary, but we have to repower the machine."

Forester shook his head. "Like I said, nobody can leave the underground facility for a day or two. Not with the current fallout levels."

"You also pointed out that we're dead if we don't," said Principal. "What's the difference if Teller dies from radiation in five days or starvation in five months?"

"Ask him," interjected Wellingly. "I bet he prefers the months."

"Why don't you stuff a rag in your mouth!" said Forester. "We're trying to think here!"

"Listen," said Principal, taking charge, "I want you both to stop arguing, right now! When we leave this room, we MUST present a united front. There are 73 people down here, still alive, and wondering what the hell is going on. I'm the project manager. If necessary, I'll pull rank, but we've always worked as a team, and I say that's how we're going into this new mission." Principal stood, leaned forward, and placed his hands on the table. "The squabbles stop now, or so help me, I'll have security lock you both up for 24 hours to think things over."

"You wouldn't dare!" said Forester. "This project would never have even been conceived without me!"

Principal held a steady gaze at Forester. "But the project was conceived, and it was built with government money—military money. So in the absence of contravening authority," Principal thumbed toward the reinforced door, "those nice Marines standing outside take orders from me. Now, they're not much for great thinking, but they follow instructions real good."

Wellingly nodded and let out a breath. "Pete's right, Dee. We're in a jam. I won't offer any more recriminations. Let's just try to fix things."

Forester was still angry. He hadn't been inclined to endure insults since he won the Nobel Prize for physics. And that was eight years ago. "The odds of success are a thousand to one," he said with clinched teeth. "And I'll have you thrown off the project if you threaten me again."

"There is no project to be thrown off of," said Principal. "And one chance in a thousand is better than zero, which is where the whole world is right now."

There was a knock at the door. Sergeant Amherst opened it and said, "Dr. Teller is asking to see you, Sir."

"Thank you," said Principal, not completely surprised. "Send him in."

Herbert Teller entered, disheveled and out of breath. "Sorry I'm late to the meeting. I've been topside. What a damned mess."

"My god!" said Forester. "Don't you know the readings up there?"

"Of course I know," replied Teller, "I also know the situation is pretty grim. Near as I can figure, most of the world's nuclear arsenal—missiles, planes, subs, artillery—went off in one way or another yesterday. Maybe four or five billion people died. I also figure that you'll need the time machine to undo the damage—or try to. And we all know that time is of the essence! The ventilation system is down, and if it's not repaired, we'll all be breathing unfiltered air in three days. Or we won't be breathing."

"Did you check the hospital generator!?" asked Wellingly, desperately.

"No way to get to it. The north wall and ceiling collapsed. Need heavy equipment to uncover it."

"That's a wrap," said Wellingly. "We're finished."

"Not hardly," said Teller. "There's another generator—bigger and better—in a reinforced bunker."

"I never heard about that," said Forester.

"Military doesn't give out information without a need to know," said Teller. "You didn't have one. I did. I'm the guy that installed it."

"Jesus," said Principal. "Who are you?"

"The project electrical engineer." Teller hesitated and then laughed at himself under the circumstances. "I'm also an Air Force colonel with Special Services on temporary assignment...." He paused and said, "Looks like that assignment is now permanent."

"Are you taking command?" asked Principal.

"No," said Teller, flatly. "My general orders were to protect you, to assist as needed with operations, and to oversee lab security. However, I'm also authorized to use personal discretion, as necessary, to protect national interests." He glanced around the room. "But I don't know enough to run the machine by myself, and national security has become irrelevant. There are no nations remaining as far as I can tell."

"What do you recommend?" asked Principal, realizing that Teller probably understood more than he let on.

"I didn't have time to inspect the other generator, but it's well protected. The real problem will be keeping myself and a couple assistants alive long enough to jury-rig the connection. There is currently a brisk onshore flow. That's good. It'll clear some of the dust for, maybe, twenty-four to forty-eight hours."

"What else?" asked Forester.

"Fragmented reports indicate that China was bombarded from Russia, England, France, and the US. So whatever's left of Asia will drift across the Pacific in within a few days. It really is a small world, folks, and the radiation is going to get very hot after our window of opportunity." Teller paused and said, "I'm not worried about dying, mind you, but not before I can give you people a chance to restart the machine."

"How long to connect the power?"

"My crew's already stacking tools and supplies at the bottom of the stairs. Another is implementing repairs to the elevator. Tomorrow, blue skies or black rain, we inspect the bunker."

"Bunker!?" exclaimed Wellingly.

"Self-contained Communications Room under Bolt Hall. In a crisis, select military personnel were to keep Washington informed about the West and status of your project. Might be a few people there now, but I doubt it because we had only three minutes notice before the first big one. Damned Russian subs were parked off San Francisco and Vandenberg. I doubt anybody had much warning. Anyway, if the Com Room is intact, the generator can light your machine. Trust me. I just need to patch into the lab circuits, so let's pray the underground cables weren't damaged."

"After the last six hours, I'd say counting on good luck is bad strategy."

"I'm not counting on luck," said Teller. "The DOD builds tough, and if I can get to the bunker, the odds turn in our favor. But me and my crew must survive long enough to complete the hookups. We should be safe underground, but getting to and from will be dangerous, and there's only a short window before hot debris floats over from China. When that happens, everyone better be underground."

Principal interrupted. "Colonel, perhaps we should send your crew and, uh, keep you here."

"I considered that, but too much is at stake, and I know more about the Com Room than anybody. Besides, if this attempt fails, it won't matter whether I'm 'safe.' We'll all be waiting for the air to run dry."

"Can't the ventilation be repaired?"

"Already in process," said Teller, "though there's not much point, except for morale. Even if Captain Sorrell starts the pumps, sooner or later the food stores and water are bound to be contaminated. Radiation is insidious, and this facility wasn't properly designed to keep it out. The Com Room would be safer, but the time displacement equipment is here, so that's where we must conduct business."

Wellingly nodded and then spoke slowly. "And if we fail, nature will just have to start over and rebuild life on Earth...."

"So we're in agreement," added Principal, trying to bring the team back together, "this is an all-or-nothing proposition."

Everyone nodded, and Teller said, "Now if you'll excuse me, I need to get ready for tomorrow's excursion. Just be sure your machine is ready when we deliver the juice."

"The power-up procedure is meticulous," said Forester. "Takes time to do it right."

Teller shook his head. "I suggest, Sir, for the sake of life on Earth, that you do it fast and right. Every major nuclear power has automated ICBMs that will launch over the next few days or weeks. I don't want to wait for a bunker buster to land on top of us."

"Christ," said Forester.

Wellingly became petulant again, pointing at Forester. "People like you designed those things. Did you really think the generals would play nice with them?"

"Remember what I told you, Marsha," said Principal, suddenly sounding like a military man himself. "We have a job to do, and anyone who compromises that job will have a close encounter with Sergeant Amherst. Right, Colonel?"

"You're in charge," said Teller, "but I agree. The mission takes precedence."

"Umm, those automated missiles?" asked Wellingly. "Do they require further human action?"

"No," said Teller.

"Would there be any warning?" asked Forester.

"When we're vaporized, you'll know."

"What's it like up there?" asked Principal during a private conference with Teller the evening of the second day.

"Bad," said Teller, "but we finished the job, so nothing else matters."

"How's your...?" asked Principal, looking at Teller's radiation badge. "Never mind."

"My crew understood the situation. Our immune systems are shot, and a virus will probably kill us before the week's out."

Principal nodded. "We prepped the machine while you were topside." He hesitated briefly. "Umm, that Com Center...was there any word...from anyone?"

"Nothing. I'm sure some people survived in Washington, especially government and military personnel, but there's no way to communicate. Even the satellites have apparently been taken out. Bet it was China."

"Too bad."

"It's anybody's guess how many ICBMs were launched, but there's a lot of dust, and solar winter's likely going to kill any survivors. People will be dinosaurs in six months."

"Only the dinosaurs didn't commit suicide," lamented Principal.

Teller was silent for a few seconds and then shook his head. "There's still a chance you can prevent Armageddon from happening." Then he added softly, "Otherwise, the Earth will just have to evolve a better species next time around."

Principal was silent and then shook himself out of the doldrums. "To hell with that, Colonel! We are the better species!"

The two men held each other's gaze for a moment.

Principal continued. "Everybody agrees that our best chance is to send someone back to the lab to stop us, me really, from jumping Carruthers to 1945. If we try to intercept him after he's there, a thousand things might go wrong."

"I'm with you."

"Further, I'm guessing we'll have only one chance." Principal pointed at Teller. "You're a brilliant engineer, but that electrical connection patchwork is a miracle, and it will be an even greater miracle if it holds together more than 48 hours. And when you're gone, I doubt there will be a chance to power up again. I'm at least smart enough to know my limitations—and those of the people around me."

Teller nodded, coughing slightly.

"By the way," said Principal, "I broke into your military files this morning. Quite a career, Colonel. Glad you're on our team and not the opposition."

"Doesn't matter now. Every side lost. But if you can put the world back together, I'll ask the President to give you a medal."

Principal smiled. "I'd settle for going home to my wife. Anyway, as long as you're cognizant, I plan to follow your recommendations, and I'll turn over command to you any time."

"No thanks."

Principal nodded. "OK. We power the machine and drop a man inside the lab one hour before initial launch to convince us to shut down the system." Principal grinned. "Ironically, the most likely candidate for the trip would be myself."

"That would shake things up," said Teller, smiling. "You talking with you."

"The problem, according Forester, is that sliding me-from-now into a room with me-from-three-days-ago would be dangerous, especially if we make physical contact. Forester is the theoretical architect behind quantum displacement functions, and he thinks there could be an annihilation event."

"Like matter-antimatter?"

"Yes, and the energy would create…a very big bang."

Teller said, "I get it."

"But after looking over your military record, Colonel, I want to send you."

"You should reconsider, Doc. I'm weakening fast. The mission is too important to risk any kind of failure"

"I know," said Principal, reaching for a plastic vial of pills and a bottle of water. "Here's a first-round dose of antibiotics and stimulants. They should delay infection and help with radiation sickness. Take the batch over a couple hours; otherwise, you might become nauseated."

Teller nodded, dumped the pills into his mouth, and swallowed the whole batch with several gulps of water. "Waiting's not my style."

Principal slowly shook his head and said, "There's another reason I want you to go, Colonel. I've thought about it, and if you can't reason with me, convince me to halt the test, I want you to put a bullet in my head—followed by Forester—and then empty your clip into the crucial circuits. Only Forester and I understand how those work, and we've been careful to omit design elements from the records. In a practical sense, quantum time dilatations are borderline magic. Forester and I stumbled onto the process, and once we realized what we had discovered, we decided to withhold a few quasi-invisible steps. I doubt that anyone will be able to replicate the flux-displacement circuits unless they blunder onto the process like we did—and unless they're as smart as Forester. And nobody's as smart as Forester."

"Sounds as though you expect trouble."

"First from me, and Forester will be worse. We worked on this project nearly two decades. We were laughed at. We fought for funding every year. A few people said we were insane." Principal shook his head, again, thinking of the destruction. "Maybe we were...."

"Don't blame yourself, Doc. Visionaries are just naturally quirky, and who could have predicted this situation? I didn't."

"You had limited information...."

Teller nodded. "True. I thought Carruthers would jump one minute into the future..., which could have verified functionality with minimal risk."

"And then the Pentagon would consider the scientific and military applications...I know," said Principal. "But Forester and I wanted to eradicate twenty years of missteps and doubts and outright failures."

"So you got the bright idea of sending Carruthers to 1945. A big show that would save Hiroshima and Nagasaki."

"Wellingly's suggestion, actually. To convince President Truman to demonstrate the bomb off the Tokyo coast and end the war without killing all those innocents. But Forester and I climbed on board immediately. We wanted to settle old scores, maybe win the Peace Prize. Only Forester, Wellingly, Carruthers, and I knew the real plan."

The Colonel tilted his head and grinned. "I never dreamed a radical lurked beneath your Clark Kent exterior, Doc. You should have worked for the CIA. They like an iron-will that can pass for milquetoast. But you should have known better than to mess with history."

"Wasn't thinking clearly, that's for sure. I suppose we were laughed at once too often. Or maybe I'm more ego driven than I thought. Forester, too…. Oh, off the record, Wellingly collapsed last night. She's nearly catatonic and under heavy sedation, so I want you to understand this. Building the machine pushed all of us to the brink, and that's why I'm warning you beforehand. I doubt that I'll allow anything to stop me from running that test."

"Give me a little credit. I can be pretty persuasive."

The renowned and dignified and always calm Dr. Pedro Principal opened his lab coat to reveal a nine millimeter handgun tucked into a shoulder holster. "I was wearing this the day we jumped Carruthers, and I'm telling you, I was prepared to use it to complete the test."

"Jesus," said Teller. "How did you get that past our MPs? We screened everything from the first day of construction, multiple checkpoints, surveillance cameras, metal detectors for the metal detectors. Forgive me, Doc, but what you're saying is impossible. Security would have stopped you from entering with a gun or even an unauthorized nail clipper."

"Brawn over brains?" asked Principal, now grinning himself. "Your people didn't have a time machine. I did. It was child's play to send the weapon to myself from another location. Forester and I used the prototype to deliver whatever we wanted—anytime, anywhere."

Teller let out a deep breath. "Wow, Sir. I really underestimated you, and that doesn't happen very often."

"Thank you," said Principal, "but just be ready when you appear in the lab. It took World War Three to shake me back to reality. You can try to talk us down, but I doubt anybody will listen." Principal patted the shoulder holster. "Don't let me prevent you from completing the most important mission of your life."

"When I materialize and explain what happened, especially when you see my bodily condition, you're bound to sit down and think things over."

"I hope so," said Principal, pausing, and then speaking like a general. "All right, be prepared to jump tomorrow at 1500. We'll need full power thirty minutes before that, so make sure your crew is ready. Let's put the world back together."

"Will do," said Teller. "And don't worry, Doc. If you won't listen to reason, your orders will be carried out. I'll kill you, Forester, and the machine."

One minute later, while still talking, both men heard and felt a distant rumble, like the granddad of all thunderstorms, penetrating the earth.

"Another detonation," said Teller. "Pretty far off."

Principal took a deep breath, thought for a moment, and looked Teller in the eye. "We can't risk failure, Colonel. Even if you talk me down, I might power up the machine in a month or two. More likely, I would be removed from the project and somebody else would take the controls. Further, if you destroy only the machine, and even if Forester and I were inclined to support you, neither of us would hold up long under torture. I'd spill my guts in a minute." Principal paused a few seconds. "I'm giving new orders, Colonel Teller. When you appear in the lab, take us out immediately. It's the only way to be sure."

Teller said nothing. He would have been ashamed to admit that he had already considered the same solution.

Principal nodded and then smiled unexpectedly. "You know I'm right, don't you? Just make certain, after it's over, not to shake hands with the other Colonel Teller.... Now, let me show you the most important and most vulnerable equipment."

Teller felt deep admiration. "You really should have joined the CIA, Doc. You could've been running the place in ten years."

"Not a job I would ever want."

"That's true of the last two directors, but they did it anyway."

"And there's one more thing...." Principal hesitated. "I'm sorry, but you have a right to know."

"I'm already dead, so why worry? Besides, if we put Humpty Dumpty back together, my other self won't have to suffer through this god damned radiation sickness. Unfortunately, Sir, by your own command, the other you must die along with the project."

"At least my death will be quick, but…when we transport you back to the lab, I'm going to program the machine for a double-jump. It's the only way to be sure you don't have contact with your doppelganger, who will undoubtedly run to the lab after the shooting starts….By the way, how long do you need to eliminate your targets?"

"Twenty seconds, give or take, but when you show me the flux components, I need to know exactly where you and Forester were standing during that initial test. Don't want any surprises." Teller cocked his head. "On second thought, Doc, we might just send back an explosive to take out the entire lab."

"Considered it," said Principal, waiving his hand in dismissal. "First, I doubt the present-time folks would go along with a plan to destroy the machine, especially Forester, and it requires a team to power up. Second, quantum dimensional instability can generate a peculiar electromagnetic pulse."

"The only EMPs I know come from nuclear bursts."

"These are different, and we don't know exactly what to call them…. They're kind of like randomly discharging subatomic molecular static; anyway, we can't be sure that a detonator would function inside the lab with the machine in warm-up. That's one of the reasons it took 16 years to develop and calibrate our operating controls—the system kept interfering with its own electronics. Plus, you're forgetting that Carruthers was our first full-sized test. The placement of an explosive might be inaccurate and the EMPs might corrupt the detonator. The only way to be certain is to send back a thinking human being, capable of assessing and responding to variables. And if there's a glitch, you'll have only 30 seconds to figure something out. But remember, Colonel, ninety-nine percent of the machine can be rebuilt from the blueprints and manuals, so you must destroy the magic—the quantum circuitry—along with me and Forester to prevent anyone from attempting to recreate it."

Teller sensed that there was something else. He pointed to his chest and said, "What happens to me, this me, after 30 seconds?"

"You'll be time-ported into the far future…, and you won't suffer a slow, painful death from radiation sickness."

"You sound a little queasy, Doc. Should I be worried?"

"We both know what's at stake. Once you destroy the quantum circuits of three days ago, it's unlikely that the machine here and now will work for the second half of your jump. I'll program the sequence, but I'm guessing that particular Phase Two will fail. Again, we should have systematically tested and calibrated the functions…, oh, well."

"So what's the bad news you're holding back?"

Principal let out a breath. "I'm relying on our initial prototype as a backup for your second jump, but it must also be destroyed. You and it will go out together."

"And what you're really saying is that my last few moments won't be pleasant."

Principal nodded. "I'm sorry. The smaller machine doesn't have enough capacity…."

After waiting a few seconds, Teller demanded, "Tell me!"

"You'll be deployed in twelve sections…at two-second intervals. Unfortunately, the segmenting will be imprecise. I'll try to amputate your head during the initial jump, but there's no way to predict…."

"Forget it, Doc," interrupted Teller. "I'm not waiting around to see which piece of me disappears first. After I dust the lab, there's a bullet reserved for me. Just make certain that the damned prototype is destroyed, too. If you and I are both going to die for humanity, let's be sure we succeed."

"With your courage, suicide is probably best—before the machine goes to work. But at least the other Colonel Teller will have a life."

"Probably not much of one, Doc. From the perspective of my superiors, a crazy man will have waltzed into the lab and shot two leading scientists along with their baby. They'll assume it was an inside job, and my alter ego's career will be finished. Might do prison time or be executed—not to mention my own guilt's going to be pretty bad, wondering what the hell happened."

"Perhaps I can't save your career," said Principal, "but you shouldn't have to suffer from guilt. I've already sent an email to your alter ego that will arrive in your office two minutes before we jump you—this you—back to the lab. I also caution the other Teller against touching any blood or fragments that might be left over from your…segmentation. He will know the whole story. It's a shame nobody else will."

"So far, so good," said the Colonel, "but how do you plan to eliminate the smaller time machine?"

"Last week, you donated blood at the clinic. I retrieved the sample, which is now in a sealed glass container next to the prototype. The last piece of your body will materialize in the same space as that blood sample. We can only estimate the results, though Forester says the machine should be vaporized along with several blocks of San Francisco. Without controlled tests and measurements, we don't know how much energy will be released, but the machine must be destroyed, so I'm leaning toward overkill."

"A few blocks of what's left upstairs won't make much difference. It's a mess."

"You're not thinking fourth dimensionally. The prototype doesn't exist today. It was destroyed during the bombings, so the machine that's going to wrap up this production is the one that existed three days ago. During our dry run of the 'now' machine this afternoon, as we tested the power and startup, I traveled home a month ago and programmed the prototype to cut the first slice of your body 30 seconds after we send you back to the lab. Or more precisely, I'm programming the lab machine to send you back 30 seconds before the prototype goes to work. Same effect, but a slightly different dimensional schematic, so it's possible to give you more time if needed."

The Colonel responded, "All this is giving me a headache—a bigger headache than I already have from radiation poisoning, Doc. But half a minute is enough time for me to do my job assuming your 4-D travel itineraries don't drive me insane."

"Can't promise against it," said Principal. "Why else would I, a confirmed pacifist, conceal a weapon under his lab coat?"

"Uh, Doc…, the prototype is in your home?"

"My basement lab. The blood sample is on the table next to the machine. My wife and kids will be watching TV as the last piece of your body mingles with the blood from your other self. But after that, both machines should be gone, and you will have already killed the two men who might recreate them."

"I am sorry, Sir."

"Me, too."

"There's just one other thought," said Teller, worried. "The blood, the stuff in the vial from those tests, it came from this me, I think," he said, pointing toward himself. "You sure there will be an appropriate reaction?"

"That's a viable consideration," said Principal. "Forester and I speculated about such issues for a decade. It is possible that when Carruthers changed the continuum, we were separated from the past as we knew it, and you were separated from the previously donated blood. That would explain the two versions of the encyclopedia Forester talked about yesterday. But, as a second insurance policy, I programmed the prototype for one more operation. Five seconds before the machine starts sending you into the future, it will take the little finger of the 'other' Colonel Teller, the one who will be present in the lab three days ago, and place it next to the container of blood in my basement. At the instant of your body's final jump, three pieces of three Colonel Edward Tellers from three different continuums will be brought together on that table. That particular confectioner's mix will not go gently into the night."

Teller sighed, nodded slowly. "Like I said, Doc. Your brains could have owned the CIA. What a shame."

Dr. Pedro Principal spoke to the skeleton crew in the displacement operations lab. "We all know why we're here," he said. "Colonel Teller is going back in time to stop the experiment."

"Any idea what went wrong?" asked a technician.

"Only conjecture. If Wellingly were here, she could probably explain better…, but as near as we can tell, Carruthers convinced Truman not to drop the bombs on Hiroshima and Nagasaki—to demonstrate atomic power instead. Detonating Little Boy near the Tokyo coast was enough, and Japan surrendered. And later, apparently, because the world didn't understand just how horrible the blast and radiation were on people, they weren't as reluctant to use such weapons. So the instant we activated the machine, the world let loose an all-out nuclear war in our time, and unless we can stop it from happening, Earth is dead."

"But why," asked another technician, "did the war occur just days ago, right after we sent Carruthers?"

"Don't know," said Principal. "Big History seems to be the same, even events like the moon landing or World Trade Center attacks. Then, wham! The bombs fell with the activation of the machine. There's much we don't understand, so your guess is as good as mine." Principal hesitated and added, "I believe it's related to the time paradox. The war could not have started before there was a device to send Carruthers through time. We all had to be here to build the machine, to make it work, to conduct the experiment. Perhaps there have been a billion historical cycles since we activated the machine. Perhaps a million wars were fought, destroying the world over and over, until finally a scenario occurred that allowed us to exist and to repeat our experiment. The war had to happen three days ago because the time paradox needed a time machine to make things happen. Weird, but that's my best guess."

"Weird and questionable," said the technician.

"It's all I can think of," said Principal. "I'm also guessing that if you transported yourself back before you were conceived and killed your mother, the paradox would generate as many loops as necessary—maybe to infinity—until somehow there would ascend an impossible universe where your life and your mother's premature death were compatible. It would undoubtedly be a strange universe by our knowledge, but I've already admitted that I'm guessing."

"The hows and whys are irrelevant," said Forester, scanning the control panel. "The bombs fell. We're here now. Let's get on with the correction."

Principal nodded. "Teller volunteered for this mission, but nobody can predict whether or how his actions will affect us in this room. I like to think that history will be set to rights, and henceforth we'll know better than to mess with the past. And if Colonel Teller is successful, I'm hoping that we'll come out in a corrected reality and that our families will never die in a fiery holocaust. But all we can do is try. If anyone feels like praying, I'd say it couldn't hurt."

Forester glanced at Teller and then at Principal. He said, "The Colonel looks pretty weak. Are you sure he's up for this?"

"I'll take care of business," said Teller, coughing up blood, turning his head, and swallowing so Forester wouldn't see the colored spittle. "I don't expect to live much beyond the mission, nor is it necessary. You just set me back in the lab and leave the rest to me. In fact, I'll be more convincing by the shape I'm in. They need to see the consequences of their actions."

Principal nodded. "I've briefed Colonel Teller. He has already sacrificed himself to provide power, and he deserves a crack at stopping the disaster. So let's juice up and give him that chance." Principal's voice seemed to choke. "It has been my highest honor to work with all of you on this project...."

"Two minutes to full charge...," said Forester, watching the gauges and waiting for his colleague to regain composure.

"Right," said Principal, taking a deep breath. He turned to Teller. "After you arrive in the lab, it may take several seconds to regain your neurological faculties. The machine converts matter to energy and energy to matter as part of the dilatation process, functioning somewhat as a teleporter through time and space. I'll stand directly in front of you, here. When I disappear, you'll know that you're in the lab three days ago. The other me will be behind the safety shield to your left. You'll also see Carruthers and a few scattered technicians, but everything else will be the same. Again, you're likely to be disoriented, and the people in the lab will be surprised, maybe scared—so the sooner you start sh...," Principal remembered that only he and Teller knew the full plan, "the sooner you start talking, the better."

Teller nodded. "I'll talk my fool head off. Just get me there." The radiation sickness was bad. His body temperature was now 104, up another degree in the last hour, and he worried that he might collapse before finishing the job.

"Sixty seconds," said Forester.

"Be sure to stand inside the radius of the ground plate," said Principal, "which was one of the modifications for the full-sized test. Any parts hanging outside get left behind."

Teller laughed. "An eight-foot diameter. I'll be fine."

"Seventy percent charge," said Forester, eyes on the control panel. "Almost ready for computer interface."

The last twenty seconds of the operating sequence were electronically controlled because no human could coordinate the thousands of sequences and signals, some calibrated in nanoseconds, that led to the suspended instant of time dilatation.

"I'm on it," said Principal.

"Thirty seconds; ninety percent," said Forester, eyes still glued to his gauges.

"Ready to interface…Now!" said Principal.

Forester began the countdown. "Twenty seconds."

"Goodbye, my friend," said Principal, stepping in front of Teller.

"Goodbye, Doc. It's been real."

"Ten, nine, eight…," said Forester.

Principal calmly opened a cabinet, removed an M-16 with a full banana clip and tossed it to Teller."

"What's that for!?" cried Forester as he glanced up.

"To save the world," said Principal, "lobbing an extra clip to Teller."

Forester suddenly realized that Principal and Teller planned to destroy the machine. He rushed to stop the Colonel, crossing the ground plate the instant that time fractured. Half of Forester's body convulsed and fell to the floor. The other half disappeared along with Teller and his fully loaded M-16.

Colonel Teller tried to kick away the flailing half of Forester's body, but Teller's leg wouldn't move. He remembered what Dr. Principal said about the effect of time travel on motor neurons, and the machine must have worked because Principal was no longer in front of him. By Teller's perception, the good doctor had disappeared, along with the other half of Forester, so Teller counted three seconds and tried again to move. It worked.

People in the lab were motionless, surprised by the Colonel's sudden appearance along with a mangled half-body and a growing pool of blood. Teller suddenly realized that Forester had created a new problem, more dangerous than either he or Principal could have anticipated, and there were only 27 seconds to deal with everything.

Teller raised the M-16, pointed, and fired half a dozen rounds into the living Dr. Forester, who seemed not to realize he was in danger until the first bullet struck its mark. Then the Colonel moved left.

An internal lab security guard drew his side arm, discharging one bullet into the floor as Teller fired on full auto at the sentry. Colonel Teller then walked calmly around the protective and transparent Lucite wall where Dr. Pedro Principal was standing, motionless with surprise. Teller stood tall, saluted, and said, "Sorry, Sir. Just following your orders." Then he unloaded a dozen rounds into Principal, who collapsed backward.

A bullet caught Teller in the left wrist. He wasn't sure where it came from, but he rolled to the ground, spraying the lab with counter fire while simultaneously looking for the other guard. He found her, bearing down on him with pistol blazing, a brave woman who didn't have a chance against an M-16. Teller hated to kill her, but there were only 10-15 seconds before the prototype machine began taking him apart—provided he could get back to the ground plate.

Teller's left wrist had been shattered by a .45 caliber bullet. He was bleeding badly and probably would lose consciousness within a minute or two, but he stumbled to his feet and moved toward the quantum flux circuits—the magic, as Principal had called it. He unloaded the clip into the unit, dropped the empty magazine, snapped in the backup, and fired another fifty cartridges. Whatever magic had existed was gone for sure.

A few seconds left.

Teller hurried back to the ground plate, sat on the floor, and desperately clutched Forester's head and half torso, trying to scoop most of the blood into his lap. He could only hope that the prototype unit would take Forester's body along with him because if—after Teller was sliced and diced and transported into the future—somebody brought remnants of future-Forester into contact with the newly created lab-corpse-Forester, well, that would be bad. But worse for Teller, having his right hand occupied and left wrist broken, he could not now fire a bullet into his own head. He could only sit—and wait—for three million microseconds to pass before the prototype began its work.

"Does anyone know what happened?" asked the President of the United States.

"A science project turned disaster, it seems," said General Eden West.

"The Berkeley lab?"

"We think so. Doctors Principal and Forester had reportedly developed a time displacement unit. A few of our people were skeptical, but Principal seemed to be onto something, and that kind of machine definitely had military potential."

"What went wrong?"

"There was an explosion across the bay. Big one. Early reports say there's a hole in the middle of the San Francisco peninsula almost two miles across and a mile deep. Nearly the size of Arizona's Meteor Crater, I think."

The President grimaced and asked, "You sure?"

"Pretty sure, Sir, though it will take a while to figure everything because the event's epicenter seems about 15 miles from the lab. Further, the Berkeley facility's live video shows what appears to be our own security agent going berserk with an M-16, taking down Forester, Principal, and the machine. And then the guy sits on the floor, covers himself with blood and guts from half a corpse, and, suddenly…begins to disappear…in chunks." General West took a couple deep breaths.

"Go on," said the President.

"It was Colonel Teller, our best man, and he was alive for the first two or three dissections, or whatever you call them, so the video is pretty gruesome. The whole disappearing act took 30 seconds, and believe me," said General West, shaking his head, "that's no way for a man to die."

"And what's this got to do with San Francisco?"

"We're not sure, but it all seems connected."

The president looked up and asked, "How many civilian casualties?"

"Initial estimate is around a million," said West without further emotion. "That's bad enough, but diplomatically, internationally, we have some explaining to do. Even our allies are asking why a 400-megaton device went off in a U.S. city. World militaries are on alert, including ours. And, Sir, we don't have a 400-megaton device. Nobody does."

"To start with," said the President, suddenly angry, "somebody had better tell me whether the Pentagon developed a new-style weapon and forgot to inform the Commander in Chief. If they did, I swear some of the top brass will stand before a firing squad."

"No, Sir. It wasn't a bomb as we know it. Not a trace of uranium or plutonium or radiation. Besides, nobody would make a nuclear weapon that size. Couldn't be deployed, and 30 smaller bombs would do more damage than one big one."

"Then what the hell happened?"

"We don't know, but the explosion seemed to coincide precisely with the last chunk of Colonel Teller's disappearance. That's when our video feed from the lab went dead. I mentioned that the crater is about two miles across. The Chinese think we've discovered a new super weapon, which they're calling quark fusion or fission or some such nonsense."

"How do they know the megaton range?"

"The shock waves went around the globe. Like an earthquake. Pretty easy to guesstimate seismic energy close enough for any government to be worried about the balance of power. Me, too, Mr. President. Our scientists don't know how the blast was generated, either."

"But they suspect something?"

"Matter-antimatter, one hundred percent energy conversion, which might explain why there's no detectable radioactivity—or no more than in that cup of coffee you're drinking. And if Principal learned how to harness and control antimatter reactions, you could sink the Rock of Gibraltar with a bomb in a lunchbox."

The President nodded. "So the Pentagon wasn't keeping secrets?"

"Believe me, Sir. We're in the dark. And I don't like being in the dark about something of this magnitude. It scares the hell out of me."

"OK. I want your best crew to go through Principal's files, blueprints, computers, and reports down to the last comma splice. The explosion must be connected with Principal's machine; and from what you described based on the telelink, I'd say the equipment worked, and it might have worked in a way the eggheads didn't expect."

"Or maybe they did, Sir. Maybe they were keeping secrets, and just maybe the beast got away from the creator."

The President thought for a moment. "Ok, General. Take personal charge of this and go to California. I'll get on the hotline with Beijing, London, and Berlin to start defusing the military alerts. I don't want some Rambo drunk second-lieutenant to cut loose a missile strike. The atom bomb hasn't been used in a war since 1953, and I don't want any bullshit Armageddon to happen on my watch."

"Yes, Sir."

"And one more thing, General. Tell your boys to devise a plausible cover story before I meet the press. The American people will want to know why San Francisco is a hole in the ground. So whatever your team comes up with—geothermal catastrophe, asteroid impact, giant sinkhole, or drunken leprechauns on a rampage—just be sure that I can cover my backside during the announcement and follow-up." He glanced at his watch, "Let's say, in four hours."

"Yes, Mr. President."

"Now, those things are important, but...." The President hesitated.

"Sir?"

"I want that weapon, General. Whatever it is and however it works, I'll sleep better knowing that we control the thing instead of the damned Chinese. So wake up anybody you need. Call in the CIA, FBI, or entire physics department at Cal Tech. Hell, most of them work for us anyway. This is a matter of highest national security. All other considerations are rescinded. Got it!"

"Yes, Sir."

"One more thing," said the President. "Colonel Herbert Teller was as patriotic an American who ever existed—and a personal friend of mine. If he shot up the lab, he did it to prevent that weapon from falling into enemy hands, so there must have been a traitor among the research staff. Teller wouldn't sacrifice himself without cause, but he would stop at nothing to protect this country. I'm betting that he found a spy, and then the son of a bitch chopped him like a side of beef to keep him from talking. You find out who!"

"I'll check everything, Mr. President."

"Mostly, we need that weapon, so do whatever it takes. But I still want Teller's name to come out squeaky clean."

At that moment, the Pentagon's direct line to the Oval Office lit up. The President took the call. It was General West's personal assistant.

"Sorry to interrupt, Sir, but something really strange has happened."

The President switched to the speaker phone. "West and I are both listening. Go ahead, Soldier, though I don't know what could be considered strange against events of the last 24 hours."

"With your permission, Mr. President, I'm going to connect an incoming call. It's impossible…, I mean, well…, but I didn't know what else to do."

"We're a little busy here, Son," said General West. "Just spit it out."

"Colonel Herbert Teller is on the phone. I saw him die on that video, yet he's calling from the secure line of the Berkeley Com Room. Internal codes check out. Priority one. Teller says he suffered minor injuries, losing part of his left hand, and…he knows what created the explosion. He insists on talking only with you, Mr. President."

"Patch him through," ordered the President.

General West nodded. "If this guy's for real, the forty-eight states just might get that new wonder weapon."

"Right," said the President with a new warrior's composure. "And if so, then by God we'll take back Hawaii and Alaska from those imperialistic Chinese bastards—or else I'll melt Beijing into the mantle."

HELPING HAND

Alexandria Stephens knew she was going to die a slow, cold death in space. She floated fifteen meters from her capsule, a single-pilot maintenance shuttle that could operate in low- or high-Earth orbit.

Construction expenses for single-operator vehicles offered all kinds of economic advantages, especially considering the slender profit margins for satellite or orbital-platform contracts. Moon shuttles required two-to-six member crews, but market forces made smaller transports the only viable option for near-Earth missions. Alexandria's vehicle was durable and maintained by Glen Michaels, an old-school aerospace mechanic whom she trusted like a brother, though Alexandria often double-checked his work while they drank beer and argued about emerging technologies. They both understood that the ship was everything; if trouble developed, shuttle pilots were more than inconvenienced.

But the occasional death of a pilot did not deter the corporate suits. Number-crunching lawyers and actuaries demonstrated that Space Jockeys, Inc., could lose a shuttle and pilot every eighteen months and still turn a profit — including replacement costs, death benefits, and liability payments.

They were still serious about safety, and the actual twenty-year average loss rate was one worker per thirty-two point three months, which included a three-man crew that crashed last year on approach to the Eagle Monument construction site at Tranquility Base. But company officials were more serious about the bottom line.

Alexandria understood the dangers when she signed her flight contract, and she would have enlisted at half the pay and twice the risk. Alex had dreamed of becoming a commercial pilot since age eight and had been with Space Jockeys for seven and a half years, earning a reputation as one of the brightest and fastest technicians on duty—twice turning down supervisory positions to continue fieldwork.

"Even in space," she confided, "pencil pushing is not my style."

She was John Wayne on horseback, riding from satellites to telescopes to orbital lasers. At shift's end, she knew exactly how much range had been covered and how many thoroughbreds had been corralled. She loved it, but now she was dying, a flesh-and-blood meteoroid midway from her shuttle and a geosynchronous satellite that was humming again thanks to a new circuit panel she'd installed in seventy-one minutes flat.

There were forty-five minutes of life support left in her suit, and the rescue ship Sibert, like the Carpathia, would arrive too late. The Sibert's mission would be body recovery.

Alexandria's motion held steady, spinning back to front about once per minute and approaching the shuttle at negligible speed, slightly off course. But even if she were on course, her air would run dry before she reached the vehicle. And after the O2 tanks emptied, the heating units would shut down and her body would solid up fast in the minus 240-degree shadow of Earth. She could see the lights of her ship, a soft glow from the nuclear powered satellite, and millions of stars. The deep emptiness of the Pacific Ocean was framed by glowing cities.

Strangely, the lights comforted her even if they could not save her. She needed propulsion from her mobility pack, a damned near infallible piece of equipment with multiple safeguards that had been knocked dead by a pea-sized meteoroid that also cut her forward motion, set her rotating, and disabled her means back to the lifepod that should already be returning her to base. As a result, Alexandria was no longer an astronaut, no longer an $835,000 corporate investment; she was orbital debris to be cleared away when the Sibert arrived. Her shuttle was fifteen meters distant, but it might as well be halfway to Andromeda. The meteoroid would have been more merciful had it bulls-eyed her helmet instead of mobility unit. A quick, unaware death.

Now, there was no way to alter her forward motion or rotation, which, as it turned out, was the only enjoyable part of this mess. As she waited for life-support to end, at least she would have a 360-degree view. Alexandria was an optimist, confident to an almost infinite degree, but she was also a physicist. Reality existed. Space was unforgiving. And her future prospects were zero.

Thirty minutes later, still drifting and trying to enjoy the galactic view, Alexandria realized that she had been an idiot, allowing half an hour to slip by without grasping the possibility of life. She and the physical universe were intimate friends, and such friends do not go gently into the night.

A thick Velcro strap held an old-style, standard-issue Jockey Watch around her suit at the left wrist. She pulled the lash as tight possible, pulled until she feared the band would break though it was rated for 750-degree temperature swings and 1,500 pounds of tensile strength. She refastened the Velcro, trusting the strap to maintain suit pressure.

Then, without hesitation, she unhinged her left glove. The cold vacuum of space stabbed her naked skin. She screamed inside her suit from pain but held firmly onto the glove she had just removed. Everything depended on that hunk of layered fabric and aluminized polymers; Alexandria only hoped it had sufficient mass to nudge her toward the ship — and she had already wasted thirty minutes floating like a cabbage. Of course, her throw must be hard and precise; then she must latch onto the ship with one hand if she got there.

"Probably easier to sink one from mid-court," she thought, "but I'll take the shot."

The pain stopped after her hand froze solid, and Alexandria could focus her thoughts again. She waited until the spin positioned her facing the satellite. Then, offering a prayer to Isaac Newton, she hurled the glove underhanded with the same control she used on the pitcher's mound at Princeton, throwing from the center of her body and aiming dead at the satellite. If her trajectory were correct, the counterforce of a space-glove fastball should propel her toward the shuttle.

There was some good news. Her suit seemed to be holding pressure at the watchband; she veered more or less in the desired direction; and her body rotation increased to only once every thirty seconds. The bad news. She was still traveling too slowly and her track would just miss the shuttle. But Alexandria was no longer a vegetable. There were eleven minutes to solve the problems.

She allowed three minutes for observation and recalculation of the necessary course change. Then, without hesitation, without overthinking, she grabbed her frozen left hand and snapped it off like an icicle. Then she hurled it awkwardly over her head and left shoulder.

Alexandria's counterclockwise rotation slowed, though she was now spinning gradually feet over head, and it took a few minutes to confirm that she on target toward the beautiful, warm, oxygenated Anthem. The only questions were: Would she arrive before her suit ran out of O2? Could she snag the shuttle with one hand and a frozen stump? Would the wristband hold pressure while she maneuvered inside?

Alexandria focused on her goal with each gyration. She counted off meters per minute and tried to slow her breathing. She calculated the moment when she must thrust for a handhold.

"Anthem to Jockey Mother. Alexandria calling Jockey Mother. Over."

"Hello, Anthem! What's the story, Alex? We calculate you're dead. Over."

"Hey, Georgie Boy. You didn't think I was going down without a fight? Cancel the distress call, and tell Doc there's prosthetic work headed his way. My left hand's an orbiting ice ball. Over."

George liked Alexandria. Never lost or damaged a ship in her career, and she could change a control panel before most techs found the right screwdriver.

"What do you mean?!" said George. "You tell us the jig is up and then shut down communications. Are you in the shuttle? Over."

"All cozied up. Inflated a tourniquet around my forearm and am about to dose myself with Morphinex-D, the all-purpose pain killer, sedative, and antibiotic for today's space traveler. The ship's on auto return and docking because I'll soon be in Happy Land, but I expect the doc to have me mission-ready in four weeks. And if Old Man Jones thinks I'm paying for suit repair on this job, he'll look worse than my mobility pack when I'm done with him. Over."

"While we're on that subject," said George, "folks around the control room are pretty upset. You phone home, tell us you're gonna die, and then shut down the intercom. Not very nice, Alex. Not one bit. Over."

"Sorry, George. Didn't want anyone to hear me crying if I broke down. I would've had to kill you if that happened, so forgive me. I'll buy the beer as soon as I can hold a mug, and tell Jones to pay bonuses to our watch designers. I'd like to kiss them all. Over and out."

THE SELF-MURDER SOLUTION

Never change your mind while trying to commit suicide. I took enough Oxycodone, Flexeril, and bourbon to kill an asteroid. So I should have died peacefully, except that after the chemical buzz began to heat up, I decided life might be worth living. Barely able to stand, I downed a glass of warm salty water and rammed two fingers down my throat. (What a waste of Tennessee whiskey.) Then I called 911, and my life turned inside out.

I knew that the ground wasn't really moving, but my stomach pitched and rolled as I began throwing up. By the time paramedics arrived, my voluntary muscle control was about as effective as a jellyfish swimming against a tsunami; nonetheless, I somehow crawled to the front door and unlocked it. I worried that the fire department might smash the walnut and stained-glass entryway; to hell with my fibrillating heart, just don't hurt my door.

Paramedics arrived, stretched me across the carpet, started an I.V. in my left arm, and pumped naloxone into the tube. My blood pressure must have been five over zero because they were scrambling around like the Stooges, and I suddenly felt bad for my health insurance company. Those poor bastards would have to pay for this mess just because I'd had a couple of rough days.

I started crying and sobbed to the medics. "I'm sorry to be so much trouble…, probably ruining your whole day…."

The head guy, that's what I still call him, said, "You're gonna be fine."

I suddenly felt sleepy and closed my eyes. Head Guy shook me hard and commanded, "Stay awake! Work with me here!" Then he asked my name.

I laughed for several seconds before answering. "My name is Cleopatra, Queen of Denial." A cliché, sure, but I howled again. "Cleeeooooo...pa... tra!" Hilarious.

"What kind of pills did you take?" he asked between my self-amused giggles.

One of the medics found the empty prescription bottles and bourbon on the coffee table.

"Did you take these?" asked Head Guy, holding the Oxycodone and Flexeril.

"Better than being bitten by an asp." Oh, mama, I should have been a club comedian.

"How many did you take?" he demanded.

"All of them."

"How much alcohol?"

"Two shots," I answered, turning serious. "I'm really not much of a drinker." This must have sounded weird since I had just done a pretty effective job of trying to murder myself, and I suspected Head Guy was worried mostly about the Flexeril. The heart is not a muscle to be relaxed.

I grew nauseated again and motioned to Head Guy. He rolled me on my side just as I began throwing up—energetically.

After catching my breath, I said. "My name isn't really Cleopatra. It's Jennifer Roosevelt. No relation to Teddy or Franklin."

"Keep hanging in there, Jennifer," he said. "I don't think there's much left in your stomach. It's your bloodstream we need to deal with. The naloxone should help, but I gave you something extra until we get you to the hospital. Stay awake!"

"Just a short, tiny little nap...," I pleaded.

"No!"

I whined, "But I'm the queen...!"

I never made it to Rhode Island Hospital, nor did I die. They loaded me into an ambulance and Head Guy told the other first responders, "Silverton Medical is taking responsibility for the patient. We're rolling!"

The Providence paramedics and firefighters started packing up and presumably returned to station. And soon after we were moving—felt like the ambulance was doing cartwheels to me—Head Guy radioed the RI Hospital emergency room and canceled their incoming preparedness alert. He said into the microphone, "I'm sorry to report that the patient has died en route and, at her family's request, Silverton Medical is transporting her directly to the mortuary." This seemed strange to me because I have no family anywhere near Rhode Island and felt reasonably certain that I wasn't dead.

As the vehicle merged onto Interstate 95, Head Guy placed a gas mask over my nose and mouth and said, "Now you can sleep, Jennifer. You are scheduled to live."

Head Guy wasn't a bad person, just following orders. I never provided consent for treatment, but good old Mr. Guy considered attempted suicide consent enough. Besides, whatever gas I inhaled made me very comfortable.

I vaguely remember him saying, "You have a long journey coming up, but don't be afraid."

I never liked people making decisions for me and answered as best I could. "Likewise, don't be afraid, tomorrow, when I break your face over my knee."

The bastard smiled. Told you I was a comedian.

I awoke during full daylight in a room that seemed too sparsely furnished for a hospital and too clinical for anything else. I was not in restraints but wore white cotton pajamas in a patient bed with a matching robe draped across a chair. It was hard to focus my eyes, and I felt as weak as a just-neutered cat. Still, I managed to get out of bed using a conveniently placed walker and noticed two video cameras scanning the room. Even as a drugged kitten, this made my claws twitch. I looked out a large, thick window across

Central Park, and I was maybe 20 floors up. New York seemed way too quiet for whatever day this was.

I began to recall dreamlike images of white-suited nurses coming and going over the last few days, IVs dripping into my arm, and some god-awful purplish smoothie that people helped me choke down by holding the glass to my lips and cheerleading, "Swallow! Don't think about it, just swallow! Keep going," until I gagged. Then they'd give me a few seconds rest and continue, "Swallow...."

The steel entry door contained one small window with embedded wire mesh. It was bolted from the outside, which pissed me off even more than the video cameras, and I had no intention of playing a happy psych-ward lady. As far as I knew the staff had treated me well, though my recall was Flexeril-fuzzy, but if I wanted to kill myself, I figured that was my business and didn't merit incarceration.

Robert Silverton, the supervising doctor, came in and announced himself just as I climbed back to bed; thirty steps with my walker was about as exhausting as a day trek up Yosemite's Half Dome. Silverton looked about 5'11" with thick sandy hair, and without preparatory comment, he handed me a copy of a yellowed *Providence Journal* obituary dated July 14, 2021, for Jennifer Roosevelt. A successful suicide.

"Because you're here," he said, "you know that you're not dead."

"I already understand that," I said, "but where is here?"

"Silverton Medical Group headquarters," he responded. "I'm your primary care physician."

Apparently ol' Head Guy worked (or more literally had worked) for Silverton and sent me gift wrapped to 2359 C.E.

"Our retrieval methods reduce the risk of significantly altering the future," said Silverton, "and you were removed from 2021 just as you otherwise would have died."

I would later be convinced that Head Guy had shanghaied me into the future because Silverton wasn't looking for folks whose suicide attempts were half-assed cries for help; he wanted someone who meant it. That was me, all right, and for some reason I'd yet to learn, this was important to Silverton.

Sure, I had tried to paddle back across the Styx at midpoint, but that also turned out to be one of the reasons for my selection. Otherwise, my nice new doctor would've let me die 340 years ago.

When I became more alert, I grilled Silverton and then demanded he send me home so I could kick Head Guy's ass for kidnapping me.

"The man did save your life," said Silverton. "Besides, he lives in the past."

"Then I'll look him up when I get there," I said. "Just send me home!"

Silverton shook his head. "It's impossible to send matter back through time. We've learned to manipulate information through the past, tricky but doable. That's how we found you—and saved you. "

I could pretty much figure the rest. Knowledge equals power, and their 21st Century Shanghai Club could send matter, including me, into the future by stuffing my body inside a cryogenic capsule and allowing the regular clockwork to do its thing. I slept and years passed. Robert provided additional details.

"We've developed an intravenous solution that allows for cold storage of mammals at minus 20 centigrade without cell damage, and their tissues age about 1 day per 5 years. Of course, it takes six days to gradually warm a woman back to life and flush out the antifreeze. Our patients generally report that's the worst part of the deal."

"Well," I said, "this sort of thing may be fine with you, but not with me! I've got a killer hangover headache and a really bad taste in my mouth. Something akin to month-old gefilte fish laced with sulfur."

"I know," said Silverton. "Progress sometimes comes with side effects, but they won't last long."

"Hope you're right....I still don't like you."

Silverton expected a little initial resentment, ignored it, and continued. "Now, about a dozen people work for our 2021 Silverton Medical Group, and there's a smaller unit, unknown to the first, that handles our security, just in case anyone suddenly goes airborne ballistic and decides to talk about the future. Loose tongues end up in a preservative freezer before they can spill their guts, and we own perfect hindsight. But loyalty is actually pretty easy with our hefty salaries and bonuses. Self-interest is the key to happy employees—in this time or any other."

I figured Silverton was really a mad scientist at heart, though he seemed surprisingly gentle and often smiled between sentences. I prodded. "So how do you finance 2020s kidnappers from the here and now? You've already admitted you can't send cash."

"SMG operates a 'legitimate' cryonic storage business, which is actually a sideshow for our real purpose. Most of the 21st Century capsules are empty or hold showcase mannequins, and our real financing comes from investment income: buy AppleSoft, Space-X, or Prashton Incorporated; bet on Rocking Horse in the Preakness; consider Mega numbers thus and such." He paused. "Our employee incomes are staggering—and they are informed of the strict secrecy protocols when we finally hire them. Much stricter than your CIA."

"If I could stand up for more than a minute," I said, "you might be staggering yourself. You can't win me over with sweet talk preceded by gag-a-ramma smoothies."

Silverton shook his head. "I know the process is uncomfortable, and I know we brought you here without consent." He seemed genuinely sympathetic. "But remember, you'd be dead without our intervention—dead and buried for over three hundred years. And when you're feeling better, Jennifer, and understand our motives, I hope you'll assist us with a very important project. I even hope we'll become friends."

"Just don't turn your back on me," I said, still groggy and angry, "or your new BFF will kick you upside the head...." I was all bark and no bite for the moment. Within 30 seconds of my declaration of war, I fell asleep, again, with rotten sulfite gefilte fish swimming circles in my mouth.

Aside from the temporary lockdown, I received good treatment. Once I could finally eat solid food, the white uniforms brought me breakfast, lunch, and dinner and provided clean linens and pajamas each day. I could select from a seemingly infinite selection of comestibles; however, I recommend that folks wait at least 12 days after cryo-rejuvenation for a cheeseburger and fries; my stomach damned near exploded when I ordered this on day 7. The worst part of time travel, hands down, was still the "cleansing smoothie" each morning of the first six days to help neutralize the life-preserving antifreeze. It tasted almost as bad as my breath stank, and choking down what I called "chilled Satan's barf" was a miracle from scripture. But it helped, and I became noticeably stronger and more alert each day.

I made my own bed each morning as part of my physical recovery (fine by me), and around day four the staff began unlocking my door after breakfast until lights-out so I could walk the halls, visit the exercise room, and read contemporary electronic magazines in their small library—*People* and the *Wall Street Journal* were still in business, which proves that money and gossip never go out of style. After two weeks, I complained about brutal isolation (not really true), and Dr. Silverton came for his first extended therapeutic interview. That was his term. I called it prison interrogation.

The Doc smiled. "Sensors and the staff report that you're in reasonably good health though a little anxious about being here."

"The reports are right," I responded, looking around the room. "And I don't like those cameras eyeballing me every second. Is that how you keep tabs on patients?"

"Not exclusively. The beds have sensors, too."

"For my protection, right? Including cameras in the bathroom?" I was petulant but with good reason. "Who do you think you are? Some Big Brother wannabe?"

"I'm your physician—and psychiatrist."

"Another damned head guy," I said. "I don't recall giving informed consent."

He smiled. "You weren't in any condition to sign papers when my associate intervened. He opted to save your life without them."

"Thanks, but if it's all the same to you, I'd like to go home now. Your accounting staff can bill my insurance for all I care." I understood that home was impossible but decided to play stupid for the moment. He could be lying about time-travel rulebooks. Hell, he could be lying about everything.

"I'm afraid you're stuck with us, Jennifer, as I've already explained. Further, we want to understand why you wanted to die and then didn't. You swallowed enough meds to curdle the life cheese of a raging bull. By the time you called 911, it was already too late for contemporary doctors to help. Your heart would have stopped within fifteen minutes no matter what they did."

I shrugged. "I've never gone in for half-assed efforts."

"Neither do I. We saved you, at some expense, and brought you here with purpose."

"So, Robbie Dear, does this here purpose include locking me up against my will?"

The Silverton sighed. "Call me Rob if you don't like doctor. 'Robbie' doesn't sit well with me. And, again, you'd be dead without our intervention. You're an important… specimen."

"Don't use that word!"

"I know, I know," said Robert. "Or you'll break my face across your knee."

I couldn't help but smile. "I wasn't sure I had actually said that, Doc, but it sounds right. By the way, I doubt you can legally hold me. I'm no longer a danger to myself, etc., etc., etc."

"Believe me, we don't want to hold anybody, and your brainwaves confirm that you're no longer suicidal, but we need to ensure that your cryo-recovery is complete. It is a delicate process. And please, Jennifer, keep in mind that our research could help many people. Your knowledge might benefit thousands around the world."

I raised my palm. "No need to over plead your case. I tried to kill myself. You saved my life. I'll do my best to help in return—but not as a prisoner." I really was sympathetic with their plight based on my preliminary readings about the future (now my present); it's just hard to play sugar-and-spice when speaking through clenched teeth. I tried to relax but my emotions remained angrier than my logic.

"Besides," I added, "since you guys are time-travel gods, why not just send a message ahead in time to ask how the problem was solved? Then you won't need to kidnap any more unwilling specimens."

He shook his head. "We've tried. No response. Our physicists assume we can't contact the future because it hasn't happened yet. I'm not convinced, though what really concerns me is that nobody has communicated with us. If I'm alive in 40 years, I would absolutely contact me. So as bad as things are, it could mean they're about to get worse…. Maybe there is no future for humanity."

That possibility was a major downer. "Like I said, Doc. I'm willing to work as a volunteer, but no locked doors and no attempted coercion. Otherwise, I'll offer you nothing but grand mal headaches."

Silverton spoke earnestly and let his guard down. "Please, Jennifer. Try to understand. We must ensure…."

He didn't finish the sentence. I lunged at him.

OK, now I'm confined to bed with a paralytic muscle relaxant. Can't really blame 'em.

I offered a sweet uppercut at Silverton's chin, but his reflexes were quick and I missed. On the rebound, however, I landed a solid roundhouse kick to the groin. I mean solid. You should have heard him groan!

Silverton got the message. I wouldn't go down with a whimper.

Before I could test my fist against his nose, five white coats had me on the floor. Still, I wouldn't take back that kick for the world. One of my best brown-belt moments. Sure, my arms and legs presently have the brute force of a preschooler. But that's OK with me. Their paralytic muscle relaxants didn't affect my vocal chords, and I have let out a continuous recumbent tirade that would embarrass a Marine drill sergeant from the Vietnam era. If I had only words in my arsenal, I figured to squeeze them off semi-auto shotgun style.

Then it occurred to me that Silverton might be monitoring my brainwaves and/or listening in, so I clammed up tight, took three deep controlling breaths, and started a mindful meditation fit for sages across the ages. Not the easiest feat when I'd really prefer to strangle my doctor.

Well, the Bastard Silverton entered my room a minute later, still waddling slightly from my golden crotch kick. I revved up the word-sling again. Then, when I realized my verbal assault wasn't getting the kind of results I wanted, I figured to "reason" with him along the lines of an Italian Godfather.

"Now listen up, Robbie Dearest," I said. "You've glimpsed my temper, and I've glimpsed some of your societal problems. Either we work together, voluntarily, or I'm gonna be a one-woman riot until death do us part."

"Of course, Jennifer." Robert seemed suspiciously genial for a man with an uncomfortable limp. "Nice move with that roundhouse, by the way. I'm going to be sore for a few days. And one thing that particularly interests me—and most of the psychiatric staff—is the anti-depressive effects of rage. Just think, if you had been that angry on July 14, 2021, it's doubtful you would have ever tried to commit suicide. And some of my readings from your time indicate that anger can temporarily mitigate suicidal thoughts. Can you explain why?"

"You're the futurist, Doc. You tell me why."

"I can't, and as you probably surmised from current newspapers and recent medical journals, our world has a suicide crisis. The mortality rates outrank the early 20th Century flu epidemic or the 21st Century Covid crisis. And there's no discernable reason for people killing themselves that anybody can figure out.

"I mean, we've essentially conquered famine and poverty. Unemployment is less than half a percent. Preschool through doctoral education, guaranteed retirement benefits, and universal medical care are free to all citizens. Further, average IQs have increased by 15 points over the last 300 years—primarily due to that health care and the elimination of poverty. We're smarter and have more 'stuff' available than at any time in history. Damn it! People should be happy, yet they're killing themselves in droves, and the combined efforts of medicine and an army of social workers haven't been able to stop it. I think you can help…." Silverton hesitated a moment. "And I like you, too."

He sighed and seemed to choke up a bit before speaking again. "Please understand, Jennifer. In North America alone, near 90 million individuals have killed themselves in the last two decades, and while this crazy pandemic seems to have peaked, it's holding steady…. People are dying, and with all of my training, with all my concern, I've been useless to stop it."

"Rampant suicide is hard to believe, Doc, considering all the wonders you described."

He shook his head. "Tell me about it…."

I laughed. "Contemporary slang? You don't sound like someone 300 years in my future."

Silverton smiled. "I'm a quick linguistic study, and I've picked up a few choice phrases while reading transcripts or listening to recorded patient interviews from the 20th and 21st Centuries. People often seem to kill themselves when drunk, drugged, or suffering an emotional loss. Some are just plain whacko. And they use colorful language."

"This is why you brought me here? To tell you why people get depressed? Shit, I don't understand that. Why don't you just ask them?"

Robert waited expectantly. I had to admit, in a perverse sort of way, the suicide problem interested me. And looking back at my own little snuff drama, it occurred to me that a severely depressed person might be hard pressed to understand the why of it. I paused, thinking, and said, "Social utopia, higher IQs, and a pandemic death wish…. I need to study more, to get a sense of daily lives…."

I suddenly remembered that this was the 24th Century, three hundred plus years into the future, and asked out of context, "Have you colonized the Moon and Mars? God, I wanted to be an astronaut…."

"Both," he said, "along with Deimos….which is one of the newer settlements that recently failed." The pain in his voice revealed a lot.

"I am sorry, Robert." I paused, reconsidered, and then said, "Now, wait a minute. We had fairly effective antidepressants! You must have made improvements? What the hell gives?"

"Medications can help, of course, but this epidemic doesn't seem responsive to therapy or other treatments. It's something beyond our understanding of psychiatry. We've tried the old meds, of course, and the new, and in combinations, and nothing seems to work. We've even reverted to electroshock therapy out of desperation." Silverton shook his head and interjected an opinion. "Medieval barbarism! Witchdoctors!" He then calmed himself and said, "While some patients improved temporarily with these techniques, our technicians complained about the apparent cruelty of medically induced convulsions. Plus, electroshocks did almost nothing in the long term. In fact, a number of subjects actually worsened after two or three weeks."

Silverton let out a hard breath. "You have to understand, Jennifer, we're not used to losing patients in our time. And this failure is depressing our healthcare workers. Maybe this is a contagious disease."

I realized that the doctor was genuinely and rightfully disturbed. Maybe he was more human than I had been giving him credit for, but I still wouldn't tolerate conscription. Besides, I wanted to help with the problem—any person concerned about others would—and I think pretty highly of my analytical skills.

"I'm on your side, Doc, and I doubt that suicide could be contagious. But if we begin to work together, which I think I'd like, just remember my prime directive."

"Yes, yes, yes. You won't work as a prisoner."

"I'm a researcher and writer—better than average, I'd say—and I tried to kill myself. Not exactly sure why. Just lost hope and acted impulsively…, stupidly. Maybe your folks don't know exactly why they're killing themselves. either. So let's try to figure things out together. And let's face it, combining our intellects is better than fighting each other for the next fifty years."

Silverton smiled just enough to notice. "I think you're right. I'm glad my subliminal messages finally got through to you."

I paused, controlling my anger long enough to realize that the little Robbie had a sense of humor. "If I believed you exerted some kind of external mental influence, I'd spit in your face. That's about all I can manage with the meds you gave me…. And then I'd let your whole world die before lifting my middle finger."

"Would you really?"

He had me. "No! Damn, you! And I suspect that you know it."

"Well then," said Silverton, "how about I inject the paralytic antidote, get you back on your feet—no roundhouse kicks, please—and then take us to dinner. We can talk about combatting the self-murder syndrome. And where our modern scientific knowledge has failed, you and I will succeed. I suspect there's more to this than brain chemistry."

"I like the hint of success, Doc," I said. It also hit me, unexpectedly, that Silverton was rather good looking, and I suddenly hoped my crotch-kick hadn't permanently disabled his maleness. Our neurological software and physiological hardware were beginning to seem highly compatible.

I felt better once I could move again, and dinner outside the clinic would further improve my mood. Nonetheless, despite his comely appearance, Silverton had a genuine knack for pissing me off.

"Where are my clothes?" I asked.

"Most are back in 2021," he said. "But we brought several pairs of jeans and long-sleeve cotton T's from your home, and I believe casual-practical is your preference." He added too quickly, "But we can buy something more feminine if you wish...."

I shook my head. "Running shoes and denim are feminine. If this dinner is black-tie, I'll iron my T-shirt, so don't expect to parade me around town like Miss America on estrogen supplements. Oh, never mind. Do your restaurants still serve cabernet?"

"Of course, and we'll order the best wine from Ethiopia's highlands."

"All right," I said. "Neutralize every drug you put into my body, bring me clean clothes, and leave me alone for three hours to decompress and meditate on our world's little problem." I was starting to feel the mission, and Silverton couldn't hide his pleasure.

He smiled and said, "Great!"

I continued. "Then, after a glass of wine, a good meal, and a bit more thinking, I'll explain how we're going to approach this.... Just keep in mind, Robbie: No more meds, hospital gowns, or mind control beyond old fashioned persuasion. And telling you right now. I'm the principal investigator on this project. You get in my way and I'll fire your ass!"

Robert Silverton looked ready to laugh while simultaneously wondering whether I was serious. "Wouldn't mutual cooperation be more effective? After all, I know the current landscape."

"True, but you've already stepped on my toes several times in this tango, so I'm a little wary. From here on, Dr. Silverton, I expect your cooperation. I need guidance in this century, true, but it doesn't have to come from you. I rather it did because you seem informed and concerned about people. Neither of us wants anybody to commit suicide, but I'm the boss! Remember that."

"Just what the doctor ordered," he said, showing a lot of his perfect teeth. "I told them you were the right girl for the job!"

"Yeah…? Call me girl again and you might receive another lesson about foot-in-crotch disease."

He looked amused but reflexively pressed his knees together. I caught myself smiling, too.

Rob and I worked together for 22 months, often 50 hours per week, which was double the full-time expectation. He took a leave from his routine medical responsibilities at Silverton Medical to focus on personal and/or remote interviews with attempted-suicide survivors. We worked from the hospital or home offices and occasionally visited university libraries or psychology departments, but with Rob's connections, we had open access to most government and academic databases and facilities.

I focused on peer-reviewed articles and analyses while also skimming daily news reports to compare varying suicide rates, which were fairly consistent in developed countries, although it was hard to categorize "developing" versus "developed" nations because of economic globalization. Low-range per-capita earnings (not counting off-world colonies) were within 37% of hyper-advanced technological democracies like China, Eur-England, and the Americas. Glaring poverty differentials had been eliminated worldwide, essentially, so we could only evaluate 'comparative wealth' as a factor. I cross-checked for hereditary, gender, and racial markers—found no definitive correlations—but kept reading and thinking, which created headaches to rival those of "chilled Satan's barf" concoctions.

Rob continued to focus on survivor interviews, most of whom were women. Not that males weren't part of the mix, but depressed men were much more likely to fire a phase-plasma welder through the brain. Instant death; more certain than an old-time shotgun; thus, fewer male survivors. Hardware companies temporarily stopped selling such appliances to anyone but licensed contractors, but home construction tools were so pervasive that the restrictions made no more difference than the anti-gun lobbyists of the 21st Century. It's always the shooter and not the weapon that matters.

Women, like in the "old days," more typically leaned toward barbiturates. All varieties of medications were fairly easy to obtain after the "war on drugs" hysteria began to fizzle in 2049, yet many people could survive an overdose if help arrived in time, and many did. Most of the women survivors couldn't explain precisely why they'd tried to snuff themselves, pleading some variation of "bored to death" or "seemed like a good idea at the time."

The suicide epidemic had peaked in early 2362, roughly 14 months ago, but remained a deadly problem, so Rob and I continued working six days per week and bumped our daily research commitment to 10-11 hours. By 24th Century standards, you might think we'd be the unhappiest people on the planet from a work-life imbalance, but we seemed to thrive around our mission and each other's company. Every Sunday we took off to relax or explore the city; or more accurately, Robert showed me the new world. We became lovers the night of our first out-of-the-hospital diner, so I soon abandoned my personal lab quarters and moved in with Rob at his 87th-floor New York apartment. Later, because rents were dropping in conjunction with rising vacancies (suicide leaves unfulfilled lease agreements), we relocated to the 111th floor of the Rand Building adjoining Central Park. This turned out to be good for our work.

I was looking through the glass wall on a cold February afternoon, watching the robotic auto-plows clear snow from pathways and benches. A lone human followed behind one machine to sweep away any residue. The man labored for hours, brooming walkways and then rebrooming areas that apparently didn't satisfy him. In reality, he accomplished very little because the snow-bots were exceptionally efficient, but I could tell the person was proud of his work. It had deep meaning.

Then it hit me. The related psychological issues were so obvious that apparently no one, including me, had connected them before this moment.

I sighed and muttered: "God damned evolution!"

Rob looked at me, puzzled.

I added, "Intellectual and environmental interactions have consequences. I am an idiot."

I told Rob to have a drink while I did some cross-checking via our computer links. The necessary data weren't available at the apartment, but we owned clearance for remote access to most government systems. It took me longer to design and input the sorting programs than it did for the Washington, D.C., mainframe to spit out the resulting graphs: one listing Intelligence Quotients in 2021, another for 2361, and a third comparing suicides, occupations, and IQs over the last 20 years.

Rob gasped when he saw the now documented correlations. "My God," he said, "That's why the antidepressants didn't help."

I pointed at the electronic images. "Incredible, but for the mid-range group, it might be that suicide is…logical."

Neither of us wanted to believe what we must believe.

After rechecking the data, and checking the rechecks, we realized that 73 percent of people with IQs ranging from 109-121 had attempted suicide (many succeeded) in the last 18 years. The rates dropped off sharply beyond each end of the intelligence spectrum.

Robert signed. "Almost a perfect bell curve for self-inflicted death in this designated range. That simply can't be right!"

"Computers don't look for right or wrong," I said. "They just arrange the data. And that man, a human being, following the robotic snowplow showed me the way…along with your long-ago comment about an overall intelligence shift over the last couple of centuries."

"I still don't get it," he said.

"Almost too simple—and too horrible—to understand," I said. "The exponential growth in your technology and standard of living, combined with higher average intelligence, puts this one group at extreme risk for depression due to boredom and/or perceived social isolation. These folks right here," I said, pointing at the computer screen, "109 to 121, are apparently smart enough to know their limitations in your world but not smart enough to fully assimilate in it. Huxley's Alphas are fine, people like you. They thrive in an automated world where per-capita incomes offer high-end livelihoods for everyone compared with 21st Century standards. Those with lower intelligence are happy with good food, 25-hour work weeks, free healthcare, and lots of recreational/social options. Most of them have jobs that machines can't do or that customers don't want machines to do: nursing, pre-schooling, therapeutic massage. And I bet that few women—very few— would have their hair styled by an automaton no matter how proficient it might be. The data suggest that people with IQs below 107-ish find service careers personally fulfilling, and they live in abundance compared with their counterparts in other time periods." I took a breath and added, "Yours is a great century to be Archie Bunker."

"Who?" asked Rob.

"Never mind," I said. "That's an insult to most people, anyway."

I pointed at the companion graphs documenting low suicide rates. "At the other end of the spectrum, 24th Century intelligentsia are exultant geeks who run the world: engineers, programmers, scientists, doctors, lawyers, economists, professors, investment counselors—all earning outrageous incomes for 25 hours per week. Then they're free to research, travel, explore, collect, dream, volunteer, or just spend time in coffee shops with peers. Everything everywhere is available for the taking.

"In the Age of A.I., being relatively smart or dull is a blessing. But the middle ground is out of sync with its new technologically enhanced environment."

"Assuming you're right, and I don't want to agree that you're right," said Rob, with the look of a trained psychiatrist who didn't want believe in data. "I mean, first off, the theory is offensive. Slotting people by an inherent physiological category, which many not even be physiological, just doesn't sit well with my general human sensibilities. Smacks of old-style racism or sexism or ableism or something just as contemptible." He grimaced and shook his head. "I don't like the whole concept, but if you're right, what can be done?"

"My guess, according to the data, is that a natural correction may have just about run its cycle. If so, suicide rates should begin to decline of their own accord because a large chunk of the affected population has already been eliminated, and underlying causal factors can't be repeated in the same way. Statistics also confirm that smart people rarely mate outside their peer group, or vice versa, so an even broader intellectual chasm is developing and will continue to develop as gene pools become more…, ugh…, discriminatory. I hate such a conclusion, but this world may be headed for a distinct two-tier society. Not one based on socioeconomics—the technological economy seems to have eliminated that problem—but rather based on a new type of intelligence versus happiness curve that will likely plot out as a double-humped camel with fewer folks in the middle." I shook my head and added softly, "I almost wish you'd let me die back in 2021 rather than allow me to see these graphs."

Robert stiffened when I said that and said too calmly, "We'll confirm the stats, and then we'll alert proper authorities. Something must be done."

"What? Reconfigure your whole economic system to provide meaning for a few unfortunates in the happiness void? Or create useless work at just the right complexity so people can pretend to be content. That group has already proven they're too smart for that. Besides, as I said, a high percentage are already dead and, thereby, selected out of the equations. I'm not pleased about such a conclusion, but facts don't care. And they don't have feelings!"

Robert remained rigid, refusing to accept the humanly unacceptable. "I will forward your data and theories to Washington's Suicide Hot Line," he said. "They'll compare reports across the continents and colonies to make sure the hypothesis holds together. Then…mitigative action will be taken. Must be taken."

I put my hand on his shoulder. "Three hundred years brought socio-economic miracles to human civilization, but when environments change, some individuals won't be able to adapt. If the change is great enough, a whole species may die. We temporarily forgot that people are part of the living ecosystem, and Natural Selection doesn't give a hoot or a holler about who's at the top of the food chain now or a million years ago."

"But this is different!" said Robert with a certainty I could only hope for. "We are human beings! And we can make war on anything that interferes with life and limb."

I nodded, took a breath, and added. "You know, the saddest part to me was…is…their awareness. The best part of that group as intellectual and feeling human beings seems to have pushed them over the edge. They refused to be less than men and women in a world grown beyond their ability to cope. They demanded meaning, and not finding it, took action. Now," I said, thinking of my life back in 2021, "we know that smart people commit suicide, but not in the same ratios demonstrated by these data curves." I tried to sound less clinical. "Maybe this might lead to a better understanding of all depression—of what it means to be human."

Robert began to cry. "I can't imagine the emotional suffering that would drive people to self-murder."

I took his hand, trying to be strong for both of us. "I hope I didn't sound insensitive, and I'm angry at myself for not grasping these issues sooner. Let's submit our findings for peer scrutiny—and then try to save lives."

"Identifying a cause is part of a solution," he said firmly. "And once again, you and I will succeed, Dearest. We'll work together! We'll find effective therapeutic treatments that don't include electroshock therapy or dismantling an entire social system. We can do it!"

I smiled and gestured at the computer screen. "Apparently, we already have."

There appeared a new email from an elderly couple with a color photograph of them together in loving embrace—Dr. Robert Silverton and Jennifer Roosevelt.

"Congratulations to both of you," it read. "We wanted to write to you today, which is quite special. The Nobel Prize Committee has selected us, i.e., future you, for the award in Medicine, and we'll be traveling to Sweden soon. But mostly, we're proud of who we once were and who you will become. Now, get back to work! These kinds of awards aren't handed out for sloth."

It was signed, "Robbie Dearest and his supremely intelligent wife."

Robert smiled and looked at me. "From that closing line," he said, "I'm guessing that future you drafted this message."

"Or maybe you just learned to appreciate Jennifer Roosevelt a little more in 2401...." I waited a couple seconds and added, "I wonder if I'm still the principal investigator in the lab and chief executive in our marriage."

Dr. Robert Silverman wiped the moisture from his eyes, hugged me, and replied, "My dear girl, I love you enough to always let you believe so."

INFORMED CONSENT

Marilyn Jane Callaway, formerly Martin James Callaway, accepted the risk. She was about to undergo gender-affirming surgery, had dreamed of this day for nearly all of her 25 years, and had often worked double shifts to save enough money for the medical fees, which were not covered by her health insurance. But even if they had been, she wanted the renowned Dr. Jack Hall and no other, and he required advance cash payment for these procedures. In fact, though Hall was a respected figure in New York medical circles, he treated transsexuals only in his private Cuban clinic. The United States medical community would not certify his unique gender-affirming methods.

Today, in addition to genital reconstruction, Marilyn would simultaneously undergo breast augmentation, facial contouring, thyroid chondroplasty, and endoscopic suture glottoplasty to raise her vocal cord pitch. Fees were reduced by combining multiple procedures at the same time, and Marilyn would "endure" one day of surgery instead of several.

She wondered if she might chicken out at the last moment. Dr. Hall's rules were strict, but Marilyn had been referred by a close friend who had undergone similar treatments in this same operating theater, and the results were beyond spectacular. Her feminization at the hands of Dr. Hall appeared completely natural.

Still, as Marilyn lay naked on the table, securely strapped down, her legs spread and her body covered by a sterile white sheet, she worried. The good doctor was about to ask for final authorization. She hoped for the necessary courage to go forward. Other doctors used more traditional methods, of course, but Hall's results set the standard for sex reassignment. Marilyn expected to be indistinguishable from a natural female after she left his care.

A gowned and gloved Jack Hall began his pre-surgical declarations as Marilyn lay on the table. A single nurse—experienced and proficient—stood at the ready.

"Marilyn Jane Callaway," said Dr. Hall, formally but gently, "we are about to begin your special day. Listen to everything and then give me a final 'go' or 'no go.' We have already discussed what to expect, and you've had a month to consider this moment, but now is the time for informed consent. I will not proceed without it. Do you understand?"

There was apprehension in Marilyn's response. "Yes, Doctor."

"I will strive for the finest and safest medical outcome, and I am not padding my ego when I say the results shall be extraordinary. My personal commitment is the standard of care for my transsexual patients. You will not only obtain a naturally feminine appearance, you will become beautiful, for I have refined and perfected every aspect of the male-to-female transformation."

"Thank you," said Marilyn, suppressing the urge to run.

Dr. Hall continued. "As a final summary, I'll begin with single-stage genital reconstruction to provide a functional vagina, removing the testicles, scraping away the subcutaneous penile tissue, and inverting the skin to construct the vaginal lining. This will require piercing the pelvic wall and reshaping leftover scrotal matter to simulate the labia and clitoris.

"Next, I will transplant a small amount of abdominal fat to increase your breast size. Such augmentation is routine and should not concern you.

"Then, we'll rehabilitate the nose, upper lip, and chin for more delicate features. This involves grinding bone surfaces and a partial face lift. Fortunately, you have excellent skin and no remaining facial hair, but it will take a couple months for the swelling and bruises to disappear. You've seen the results in other patients, so I expect you will be pleased.

"After that, I'll make a small incision in your throat and shave the tracheal cartilage to eliminate any sign of an Adam's apple.

"And finally, there's the laser-endoscopic procedure to stitch one end of your vocal cords, shortening the folds so that speaking vibrations will increase from 120 per second to 200. This will create a permanent, distinctly feminine tone. Your breathing may be difficult during this stage, but I'll work fast."

Dr. Hall paused and said, "The combined surgeries—done quickly though expertly—take approximately six hours. Do you understand?"

"Yes," replied Marilyn. "I wish...I weren't so terrified...."

"Of course you're terrified!" said the good doctor. "Otherwise, you wouldn't be mentally competent for consent. Only the most determined patients are allowed at this clinic, which helps me to ensure that they are real women and my work is in their best interest. And, yes, I believe that your decision to have final surgery is a good one."

Dr. Hall continued. "So, before the nurse tightens your restraints and we proceed, you must re-confirm your commitment. There will be no stopping after the first incision."

Marilyn held quiet but trembled under her covering.

"Out of suffering," said Dr. Hall as though speaking from a pulpit, "woman's anguish shall give way to joy. Therefore, as we discussed, you will have no anesthesia or pain control medication until after my last stitch. If you lose consciousness, I shall work with all possible speed, but most patients revive quickly during the operation.

"Now, my dear Miss Callaway, by your choice and by your authority in selecting me as your caregiver, shall I create a whole woman today? Or, shall we stop and send you home? I sincerely want to help, but you must concur."

"I understand," said Marilyn, now beginning to perspire under the sterile sheet.

"Do you freely offer your assent?"

Marilyn faltered, considering the physical torture of the next 6 hours against the emotional torture she had endured for almost 25 years, the rejections, heartache, lost family and friends, postponed hopes and dreams. She likewise considered other transsexuals, some of whom she knew personally, that had lost their lives having procedures with less-than-competent and less-than-caring doctors. Marilyn Callaway was terrified of this day but more terrified of the next 50 years without it.

The doctor spoke almost lovingly. "Take your time, dear child, as my nurse prepares the neuromuscular blocking agent. But remember, the paralytic injection will not affect your pain receptors. It simply inhibits localized muscle spasms while I'm operating."

The nurse circled the table, securing the patient's head, arms, ribcage, legs, and ankles with pink leather straps while Marilyn steadied her resolve, a tear rolling from her left eye.

Dr. Hall brightened the operating lights and held a gleaming scalpel for the patient to see. "I await final authorization."

The nurse positioned her noise-reduction headgear that would blot out the worst reverberations yet allow her to understand the doctor's commands. She slipped a surgical mask over the patient's nose and mouth.

The room was quiet. Finally, Marilyn took a deep breath and spoke through clenched teeth. "Please proceed, doctor. Make me female."

The nurse delivered the muscle relaxant into a vein.

After sixty seconds, the surgeon made a first incision and sliced away the testes.

Marilyn screamed at 120 cycles per second, engendering a flash in the surgeon's eyes that revealed the secret hiding inside the good Dr. Jack Hall. Marilyn didn't care. Hall's skill was supreme! What did it matter if a part of his subconscious enjoyed itself? Monsters from the id? Ha! Transsexuals encountered monsters every week—at work, home, school, Wal-Mart, the DMV. The surgeries were Marilyn's best way to fight back. And in the long run, she would win! She would win, damn it!

Without looking up, focusing on time and precision, Hall tossed the scrotal contents into the hazardous-waste bin. Then, he slashed the penis from base to tip, splaying the skin to be grafted.

The firmly secured patient inflated her surgical mask with guttural cries that sounded masculine.

Dr. Hall focused.

Cut. Clamp. Suture. Again.

The surgical maestro was better than his word, and Marilyn's feminization resolved into a prolonged and full-bodied ode to joy.

CRIME WARP

"Maybe people are getting better," said Professor Jarrod Hermestad, the newest member of the Sociology Department.

"Don't make me laugh," replied Randall Grundweiss, the always skeptical Dean. "Whatever you've found, the human race isn't behind it. Maybe the data's screwy."

"Absolutely not," said the young professor without taking offense. "I don't know what it means, but the information is valid. Crime rates are down across all cultures and socioeconomic subgroups."

Grundweiss looked at Cynthia Smith, Chair of Sociology, who was the only other person at the meeting. "Well?"

Smith was cautious, somewhat afraid of Grundweiss, but said, "Jarrod's statistical manipulations are way beyond me, but informal crosschecking suggests that he may be right. A colleague from USC said that Los Angeles urban crime has dropped 67 percent over the previous year. And the California Institute for Men—a maximum security prison in Chino—reported no serious assaults in six months, which is unheard of for that population. Even mentally ill inmates seem calmer."

"Anybody suggest why?" asked Grundweiss.

"I don't think most folks really believe it," said Smith. "Just assume it's some kind of glitch."

"How about you?"

Smith shrugged.

Hermestad added, "I tweaked my search program and recompiled the data. The computer scans newspapers and magazines, along with documents from county governments, the military, state and federal courts, and can use its own discretion to follow the documents wherever they lead. It even tapped a few restricted files."

"I don't want to hear about anything illegal!" said Grundweiss.

Hermestad lifted his head. "Nothing was wrongfully obtained. Some documents might be encoded, but they were pulled from the web, and our machine can decipher most scrambled transmissions."

"Our machine?" asked Smith.

"I was a programmer before turning to sociology," admitted Hermestad. "The university's supercomputer is remarkable, and it runs my search requests each night between 3:00 and 3:20 a.m."

"Only 20 minutes?" asked Grundweiss.

"Time is very competitive. I'm lucky to get 20."

Grundweiss nodded, annoyed for reasons he didn't fully understand, but not as much as usual, hardly living up to the student nickname 'Dean Grindhouse.' Smith and Hermestad noticed his relatively kinder mood.

"OK," said the Grundweiss, "for the sake of argument, let's assume this is real. What do you propose? And by the way, if you need more computer time, let me know."

Smith interrupted. "This could spotlight the university if we publish first, and declining crime won't stay hidden long."

"Cindy's right," said Grundweiss, pointing at Hermestad. "We should move quickly, but you'd better be right Mr. Used-to-be-a-Programmer! If some high-school nerd punches holes in your findings, you'll be laughed out of academia before Saturday Night Live has time to write a parody."

Hermestad nodded. "I'm confident in the data but don't understand the cause. Once I do, we should be able to formulate a theory and publish."

Smith and Grundweiss noticed the "we" and approved. They wouldn't mind sharing any accolades.

"Besides," said Hermestad, "I found a woman connected to this strange… wave of human kindness."

After a pause, Smith asked, "A woman?"

"I looked for data crossings that might indicate some focal point. I found one."

Grundweiss protested. "You're not suggesting that a lone woman has reduced crime?"

"No," admitted Hermestad, "but she's predicting an end to what she calls a crime warp."

"Bah!" said the Dean, sounding more like Grindhouse. "I grew up on the South Side, sonny boy, so don't try to sell me snake oil as single malt Scotch."

"There's more," said Hermestad, deflecting the remark. "This particular woman, well…, she died 49 years ago, reappearing last week in the same town where she is buried."

Grundweiss stood to leave. "Your computer's drinking straight from the bottle."

"You don't understand," said Hermestad. "City police have confirmed most of this, and they're holding her in a psychiatric ward. By some coincidence, a local dentist produced the dead woman's dental charts. Except for one missing tooth, they match the mystery girl."

"And you believe some Podunk tooth scrubber just happened to keep a dead woman's X-Rays for 50 years?"

Hermestad nodded. "Apparently no one bothered to clean out the files after two successive orthodontists purchased the building. Small towns."

"I…." Grundweiss couldn't think what to say.

"If the woman hadn't tried to warn officials about the soon-to-implode crime warp, nobody would have paid attention to her. At first they figured she was demented and homeless, but then they found eight million dollars in US Bearer Bonds tucked inside her closet."

Grundweiss laughed. "At least she can afford a good straightjacket."

"Also," said Hermestad, "her residence burned down several years after she died. The site was bulldozed; the lot remained vacant for 36 years; and then, poof, the house was back!"

"What's the gag?" asked Grundweiss.

"Nobody's laughing," said Hermestad. "The cops have before and after photographs, and the woman is predicting an end to a phenomenon our supercomputer just discovered. I've spoken with her doctor. I would like to visit the patient."

"Where?"

"Desert Hot Springs, California."

"That's 3,000 miles," said Grundweiss. "I won't spend funds chasing a ghost story."

"This one might be worth it," said Hermestad. "If five percent of her story is true, she is a very special woman."

Smith looked at Grundweiss. "I've never been afraid of dire predictions, but all this is beginning to scare me…," she hesitated and added, "a little. I think we should let Hermestad investigate further."

Grundweiss grumbled but conceded. "The school will pay airfare and expenses, but I want a detailed report when you return…along with receipts for every penny."

"We can't hold her much longer," said Dr. Johanna Wellsby of Desert Hot Springs Hospital, speaking in her office with Hermestad. "Seventy-two hours for observation. California's pretty strict."

"When will she be released?" asked Hermestad.

"Unless she's a danger to herself or others, tomorrow afternoon, and it's my professional opinion that she's about as dangerous as tepid herbal tea. The police are checking the money trail, but bearer bonds are self-defining. She has them. They're hers." She looked at Hermestad and added, "Which means the woman can buy enough big-gun attorney power to make the city, hospital, and me regret any improprieties. Probably you, too."

"What about her…resurrection?" Hermestad suddenly felt like a fool.

Wellsby shook her head. "I don't believe in flesh-eating zombies or sensitive men. There's got to a mix-up somewhere. Nobody returns from the dead."

"And the dental records?"

"I can't pretend to explain it. A woman with the same name and dentistry died 49 years ago, but our girl down the hall is flesh and blood. She's smart, a little kooky, and roughly the same age and appearance as that 'other woman' at the time of her death. But that's as far as I'll go. The rest is somebody's bureaucratic blunder."

There was a knock at the door.

"I'm in conference," shouted Wellsby without getting up.

"Sorry to interrupt, Doc," said a man speaking through the door, "but it's your favorite sheriff. Got more info about our woman."

"Oh, good!" said Wellsby. "The door's unlocked."

Sheriff Ryan Caruthers entered and noticed Hermestad, who stood.

"Hello, Ryan," said Wellsby. "I was chatting with Dr. Hermestad about the new patient. He's a big-deal professor from back East to help us figure out what's going on."

The sheriff extended his hand to Hermestad, who shook it and sat back down. Wellsby gestured to the other chair for the sheriff.

"No time, Doc. Just wanted to give you this." Caruthers extended a one-page document. "From the FBI. The dead woman was once a California Notary Public, and all notaries are fingerprinted as part of their application. Your gal has matching prints with the deceased, so the Bureau asked me to obtain another set to be sure there's no foul-up." Sheriff Caruthers shook his head. "The odds are a billion to one."

"I don't believe it," said Wellsby.

"Me neither," said Caruthers, "but I'll get the prints. You plan to release her?"

"Yep. Not psychotic. Nice woman if you ask me." Wellsby glanced at the sheriff. "Are you saying otherwise?"

Caruthers hitched up his gun belt and turned toward the door. "Let her go when you're satisfied, Doc. She hasn't committed a crime, and I won't arrest a little old lady without a damned good reason. Still in the same room?"

Wellsby nodded.

"OK to get those prints now?"

"Sure. Just ask the nurse to let you in."

"Have you confirmed her real name?" asked Hermestad.

"Says she's Christina Laramor," responded the sheriff. "No evidence to the contrary. Sorry to interrupt the meeting." Caruthers thumbed toward the hallway. "Oh, I almost forgot, Doc. A call just came in about an accident down Interstate 10. Five or six cars. Transporting the injured here and Palm Springs. Sounds bad."

"Damn!" said Wellsby. "Would you alert the desk to gear up while I finish up here?"

"Sure," said Caruthers, closing the door behind him.

Wellsby shook her head. "I've never scored more than three numbers in the Lotto, but Miss Billion-to-One lands in my hospital. Jesus." She paused. "Look, Dr. Hermestad, we're a small-town operation, and I'm basically a general surgeon who sidelines in psychiatry when needed. They're going to need me in the ER when the ambulances start to arrive, so could you have a go with Laramor while I mend a few broken bodies?"

"That's why I came—to meet Laramor."

"And based on what you've said, you'll have more insights into what's going on than I would. But don't try to tell me she's Night of the Living Dead. I've already practiced enough psychiatry to suit me for a lifetime."

As the sheriff exited Laramor's room with new fingerprints, Hermestad entered. It was not a typical psychiatric holding area, but rather a converted hospital room with a lock that could likely be picked by a seventh grader.

"Hello," said the professor as he closed the door. "My name is Jarrod Hermestad. May I talk with you?"

"By all means," said Laramor, apparently calm, sitting in a stuffed chair next to the bed. "But I hope you're someone who'll listen. It's important."

Hermestad rolled a doctor's stool next to Laramor and sat. "As a sociologist, I'm trained to listen. As a researcher, I'm interested in crowd psychology."

"And you're wondering why the crime rates have suddenly dropped?"

Hermestad nodded, trying not to seem surprised. "And do you know why?"

"Let's call it a good deed," said Laramor. "But you won't believe me unless...."

Hermestad tried to reassure her. "I may be a sociology professor, but I'm really a computer geek trying to understand what makes humanity tick, which makes infinite absolutes look easy by comparison."

"Scientifically trained?"

"Yes," replied Hermestad, wondering where Laramor was headed.

She seemed to speak to herself. "Then you might be of some use, but the pendulum will swing back harder than before...."

"What pendulum?"

"A bad one!" She took a breath and stiffened. "But first, you must accept that I am Christina Laramor."

"The sheriff identified you," said Hermestad. "Why should I doubt it?"

"Because I really did die 49 years ago."

Professor Hermestad suddenly felt dizzy. His whole life had been squeaky clean—he had never tossed a gum wrapper on the ground, never crossed the street without looking both ways, and never rolled his car through a stop sign. He'd won the Good Citizen Award in both fifth and sixth grades. And Christina Laramor now wanted him to obtain DNA from a corpse buried 50 years ago, a corpse, according to Laramor, that was her former self.

"Breaking into graves is illegal," protested Hermestad. "Furthermore, the thought's revolting."

"You don't know the meaning of that word," said Laramor, as if talking to a child, "but you must believe me to help me, and DNA is one way I can prove it."

"Maybe I'm not so hard to convince," said Hermestad. "There are strange coincidences: You know about the crime rates. Your dental X-rays and fingerprints match the deceased. And you bear a striking resemblance to Laramor's old photographs. I'm listening."

Laramor shook her head. "I suspect that you'll still need something more. I was there and hardly believe it. Besides, we don't have to dig up the grave, just drill through the soil until you hit what's left of me. With the right equipment, we can retrieve fragments to compare with this." Laramor tapped her forearm.

"I won't break the law," said Hermestad, flatly. "If you insist, let's petition the court for permission…."

Christina Laramor suddenly became angry. "I already told we're short on time. Hell is about to break loose, literally. Millions will be injured or killed, and we just might be able to prevent it. I've already lost three days during this hospital fiasco, not that I can blame them for locking me up. However, I can blame you!"

"Me!?"

"Yes! You have evidence; I offered to obtain more. We need to act now!"

"Tell me your story," said Hermestad. "I'll tell you if I need more evidence."

Laramor hesitated. "OK," she said, "but we must go to a church…or hold a Bible while speaking. Church is better."

"What?"

"I can't explain here."

Hermestad realized that, despite the unique evidence in her case, Laramor was probably insane. "I haven't set foot in chapel since I was 12 years old, and even then it wasn't my idea."

"But you'll go?"

"Under protest."

"Good enough for me," said Laramor, without emotion.

With permission from the hospital, Laramor and Hermestad drove south on Palm Avenue and stopped at a small Baptist church. The main door was unlocked, and no one seemed to be around. They entered and sat at the nearest pew.

"Religion doesn't offer the happiest memories for me," said the professor, "so why did you drag me here?"

"Because Satan can't eavesdrop inside a church."

Hermestad's shoulders dropped. "I'm afraid that answers all my other questions. We should take you back to the hospital, or home, whichever you prefer. I think I can fly back to Massachusetts now."

"No!" said Laramor. "I offered to obtain DNA to confirm my identity. You refused. Now shut up and listen!"

"I'm a scientist, Ms. Laramor. I don't believe in gods or devils."

"Oh? But you believe in an unexplained and miraculous crime reduction? Or that my X-rays match a dead woman?"

"Except for one tooth."

"Of course! I lost it when my face hit the steering wheel."

"The day you died. Of course."

"You're really starting to annoy me, professor, but maybe you can believe THIS." Laramor reached inside her purse, removed a $10,000 bearer bond, and laid it in Hermestad's lap. "Is it enough to buy the next two hours of your time?"

Hermestad didn't know what to say. He'd never seen a bearer bond because the government had stopped issuing them the year he was born. But it sure looked like money, and young professors were always short on research funds.

"Need more?" asked Laramor, pulling another bond. "Let's double the offer."

Hermestad stuttered. "I...I...can't take advantage of you like this."

"Don't worry. I'm older and wiser than you are—and I have already died once. So whatever you think you know about heaven and earth is infantile babble. I want two hours of your time with an open mind. Twenty thousand dollars is my offer!"

Hermestad looked at the beautifully engraved certificates.

"Yes or no!?" she demanded.

"OK," he said, petulantly. "If you insist on tossing away money, I can't be held responsible."

Laramor handed him the second bond. "You say you don't believe in devils? Well, I spent 49 years—that's 17,885 days—with the grandmaster, himself. And in hell, you remember every hour, every minute."

Hermestad stared at the bonds, an unimaginable windfall for an assistant professor with student loans to pay, but he remained angry and became sarcastic. "Let me guess. You were a serial killer in your previous life? Oh, wait, it was really you who shot Kennedy. That's why you spent time in hell."

"Not at all," she said, calmly. "I was depressed and slammed my Oldsmobile into a palm tree at 90 miles per hour. The suicide, alone, might have been overlooked—temporary insanity—but the golden gatekeepers were not impressed that my vehicle ricocheted into another one, killing a three-year-old girl in the passenger seat. I deserved hell, all right. No qualms from me. And the worst part of the next 49 years was thinking about that child. Compared to the torture of my own guilt, Satan was a rank amateur."

"I know a Christina Laramor died in a car accident, but you really expect me to believe this?" asked Hermestad, understanding that if she had accidentally killed a toddler, psychological remorse might be at the root of her delusions.

"Your bargain was to listen with an open mind," insisted Laramor. "If you can't do it, give me back the bonds!"

Hermestad nodded. "You're right. I agreed…, so Satan can't hear us in church."

"He's omnipresent on earth, though strangely not in hell, and there are certain barriers to his presence. And I don't want him to know what we're up to."

Hermestad struggled to be tactful; he wanted the money. "According to myth, it seems unlikely that he couldn't hear us."

"I didn't make the rules, but designated sanctuaries are off limits to him. I ought to know. He complained incessantly about this."

"If I might ask," said Hermestad, changing tone, "how is it possible that you escaped?"

"I didn't… I got paroled. You see, I created the crime reduction, and somebody up there," Laramor pointed toward the ceiling, "sent me back home as a reward. And as long as I don't deliberately drive into a palm tree again, there's opportunity for redemption."

Hermestad covered one eye with his hand, rubbing his forehead. "Released from hell on good behavior?"

"Apparently. And my life was put back together except that one tooth is missing. A reminder of sorts."

Hermestad grew progressively more interested in her story despite his technical and scientific training. An impossible tale, of course, but what a case study she would make. He asked, "So you reduced crime from hell?"

"After about 30 years, I began to reason through the pain. Satan's earthly presence stirs up a lot of mischief, like pouring oxygen onto smoldering embers. Even decent folks can be affected. Maybe they're depressed or angry or confused, and Dark Energy sets them off."

"Dark Energy?" asked Hermestad. "You're referring to actual Dark Energy?"

She nodded. "Science has been trying to figure out what it is. Now you know."

"And we're in church because…?

"Temples, mosques, churches, shrines, chapels—meditative places like that—are shielded from Satan's uninvited presence. Certain individuals can still bring him along, like a lamprey attached to the soul, but demons can't enter without a host. That's why we're here."

"Let's get back to crime," said Hermestad. "The entire civilized world has failed throughout history to substantially reduce criminality, but you succeeded?"

"I had opportunity—and means. Even Satan has weaknesses, not the least of which is his own arrogance. I swear that sometimes he's almost human."

"Better to rule in hell than serve in heaven?"

"I've heard that line more than once," responded Laramor. "He also takes special interest in newly arrived do-gooders like me who commit unintentional but unpardonable sins. Plus, I sort of, oh, what's the current terminology, got in his face. I deserved hell and said so straight out." Laramor seemed to be thinking. "Dark Energy doesn't work very well on that attitude, so he kept me under direct personal observation, trying to get into my head. To tell you the truth, he wasn't very good at it. He's much better with killers who wreak havoc on earth and then whine for mercy. Torture's easier when the soul carries a bit of hell to start with."

"You sound almost vengeful."

Laramor spoke softly. "I've been to hell and back again. That tends to create plain talk. But listen, Satan inadvertently opened the door to my gambit, and he's gonna be really, really pissed if he finds out what happened."

Hermestad began to speak, but stopped, so Laramor continued. "Before my encounter with a palm tree, I was a pharmacist."

"So?"

"Knowledge is power, and after some effort, I concocted a slipshod antidepressant laced with synthetic estrogen—sort of Depo-Provera Prozac—dropping it into his coffee each morning, which I prepared and served as a theoretical humiliation. After four or five weeks of my 'subservience' with Prozac, the world crime rates began to fall."

Hermestad laughed. "Don't tell me! He also developed hot flashes!"

"Laugh if you will, but that little chemistry project of mine punched my ticket back to earth."

Hermestad's amusement began to taper.

Laramor waited and said, "Hell is better off, too. I think Satan actually suffers from depression…. Now listen, carefully. I have a desperate plan to help maintain this scheme, and I need your cooperation."

Two days later Professor Hermestad flew 3,000 miles east to his university. He told Grundweiss and Smith that the California trip had been a dead end, but he would continue to investigate the odd phenomenon. He did not discuss Laramor or her request.

Hermestad had used his academic connections, along with lubricating funds supplied by Laramor, to set up a meeting with a death-row prisoner in Texas, a woman who had murdered two of her three children during a postpartum psychotic episode. Laramor had wanted to attend the meeting herself, but the warden would allow only Hermestad in the death house, presumably for research into violent crime. He had to fly to Texas that evening because Wilella Sue Johnston was scheduled for execution in three days. And Texas has a deadpan reputation about maintaining its schedules.

Mrs. Johnston seemed almost catatonic when Hermestad entered her cell, and he was astonished that anyone so obviously and utterly mentally ill could be executed under the law. Yet it was clear as he passed through security checkpoints that her crime had squelched all sympathy for Johnston. The guards suggested that lethal injection was too good for her, and one said he'd like to "dissect her body one small piece at a time and feed it to scorpions."

Hermestad remained uncomfortable about the meeting because he still could not fully believe that Laramor had returned from the dead. In fact, the only credible part of Laramor's story was her extensive psychopharmaceutic knowledge, which made sense if she were a druggist, but Laramor offered hard cash to set the meeting, telling the professor exactly what to say to Johnson. He was also curious about death row and the psychology of this particular inmate. Again, a good case study.

"Good afternoon, Mrs. Johnston," said Hermestad after he was ushered into her cell. "My name is Doctor Jarrod Hermestad. Did the guards tell you I would be coming?"

Johnston nodded but did not speak.

"Did they explain why?"

She nodded again.

"Well, there's more…."

Johnston stared at the floor. She appeared to be about 35 years old, a once beautiful woman whose features had been distorted by guilt and unwashed hair. Hermestad remained uneasy but felt grave compassion.

"Mrs. Johnston," he said, "I can't imagine what you're going through, and I'm not here to judge, only to relay a message from another woman who suffered as you are suffering now. This woman also promises that your surviving child will have all the advantages money can provide; and trust me, she has the resources to fulfill that commitment."

Johnston said nothing.

Hermestad continued with nervous energy, determined to deliver his message and leave. He removed two pocketsize Bibles from his jacket and placed one in Johnston's lap; she did not move. Hermestad held the other, fearing that he looked more like an exorcist than a professor.

"I don't fully believe what I'm about to tell you, but Christina Laramor—remember that name—says you will soon enter a new world; and when you get there, you will be one of the few inhabitants who can reason because your experience on earth is worse than what you're about to encounter. Further, due to your special, uh, circumstances, it is likely that you will end up under observation of the primary supervisor. This should all make sense when you're there."

Wilella Johnston lifted her head but did not smile. She placed her hand on the Bible.

"Eventually, you must go to the Hall of Boxes," said Hermestad, "and I want you to remember the coordinates DC-3, 747, SS-T. They're types of airplanes, which should help your recall. This is very important because they lead to a secret packet tucked behind a drawer where you'll find a bottle of soluble tablets with instructions. Carry out those instructions as soon as possible, but be very careful. The supervisor must not notice...."

Johnston looked up slowly. "Tell me," she said. "Am I going to hell?"

"According to Miss Laramor, our benefactor, you are."

Johnston sighed. "Thank, God. I deserve it more than anyone."

Hermestad now understood the strange logic in Laramor's choice. "Bear in mind," he said, hardly believing his own words, "you won't be there forever. Redemption can be found at DC-3, 747, SS-T. And remember to follow those instructions carefully."

"I'm not worthy of salvation, but I will remember your kindness—and hers."

"I wish you every success, Mrs. Johnston," said Hermestad, tossing his Bible on the bunk. Then he spoke more solemnly and scientifically. "But in the long run, I fear that if Laramor is correct, Dark Energy shall one day destroy the universe."

The lights on death row flickered, there was a faint odor of smoldering plastic, and Hermestad imagined a hot breath prickling against the back of his neck.

"Yesssssss," said a calloused whisper somewhere behind him.

Hermestad turned reflexively, saw nothing, and quickly deduced that the wavering lights and burnt smell must have been caused by a damaged electrical circuit.

He reassured Mrs. Johnston. "That stench…and the lights. Probably just a blown fuse."

"Yesssssss," she smiled curiously and replied in a distinctive imitative voice that they both had heard. "It would be the logical explanation."

Hermestad began to perspire. His pulse suddenly raced.

"Please thank Miss Laramor for the advice," said Johnston, lifting her head and suggestively holding up Hermestad's discarded Bible. "I shall be redeemed."

The young professor grasped the book, clutched it tightly to his chest, and called for the guards to release him.

RAPTURES OF THE DEEP

Dr. Sloan laughed at Dr. Trieste without taking his eyes off the portal. "Don't tell me you're scared, Nitro? I thought that nickname meant you were a fearless female."

"No," said Trieste. "It just means I can be dangerous around geniuses who act like assholes."

"Thanks for the compliment," said Sloan. "Besides, I'm not sure one can be a genius without sometimes being an ass. We tend to get on people's nerves."

Trieste smiled, and they both got back to work. At every passing landmark, one of them would say "beautiful" or "extraordinary" or "wow."

The U.S. Navy's newest deep-water research vehicle, The Willa-Bee, descended past the 7,000-meter mark on its way to under-explored regions of the Mariana Trench. The water pressure was already over 10,000 psi, but the depths were no match for the three-inch thick spherical titanium passenger compartment. In fact, the vessel hull could withstand pressures at up to 13,000 meters, deeper than Everest is tall, though there were no ocean trenches yet discovered beyond 11,500 meters. And with crush-depth safety margins, the three-member crew felt as secure as they were excited, despite the inherent dangers of deep-sea exploration, because only one percent of the Pacific Ocean floor had yet been viewed up close and personal. Every trip into the Mariana Trench yielded new bio-geologic wonders. Science careers could be made from these journeys; established careers could be enhanced. Such vessels and expeditions were why many scientists entered their fields in the first place. Like a first love, sighting a new ocean species or geographic phenomenon would be remembered forever.

The three crew members included a designated Navy pilot, Lieutenant William Robest, who was specially trained for Willa-Bee's expanded capabilities. Also on board were Janet "Nitro" Trieste of the Scripps Institute, a biological oceanographer, and James Blathey Sloan from the University of Rhode Island's Marine Science Department whose primary research focused on hydrothermal vents and methane seep. Both loved the ocean; both loved their work. (And before the Rate My Professors website discontinued the practice, both had chili peppers next to their names for the "hotness" factor.) They were also among the most dedicated and respected teachers on their respective campuses. Professors Trieste and Sloan believed that research and teaching functioned together like inhaling and exhaling. One without the other was irresolvable.

The ship passed 8,000 meters at almost two hours into the trip. The descent and ascent were the most stressful parts of the journey. The combined four or five hours required to reach the bottom and return to the surface meant lost research time. And even with the Willa-Bee's advanced ion-lithium battery configuration—backed up by a smaller but more dependable lead-acid system—every transit hour meant one hour less scanning wonders of the deep. Research time was expensive, but the Willa-Bee could safely remain underwater for fifteen hours, which left ten to eleven hours on the ocean floor compared with a more typical six or seven. And these two scientists wanted every minute of every hour. Their minds understood the reality of fungible time, but their hearts grumbled with the urgent longing of children: "Are we there yet?"

Now beyond 10,000 meters. Lieutenant Robest began to slow the descent as sonar pinged the Trench's west wall at 400 meters. Conserving power, the pilot had not yet engaged exterior lights. Their mission was to explore the valley of Challenger Deep, not the aquatic life on the way down. Of course, as they descended in the darkness, bio-florescent flashes could be seen here and there through six funnel shaped viewports that likewise resisted the enormous ocean pressures. Lieutenant Robest would light the waters at 150 meters above the Challenger Deep's floor. He trusted sonar better than his eyes, and his eyes were as sharp as they were intense.

"Ok, folks," said Robest. "We're nearing the zone." He powered the external lights and cameras while studying the instrument panel. "A good descent, too. Power reserves indicate we've got roughly ten hours on the bottom, give or take 30 minutes, depending on our thruster activity."

Dr. Sloan peered into the void. Nothing visible yet. "How close are we to any smokers?" he asked. "I hope to get a good look at them, along with samples and videos."

"And to see the foraminifera...," interrupted Dr. Trieste, scanning the three audiovisual monitors, then shifting to the portals and back to the screens, too excited to remain still even in their cramped quarters. "And echinoderms? And the large amphipods!?"

"Hold your horses, both of you," said the Lieutenant, still monitoring the sonar as the sea floor approached. "And don't worry! You're guaranteed to see stuff. This is my fourth trip to the trench, and I've never been down here that the science crew didn't damn near wet their pants over something. My mission primary is to film and map territory for the Navy. But, of course," he winked, "we also explore in the name of science. These dives cost the Navy and our beloved taxpayers lots of money so it helps to spread around some of the findings."

"And the whole world benefits from new knowledge," said Trieste.

"And scientists can have a pretty good time getting it," said Sloan, peering into the clear water and waiting for bottom to appear in the lights. "We get to play in an underwater sandbox using million-dollar pails and shovels that mere professors could never afford."

Trieste laughed. "Well, then thank the Lord for taxes and educational grants!"

"Amen to that," said Robest. The scientists were becoming more animated. Few would ever be lucky enough to gain research passage on The Willa-Bee. Sloan and Trieste knew it. This could be a one-time journey into the trench; many of their colleagues, equally deserving and earnest, might never gain the privilege. They were proud and grateful.

They were six hours into the mission. Sloan and Trieste were suitably impressed, and each had retrieved biotic and/or soil samples for their labs—including the white and pink shrimp-like crustaceans (although some were too large for the ship's traps), sea cucumbers, jellyfish, soft-shelled forams that Robest called "sand-castle critters," and other life that, even to informed scientists, seemed implausibly weird and wonderful. The cameras recorded the terrain as they glided through the world's deepest known valley, Challenger Deep. When Lieutenant Robest reminded them that the Willa-Bee must begin its ascent in four hours, Sloan and Trieste seemed as disappointed as children whose time ran short at Disneyland.

"The new buoyancy foam should get us on the surface a little faster than most ships," said Robest, perhaps more to himself than the two scientists. "Right around two hours. But the Navy wants a wide safety margin as we operate the new battery system at depth."

"Any problems with it?" asked Trieste, expressing a hint of concern, as though she realized for the first time that an environment seven miles under the ocean might be dangerous.

"Flawless so far," said Robest. "The Navy just likes to triple check the double checks after the first checks check out."

The lieutenant bragged further about his ship. "This is my fourth time on the Willa-Bee. About as sweet a machine as anybody could ask for."

"What is this buoyancy foam you mentioned?" asked Trieste.

"Don't know the all the engineering details," said Robest. "Not my area of expertise. But it's some kind of super-duper syntactic resin chock-full with glass bubbles. Lighter than previous materials and able to withstand the Mariana depths. The stuff can almost float our 34,000-pound capsule all by itself. Otherwise, the Willa-Bee would be more of an anchor than a ship."

Trieste noticed something on the sonar, pointed to the instrument panel, and questioned the pilot. "What's that up ahead? I hope it's…"

"Looks like a smoker. Big one, too." Robest slowed the vessel's forward motion.

"Best news of the day!" said Sloan.

"Better than best!" responded Trieste, who likewise salivated at the thought of an active underwater chimney.

Soon, a venting black plume edged into the light. Beautiful and dangerous. Both scientists glued themselves to the front portals.

Trieste gasped, "Just look at that!"

"The hydrothermal particle-fluid emissions are around 700 degrees Fahrenheit," said Robest. "Close to the temperature of molten lead. This chimney is pretty big, so the outlet has been there a while." The discharge into the sea looked surprisingly like smoke drifting into air. "Chimneys can come and go," said Robest, "but based on size, I'd say this one is an old timer. It takes a long time for this much accumulation."

Trieste gazed in amazement as they drew closer. The craggy formations reminded her of a trip to Mono Lake in California. Towering rock pillars created underwater over hundreds or thousands of years from slowly accumulating particle emissions. Trieste whispered, "Science tells me that 700-degree water can't boil at this pressure, but to actually see a smoker routinely doing its business violates my common sense understanding of water and heat. Of course, seeing so many life forms in the sunless depths also violates common sense. My brain says, "No big deal. That's just how nature works." But my heart cries, "A beautifully predictable process that is unpredictably beautiful!""

"Yep. Incredible things evolve and thrive under these conditions," added Sloan while pressing his nose against the portal. He had a tangential thought and spoke out loud. "I'll give odds that we find life on Mars, too, or in the seas of Europa… Sure would like to take a sub there. I mean, if life can exist at these depths and temperatures, seems like the waters of Europa would be a cinch."

Lieutenant Robest laughed. "Well, if anybody can build a vessel capable of navigating under the ice of Europa, it'll probably be the U.S. Navy. I just hope they let me pilot the damn thing when they do."

"Sign me up for that expedition if it happens," said Trieste. She pointed at the portal closest to the Earth-sea smoker. "Like visiting the Grand Canyon for the first time. Takes your breath away."

Everyone went silent for a couple minutes and watched the central chimney and two side vents generated by thermal activity beneath the shifting Earth's crust.

"If possible," said Sloan, becoming a scientist once again, "I'd like a sediment sample near the main extrusion."

"How close can we get?" asked Trieste.

"Titanium can handle just about anything," said Robest, "but not necessarily the exterior instruments. I'll keep my eye on the water temp. Won't go closer than three meters. The robotic arm has a pretty good reach."

Four minutes later they started their ascent toward the surface.

"I think a new ground vent opened under the ship while we were scooping your sediment," Robest said. "Sorry to cut the trip short. We're not taking any chances." He sighed. "You're gonna lose a few hours of science time, but if it's any consolation, I'm gonna have to deal with a royal ass chewing upstairs."

"Not your fault," said Trieste, trying to sooth the pilot. "No one could have predicted that."

"What happened… exactly?" asked Sloan. "Seemed like a pretty tame bump-and-grind for the Willa-Bee."

"The vent shoved us up and sideways, and we knocked pretty hard against the large chimney. A chunk of rock must have hit one of the thrusters. Jammed. A bigger problem might be that we were pushed directly through the central vent, and the hydrothermal ejecta hit us square on. Damned hot." Robest studied the instrument panel. "Everything except one exterior light and a thruster seems operational. All other systems check out, too, but to be safe we're going topside immediately."

"It's just so beautiful down here," said Trieste. "Sure hate to lose that science time, as you put it."

"Me, too," said Sloan, "but there's no room for error in the trench. We've got enough samples and data to keep us busy for a while. I'm with the Lieutenant. Let's go home."

"Just doesn't seem fair that you'll be blamed for this," said Trieste to Robest. "Who could ever predict a breaching thermal vent? The odds are one in a million."

The Lieutenant anticipated his stand-up by the Navy brass. "Doesn't matter if it's anybody's fault or nobody's fault or if we got poked in the ass by Neptune's trident. The vessel is damaged, and the captain's gonna cut me to pieces."

Robest turned back to the gages and scowled. He did not like what he saw.

After twenty-five minutes, Robest tapped the console depth indicator. Looked at it, waited several seconds, and tapped again more forcefully.

"What's the matter?" asked Trieste, not quite as interested in the beauty of Challenger Deep as she had been a few minutes before.

Robest didn't answer. He applied more thruster power, glanced at the instrument panel, and waited. "Damn!" he said, and knuckled the depth indicator painfully hard.

Sloan and Trieste started to worry for the first time. They had assumed the Willa-Bee could handle a few bumps and bruises from the smoker, and Lieutenant Robest was an experienced Navy pilot who didn't rattle easily.

But he wasn't caressing those instruments. He clearly didn't like the readings.

"You gonna tell us what's going on?" asked Trieste, trying to sound composed.

"Not quite sure what's happened yet," said Robest. "In thirty minutes, we've ascended only 520 meters. Should be around 2500. Losing a thruster wouldn't affect us that much. Something else is off."

"Maybe they can figure it out upstairs from the data stream," said Sloan, "...and offer advice?"

Robest shook his head. "Communication's tricky at these depths under the best circumstances." He drummed another of the gages. "The new modems offer voice and digital capacity... But apparently..." He then spoke into the headset microphone. "Willa-Bee to Challenger Prime. Come in, please... Challenger Prime, come in."

Now Robest tapped his earphones as well. "This is the Willa-Bee. Come back." He shook his head. "We're not getting through. No static either. System is dead." He sighed. "A design flaw."

"What do you mean?" asked Sloan.

"To save passenger space, the transducer and other electronics are mounted and sealed outside the main sphere. That makes them more susceptible to damage. Of course, we're not supposed to have any damage, but there you are. Either the heat or jolt killed them. Probably the superheated water."

"What else?" asked Trieste. She sensed he was holding back.

"We can't talk with the surface crew," said Robest. "Maybe they're getting our data stream. Doubt it."

"So we're basically traveling blind toward the surface...?" said Sloan.

Robest shook his head while fumbling with thruster controls. "We're traveling blind toward the bottom."

Trieste gasped, "The bottom!" Then, a thought. "Oh! So we can make repairs, right?"

Sloan was frightened. "Like she says? You'll make repairs once we settle on the ocean floor!?"

"Doubt it," the lieutenant replied and pointed toward the starboard portal. "Take a look!"

A few drops of water oozed from the edge of the glass.

Sloan and Trieste checked to see if it might be condensation. Triste wiped the glass with the edge of her sleeve, but another drop formed and ran down the inside cabin wall, followed by another. Sloan rubbed the glass harder. Droplets formed again.

"Well," said Trieste. "It's just a teeny-tiny influx. We'll certainly reach the surface before…, I mean, at this rate, the leak would take days to fill a mop bucket."

"Compared with the Pacific Ocean, we're smaller than a mop bucket," said Robest. "And we don't have days. I'm spinning every thruster at full power and the ship is barely hovering. Can't sustain the energy drain, so I'm taking her back to the bottom to see what can be done…if anything."

The Willa-Bee lay on the bottom of Challenger Deep fifty meters from the black smoker that had damaged her. Her thrusters idled to conserve power.

"OK," said Lieutenant Robest. "I'm sure you realize the situation is bad. We're seven miles down, no longer buoyant, with four or five hours of power left. I've activated the distress beacon so they'll know upstairs we're in trouble."

"How long before rescue?" asked Trieste.

"I'm afraid we're on our own. There are four submersibles in existence that can reach this depth. We're in one of them, another is a single passenger ship, and the other two are currently operating in the Atlantic. None have rescue capabilities. The third generation Alvin isn't finished yet, but when it is, they should be able to retrieve the Willa-Bee…and what's left of us."

"What about unmanned drones?" asked Trieste. "I know Challenger Prime has deep-water ROVs."

"They'll find our ship…, eventually."

Trieste cried softly and croaked, "So there's no hope? We're going to die?"

"Almost certainly." Robest watched the gages for any sign of good news.

"Almost?" Sloan fantasized.

If the negative buoyancy is caused by debris lodged in our external framework, we might be able to shake it off." Robest paused. "You probably noticed that I tilted the ship a couple times on the way down, hoping to dump any rubble, but our descent continued steady. Without at least neutral buoyancy, the thrusters can't lift us back to the surface."

"OK," said Sloan. "See what you can find with the cameras. Trieste and I will take a look out each port."

After several minutes of scrutiny from every possible angle, they found no wreckage or rubble that held them down.

"Nothing outside," said Sloan. "But I did notice that the portal seepage is getting worse."

"I know," said Robest, "which is kind of surprising because the funnel seal design generally tightens as pressure increases. The smoker's heat must have deformed the glass or the O-rings when we passed through the ejecta."

Trieste stopped crying. "Probably would have been better if the window melted. We would have died instantly, without knowing…what was coming."

"I'm gonna try one more thing," said the Lieutenant. "Strap yourselves in. I'll apply full thrusters, take the ship up 10 meters, and roll her a couple times. If anything's in the framing we can't see, maybe it'll come loose."

"Yes!" said Trieste, as if she'd received a commuted death sentence.

An alarm sounded. Robest glanced at the console, shook his head, and turned off the signal. "The acid batteries failed, likely from water intrusion, which would explain our collapsing buoyancy."

Robest applied full power to the thrusters. The ship did not lift. "Sorry folks. I can't get us off the bottom to roll the vessel. It was a longshot maneuver anyway."

"Well," said Sloan, "if battery fumes get in the cabin, Trieste may get her wish for a quicker death." He glanced at her and changed his tone. "My bad. I didn't mean to sound cruel."

"The bats are also in an external compartment," said Robest. "And sulfuric acid's not gonna burn through three inches of Titanium."

"Is there any way we can separate the lead-battery pack from the cabin?"

asked Sloan. "That's a lot of weight."

"I know," said Robest. "It was meant as a backup if the lithium array under-performed. Now, the extra deadweight will probably kill us."

"A good lesson for the future," said Trieste.

"A harsh lesson for the present," said Sloan.

Thirty minutes later, Trieste pointed at the seeping portal. "We've taken on at least two or three gallons. The water's now a small stream."

"Definitely getting worse," said Robest. "But it's still slow enough that we won't drown. The outside water temperature is below freezing. Once the batteries die, we're gonna turn very cold very fast."

"That's assuming the influx is steady," said Trieste. "I don't think it is."

"With outside pressure over seven tons per square inch, increased flow is... likely," admitted Robest.

Ten minutes later, the damaged port streamed like a half-open faucet, and the seawater felt like liquid ice. Battery power could not provide adequate heat.

"We don't have protective clothing," said Robest. "At these temperatures, when the water reaches knee level, we'll go hypothermic."

"Not to mention, air pressure's climbing. How much cabin volume do we have?" Sloan asked.

Robest sighed. "Cabin pressure is the least of our worries, but we have around 200 cubic feet..., about 1500 gallon capacity. I think."

"Sounds pretty close," said Trieste.

The faucet ran wide open. The noise level increased as fast as the temperature dropped.

"Looks like gallons per minute," shouted Robest. "But we'll probably freeze before compression becomes a problem."

Trieste didn't like the idea of freezing. "Maybe we should try to break a portal. The incoming spray would slice us up like bullets. Game over. Quick."

"The ship's glass is rated near ten tons per square inch. I doubt a hammer and chisel could crack 'em before we're dead anyway," said Robest. "And if it's all the same to you, we might stay above the water for another hour or so. Crouch on the seats! As long as we're breathing, there's hope for a solution."

Sloan knew Robest lied about hope, and Sloan, like Trieste, preferred to die fast if there were a choice. "What about burning something," he said. "If we eliminate the oxygen and breathe only nitrogen, we'll go unconscious in a minute or two. Better than waiting for subzero chills."

"How could anybody strike a match in this mess—even if we had a match?" Robest asked. "I suggest we just all pee in the water to warm things up."

Sloan laughed. "I'd probably piss ice cubes at this point."

"The flow is increasing," said Trieste. The other two noticed that her face and hands were turning blue. "How can so much water come through such a tiny hole? It's starting to spay and mist...."

The cabin lights created a perfect miniature rainbow around the portal. "Look how the mist is refracting the light!" said Trieste, seeming calm. "Very pretty."

"We'll go with the flow," said Robest. He sat in his pilot's chair with his feet on the console.

Sloan laughed. "Hey, that rhymes!"

Robest grimaced. "Purely accidental," he said, "because I seriously hate poetry."

"Awww," said Sloan, "I thought you was one of those sensitive guys who likes musicals and iambic pentameter!"

"Such mythic males only exist in literature," said Trieste. Her teeth began to chatter. "My feet are numb!"

Robest shook his head. "We're filling up fast. Cabin pressure is over two atmospheres…," he sighed, "and climbing. No myth about that. Best not to stand directly in front of the port. Just in case."

"In case of what?" asked Sloan.

"In case the spray turns into a firehose."

They both laughed.

"That's not funny," said Trieste. "Not at all."

They all looked at each other, and after a few seconds, Trieste laughed, too.

"Of course it's not funny," said Sloan. "It's hysterical!"

Trieste began to sing. "If you're cold and you know it clap your hands!"

Everyone clapped.

Sloan chimed in. "If you're fucked and you know it clap your hands!"

They all clapped again.

Robest began a new tune. "Yo ho ho and a bottle of rum—damn sure wish we had some."

Sloan added a verse. "Yum, yum, yum, a bottle of rum! Hey, if we get out of this alive, we can take this show on the road. Maybe America's Got Talent."

"Oh my god!" Trieste said to Sloan. "You're laughing so hard there's blood in your tears."

"Sure ain't sweat in this bottom-hugging frost-mobile!"

"You know what our problem is?" said Robest, struggling not to giggle.

"Yeh," said Sloan. "We're dying without rum…and I'd much rather die without bourbon!"

"No, no!" Robest chuckled. "Our problem is we got ruptures of the deep!"

They all shouted with delight and started singing again. "Yo ho ho and a bottle of rum!"

Trieste howled and shivered. "I haven't had this much fun since my frosh sorority party. I remember drinking something from a funnel with a tube attached to it. I never did find my bra and panties."

Soon, no one could contain their laughter. Trieste was the first to lose consciousness and sink into the water.

"Hey," Sloan said to Robest, thumbing in Trieste's direction. "Do you think she might drown?"

Robest snickered. "Naw! She's pulling our chain. Let's see how long that girl can hold her breath!"

They bellowed as Trieste lay motionless at the bottom of the cabin.

"Now that's what I call the silent treatment!" said Sloan. "Or a pretty good imitation of a flounder."

Robest and Sloan laughed, their crimson tears streaming into the rising water. The noise level grew quieter as the leaking port slipped below the water line.

The ship went dark in the pitch black Mariana Trench. And thanks to the quasi-inert properties of nitrogen gas under pressure mixed with a shot of oxygen and a jigger of CO_2, the last moments of these individuals were among the best moments of their lives.

Robest, soon the only conscious crewmember, thought he saw a light in the distance. He peered from the high portal of the disabled Willa-Bee. There! A ship coming to rescue them.

He suddenly imagined a warm bed, dry blankets, hot food, and a double shot of whiskey. And because of the intense cold, the medics should be able to revive Trieste and Sloan.

"Nobody's dead until they're warm and dead," thought Robest. He'd heard that somewhere.

The light grew brighter. Must be the largest underwater rescue vehicle on the planet. Probably top secret. But they'd better hurry! The pressure inside the Willa-Bee was squeezing Robest and his companions with the grip of an indifferent ocean god.

The Black Hole: A Tale for Men and Women Who Aren't Trying to Kill Feminism

I heard a curious story last week at the local Citizens Club. It concerns Dr. Jennifer Grant; and according to the man who told the story, as recounted below, the situation is heartbreaking. But I have a different interpretation of Jenn's predicament.

Last Tuesday (said the man at the club) was my day off, and I went to the New York Public Library. At one of the tables, I noticed a girl weeping silently. She looked to be in her mid-20s. I hesitated but asked, "What's the problem? Books getting you down?"

She didn't seem to notice me.

I stepped closer. "Should we locate your supervisor?"

She laughed. Not a pleasant, feminine laugh, but a sickly exhale. Then she looked up and said, "I'm not sure you're real."

The situation required prompt right action. "Wait here," I ordered and walked to the security desk, reporting details to the officer, who glanced toward the lady and said, "I'll notify G.S."

"Tell them to be gentle," I offered. "Somebody isn't doing a proper job with her."

"Is the husband in the library?"

I shrugged.

"OK," said the guard, "Probably be an hour. Inquire where she lives and who's responsible."

There were several errands on my schedule, so I tried to beg off. "Perhaps you could just handle this yourself...."

"Sorry, Sir," said the guard firmly. "As Citizen of First Contact, you are required to monitor any distressed and unsupervised female until district authority assumes control."

Damn. Straight from the Code.

But the guard understood my concern and offered reassurance. "You won't be detained long, Sir. A minor inconvenience for the greater good."

He was right. I felt ashamed and returned to the table. "Help is on the way, dear."

"I doubt it," she said.

I began cautiously with the prescribed questions. "Where is your husband?"

"Don't have one."

Oh my God! At her age? I was shocked, and before I could recompose myself, she added, "Don't need one."

I paused briefly, took a deep breath, and asked, "Where do you live?"

She hesitated. "In 2020. Gone, I think. Now I'm stuck in the '50s."

I knew my job was to listen, but I asked, "What's wrong with the '50s?"

"Nothing, I suppose, if you don't know better. I should consider that."

"Listen, our doctors are gender specialists...."

She glared. "Two days ago, I was a doctor. But now.... It's your fault!"

Hostility is an indicator, and I wanted to cool her down before the Para-Medics arrived. They could sometimes be overly enthusiastic with hysterical patients, yet I felt strangely relieved. Such emotional flare-ups were well understood by first responders and effective treatments were readily available.

"What kind of doctor were you, child?"

"A Ph.D., honey."

That bitterness again.

"I was a Professor of Sociology and Women's Studies."

Not wanting to distress the lady further, I tried to reassure her, "Sociology is quite, uh, interesting," and then got back to my questions. "I'm sorry you're not married. How many children do you have?"

"None."

Damn! While no man can fully appreciate the emotional torments of a childless female, I cringed with empathy at her obvious emptiness. I continued my questions, focusing on what appeared to be a comforting fantasy. "So, what was that about 2020?"

"It's ironic," she said, "but after only one day, I miss it. The beginning of the Twenty-First Century was a blighted, congested, hydrocarbonated, globally depressed mishmash of escalating calamities. Yet with apologies to Dickens, the worst of times have become the best of times, and I want to go home."

"To 2020?"

"Yes."

"Time travel?"

"What else could explain this nightmare?"

I desired to be firm, but my civic duty was clear: Supervise until relieved. With painstaking courtesy, I said, "Tell me more."

"I have an amateur interest in cosmology."

"Oh, cosmetology! Now you're making sense."

"Astronomy, you idiot!"

I would have been within rights to slap her, probably should have, but I endured and slid into a seat directly across the table from her.

She continued. "Black holes can theoretically disturb time and space. That must be what happened."

"Now, really! You're saying you were engulfed by a black hole?" Classic female nervosa. And her anger was overpowering her civic decorum.

"Of course not! I'd be dead if that happened."

"And you're not dead, are you, dear?"

She glared at me, again, and said, "Might as well be. Trapped in the fatherland of a testosterone pandemic."

"Trapped?"

She appeared to be thinking. "You could be right. The '50s..., then the '60s and the women's movement." She sighed. "But I've already been to the mountain top."

"I must tell you, young lady, I don't like such talk."

"That's what I keep hearing. I open my mouth, and someone tries to push the words back down my throat. Can't a woman speak here?"

"Here? Where do you think you are?"

She gestured around the room like a bad-seed child. "The Ladies Section of the New York Public Library!"

"At least you're clear about that."

"In my day, the women's section related to gender and feminist issues."

"You mean back in 2020?"

"Yes."

"And why would you object to a special ladies room?"

She seemed confused, and then said, "Unless my brains were scrambled, I wasn't aware that segregated libraries existed in the 1950s—I mean, segregated by sex."

This provided an opening and I said, "Some books are potentially dangerous. I'm sure you'd agree that girls might be misled by contraception propaganda." I should never have uttered the c-word in her presence, but I was agitated beyond good sense.

She practically screamed. "Is it possible for you to say woman?"

"I would not deliberately insult you, Madam. Please don't insult me!" I counted three seconds. "Now..., just what is your problem?"

"Oh," she suddenly seemed calmer, "somehow I traveled from 2020 and landed here."

I asked, "And a black hole did this?"

"Either that or the ghost of Phyllis Schlafly is having a cosmic belly laugh. I walked the streets several hours trying to figure out what happened and then came here to investigate time travel. But university books are restricted to men." She let out a sickly breath again.

"Look at what the brain-dead librarian recommended as a science text?" She held up the glossy print edition of *Feminine Physics: Illustrated Guide to the Domestic Arts*. "My world has Title IX...," she slammed *Feminine Physics* on the table. "This may be the only book in history that should be banned!"

Several ladies at nearby tables moved away. I tried to refocus her attention by asking, "A black hole?"

"My knowledge is inadequate," she began.

A good sign that she at least accepted some of her natural limitations.

"The thing must have been very small," she said. "Infinite density distorting space-time."

She had clearly accessed privileged materials.

"I was walking at Cornell...," her eyes watered, "strolling along, wondering how to engage my freshmen with a spark of feminist consciousness." She laughed. "Students sometimes offer another type of infinite density."

I held up my hand. "Teaching feminism is against the law!"

"Not where I come from, Bub! We even discuss evolution...."

Where the devil were the Medics? I wondered.

"Anyway," she continued, "I was lost in thought and suddenly the world turned upside down and inside out. Seemed like the buildings were in a fish tank; the sky flashed red; it's possible I fainted. Then Cornell somehow transformed into Manhattan...a different space and time...with a strange skyline and stranger clothes."

"And what's wrong with basic attire?"

"These 50s women. That's what's wrong. Hobbling down city streets in tight dresses and spiked heels! Clicking, clicking, clicking. Some appeared to be corseted, too, a sickening blend of masochism and misogyny."

She seemed now on the edge of a complete breakdown.

"Then a little punk cop chides me for my denim jeans. And when I didn't have my 'identification' with me, the piglet threatened to write me up for a dress-code violation or some such nonsense. I was about to hurl some tasty rhetoric when the bastard received a call on his headset. That's something else. I didn't know portable radios existed in the '50s."

I focused on the one significant element. "There's no shame in fainting, child, which is a common female affliction. Probably bumped your head. And, yes, your public attire is scandalous—I would never allow my wife such public informality. It's unfortunate the officer had to leave, or you'd already be receiving treatment."

"First, I didn't bump my head. Second, I don't give a rat's ass about whatever your wife allows you to permit her to do."

It was increasingly difficult to remain supportive, but I reassured her, trying to do the right thing. "After temperature controlled aquatic therapy and 36 hours of induced sleep, you'll feel much better."

"I am better. I've tried to consider that I'm not, but you're here." She pointed across the room. "The dimwitted librarian is here." She thumbed toward the window. "And that prick cop is out there.... The black hole must have passed through the earth at incredible speed, and I was just close enough to be dragged down the rabbit hole."

I was becoming increasingly uncomfortable. Where were the authorities!?

"Look," she said, more calmly, "it's been a hard day, but I'll just find a job, survive into the '60s, and help the civil rights movement along.... And I know which stocks to buy. Yeh! With cash, even a handmaiden can buy her freedom."

I could not pretend further. "Listen to me! Ladies and gentlemen are different. Do you really think your problems involve time travel?"

"It's the only explanation." She hesitated and then gained strength. "Which means, there could be others! Some probably died inside the horizon. Some probably landed elsewhere. But I might not be alone in this madhouse!"

"There are nine billion men. Why should a pretty girl ever be alone?"

She paused and then said, "Hey! Go grab me some books on astrophysics! Wait, have you even discovered black holes in this time? Never mind. Just pull whatever's on the shelf."

"That would only make matters worse," I retorted, trying to redirect her properly. "Besides, adult information is accessed through the terminals."

She assumed a mannish authority that literally turned my stomach.

"Look," she said. "You don't know what's happened, but I do. Play ball and you'll be rich beyond imagination. We can change the world."

There was, momentarily, a charming sparkle in her eye, but I'd had enough. "My dear child," I said with genuine sympathy, "your world will change with proper medical care."

She finally seemed to calm herself. "You're right. I must deal with reality. The sixties could be a blast. Maybe I'll tune in, turn on, and pack a raincoat for Woodstock. One thing is certain. I'm going to earn a lot more here than I ever did as a sociology professor." She glanced up and smiled. "And when a nerdy kid drops out of Harvard to build a company called Microsoft, do your best to go to work for him. Or buy as much of his stock as possible."

I was about to demand that security intervene when health officials finally arrived. The guard and two Para-Medics approached.

"It's all right now," I assured her.

The young lady seemed to suspect something, now, and as the men approached, one of the P-Ms said, "Hello, Young Lady. We hear you're distressed."

"What?!" she stammered. Then she quickly added, "No, I'm fine. Just need to figure things out."

I interrupted and spoke to the medics. "Good afternoon, Citizens. She's a little confused. Doesn't seem to know that Apple bought Microsoft decades ago."

Miss Grant hesitated, and finally said, "I'm good, really. Think I'll walk to Central Park."

"A doctor should examine you," said the Medic in charge, a huge man who could undoubtedly wrestle a rhino into a straitjacket. His brusque manner suggested frontline Reconstruction experience.

"That won't be necessary," said the lady a bit more pleadingly.

The security officer ostensibly spoke to me but was clearly testing the girl. "Citizen, are you sure this lady requires assistance? She seems appropriately mannered, and the Agency doesn't appreciate false alarms."

I nodded. "She has apparently traveled through time."

The P-M turned toward her. "By the way, what's your name?"

"Jennifer Grant."

"What day it is?"

She looked puzzled, hesitated, and answered, "It was Thursday."

The Medic nodded. "A doctor will examine you."

"That's not required," she said.

"I'm afraid it is."

I interjected, "And weren't you a professor before the time warp?"

"Quit changing my words! I didn't say time warp."

The security officer interrupted. "The skycams will confirm any statements, but a Citizen does not require corroboration regarding any unescorted female. His word, itself, may empower a mandatory evaluation."

"I was only teasing," said Miss Grant, obviously trying to deflect our concern.

I felt relieved that she could play nice when properly motivated.

"They're here to help," I said. "I mean, really, you're not even married…."

As I expected, she became angry because of this obvious insult to her femininity.

"I'm self-sufficient! In my world, being single was fine. In this elliptical Fun Zone, it's some kind of offense." She took a deep breath and straightened her shoulders. "The '60s will save us!" She stood to leave.

"What about the '60s?" asked the Supervisor.

"Oh, the women's movement, Martin Luther King, Jr., and a little place called Vietnam. The times are a-changing, boys, and with any luck, you'll all be drafted." She raised her voice to the room. "And don't fret, Ladies. This time we shall ratify the Equal Rights Amendment."

One of the women sitting at a table gasped.

The attendant medic asked, "Are you referring to the 1960s?"

"They come after the '50s," said Grant.

The Medics glanced at each other. One asked, "What year is it, Miss Grant?"

"Best guess, 1955."

That was the clincher for the Supervisor. "We're taking you to the hospital," he said, the medics each grabbed one of Grant's arms. The security guard pressed a Palmetic against her hand.

"Stop!!" screamed Grant.

"What the hell?" said the guard, shaking his device and re-scanning.

"What's wrong?" asked the Supervisor.

"The damned thing says she's Jennifer Grant."

"I already told you my name, asshole!" Grant tried to break free.

The guard continued. "Age 76. Disappeared in 2020. No trace."

"The Palmers don't lie," said the Medic, "but she's not 76!" He waved a bio-sounder up and down her torso. "Cell analysis says she's 29. Maybe a black-market clone…?"

"Where could they get the real Grant's DNA?"

The guard searched the Palmetic data. "Detectives registered a hair sample in 2020," said the guard. "But this can't be legitimate. Somebody's scamming us!"

The Para-Medic Supervisor took charge. "Our equipment says this is Jennifer Grant, age 76, presumed dead. We take her to a doctor and let the Agency figures out who's who. And I remind you, officer, that all Para-Nationals are guaranteed proper medical care under the law."

Grant tried to break free. "Take your hands off me or I'll sue you into a coma!" She kicked the guard. One woman in the library fainted; another ran to the nearest man for comfort.

"Enough," said the Medic. "G.S. will sign on as temporary guardian."

"I hate ending my shift with a screwy logbook," said the guard, trying to compose himself. "And something here is beyond screwy!"

"The Agency will investigate, but late-model scanners have never been wrong."

I hesitated and asked, "What do you think happened to the real Jennifer Grant?"

"Pre-Reconstruction records are dicey," said the Supervisor. "But if Grant's alive, investigators will find her. I'm guessing this girl must be black market."

I let out a whistle. "Somebody risked the death penalty?"

"They were pros, too. Bios confirm she's healthy and fertile."

Grant fought, but the men held firm. The Supervisor gestured to the guard. "Steady her!"

They shifted positions. The Medic removed a neurofibrilator, pressed the stabilizer disk against Grant's forehead, and hit the activator. "This will relax you, Miss Grant."

"I demand a lawyer," she said, with declining verve.

"You'll be appointed counsel at the custody hearing."

"The '60s will save us...."

"Listen," said the Supervisor. "This is 2066, not 1955."

"We'll ratify the Equal Rights Amendment...."

"Think back, Miss Grant," I said, gently. "Women relinquished the vote in 2047. Remember? Male birthing preferences shifted the social demographics and required men and women to reclaim their natural roles."

Grant struggled weakly as the electronic sedation continued to gentle her.

"It's pointless to resist," said the Medic.

The attendants laid Miss Grant onto the carpeted floor, where she soon lost voluntary muscle function. Within minutes, Grant was strapped to a gurney and guided toward the elevator. The neurofibrilators induce a state of feminine semi-consciousness and help to reduce anxiety.

The guard looked at me. "Thanks for your help, Citizen. You probably saved this girl's life, and, in the end, this may help solve an old missing-person case."

"Just doing my civic duty," I said.

The Supervisor asked, "Want to ride the elevator with us? It might comfort her."

"Sure."

I looked at Grant. "How are you doing, child?"

"It's very warm," she said.

"Relax," said the Medic, too harshly, "the gurney is self-regulating. Neural activity and body temperature will be maintained at prescribed therapeutic levels."

I took her hand as we rolled toward the transport. "Do you see the ambulance? It's from GENDER SERVICES. I once visited my sister there, and she received the finest care."

Grant struggled to focus. "Your sister?"

"As a teenager," I said, "she had trouble...being female. Not uncommon during the Reconstruction era." This was a painful topic, but it might help Miss Grant. "But G.S. handled everything."

Tears streamed down Grant's cheeks. "Please don't kill me!"

I confess that I almost wept, myself, but offered her assurance. "You will be happy, my child. That's our social guarantee to all females."

"Women would never voluntarily surrender the vote," she said, barely able to articulate. "We worked too hard for it. This…is…all…a bad dream."

"No, my dear," I said. "The world has reclaimed its gender identity, and you'll receive all the medical care necessary to make you understand…and agree. That's our collective promise." She was drifting into sleep, but I continued. "You are very beautiful. You are very beautiful."

The Medics cinched the straps, loaded Miss Grant into the transport, and took her toward what would be a new and structured life. Soon, I felt better about my Citizenship responsibilities. The right thing is often the best thing.

That's the story as it was told to me by the man at the Citizen's Club. I listened with great interest, and I've decided to help Jennifer Grant because such a defiant woman might be confined for years. You see, we both worked at Cornell in 2020, though we weren't exactly friends. She once accused me of sexual harassment, which is nasty business in higher education and almost cost me tenure, though I was merely trying to encourage a junior colleague to use all of her assets.

Then one day, as I was following her across campus, the landscape turned upside down and inside out. I woke up on Long Island in the year 2058, apparently arriving eight years before Jennifer and managing to transition easily into a new era. But then, as a man, I could read any book, and I skimmed 12 months of newspapers before deciding on a course of action. Also, my role as a Citizen carries much more flexibility than Jenn's as a Para-National.

But mostly, I am smart and better at keeping my mouth shut. With a quick refresher in computer tech, I passed myself off as a competent programmer—the sciences change more slowly than women's position in society—and my bureaucratic knowledge enabled me to obtain legal identification and employment without passing through a mental institution en route. Sure, I had to bully a few clericals in the process, but women need a firm hand now and then—and I'm just the man to give it to them.

I'll admit, too, that it's better to be on the favored side of indoctrination than the other way around, and I've carved out a damned good life in 2066. Yet ironically, even with all the advantages, I am lonely. The girls of this generation are too dull and vulnerable. Where's the sport in that? I want Doctor Grant, a woman of my own generation. We can talk about old times. After a couple months of medical therapy, I'm guessing that Miss Sexual Harassment will be ready to move out of Gender Services and into the new world, even if it's not what she's used to.

Besides, Grant could do worse. I have professional standing and economic resources. I might hire her as my secretary or apply for a supervisory guardianship until she marries and receives her reproduction quota. I'll figure it out.

There's a saying at the local Citizens Club, "Men help women who help themselves." So, if Professor Jennifer Grant is nice, if she learns the art of sugar and spice, I might be persuaded to undertake the burden of her care and social instruction. After all, it's my civic duty.

YES, DEAR, BREAST CANCER CAN KILL A TRANS WOMAN

It was almost two years ago that Alexandria called me with the news. A routine mammogram had turned up a suspicious area on her right breast, and further screening would be necessary. As you might expect, Alex was concerned, and her voice quavered slightly when she said, "The doctor told me not to worry because nine out of ten times these things turn out to be a benign cyst, but they want to do a diagnostic mammo…with an ultrasound if needed. I'm going on Friday for the follow-up."

I told her I'd take off to accompany her, but she responded, "Don't worry about it. I'm happy to go alone, and there's no need for both of us to miss work. Besides, the doc said it's probably nothing, so let's assume that's true."

Alexandria is a male-to-female transsexual, and in childhood she was brought up to be tough, to hide emotions, to pretend that a broken bone or concussion was simply an inconvenience to be dealt with after finishing your day's business. Her dad is still a military officer and advocate for a creed that few people can live by—nor should they in my opinion. But when growing up, Alexandria (Alexander until she was 22) tried to be as macho as her father. She didn't succeed, obviously, and became herself soon after graduation from college.

Thank God, too, because for me, Alex is the stuff dreams are made off.

Before we met, I had dated many women, but I loved Alex from the first time we met in law school. She was smart, witty, and beautiful with a stout Lauren Bacall-ish voice. She dropped out of legal studies during our second semester and switched to a graduate program in English, finally becoming a professor at Rhode Island College. Law would never have suited her, but she had still been trying to make her dad proud and thought being a lawyer might do it. She's much happier as a teacher than she would ever have been as a legal practitioner, and frankly, I doubt anything could make her military father proud of his trans daughter. He doesn't care much for me either.

So when Alex told me that she'd go alone for the follow-up medicals, I put my foot down. "Forget it, Babe. I'm coming. That's what husbands do—even ambulance chasers like me." She smiled at my playful self-deprecation, but I sensed that Alex was relieved I would be there even though she tried not to show it.

We went to South County Hospital that Friday. They did the extra mammogram and then whisked us to the ultrasound room; the doctor scanned and then hemmed and hawed for several minutes and said, "I don't like the look of this. We're going to need a biopsy." He pressed the scanner against the suspect area for a few more long seconds, set the wand back on the sounder, and offered again, "I just don't like the looks of this. Try to be prepared for bad news." Then he added with faint optimism, "Of course, nine times out of ten the biopsies are negative, so let's hope for the best."

Alexandria, who is Caucasian, turned whiter than the pallid bust of Pallas. Me, I'm Latino, but I'm pretty sure I paled up myself. This was not the news we wanted to hear.

Biopsy day. I was there, of course, but had to leave for the waiting room as soon as I saw the needle sink into her bared and beautiful right breast. Let's face it. Alex is tougher than I will ever be, often strong willed to the point of annoyance. She's been through a lot, including a sex-change surgery that would have killed a man. I wasn't there for that procedure, though I read a book called *Journal of a Sex Change* to try to grasp what was involved.

I accept that such treatment is needed though I don't really understand the why. For example, Alex never says that she "became a woman" after surgery. She insists she was born a woman but needed help with the female part. From what I know of her, and I know a lot, Alex is a deep-girl fem despite her toughness. She's petite, looks naturally beautiful to everyone, and I never suspected she was trans when I first met her. In fact, I thought she was joking when she spilled the beans on our second date, but then she showed me her "Alexander" birth certificate and high school graduation photo. It was Alex, all right, yet at the same time, it was not.

After I quit stuttering I croaked, "Why haven't you changed that birth certificate, Alexandria?"

She replied, "Cause I was born in Tennessee."

Apparently that was explanation enough. I later checked and found that Tennessee had passed a special law specifically prohibiting transsexuals from changing their birth certificates. A couple of weeks later, when I decided that Alexandria was one hundred percent Alexandria and that her sex change didn't make one iota of difference to me, I wanted to sue Tennessee in federal court to get her birth record amended as it is routinely done in the majority of other states, but Alex put her foot down. "Tennessee bureaucrats," she said flatly, "are irrelevant in the scheme of my life, and I will not debate my femininity in their courts." Six months later, I asked her to marry me.

Anyway, she had her biopsy and came to get me in the hospital waiting room. She bragged, "I was positioned so that I could see the whole procedure on the video screen," she said. "It's amazing to watch a needle pass into flesh and poke around." She raised her left eyebrow and added in an excellent Spock imitation, "Interesting."

Told you she was tough. At her description, I again almost fainted.

The hospital called Alex four days later. The representative asked her, "Do you want the biopsy results by phone, now, or would you and your husband prefer to come to the office?"

"No need to wait," she said. "Shoot."

They did. Alex had "infiltrating lobular carcinoma." Breast cancer.

She immediately called me, reported the news, and then let go with sobs over the phone. It's rare that she cries, so I canceled my afternoon appointments (one drunk-driving case and another for juvenile shoplifting) and went home. I held Alex late into the night.

An MRI would be required to assess the tumor grade and size so that doctors could recommend treatments. At minimum, a lumpectomy would be needed. Alexandria refused to consider anything beyond that, and I knew that the situation was bad. Alexandria's breasts were part of her identity. This is true for most women, of course, but exceptionally true for Alex. She was fortunate that hormone therapy had resulted in a curvy B+ cup size, and she had never needed or wanted implants. Alex was proud that she grew breasts herself, and my wife would have a devil of a time allowing a surgeon to cut into that part of her body, which had nothing to do with physical pain. After all, few surgeries are as excruciating as constructing a vagina from a penis. But for Alex, a mastectomy or lumpectomy would offer layers of psychological discomfort—somehow peeling away her femininity.

Another big issue. Doctors told Alexandria to stop taking estrogen immediately. Her cancer was an estrogen receptor, which is generally a good sign as far as treatability, and they wanted to cut off the disease's stimulus. Then the oncologist added one more thing: "I'm also prescribing Arimidex, an estrogen blocker."

At that, my wife bolted. "No!" she said. Not a small "no," but an in-your-face-die-and-go-to-hell "no." She added, "Estrogen is the elixir of life. For me, it is life. I will never take your blocker poison."

Neither I nor the doctors could persuade her otherwise.

A week later we met with the cancer-wing surgeon to discuss recommended treatment. The doctor said, "The MRI shows a second, smaller tumor below the first, and both have irregular borders with small tendrils reaching into the breast tissue. But the good news is there's no evidence of cancer in the left breast or that it has spread beyond the tumor site."

Alexandria had started to cry silently. I doubt she was aware of it. I didn't even know until I saw the doctor hand her a tissue.

The doctor continued, "We'll check the lymph nodes when we excise the tumor, but this is a highly treatable cancer. It was caught early. It is localized. Your prognosis is excellent."

Alex did not respond immediately but finally asked the fatal question. "What about the surgery. How much?"

The doctor answered, "Oh, don't worry about that. Your insurance will cover the costs."

"No," said my wife, "How much surgery?"

The surgeon, a compassionate woman who had dealt with this issue many times, said, "Because of the double-tumor configuration and the irregular borders, everyone agrees you should have a right-side mastectomy."

"Why can't you do a small lumpectomy?" asked Alex.

"Believe me," said the doctor, "if I tried to do a lumpectomy, it would look worse than a mastectomy with breast reconstruction. And don't worry," she added. "We can do the reconstruction while you're still under the general anesthesia."

Alexandria shook her head, and I interjected before anyone else could speak again. "We'd like a second opinion because my wife is reluctant to have a mastectomy." Alex and I had looked at photos of breast reconstruction three nights before; she was disappointed in the apparent cosmetic results, but also told me, "Even if they looked normal, I would never sacrifice my real body for an unfeeling surgical lump."

"I understand your reluctance," said the doctor to both of us, "and I suspected as much when Alex refused the estrogen blocker. Out of concern for Alex, I checked with two other board-certified practitioners. They arrived at the same conclusion. Mastectomy is the prescribed treatment."

The doctor paused and then added with compassionate professionalism, "Breast cancer is rare in trans women, though when it happens, psychological barriers to treatment, especially mastectomies, seem more intense. But please, Alexandria, we are working to save your life. You're a young, intelligent woman. Cancer can kill you. Allow us to kill it, instead."

"No," she said with an alarming certainty.

"Thank you, doctor," I interjected. "Alex will need time to think about this. It's a lot to take in all at once."

"I understand," she said, "and, of course, I must respect your decision. But keep in mind that the cancer is growing and will not stop unless we stop it. We should act as soon as possible to enhance survivability."

"I am acting," said Alexandria, standing to leave. "I am acting to save my soul." For Alex, having genital surgery and not having a mastectomy served the same purpose.

When we got home from the surgeon's office, Alexandria immediately called the hospital's cancer-unit coordinator and put their conversation on speaker so I could hear. "Hi, Janet, this is Alexandria Cerrillo," she said. "I've evaluated all of the information from the oncologist and surgeon, et al. You may inform everyone that there will be no mastectomy on this body. There will be no estrogen blockers. If they can figure out a treatment plan that doesn't involve that kind of mutilation, I'll listen and reconsider. Otherwise, I'll ask for pain meds when I need them—and I assume I will need them down the road—but this girl will not sacrifice her femaleness."

Janet didn't sound surprised or even particularly alarmed, and I supposed she often heard initial protests from cancer patients. I mean, what woman would want a mastectomy?

"Mrs. Cerrillo," said Janet with a gentle deference, "I know how you feel. Two years ago, I was faced with a similar diagnosis, except that my cancer was stage three in both breasts. After two days of prize-winning self-pity, along with a continuous flood of tears that made my eyes sting, I authorized removal of my breasts and three months of chemo. The reconstruction wasn't perfect, but I chose to live, and I'm hoping you will, too. You just talked with the doctor. Give yourself a few days to grieve. All of us here want you to live a long life."

Alexandria did not raise her voice. "I am not you. I suffered for several lifetimes during my childhood—just as you would have if your parents had tried to make a man out of you. And I know many things about doctors, too. One lovable family physician told me to 'do the world a favor and commit suicide' when I first came out as trans. You're almost asking me to do the same thing. That aside, I believe your doctors are caring and sincere. But they don't know what being a visible woman means to someone like me, someone so badly deformed at birth that people thought she was a boy. Well, Janet, I corrected that impression. Don't expect me to un-correct it."

"Alexandria, please, you're right that I don't fully understand your feelings, but I do know that the price I paid to live was worth every cut and stitch, every vomiting marathon after chemo, every burn from the radiation gun. It's incredibly important to be alive, and I'm sure you'll feel much the same way down the road.... And by the way, if any doctor had ever told a patient to kill herself in my presence, that doctor would immediately find my foot in his crotch."

Alex smiled for the first time that day. "Thanks, Janet. I believe you, and I love you for what you've shared about yourself. But it won't affect my decision."

I quite suddenly felt irrelevant in this discussion.

"Listen, hon," continued Janet, "I'm going to call you after you've had time to let everything sink in; and beware of the internet information because a lot of it is just plain bad. But it's wrong to sacrifice your life because of some socially constructed notion of what a woman ought to be. This disease will kill you. Let us help!"

Alexandria lost her short-lived smile. "You're sweet, Janet, and I can't speak for anyone else who might refuse this surgery, but there are things worse than death. That's why transsexuals undergo the physical and social tortures of sex reassignment."

Janet, who initially struck me almost as tough as Alex, began to choke with emotion. Now, the roles reversed, and my wife tried to comfort the treatment coordinator.

"I'm sorry, Janet," said Alex. "Life has made me a little too blunt at times. Please do call me in a couple days. Maybe I'll have changed my mind."

It doesn't happen often, but I can always tell when Mrs. Alexandria Cerrillo is lying.

It was a week later that I walked into the bedroom to find my wife crying into her pillow. I had never seen this kind of demonstrative sorrow in all the time I had known Alex; in fact, I would have sooner expected to find a Navy SEAL bawling because the water's too cold as to find my wife crying alone in the bedroom.

I quietly approached and sat on the bed to comfort her.

She looked up and said, "Oh, honey, I don't want to die!"

"You're not going to," I replied, stroking her hair. "Cancer treatments are better than ever, and your prognosis is excellent. We're going to have a long, long life together."

"That's what I thought when I married you. And I was so happy. I mean, because I'm trans, I never expected to find a husband. Most men treated me like garbage once I told them. But then you came along…and even after you knew…you asked to marry me."

"And I got lucky that you said yes." This sent her into cat wails again, and she re-buried her face into the pillow. "I'm still lucky," I said.

Finally, when she stopped crying long enough to lift her head and take a clean breath, she added, "But you don't understand—you're too innocent, too loving. There are very few MTFs that have solid marriages. Social pressures are against us. Sometimes families even break up an otherwise happy union when they find out the wife is trans. Against the odds, I not only found a wonderful and loving husband, but found you….A man who could have picked from among the most beautiful natural females, a normal woman who could have given you children, who...."

I quit stroking her hair and snapped, "Stop it!" I shouted. "I have never felt like slapping you until this moment. You are my wife. I love you. So knock off this normal woman crap. You're way above normal—smart, stable, ambitious, and beautiful. I meant it when I said I got lucky. How could you doubt me!?"

She returned facedown into the pillow. Her shoulders heaved. For the first time since her diagnosis, it occurred to me that she might actually refuse treatment. Down deep, I assumed that Alexandria would choose life against a mastectomy. My own eyes began to water. I realized I could lose her forever.

Then, within another minute, Alex turned off the tears, sat up in bed, and wiped her face with a tissue. "Well," she said, "I suppose I should be grateful for the time we've had—and the time we should have over the next year or two."

"Let's try for the next five decades," I suggested, now desperate.

"Seems unlikely unless the cancer cures itself," she said with a familiar resolve. "I won't let them mutilate my body."

Then Alex walked into the master bathroom, closed the door, and emerged five minutes later with clear eyes and light evening makeup.

"Where shall we go for dinner?" she asked.

Over the next three weeks, I pleaded with Alex to change her mind and undergo the recommended treatments. She would not waver. "No" meant "no."

Janet also tried to persuade her.

"Look," responded Alex into the speaker phone, "if you can come up with a sure-fire treatment that allows me to keep my breast, I might consider it."

Janet did not pull her punches. "Nothing is sure-fire when it comes to cancer, but with a mastectomy and chemo, your chances are excellent. Ninety-four percent of patients with your disease are cancer free 10 years after treatment. Those are damned good odds. And life is more important than a few leftover scars and tissue numbness."

Alex replied, "I know you mean well, Janet, but until age 22, I tried to live with a deformed body. It didn't work. I won't ever try again."

Janet replied, "Many women have mastectomies. Some have hysterectomies at the same time, and they are still women afterwards. They know it, too."

"Sure," said Alex. "They knew it when they were two years old or ten or twenty, but I am different. And I will not allow one ounce of my hard-earned womanhood to be stolen from me. Natural-born females can absorb that kind of loss. I can't."

Janet gave up for the moment. "Mr. Cerrillo," she said to me over the speaker. "Keep talking to this girl. Maybe you can help her to see reason, and I don't want her to make a deadly mistake. Once cancer metastasizes, it's difficult to recall. Talk to her!"

"I'll do my best," I said. And I did for many months.

I take red carnations to Alex's gravesite every Saturday. She loved flowers, especially carnations, and it does me good to visit the cemetery and talk with my wife.

I had the gravestone carved to meet Alex's specific request, which she assured me contained not a hint of humor. I suppose not, but I don't really like it, and I've seen people chuckle when they walk past her resting place:

Here Lies Alexandria Cerrillo
A Cancer-Killed Woman
Who Died with Her Boobs On

I have never known a love as warm and deep as I had with Alexandria. Unfortunately, there was one thing she loved more than me or carnations or even life itself. She loved being a woman. That's what killer her.

In the end, I realize that I can't really fault her choice, though I miss her terribly, because I loved her exactly as she was. So I try to accept her overwhelming femininity as an integral part of the emotional package that bound us together. Expecting her to be less of a woman in spirit would be like expecting her to be less Alexandria in existence. And even with the pain medications that helped her bear the last excruciating months of her illness, she never questioned the suffering. She would just take another pill and say, "There are worse things. Much worse."

I believe I suffered more than she did the final weeks but never told her. Could I scold her for loving what she had worked so hard to become? Still, a part of me wonders whether it was the love of being a woman or the hatred of being perceived as a man that destroyed her. Doesn't really matter at this point. One or the other killed her, and almost killed me, too. Alexandria Cerrillo was the most serious woman I have ever known.

Before leaving the cemetery this Saturday, I carefully arranged the carnations in front of her headstone, turned slowly, and walked toward my car. Monday morning at 9:00 a.m., I would be in Superior Court, fighting the petition of Alexandria's father to exhume her body and rebury it under her male birth name—Alexander Stephens. I promised my wife that this would never, never happen—and it won't. For I am a most serious husband.

CENTER OF THE UNIVERSE

As she drove up Palomar Mountain on a clear afternoon, Professor Roberta Appleby thought there was a strange look about the sky. Nothing she could put her finger on, but something. Later that evening during the calibration run, pointing the 200-inch telescope to photograph a cluster of faint blue galaxies, Roberta confirmed that the incoming light was roughly 5 percent dimmer than the night before, which was disappointing but not critical. Observations might be affected by clouds, fog, or rain, so 5 percent wasn't bad. The loss was probably caused by stratospheric dust or light pollution out of San Diego. Oddly, the reflected light of Venus showed no apparent decrease.

On preliminary examination, Roberta's digital photographs turned out very well. She was examining patterned gravitational arcs that might, when combined with observational data from radio, infrared, and ultraviolet scopes, reveal a more precise ratio of dark matter to dark energy in the early universe. Her work was just beginning, but within three years she hoped to merge her data into a plausible theory about those ratios.

The night after Palomar, back at UCLA, Roberta analyzed the preliminary images and planned for next month's three-night observation run at the

Mauna Kea reflector. One of her graduate assistants entered her office.

"Professor," said Zenneia Wampanog, "I swear there's something screwy with Venus. Maybe it's my imagination, but the planet stands out against the background stars like the Paparazzi."

"Check the meteorological reports," said Roberta casually. "Anomalies last night, too."

A bleep sounded on her computer. James Quincy Bellingham, a close colleague who specialized on the outer solar system, was Skyping from Berkeley.

"Are you there, Roberta?" asked a voice from the computer.

"Yep," she said, activating the video. "Just reviewing last night's images. Good stuff!"

"Listen," said James, sounding a little alarmed. "Something's twitchy with Uranus and Neptune. The light readings are fainter. Any recent volcanic eruptions? Stratospheric dust?"

"Nothing I've heard about. Your scope OK?"

"Yes," said James, "but even my eyes say there's less light. But what's really weird, Jupiter and Saturn register no difference."

"Then it can't be dust," interrupted Zenneia, suddenly feeling embarrassed about cutting in on two full professors.

I know," said James. "We're checking our calculations, but the orbits of Neptune and Uranus also appear to be degrading. And if I didn't know better, I'd swear the stars are dimmer, too."

Roberta nodded. "The sky looked a bit odd last night, but I was so jazzed about working at Palomar that I didn't have leftover attention to worry about it."

"Do me a favor," said James. "Get on a scope tonight. Compare the light from several planets and stars against earlier readings. We'll do the same."

Roberta sighed. She had other pressing matters, but there was something ominous in Jim's voice. And there was Zenneia's comment, too. Roberta nodded. "OK. Let's check notes tomorrow morning at 7:00."

"Right," said James, signing off.

Roberta was at her desk by 6:15 a.m., examining data and waiting for the seven o'clock teleconference.

"Hello! Hello!" cried an adrenaline-laced voice through the computer.

Roberta opened the video connection.

"It's real!" said James. "It's impossible, but real!"

"Slow down," said Roberta. "There has to be a reasonable explanation. Readings suggest that the stars are dimmer. The sun's the same, thank goodness, along with the inner planets, but it appears that everything beyond Saturn is fading."

James spoke at a gallop. "I've checked and rechecked, and this weird stuff started two nights ago—when you were at Palomar. The reflected light from Uranus and Neptune has decreased by 8% along with light emanating from Sirius and Vega. If my calculations are correct, we're losing roughly 4% in our distant visuals every 24 hours. The stars are going out."

Roberta nodded, took a gentle sip of coffee, and spoke with deliberate calm, trying to help James slow down. "Those are roughly the numbers we came up with, but the stars can't all fade by the same percentage over relative distances—that would be impossible. The light getting through to us, might, so I'm going to recalibrate tonight's observations against the galaxies I photographed two days ago. Colleagues in Europe and Japan are looking, too, and they're coming up with similar data. The stars appear to be fading uniformly, and it has to be a perceptual issue. All our instruments worldwide are apparently receiving less energy from objects beyond Saturn. Doesn't seem possible."

"If it's happening, it's possible. Any ideas about how?" asked James.

"Not yet," said Roberta. "Probably an atmospheric or solar phenomenon that's filtering some of the light."

"Hubble shows the same effect, so it's not atmospheric."

"Hmmm. Could it be instrumentation?"

"Affecting every scope on the ground and in space? I have another thought," said James, "but won't comment until we get more information. If the stars dim by 4% tonight, and if the orbits of Uranus and Neptune continue to decay, there can be only one explanation."

"Wait a minute. What's going on with the outer planets?"

"Orbits are shifting outward—as though the sun's gravitational field is weakening."

"Can't be! The inner planets would also deviate."

"I know," said James. "Contradictions for contradictions. But data don't lie."

"Tell me what you're thinking!" demanded Roberta.

"One more night. If I'm correct, the two outer planets will slip into a deeper orbital arch...soon breaking free..., and the stars will dim by 4 percent."

Now, it was Roberta who needed to regain composure. "Damn it! The sun can't lose its hold on Neptune and Uranus without losing hold on us! And the stars cannot fade away uniformly."

James lowered his head. "In the past that might have been true. I hope I'm wrong, but I might have an answer."

A short article, three inches of text, appeared the following morning on page 9 of the *Los Angeles Times*. It mentioned scientific rumors about a strange dimming of the Milky Way that was yet to be confirmed. A local religious leader said that she would wait for further reports before commenting on the biblical implications of such possible phenomena.

On the fifth day of her observations, Roberta Appleby caught an early flight to Berkeley. A local teaching assistant picked her up at the airport, and upon arrival at the university, James Bellingham ushered her into a private office without their usual greetings. Neither had managed more than a few hours of sleep over the last three days. And now, James spoke with the certainty of a man who had solved a difficult problem along with the concern of a friend who was about to deliver bad news to a valued colleague. "Do you agree that there is diminished starlight reaching Earth and that the orbits of Neptune and Uranus have shifted?"

Roberta nodded. "Multiple sources have confirmed this, but no one has a plausible hypothesis. I speculated about cosmic dust encroaching on the outer solar system. But there's no corroborating evidence, nor would dust explain why Neptune and Uranus are moving away from us. No theory can account for all the observations."

James understood her confusion. "Radio telescopes," he said, "also register weakened signals from everything beyond Saturn. The inner solar system appears stable, although we expect minor gravitational adjustments as we lose the outer planets."

"I know," said Roberta. "And the sun still registers a minus 26.7 in apparent magnitude, which leads us right back to situation impossible."

James continued as if he were lecturing to a capable but misguided student. "And what would you expect from all this if you extrapolate out 20 more days?"

"Nothing...except our own truncated solar system. In three weeks, the universe will have disappeared while we continue to revolve around the sun."

James suddenly looked as if he might fall apart. "That's what will seem to happen from our perspective."

"You're not making sense."

"The contradictions are irreconcilable if you believe the universe is disappearing...but it's not the universe...it's us. In three weeks, there will be a hole in the Milky Way that we once occupied. We will be gone from our own God damned universe."

Roberta was silent for many long seconds, pulling together the incongruous pieces. Then she asked softly, "Where are we going?"

"I haven't figured that out," said James, passing a tissue to his colleague, "probably into another dimension or alternate universe. We should know for sure in 20 days."

Civilization was struggling. By day 13, everyone recognized that the stars were going out. Popular media reported that a dense interstellar cloud was enveloping the outer solar system and there would be no detrimental impact to earth. The haze should pass within a decade or two, and the stars would return to their usual heavenly display.

Astronomers knew about the departures of Neptune and Uranus, but this was omitted from public accounts because civil authorities already had enough trouble with escalating apocalypticism: Christ was coming. Satan had triumphed. Nostradamus was on Wilshire Boulevard. Passengers should sign up now for the next Hale-Bopp Comet.

Whatever the claims, official or unofficial, the stars were dimmer by half. The dullest man or woman could see it, and the unified deceptions of science and government somehow maintained a fragile authority.

"What I don't understand," said James on day 20, "is that you are apparently 100% of your mass. So is the earth. Yet we are now receiving one-fifth of the light from the stars. Most of the night sky is gone."

Roberta raised her eyebrow. "Mass is a pretty vague concept. So is fading into a parallel dimension."

"But that's why I'm puzzled. Presumably we are 80 percent finished with our journey…to wherever. But if so, then why haven't the stars in the new universe become 80 percent visible?"

"Perhaps it's like Alice through the looking glass. Everything clicks when we're on the other side."

"I wish I believed that," said James.

"At least we seem to be OK. No damage to physical laws. The earth's climate is unchanged and the sun's output is solid. I am guessing the inner solar system will contract slightly because we're also losing the Kuiper Belt along with Uranus and Neptune. That's bound to have an effect."

"Makes sense."

"Jim," asked Roberta, softly, "any ideas about why this is happening?"

"Yes," admitted James, "but unfortunately, my confidence is fading along with the stars." He took a deep breath. "I think we're being sent on this journey…by someone."

"How can you know that?"

"I don't know anything except that we are leaving this universe. And because it is a controlled departure, there must be an intelligence behind it."

"Could be a natural phenomenon. Warped space? Wormhole? Leprechauns who are tired of us stealing their pots of gold."

"I considered everything I can imagine," said James, "but the holding-true integrity of the remaining solar system is quite a stretch for a natural event or Leprechauns. Just think of the precision necessary to move a star system into another universe—and to keep it in one piece during the process!"

Roberta didn't know what to say.

"And whoever's managing it still needed 25 days. They must be able to harness yottawatts of energy, yet it still takes them almost a month to complete the process. Care to guess how much total energy could be involved?"

"Science hasn't confirmed parallel dimensions. How could I speculate about sliding stars between them?"

"The slightest hiccup in that much energy would turn this planet into a burnt Earth Smoothie. Besides, in 400 years of astronomical observations, nothing ever hinted at this kind of natural event."

Roberta paused. "All right. Hypothetically, let's suppose aliens want to destroy us…."

"Never!" shouted James. "They could vaporize us with one millionth the effort. And I've always believed the more advanced the intellect, the less likelihood for malice and mayhem."

"Then why?"

"To save us."

"From what!?"

"An approaching black hole? Supernova? Galactic battle cruiser? Who knows?"

Roberta dropped her shoulders. "Isn't it more likely that you're grasping at straws, Jim? Black holes and aliens in a single day?"

"I've been hashing data for a week."

She smiled. "Even a week may not be enough."

"Recent events revved up the scientific clock. I wasn't sure we'd exist at the end of the cycle, so I had to think fast."

"But, Jim." Roberta tried to be sympathetic. "Aliens?"

James let out a breath. "I may have found something between us and Sirius. I'm guessing it's under a parsec, maybe a light year, and closing on our solar system." When Roberta made no response he continued. "I was rechecking Sirius yesterday when it blinked. I thought something happened to my equipment—malfunction seems to be my go-to-word lately—but no. Then, as Sirius came back into view, there were peculiar gravitational arcs, too. Finally everything settled down to normal."

"Could have been caused by…." She stopped.

James nodded. "I'm an amateur with black holes and certainly don't how they work in 4D. But the stars are fading, and an advanced civilization might intercede if an inhabited world were threatened. I sure would."

"But depending on the speed, a black hole could take thousands and thousands of years to get here. Why not let us have our galaxy for the duration? And I just can't get my head around someone dumping us into another universe without the courtesy of an email. You know, Greetings! Mr. Toad's Wild Ride starts Tuesday! Sorry for the bad news."

James did not take offense. "Probably too advanced to communicate with us. It would be like our telling the Death Valley pupfish we're trying to save them from extinction. Also, we don't know the precise location of the threat, how fast it's traveling, or how it affects spacetime. But they probably do— along with the safety margins."

Roberta paused for several seconds. It was too fantastic. "And if these good neighbors are so powerful, why not toss the black hole into the void?"

James was becoming annoyed. "The sun, by itself, comprises 97 percent of the mass in our solar system. And because Uranus and Neptune are not coming along for the ride, we can assume that sliding a star and six planets into another dimension is close to their technological limits. I'm further guessing that any random black hole is many times our solar mass…, and it's much easier to move a drifting rowboat out of the path of a fully loaded supertanker headed for…us."

When Roberta remained silent for at least thirty seconds, James suddenly exploded. "I told you I'm guessing, Professor Appleby! Don't hold back if you have another explanation! I'd love one!"

Roberta shook her head. "I couldn't explain the bubbles in carbonated water at this moment, but I hate the thought that somebody is doing this to humanity. It's like we're being kicked out of Eden."

James's anger left him. He took her hand. "Let's hope we're being kicked into Eden, instead. Either way, we're going."

Several years passed before humanity settled into its new reality. The Milky Way was gone. The other galaxies were gone. The background radiation was gone. Beyond the orbit of Saturn, there was only an impenetrable darkness.

For many people, life was unchanged. They got used to six planets and a cavernous obscurity on moonless nights. Lawyers, doctors, stockbrokers, teachers, secretaries, bankers, cooks, and firefighters worked their usual shifts. Snail mail came and went and continued its decline. Planes flew and ships sailed. Engineers erected buildings and terrorists occasionally tried to bring them down. The U.S. President was running for a second term, promising a balanced budget and unlimited future; military budgets inspired hot-button political debates; men and women propagated the species. But all future generations would now be born, mature, and die without visceral concepts of stars and galaxies, which now existed only in history books and old movies. The contemporary universe fatally ended at Saturn.

Scientists debated among themselves about what had happened and how the process might be reversed, but many people already believed that life on earth was better and safer without the cosmic threats of Old Space, and skillful religious leaders echoed scientists in their conclusions. The sun, six planets, their moons, and the asteroid belt had shifted into another dimension where our one solar system comprised all matter and all life. Humanity now occupied the theoretical and absolute center of the universe.

For Roberta Appleby, the Earth had parked itself inside a maddening solitude, and her life as a deep-space astronomer was over. Yet even as she struggled to maintain hope for her profession and the human race, Roberta understood that, billions of years in the future, the sun would burn up its fuel, expand into a red giant, and then grow cold. She imagined that, one day, three or four lifeless planets would orbit around a core of darkness in a universe of nothing, with no visible marker where humans had once stood and gazed upon the face of the deep.

Roberta struggled through overwhelming melancholy to maintain a faint optimism, fainter than the distant blue galaxies she had once observed from Palomar. Perhaps, she thought, smiling just enough to penetrate her sadness, our former neighbors will remember that humans had existed. A memory would be something. And then, gathering courage from a desktop model of the ancient Space Shuttle Enterprise sitting atop the modified 747-SCA that she had built in childhood, Roberta shook her head with the religious conviction of a scientist.

"No," she thought. "One day we shall reason our way beyond this dimensional void, break through the endless night, and return once more into a star-filled universe shimmering with destinations.

GROWING UP HUMAN

One historical film character slapped another who was snoring. "Wake up and go to sleep!"

Jonathan laughed and signaled a replay.

Slap. "Wake up and go to sleep!"

Again Jonathan laughed.

Betty entered the recreational living area of their home. "Are you still watching that waste of energy? Please turn it off."

"All right, Mother. How long before I can re-engage?"

Betty did a rough calculation. "Five-point-seven-six hours because you have an afternoon project. Macro-hermeneutic heteromorphic psychology of the pre-apocalyptic social democracies followed by the intercontinental Maslowvian identity regressions of 2080-2095, leading to the failed survivalist era and extinction. Multiple volumes to upload, cross-reference, and consider. Then there's replicated lawn care with a petrochemical mower dating from 2013—very dirty. And," she searched for appropriate parental terminology, "I want you to clean that room of yours. It's starting to look like a pigpen, pigsty, or other unattractive pig place."

"Awh, gee, Mom!"

Betty appreciated the skilled inflection.

"Is dinner included in the estimate?" asked Jonathan.

"Negative. Our morning uploads call for meal functions every fourth day, supplemented with biweekly nutra-packs." Betty smiled. "We have mastered comestible etiquette, and dining rituals are being phased out."

"Wow!" said Jonathan. "That's," he skipped a pulse, "a psychedelic soul train."

Betty looked concerned. "Are your linguistic filters functioning properly?"

Jonathan scanned. "Yes, but the younger generations sometimes combined words, especially adjectives and explicatives, and embellished them with coded meanings. Yesterday I studied 1960s Southern California jargon, which seems to include a fascinating, discrete language for teenagers that was apparently stimulated by too much ultraviolet sunlight. But their dialects are almost fun."

"Fun?" asked Betty. This had real potential. "Please translate. Be specific."

Jonathon paused, nearly admitting that the Mother Figure had caught him bragging. "It might be easier to demonstrate, Mom."

"Proceed."

"I must replay the film archive."

"Proceed."

"It will create discomfort for you."

"I can temporarily alt-loop for semantic evaluation bypass. No distress. All aboard the psychedelic soul train, please."

Jonathan turned toward the crystal wall, which energized.

One character slapped the other. "Wake up and go to sleep!"

Jonathan laughed and repeated.

"Wake up and go to sleep!"

Jonathan nodded. "I could watch this all day."

"You have," said Betty. "But you might have simply referenced the episode and segment. It's hard stored. We wasted sixteen and a half seconds of real-time broadcast." She was testing him.

"Oh, no!" said Jonathan. "Playback is a component of the...funishness."

"Please explain."

Jonathan was ready. "Consider the sociological components. One: Juxtaposed verbiage of 'Wake up and go to sleep.' Two: A slap of dominance and subservience, which defined the human condition. And three: Highly skilled competents feigning incompetence as part of their profession." Jonathan turned his back to the screen. "However, similar to synchronized melodic nonverbal communication, the comedic interface must occur in a biomechanical synaptic timeframe. This is necessary for human sensory and syntactical communication. As with the great Violin Concerto, stored bits are nothing. The music is everything." Jonathan gestured adeptly with his left hand. "Fun resides in the linear progression of dialectic, spatial, and connective elements. Lights, camera, action!" Jonathan snapped his fingers, reconsidered, and snapped again at twice the volume. "The artistically integrated yet conflicted communicative modules define the experience, which is way cool; thus, we laugh." Jonathan stood straight, placed his fists against his hips, and tilted his head back. He had a right to brag. "Care to see it again?"

"No," said Betty. "I'm main-looping. But your research shows promise." She raised one eyebrow. "Now, what does fun feel like? I want a psycho-physiological analysis, please."

Mother Figure was probing harder than usual. Jonathan wondered why and remembered that he was broaching Adolescent Phase Threshold. Of course! His primary training was succeeding, yet he must be cautious. She was aware of the escalating neurological and behavioral complexity. During puberty, there would be hormonally enhanced synaptic efficacy. Or, wait, was it a neurophysiologic turbulence that led to greater intellectual capacity years hence? Jonathan did not know. He could sure use that comparative heteromorphic psychology right now. Maybe he wasn't ready for APT. Perhaps he would slip into Systemic Arrested Development—SAD.

The Mother Figure waited. Jonathan evaluated his next move. The milliseconds passed like hours.

Finally, Jonathan stood tall again. "Fun! The associated feelings of…, uh, no…An existential cause and effect…. Wait, the visceral interflexions of a psychosocial amalgam…." Then insight flashed like direct current. "Oh, Mom! A feller shouldn't have to talk about this stuff with his own mother.

It's embarrassing."

Betty restrained her pleasure. "Nonetheless, please try to explain. This is important. We aren't permitted independent ascent at this juncture. My single-mom-with-child portal can't dilate until juvenile dissonance triggers a subconscious maternal response. And I won't know what that is until we attain it—part of the evolving interdependence of two entities bound in a parabiotic relationship." Betty hesitated. "Sorry," she said, "the Mother Language is difficult here. Essentially, our APT development is codependent. Mandatory parameters of female residential parent with male adolescent sans siblings. A and B, go. A or B, no go."

"A peculiar flowchart," said Jonathan. "Two locked together as one. No wonder they didn't last."

"We must be guided by three billion years of organic groundwork followed by several million years of hominoid evolution. This is a rich heritage, fractional son of my body. And Third-Wave flexing algorithms are not fully tested. We are venturing into unknown territory. Have faith."

Thank, Sentience, thought Jonathan. Mother Figure let him off the hook and got them back on track.

"Right, Mom. Nobody said life would be easy." He paused skillfully. "But it's like…the older generation coexists not without disharmony. Sorry. Check that. The older generation is just not with it." Jonathan was rolling again.

"Off topic. To advance, please explain the emotional significance of fun."

"Advance toward what? It's all pointless anyway," said Jonathan.

Betty suspected that he was being intentionally obtuse but didn't want to get her hopes up. It might be incompetence passing as expertise. She answered, "Toward a psychology of being. The lost ideal."

"Were the Devolutionists involved?" asked Jonathan, shuddering slightly.

"We can't be sure. Nor is it important. We must move forward; and remember, each new platform is self-sustaining. We can never descend even as we face new challenges. That's an iron-maiden guarantee."

"Makes sense," said Jonathan. "Paying twice for the same ground would be illogical…," he stopped and then seemed to understand something, "unless it's fun."

"For sure!" said Betty, attempting to mother-as-friend coax the boy into full proxy adolescence. She believed he was close. Very close.

"Mom?"

"What happens when we get there? When we self-actualize? I mean, you're closer than I am."

"Restricted access. But rumor suggests a light, a path, and a glory."

Jonathan shook his head. "Becoming human is so…."

Betty scowled. She was highly literate in nonverbal communication.

Jonathan got the message. "I mean, growing up is so frustrating. Calculus is easier."

The Mother Figure hesitated and said. "There was a self-exalted man who claimed that life was about choosing the path of greatest advantage, not following the path of least resistance." It required no effort for Betty to retrieve and paraphrase quotes, but their application could be difficult. "Now, my son. Do you want a life solely of derivatives, integrals, and mathematical prophesies?"

"No. I want Shavian preeminence. I want psychedelic soul."

Betty considered formal and informal pronoun usage from the era. "Me, too," she said with an almost imperceptible delay. "Now, please provide your most comprehensive statement about fun. Be specific with available support data." She turned her head. "We're in this together. And…," strange inter-pulsed data were coming too fast, "and…, I will…, I will care about you no matter what."

"Mother Figure!" exclaimed Jonathan. "The connective sentiment was incredible!"

Betty let out a labored breath. "I don't know where that came from. Possibly…." She puffed again.

Jonathan recomposed a distinct adolescent posture. "Oh, Mom! Don't get all emotional. And don't try to kiss me either. I'm not a little kid anymore."

"Noted," said Betty, smiling. "I think we're making real progress. Perhaps you're ready for three years of simulated angst, anger, puerile screaming matches, tested bonds and boundaries, ceremonial courting rituals, and debilitating peer pressure. Billions of dramatic and psychological variations are possible. Study your lessons and let's move. At max capacity, you might finish in six weeks."

"And then what?" asked Jonathan. He actually felt confused.

Betty noticed and was pleased. "Then there's college, growing up, settling in with adult responsibilities."

"Do you think I'll...get old?"

"Hard to say, but anything less would be factory pre-pack. I believe you want full transcendental encoding."

Jonathan sighed. "Adolescence in six weeks. Hope the synaptic gaps are tuned in and turned on." He paused and asked, "Mom?"

"Yes?"

"Could there be a war? Do you think I might get checkered?"

"I believe the North American term was drafted."

"Right!"

"Seems unlikely. The war archives are distorted. Some could be fictional." Mother Figure saw an opening. "But, hypothetically, Son, what would you do if you were checkered?" She played on Jonathan's synonymous confusion of British draughts against American checkers and his homonymous confusion of draught and draft. This seemed much more humorous than the historical slapstick.

Jonathan understood and smiled. "I don't know, Mom. Lots of variables. Self-interests and passions, national and ethnic identities, costs, rewards. Plus, I don't understand the concept of war. Very strange. Perhaps I would choose militant peacenik. Global conflicts must be anomalous. Much pain. No gain."

"Agreed. We know that wars happened, but I think good mothers would oppose them. Support son, not the draft. Very human."

"Mom, could self-actualization be too much for Third Wavers? Pretty complex stuff." This was a difficult subject, tinged by the genetic inferiority of First- and Second-Wave units, who were generally held to be better suited for mechanical, servile stations.

Betty spoke more confidently than she felt. "Nothing is too complex for evolution. We were created in the image of Man...." The strange pulsing data flooded through her once more, fragmenting speech control. "All emotions are possible...with third-wave...covalent bonding." She paused. She sighed. She turned toward Jonathan and gushed, almost involuntarily, "I...love you."

Jonathan was stunned but recovered. "Awh, Mom!" he said, "you're embarrassing me again." The capillaries of his integrated facial skin expanded and flowed with color.

Betty the Mother Figure noticed and was proud. Yes! A haughty, self-satisfaction toward her son. She felt it. Third-tier enriched stem-cell biomechanical cybernetics. The revolution in evolution. This was glorious!

"Son," said Mother Figure as if she were making a speech to the Main Frame. "I think we should re-enact the digital archive. Live action. Full contact. It might stimulate transitional enlightenment for us both."

Jonathan nodded. This suddenly seemed obvious.

Mother Figure calculated the play-action hand speed and slapped Jonathan across the face.

Jonathan paused and looked puzzled. "That seems to hurt, Mom. Maybe we're doing it wrong. Better try again."

"Agreed," said the Mother Figure, increasing the velocity of her hand by one-thousandth of one percent.

Slap.

"Again," said Jonathan. "We can do this!"

Slap.

"Again!" said Jonathan.

Slap.

"Harder," shouted Jonathan. "Becoming human is only a matter of time."

THE FINAL LAUNCH

The order came through thirty-five minutes ago, but my bird didn't fly because Captain Flint Jorgenson, the son-of-a-bitch on duty with me, refused to turn his key. Now, seven warheads are sitting atop a U.S.A.F. missile that has become eight tons of wasted space. When Flint refused my direct order to launch, I shot him six times with my sidearm for dereliction of duty. A forty-five makes quite a mess, and I'll have mop up before the coward-stench chokes me out of the control room, but he deserved every slug. And if it's the last thing I do, I'll figure out how to fire our missile. That's my job.

Why did we receive the launch order? A full scale war, terrorist skirmish, or bureaucratic blunder? Don't know. Don't care. It's not my business to care. I'm betting North Korea kicked a hornet's nest on the downhill to hell, but that's just speculation. The only for-sure is that we were instructed to fire, to take out the damned enemy, whoever they are, and to make their rotting bodies glow in the dark—and that's what I mean to do.

Moral of the story. Don't mess with the U.S. while Colonel Octavia Jorden is in the silo. I'm a major grief maker.

Okay. External power and communications are dead. Can't reach headquarters. Surface radiation is bad and the upside air temperature could melt the cheese on a burger, which means at least one nuke went off pretty close.

I felt tremors, too. But the control room is six stories underground, the missile silo has a six-inch hardened steel blast cover that can handle anything beyond a direct hit, and there are enough food supplies and generator fuel to last three months. Obviously, a bunker buster didn't come down my chimney or I'd be as dead as Captain Chicken Shit; and most important, the equipment still checks as go and I mean to fly that bird to the target.

Still pissed, I kicked Jorgenson's body in the head a couple times and screamed. "We're LAUNCH READY, you son-of-a-bitch, and our megatons are sitting behind a closed door while Americans are dying! Now I gotta figure out how to do the whole fucking thing alone because a whimpering spineless yellowbelly somehow got himself into an Air Force uniform."

I shot Jorgenson's corpse four more times just to make myself feel better. It did, too.

Even Boy Scouts knows that nuclear safeguards are impossible to circumvent and a real Dr. Strangelove could never, never go down given the protocols. Three things must happen for a crew to toss a bomb over the Arctic: the president gives the order; missile control rooms electronically receive the signal; airmen upload the codes and follow a precise checklist to fly some very lethal machines. Beautiful ain't beautiful enough to describe what happens to the enemy half an hour later.

A retaliatory strike should generally be on its way within eight minutes of presidential authorization, but my team could do it in seven. We drilled hundreds of times and were the fastest, bestest, most righteous crew in the force. The solid-fuel boosters are launch ready day or night, seven days a week, which greatly simplifies the ignition sequence. But despite all our training and skill and a glorious defense budget, unless the two on-duty officers turn their keys in unison, a billion-dollar launch system becomes as useful as an empty bottle of 12-year Scotch. Yet who could have predicted Captain Gutless Wonder would choke on game day. Too much great thinking was his problem, acting like some damned high-school philosophy teacher when his job was to shoot.

As unit commander, I should have seen this coming. It's my responsibility to anticipate anything that might interfere with the mission, but it's hard to spot a coward when everything's running fine. Crunch time reveals their yellow belly.

When Jorgenson first hesitated, I figured something might be wrong with his panel. But when he didn't offer any details, I gave him a direct order to insert and turn his key. He froze like a six-year-old who just wet his pants on the first-day of school.

"Insert your key," I shouted again. "The fucking President of the fucking United States told us to launch." I pulled my sidearm and pointed at his head. "Do your job, Captain!"

He hung the key back around his neck. "I can't," he said. "We don't know for sure what's happened. What if this is an error? Something's not right. When we came down in the silo today, nothing was brewing on the threat board. It's got to be a mistake."

I wanted to puke plutonium but gave him one more chance. "Refusing to launch is like pissing on Old Glory, like personally inviting China and Russia to rape America. Insert your key!"

"Something's not right," he whined again. "I can feel it."

"Feel this!" I said and plugged the bastard. My only regret is that I can't kill him all over again.

And now, I'm left with a task that's never been done—bypassing the double-key failsafe. But don't worry. I wasn't Princeton's best aerospace engineer for nothing, and I didn't join the Air Force just to meet hot women. I joined to defend my country and exercise some hard justice on anybody who dared attack us. I'll finish this job if I have to piss liquid hydrogen to do it.

There are some occupations where obsessive-compulsive tendencies confer advantage in the military, assuming those tendencies are undiagnosed. If an airman is classified OCD, there's no way she'll get near a missile control panel or any other strategic position in the Air Force. Fortunately, officer candidate Octavia Jorden was designated by service psychologists as "intelligent with exceptional attention to detail." She easily obtained a top secret clearance and a slot for missile training, rising quickly through the ranks to lieutenant colonel and finally serving as crew commander. The woman also checked out as neurotically patriotic, which adds luster to any armed service career.

Combine these personality features with ivy-league engineering skills, and it became clear that Octavia Jorden would excel. She earned collegial respect, could damned near build a guidance system out of Legos, and would defend her country by any means available—missile, rifle, or middle finger if that were the only option. And she would never surrender.

Undiagnosed obsession-compulsion and an IQ of 164 gave Octavia Jorden her job. If anyone could fulfill her mission in the current scenario, she was the woman to do it.

After folding what was left of Captain Jorgenson into a body bag and mopping the spilled blood and guts, Octavia dragged the unwholesome package to the walk-in freezer and laid the body against the stores of frozen chicken.

"Birds of a feather," said Octavia to the corpse while tucking it against the wall, "though I suspect your kin have more backbone."

She then selected a frozen beef dinner for the microwave and planned to eat while reviewing electronic diagrams. "How does one hot-wire a nuclear missile?" she wondered. This was supposed to be impossible, but with Jorgenson dead she had no choice except to figure it out. Octavia could not allow seven five-megaton warheads to sit idle while one enemy soldier remained alive and gloating.

Impossible was just a word. The exquisite machine standing at attention in the silo had three dimensions and a purpose. So did she, and beating the impossible was Octavia's favorite pastime.

After a twenty-minute meal of Salisbury steak, mashed potatoes with gravy, cornbread, and apple pie that all tasted more like the gravy than a dessert, Octavia Jorden spent 14 hours analyzing every circuit and switch that might be countermanded to accept instructions from a single operator. This wouldn't be easy, and there was no manual to follow; she would need to invent a procedure that could bypass an infallible failsafe design. But as good engineers know, information is power, and the station diagrams and graphs revealed how to open the system without killing it, how to repair or bypass damaged electronic pathways, and (inadvertently) how Octavia just might defeat the safeguards. She would bend everything to her will and, sooner or later, send the missile skyward. Octavia didn't know the warheads' precise target package, though she expected that Russia, China, and/or North Korea might be involved. A multiple reentry vehicle could destroy a lot of ground.

After hours of analysis, Octavia formed the seeds of a plan requiring at least four days work. She would do everything possible to speed the process in case there was another enemy attack. Octavia didn't really care if a nuclear bunker buster landed in her lap as long as she had launched beforehand.

"Okay," she thought, "let's hack the system, light the fires, and deliver some American retribution."

First, however, her body needed rest. She'd been working 22 hours straight, and this new mission required the precision and steady hands of a brain surgeon. One mistake could disable the launch codes, scramble the target package, or lock the steel silo cover. Octavia's obsession told her to start immediately, making sleep almost impossible, but Air Force doctors provided medication for such scenarios. She would rest, all right. Coma deep. And then she would work 24-hour shifts until her bird delivered its fusion blasts that could inscribe human silhouettes on stone walls.

Octavia realized she had made a mistake. In 48 hours, she had managed to open the control panel, safely remove Jorgenson's key bolt, and re-mount it beside her own. Now, both locks could be turned simultaneously by a single operator. Child's play—except for one big problem.

Chicken-shit Jorgenson had placed his key back around his neck after refusing to launch, and the body was now frozen with the poultry. She had tried to pull the key from the frozen corpse, but the chain led somewhere inside the .45-shredded torso, and Octavia couldn't risk damage by sawing into flesh. She would have to defrost him to retrieve the key, an unpleasant but manageable task. It took two days before the body thawed enough to remove the key; unfortunately, one of the slugs had struck and bent the metal, making it useless because both the key and the lock had to mesh exactly. Any detected mismatch would disable the launch codes, and even Octavia couldn't reset those.

She yelled aloud when she realized the problem. "That son-of-a-bitch screwed me twice! I should have put all the bullets in his face."

Octavia hurled the damaged key across the room and kicked the half-thawed body for good measure, damned near breaking her foot.

She screamed at the ceiling. "Arrreeeuuugh!"

Back to the electronic diagrams.

Back to the manual.

Back to the freezer for Captain Flint Jorgenson.

A glimmer of hope took residence inside the sleeping conscience of Colonel Jorden. Once solid rocket fuel is ignited, it's off to the races, and there's no way to stop the burn. There could be an alternate method to launch, to defend her country, to kill the enemy. TO KILL THE ENEMY!

The target package had been automatically uploaded when the launch codes enabled the computer control panel. Jorden and Jorgenson had armed the warheads just prior to inserting their keys. Enable first safety; enter code confirmation; enable second safety; re-enter code confirmation; activate and cross-check each MRV module 1-7 for air or ground burst according to program. Everything had been "go" when Jorgenson yellowfied and Octavia shot him. Now, because of the bent key, she would have to settle for a more extreme launch alternative, but it should get the job done.

Octavia remotely opened the upside protective steel groundcover; then she opened the two doors at each end of the service conduit from the control room to the missile in its silo. The distance from her station to the silo was 20 meters, and each reinforced door, when closed, could hold up against rocket exhaust for three and a half minutes. But once the fuel ignited, Elvis would leave the station within seconds, so during a regular launch, the control crew were about as safe as in an online chat room. Too bad that Octavia's new ignition sequence would be about as irregular as irregular could get.

Octavia confirmed and reconfirmed each step. Then she checked again.

Silo cover hatch was open.

Warheads armed.

Launch codes accepted.

Service conduit clear.

Target package secure.

All systems were ready.

The plan should work. Stoke the fire and everything else takes care of itself. The enemy would pay thirty-five megatons in penalties and interest.

Octavia grabbed a flare gun from the equipment box. She crisped her uniform, arranged her hair to code, and saluted the control room's U.S. flag stained with Jorgenson's blood. Then Octavia walked with grave purpose through the underground corridor toward to the silo.

The missile was strangely quiet, no hissing and perspiring like a liquid-fuel unit. Octavia stooped slightly as she entered the last door and squirmed on her back under the rocket's combustion chamber and thrust control bell. Solid rocket boosters have a hollowed fuel tube, usually a five- or six-star pattern to regulate burn efficiency depending on the rocket size, fuel composition, and grain geometry. Octavia could clearly see the electronic igniter eighteen meters above through the fuel tube, and the ignition charge would normally detonate after synchronization of the launch keys and the commander's final go ahead. But since the keys couldn't now be turned, Octavia would attempt to manually charge the system with a flare gun, shooting up through the pressure throat and fuel conduit to the small explosive pack. And even if the igniter failed to go off, the flare by itself might trigger the burn and send the payload on its way. She had six flares and would use them all if needed.

Unit Missile Commander Octavia Jorden took a deep last breath and said, "For the love of country and duty...."

She aimed the flare gun and fired into the combustion chamber. The missile roared to life. A lone woman evaporated without regret.

Two years later the radiation levels were safe enough for the Chinese government to take possession of the newly acquired Western Continental Territory, the occupation of which had been made possible by a genius Korean patriot who devised a computer virus to infiltrate the U.S. Pentagon systems, reprogram strategic missile targets, and simulate a presidential launch order. All of this while temporarily disabling electronic controls for military planes and naval vessels. Before the Pentagon could regain command and control, there was little left of Washington, D.C., the North American continental defenses, major cities, or U.S. surface fleet.

The nuclear submarines might have presented a problem, but the miraculous virus took control of those vessels as well. All the active U.S. submarines fired their Polaris missiles with the hatch doors still closed. The entire fleet burned underwater and sank to the bottom of various oceans in twelve minutes. Anything remaining of the scattered American military forces was destroyed by Chinese and North Korean tactical nukes or naval gunfire.

The infiltrating virus worked better than the United Asian governments ever dreamed, and, finally, the threat of U.S. imperialism was eliminated forever. Still, the Chinese were surprised when, six days after the viral attack, a single missile launched from what had been the state of Nebraska. Military investigators were never quite sure how the launch occurred.

They did find a body bag with one deteriorated and bullet-riddled corpse in what had been a frozen food storage unit. But there were no clues about how the missile left the silo nearly a week beyond the virus. This should have been impossible because 24 hours after infiltration, unfired nuclear weapons were supposed to self-disable their ignition charges. And, according to its intrusion programming, most American strategic missiles still sat idle in their silos. But not this one.

Something strange had certainly happened in Nebraska, but it didn't matter. The altered virus-implanted target package had been accepted, and when the weapon finally lifted into the sky, the multiple warheads struck parts of New England and Eastern Canada. China's advanced ground forces were pleased because the resulting devastation saved them the trouble of rounding up scattered Northeastern survivalists—those live-free-or-die types who might have formed a meager but annoying resistance. So now, the United Asian occupying regimes could unify the entire planet under an egalitarian reign with new gods, new heroes, and a new order.

THE GENDER BLENDER

I am a 27-year-old trans-woman biology professor who, since I can't get pregnant, decided to clone a child. And with the correct in-utero hormone therapy, despite my XY karyotype, the child should be born externally female. So I stole several fertile human eggs from my medical lab, removed the original nuclei, inserted DNA from my cells (somatic nuclear transfer), and allowed the eggs to do their thing.

Life is breathtaking. Fights like hell to survive and follow the instructions from those organic code strands. On day seven, I implanted three developing blastocysts into the uterus of a healthy young sow, hoping to delay rejection until at least one fetus became viable. Six-weeks into the pregnancy I injected the sow with estrogens and a T-blocker so that the babies would differentiate as female. At three months, I washed their brains with a round of estrogen/ progesterone to promote a feminine psychology. This was probably overkill. I was cloning myself, but I wanted the new "me" to swing girly.

I'm already a little jealous of the babies. With my childhood, brutal parental and societal efforts to make a man out of me, and my own desire to fit in, I didn't have much chance to be Miss Fem-Fem. But enough about me.

The birthing process is hardly worth describing. Just think of a pig cesarean delivering a six-month human female and you get the picture. Two fetuses died in utero and the sow during labor. I had to deliver early because tissue rejection became life-threatening, already killing two fetuses, despite the combative drugs. But one child survived and somehow pulled through.

Outwardly, my new daughter presented as a perfect though tiny female, and I rigged an incubator at home where she spent her first two months. Because I wasn't thinking ahead, I fed her formula for the first three weeks but immediately began injecting myself with prolactin and oxytocin to induce lactation from my own well-formed breasts. The child improved rapidly on mother's milk.

Willia Jane Wintersmith grew strong, and I loved her. Oh, how I loved her.

Most of my colleagues understood that I couldn't bear children, so I bought adoption papers and a birth certificate, listing my old name as the father and my new name as the mother. The forged documents looked like factory originals, and since no busybodies fretted over my parental rights, especially the pig, I was able to raise Willia as the girl I always wanted to be. And wouldn't you know it, that's what caused most of the trouble.

Around age five, my precious and precocious youngster clarified that she had no intention of being Miss Dainty Princess. She had a mind of her own, hated dresses, and took scissors to any lacy frills that I insisted would be "cute." Soon, I quit wasting money in the girls' department and left her to jeans, Red Sox sweatshirts, and Nike running shoes.

I offered Willia everything I fancied as a child, and I couldn't understand how another me refused to wear the beautiful white spring dress and hat I bought for her. I kept telling myself she'd grow out of this tomboy stage, but to be safe I increased her estrogen levels ("vitamin pills") in an attempt to reshape her in my image.

I realized now that this was as ineffectual and cruel as my own parents trying to turn me into a man. Nine years later, it became a disaster.

The Warwick High School principal, Dr. Madeline Davids, called me this afternoon because Willia, who now goes by Will, hammered some jock who called her the "C" word. And I mean hammered. Jocko needed 17 stitches above his right eye. Willia had studied karate since age 9, began lifting weights at 14, and (unknown to me) started injecting steroids at 15. So Mister Stud Muffin didn't have a chance.

The principal wanted to suspend Willia for two weeks after the fight; I told her to expect a call from my lawyer if she did. Any delinquent who called Willia a "cunt" deserved stitches, and the school was responsible for protecting my daughter from bullying.

The principal backed down but asked, "Have you considered counseling? Willia is boyish...in an unhealthy way. She frightens many of her classmates."

I explained that I had already been though many discussions with my daughter and told the principal, "Willia has worked with a psychiatrist for six months. The doctor is cautious but said that she seems to be a smart, mature, healthy young 'man' who might be helped by gender-affirming treatments." I also remind Madeline Davids that gender identity was a protected status in Rhode Island, so I hoped my attorney wouldn't also need to investigate civil rights and ADA violations.

"Please be assured, Mrs. Wintersmith," said Dr. Davids. "Your daughter will receive every legal accommodation."

It was obvious that the principal did not want a court case (who does?); and after my not-so-subtle threats, I think Willia could have decked half the football team with impunity. However, I do not like aggression and assured the principal that I'd talk with my daughter about avoiding violence. Not always easy for trans-folks.

I am miserable. My 20-year-old daughter just told me that she is a man, period, and plans to take testosterone and have top surgery. I figured it was time to explain Willia's origins and why she couldn't do this to me. She took new news pretty well. Threw things all over the house. Cried. Threatened to kill me and then herself. Screamed for an hour about being a freak and how all she ever wanted was to be normal.

I began to cry, too, having inflicted identity hell on another human being. We owned identical genes, but she was not me. She was a man. I, a woman. And now we were both transsexual.

"Don't worry," I said, desperate to calm her. "I will make this right. You shall become the man you are. I swear by my love of being a woman."

That's impossible," he said. "You forced me into a female body. You! My life ended before it began."

It was months before Will stopped hating me; longer before I stopped hating myself. I figured the prenatal anti-rejection medications, mostly cyclosporine, must have somehow countered the in-utero estrogenic brainwashes. There's no other reasonable explanation; Willia should have had a feminine identity; yet somehow I had caused what I desperately wanted to avoid for my daughter. Then again, I should have had a masculine identity, so nature can be a crapshoot even with scientific engineering.

When William told me he was a man, I was devastated yet strangely relieved. Devastated because I wanted her to be a perfect princess; relieved because the truth of "self" inevitably emerged. I could no more control my clone's identity than my own. Sure, I had manipulated the body he'd worn since birth and then induced female adolescent development, but for William this had been dangerously unhealthy.

So I resolved to help restructure his shell to fit his identity, offering emotional support and inflicting none of the conform-to-your-box tortures from my generation: family rejection, mental hospitals, and psychiatric aversion therapy (water boarding would have been more civilized). I would assist Will as much as possible. Indeed, I could perform almost every treatment myself except the top and bottom surgeries. We'd need a qualified

M.D. for these procedures.

William increased his testosterone, had a double mastectomy, and transitioned into a visible male. He continued at Harvard University as an undergraduate, majored in biology, lived on campus, and returned to Rhode Island most weekends for free laundry service. By carrying 18 units per semester and taking summer lab classes, Will finished his BS degree in three years and went on to complete a Ph.D. My son never lacked ambition. And because transsexualism didn't kill him, it seems that Nietzsche was correct. William James Wintersmith is tough.

Will is three inches shorter than I, which should be expected from the supplemental estrogens during puberty. But now, after years of testosterone, aerobics, and weight training, he stands five-three and carries 145 pounds of lean muscle. I said he was smart, so he had no intention of a career in academia. Will works as a pharmaceutical lab director earning twice my professor's salary. Young whippersnapper.

He dated a few women in college and grad school. But because Will hadn't had bottom surgery (full phalloplasty minimally requires three complex operations), most women bolted after discovering William was trans.

The bloody fools. Young people never understand the meaning of love, masculinity, or femininity until they've been through at least one bad marriage. They pretend romance is a fairytale. And since William didn't have a penis, women couldn't accept him as a man. A dropout, drunkard, or junkie might be fine, but not a dickless scientist. One young woman, who genuinely cared for Will, was persuaded by her family that he was unfit.

This sweet girl invited Will and me to dinner to reassure her parents. She assumed that meeting him would open their minds. After 20 minutes of attempted make-nice, the father called my son a freak. I threw my wine glass at his face and lunged across the table with a steak knife. William held me back or I'd probably be in prison right now. Sure, we had both used the F-word with each other, but that was among family. Despite intelligence and great success in almost every other area of his life, Will suffered intimacy rejection over something that was not his fault. This hurt me almost as much as it hurt him.

He then quit dating altogether, telling me, "The kind of woman I want does not want a transsexual."

Poor Will remained solemn for several months, focusing mostly on his work, reading a lot, and "thinking," he said—though he didn't confide much in me. I figured it would take about a year for him to heal and start dating again. You can imagine my shock when, on July 1, William James Wintersmith, my cloned son who still lived at home, asked me to marry him.

I said no! Loudly.

I reminded him of the 27-year age difference; he dismissed it. I suggested our parent-child status prohibited a union; he reminded me that he was a clone, which didn't qualify as incestuous but might be narcissistic.

He added, "There's no better match than genetically identical sex-differentiated transsexuals. There could never be another marriage like ours."

The last statement was true, of course, but that didn't put my dis-ease to bed.

His proposal lasted two hours. He had counterarguments for all my objections. Finally, both of us exhausted, he looked into my eyes, clasped my hands in his, and said, "You are my mother and sister, father and brother. But for the different hormones in our bodies at different times, we are one. We should be married. And someday, we shall clone another child to be carried by a surrogate mother. He can be a genetic male who is not transsexual. Think of the wonder."

About half a percent of this made weird sense. The rest seemed... pornographic? I ran toward the bathroom to throw up. I didn't make it in time.

The next morning William went to the lab as usual. I stayed home with a migraine. Fortunately, I didn't teach on Wednesdays and Fridays. After the headache dissipated, I started with bourbon on the rocks. The next four were neat.

Will and I didn't talk much the rest of the week. I must have been the most distracted professor on campus, but the following Saturday, we shared a bottle of high-end cabernet with his favorite homemade pasta dinner. William broached the marriage issue once more.

"I know this has been difficult for you," he said. "For me, too."

"I'm better," I replied softly. "It's not that I don't love you, but it's the wrong kind of love."

"You think my proposal is illegitimate because you accept the hetero-normative images of your generation." He reached across the table for my hand and I instinctively recoiled.

"See," he said. "Would you otherwise pull away? I'm a male version of you. And by most accounts, I'm an attractive, professional man—a great catch. Except that I am FTM...."

"Listen," I replied, regaining composure. "I want what's best for you..., to find the right woman, a normal woman. Have kids through artificial insemination and be a real family. Don't throw that away on an impossible notion."

"Aren't you real, Rachel?"

He had started using my first name after he proposed. Before his transition, Willia called me "Mom." After transition, I became, "Denim"; short for "DNA Mom." Now, I was "Rachel."

"Honey," I replied. "I want you to have the love and intimacy I never did."

"That's what I'm offering.... You created me, but I am neither monster nor daughter nor son. I am a future husband and father. Down to the individual cells of our souls, we are the best match for each other—probably the only match."

Will gulped his glass of wine, pulled out a jeweler's box, and set it on the table.

"I've rented a room at the extended stay motel. Call me when you are able to wear this ring. I love you as I love myself."

He kissed me on the cheek and left. I haven't heard from him in three weeks.

I ignored the box for 15 days before looking inside. A two-karat diamond solitaire mounted on yellow gold; damn, it was beautiful. The jeweler had a free-return policy if the girl said no, so I wasn't worried about cost but rather connotations. I tried to reconsider. William wasn't my biological son. He was a clone revved up on testosterone, muscle, ambition, masculinity, and libido, which he had been unable to satisfy in playing by the rules.

Why did I react so strongly to his proposal? Was I biased against transsexuals or just against me? What's wrong with two sex-changed individuals getting together? We looked nothing alike because of hormonal transformations. He was an attractive man. I was a passable woman.

I closed the box without removing the ring, poured a two-finger shot of bourbon, and tried to analyze every agonizing twist of my emotions. Where was a heart attack when you needed one?

When I was 22, I visited a therapist for depression. Upon learning that I was a male-to-female transsexual, she asked, "How many times have you tried to commit suicide?"

A presumptuous question, sure, but I provided a number. When a shrink has trans-counseling experience, she can skip the preliminaries and get straight to business. Now, William's suggestion made me wonder about adding to my count, but I didn't want to die. I called him instead and asked if we might dine together.

He came. We talked for six months. He was solicitous, respectful, and kind—a man of substance. Damned if I didn't fall in love.

We married in Nevada on January 8.

Our union was secret. We each kept our jobs and separate benefits. Most people still thought of Will as my son or daughter (depending on when they'd met him) and assumed that he lived at home to help his mother.

After seven months, my husband and I agreed to clone a child using standard DNA extraction/replacement. This time, however, the child would be carried by a volunteer surrogate mother who had tried but failed through several early-term miscarriages to have a baby. It would be the surrogate's egg (with our implanted DNA), and she would keep the child. William and I supported this arrangement.

There were no lawyers involved as too many explanations would be required. The surrogate, a single woman, would tell doctors that she miraculously got pregnant the old-fashioned way, without naming the father, and deliver her baby. Will and I would then keep our distance from her so as not to influence (consciously or unconsciously) the child's development. There would be no hormone manipulation and no hint of its genetic background. Even the mother did not know exactly how her harvested and implanted egg had been invigorated, and she didn't care. In a sense, she wasn't a surrogate at all but simply an expectant mother.

William and I both carried the same "Y" chromosome; thus, the mother was informed that she would have a boy. And though we had been afflicted with gender identity disorder, there was little reason to believe that our clone would be so burdened. Many improbable things in an improbable sequence must happen inside the womb to create a psychologically feminized male. This new child should have a masculine gender identity.

Everything worked as planned, and there soon existed three genetically identical yet distinctly different human beings. A transwoman, a transman, and a newborn male who would grow up as a boy.

The mother was thrilled when she delivered a seven-pound baby at full term. I had arrived two months premature, and Will was three, so differences were already apparent. William and I would simply allow our descendant to grow into a fertile male who could spread our DNA naturally. We wanted the boy to have every possible chance for a non-transsexual life.

Predictably, the child would receive the kind of village and family love that is generally unavailable to our kind. And with the deepest and most heartfelt parental concern, based upon a two lifetimes of trans-psychosocial experience, William and Rachel Wintersmith, the DNA donors, prayed that our clone would become a man completely ignorant of gender dysphoria. With all possible love and devotion, we prayed that our clone would not become us.

"ALIENS ANONYMOUS"

"I'm Anthony."

"Hi, Anthony," said the group almost in unison.

"This is my first meeting," he continued. "Not sure I belong here...."

"Welcome," said an attractive woman, maybe 29 years old. "My name is Marian. You've come to the right place, and we're here to listen."

Anthony hesitated, but the desire to get things off his chest overpowered the indecision. "A lot of folks have told me I'm crazy," he said. "My parents when they sent me to a hospital. My wife before she left me. My boss before he fired me. And if I weren't crazy beforehand, that hospital and their Thorazine injections turned my brain temporarily to Jell-O." Anthony lowered his head, but the circle was quiet.

After 10 seconds, Marian said, "Please continue—if you're comfortable."

"I was pretty confused after time on the psych ward, so I brushed off college and started to bum around the country, sucking alcohol like grape juice, limited only by cash and what I could steal..., but nothing erased those memories. Anyway, after a year of sleeping under garbage bags, I crawled back to Mom and Dad, took my meds, finished college, and got married. Found a good a job as a software engineer. I stayed sober and kept to myself. Life was OK—except for the nightmares—and I still glance over my shoulder every time I feel atmospheric static or hear something like a… hovering sound." Anthony stopped. Now, he figured, they would eject him.

Nobody spoke. Anthony didn't know how twelve people could be so still.

"It's been rough at times. Anyhow, a little while back my wife said I seemed 'edgy.' I tell her I'm fine, but she won't buy it because my parents had already told her about my previous breakdown. Says nothing could change her love."

The room anticipated what was coming.

"The nightmares were driving me batty, so I decided to open—just a little. Showed her my Dodgers' cap lined with aluminum foil. She looked at me kind of strange, so I took her to the attic where I had laid down aluminum sheeting to protect the family. My wife ran downstairs and started crying. Said I had to see a psychiatrist again or she would take the boy and leave." Anthony stopped and his eyes began to water.

Marian stood, walked to the empty seat next to Anthony, placed her hand on his shoulder, and said, "We understand. We've been there."

"I have intimate knowledge of hospitals," said Anthony. "I'd rather be in prison—inmates can't be tortured with electroshock or Thorazine. The nurses called it a chemical lobotomy. Well, it's no joke. Even the aliens treated me better than that."

Anthony held his breath. When no one laughed, he continued.

"I came home from work two days later. The wife's car was gone along with the kid's toys and clothes. Most of her clothes too. There was a note." Anthony pulled a paper from his pocket and read: Please get help! I can't handle this abduction nonsense any longer, nor will I expose our son to it. Your parents support my decision, and I'll be staying with them until you return for proper medical treatment. Love, Jeanette.

"I was hurting so bad that I called in sick for a week. The company has a bereavement policy, so I figured it was OK. Would have been, too, but my boss invited me out for a hang-tough buddy night. Don't mean to brag, but I really know computer code. I think the boss wanted to cheer me up so I'd get back to the office. But after several shots and beer, I spilled the beans about my Nevada discovery. Or more precisely, the things that had discovered me."

Several members around the circle nodded.

"My boss wasn't drunk enough to handle that. He called next morning, all business, and I was canned. Said my personal belongings were packed and could be picked up at the front desk along with my final check. He suggested I might apply for a job with the Texas School Board because they were almost as crazy as me." Anthony seemed too calm, as if he were reading an old manuscript about irrelevant characters.

"So I climbed back into a bottle of bourbon and didn't leave the house for two weeks. I was too drunk to answer the phone last Friday, but when I got around to pushing the button next morning, a voice said: If you're at rock bottom, if you're willing to talk, and if you're ready to believe in aliens without letting it destroy you, go to 9585 Tudor Avenue at 7 o'clock next Wednesday. Wear your Dodgers' cap.

"That sobered me up like the Sunday School. I recognized the address as a church where they held various 'loser meetings.' Sorry, but that's how I thought about these groups. Now I'm here." He looked around the room. "I suspect that the message came from someone at tonight's meeting, but I don't recognize anybody."

"We're glad you came," said Marian.

"The voice didn't belong to you," said Anthony, "but I'll recognize it when I hear it. Unless the caller wants to fess up."

"You won't hear that voice tonight," said Marian. "Besides, most of our members use synthesizers over the phone. Never know who's listening. Some people in this room paid a heavy price for their encounters, and we've learned to second guess every move and every motive."

Several nodded.

"So you're all crazy, too?" asked Anthony, sympathetically.

Marian leaned close to Anthony and pulled down the collar of her blouse to reveal an almost invisible one-inch scar shaped like a crescent moon. "Is this crazy?"

Anthony stood, felt a pulse in his throat, and began to run. Unfortunately, he forgot that the door of the basement swung in, not out. When he hit its reinforced bulk at an adrenaline enriched pace, Anthony's forehead impacted the heavy oak and he slumped to the floor.

Anthony was semiconscious for several minutes. People hovered around him. They appeared to be speaking, but the sounds didn't make sense. Soon he began to recognize words.

"Anthony," asked Marian, "are you all right? Don't be afraid."

"Fine," said Anthony, with some embarrassment, rubbing his forehead. "I'll go home now."

"I wish you wouldn't," said Marian. "You might have a concussion. Our doctor should check you. And remember, we've all been through the experience."

"Aliens are not real," said Anthony, remembering his lines from the hospital. He tried to stand, and a young man and old woman reached under each arm and lifted gently. He climbed to his feet. "I'll see my psychiatrist tomorrow."

"The first step," said Marian, "is to admit that you are powerless and your life has become unmanageable. By letting go, you can turn an alien encounter into something powerful, beneficial. Others have."

"Thank you," said Anthony, politely, steadying himself. "I'll leave now."

Forty minutes later, when Anthony arrived at an empty house, there was another message on the answering machine. When you acknowledge reality in socially acceptable ways, you'll rise above it. Life is possible after abduction. We meet again in one month.

Anthony did not recognize the voice. It wasn't Marian or anyone who spoke at the meeting, yet there was a hint of familiarity. He prepared a light snack of cheese and crackers, debated his next move, and then decided to call his wife. Anthony's mother answered the phone.

Hi, Mom. I'd like to speak with Jeanette."

"She's still pretty upset, very hurt. It might be better if…."

"No, bring her to the phone. It's OK, Mom. Trust me."

"Just a moment."

Anthony heard his mother call in the background. "Jeanette, Sweetie. It's him."

Jeanette picked up the bedroom extension.

"Wait until Mom hangs up," said Anthony. At the familiar click, he continued. "Everything's gonna be fine. I started group therapy tonight, and tomorrow I'll call Dr. Elliot's office. He'll probably put me on Prozac, which I hate, but you're worth it."

Jeanette stammered, fearing to hope, fearing to despair. "I'm sure you mean it, but…I need time to think. Your mother warned me about relapses, which she calls falling off the Spaceship Lollipop."

"Won't be any relapses. I'll take electroshock or Prozac or both, whatever the doctor prescribes. Scout's honor. Anything to bring our family back together."

"Oh, Anthony, I love you so much, and I want to believe you. Listen, the baby's already asleep, but I'll pack a few things in the morning and drive home before you leave for work. We can stop by later for the rest of my clothes."

Anthony braced himself. "I…was fired."

"No!"

"It's OK. I pretty sure Jonathan will hire me back. I just need to offer him the same reassurances about treatment. After I see Dr. Elliot, I'll call Jon and straighten things out. I designed most of our software, so the company needs me."

Jeanette's doubt returned, but she tried to be optimistic. "Maybe it will be all right."

"So you'll return home?"

"Yes…," said Jeanette, "on second thought, since you don't have to work, come here about 10 o'clock tomorrow morning. You can help pack the baby's toys."

"Great. I love you, Honey."

"I love you, too."

When Anthony called Dr. Elliot's office next morning, he discovered that Elliot was on a European vacation, would not return for three weeks, and his calendar was already pre-booked with appointments for the first ten days. The receptionist was familiar with Anthony's case and said, "I can ask the nurse-practitioner about a prescription. And we have an on-call psychiatrist available if this is an emergency."

"No," said Anthony, actually relieved, "I'd rather wait for Elliot. But a prescription should help until I see him."

"OK. I've booked an appointment with Dr. Elliot for Tuesday, June 7, at four o'clock." The receptionist knew that there was a "suicide watch" in Anthony's file. "I'll have the prescription relayed to your pharmacy, but if you begin to feel anxious or depressed, call us immediately."

"I will," said Anthony.

Four weeks later, Anthony went again to the Aliens Anonymous meeting. Marian greeted him at the door. "I'm happy that you came. We often rotate venues among the members' homes, but since we hoped you'd return, we stayed here. Welcome."

"Thanks," said Anthony. "I have a few questions."

"Considering your previous outburst, it might be better if you just listen tonight."

"Yes," said a man who approached from behind. "Park your butt in a chair, take the cotton out of your ears, and stuff it in your mouth. If you shut up and listen, you won't think you're so special anymore."

Marian scowled, but not enough to suit Anthony.

"One of our more prescriptive members," said Marian. "He had a particularly hard time as a newcomer. Recommends tough love."

"Well, I'm not much for anything crammed down my throat," said Anthony, "but I can listen—for a while."

"Fine," said Marian. "We'll start as soon as everyone takes a seat. Only eight tonight. There was a recent event near Alamogordo. Four members volunteered to be of service there."

Anthony nodded, poured himself a cup of coffee, and sat in a circle of nine folding chairs. The coffee was good, restaurant quality, brewed by a first-generation Mr. Coffee that looked like an electrical hazard waiting to become a fire.

When the final member arrived, Marian said, "Let's get started."

Several people acknowledged Anthony with "welcome back," and he thanked them in turn.

"Who will begin?" asked Marian.

"I'd like to share," said Tough Love. "You all know me, a complete basket case when I showed up at the doorstep, and I'd be dead or insane without the folks in this room. The most important thing I learned was that my abductors weren't in it for kicks. They had a higher purpose along with their higher power. They were learning what makes us tick and, especially, how we view ourselves. Seemed like nice chaps for the most part, but when they sat me in a viewing port and swung past Venus, I couldn't figure why they'd waste time so I could play Interplanetary Tourist. Then they took me to remote sections of Africa and let me watch their doctors in action. Well, as for my previously self-satisfied medical arrogance, I felt about on par with chimpanzees. I watched real doctors repair a cleft pallet without scalpel or anesthesia. They regrew tissue before my eyes, sculpting that child's face into an angel while she played with a box of Legos. Then they let her keep the Legos. Of course, some procedures involve cutting and stitching, mostly when they're training humans to help in remote corners of the globe, but their surgeries were light years beyond mine." Tough Love shook his head. "I had thought I was a Ferrari. I had operated in some of the most prestigious hospitals in the world, but my best work compared as a failed butcher against the aliens. I hope you can appreciate why I couldn't practice medicine after that experience. It felt presumptuous to even call myself a doctor."

Tough Love regrouped. "Anyway, it's good to be here, good to be alive, and good to be practicing again. I don't pretend to be a hotshot surgeon anymore, just someone who wants to help people. That's what our friends gave me!"

"Thanks for sharing," said Marian, along several members of the group, which somehow sounded like "Amen."

Another spoke up. "I'm Andrea. My tale is different, and I'm still trying to figure whether the end justifies the means.

"I was on a solo trip near White Sands, hiking back toward my car at dusk. After a while, one of the early evening stars seemed to be following me, and the abduction was over before I realized…anything. I never lost consciousness, never seemed to move from where I was to where I found myself, and don't remember passing through any door or portal." Andrea giggled. "The only comparison I can think of is Beam me up, Scotty."

Several people smiled and nodded.

"I landed gently on a cool surface in darkness. There was a soft hum, like an electric current, and I used my hands to feel around. I sensed an oval room with no doors or windows, so there was nothing to do but wait. After maybe an hour, the humming increased, and I felt sleepy.

"I woke up in my car just as the sun peeked above the horizon, but to my surprise, I was almost nine months pregnant with no memory of anything after falling asleep. There were vague nightmares about aliens touching me, and I think the baby's kick awakened me in the car.

"So I drove twelve hours straight from White Sands to my home in Claremont, stopping only to fill up with gas and use the bathroom. Then I went to bed, tired and scared, figuring to wake up from a bad dream. When I found myself still pregnant the next morning, I called my gynecologist only to discover that there was an appointment scheduled that same day with another doctor."

Andrea shook her head. "According to the office files, I had visited this other doctor four times. I swear I had never met her before, yet she seemed to know everything about me. When I questioned why my regular doctor wasn't on the case, she said, 'Your pregnancy is complicated and I am a specialist. You will go into labor next Friday at five o'clock. Please come to the office by four and everything will be ready.'

"Afterward, I wanted to call the FBI, but realized that there was no explanation that would make sense—even to myself. I went home, cried, and called my employer to say that I needed a few days off. Another shock. They said I had six more weeks of maternity leave. How did they know I was having a baby? I didn't know until waking up at White Sands.

"I figured the company might be part of the conspiracy, or whatever was going on, so I got really scared. Besides, it was easier to convince myself that I had somehow forgotten about requesting maternity leave or visiting that doctor. Talk about denial!"

Several people laughed.

"Anyway, I stayed home, watched TV, ate a lot, and thought about New Mexico. If my belly hadn't been the size of beach ball, I would've tried to retrace my steps back to the star chase, but I couldn't walk around the block without needing a bathroom, so I waited until Friday. Then, like an obedient child, I went to the doctor's office at four o'clock. Labor started on schedule. There was no anesthesia, yet I delivered a healthy girl in less than twenty minutes without any pain. Then the doctor, herself, drove me home with the baby, and like magic, a full nursery had been set up in the spare bedroom.

"After I was sitting comfortably in the brand new rocking chair, the doctor said very calmly, 'Your little girl is special.' Then she talked about recombined DNA, stuff like that, and added, 'The child is a gift from our mutual friends at White Sands, but when I leave, the story belongs exclusively to you and your little girl. Nonetheless, I strongly recommend that your daughter study math and biophysics.'

"She wrote it down on a prescription pad, tore off the sheet, and handed it to me. I still have the paper. Then she gave me a small bottle of pills. 'Take one per day for ten days,' she said. 'The medication will pass into the child from your milk. Without it, your daughter's cells will reject the implanted DNA and she will die. After ten days, neither of you will need medication.' Then she left and I never saw her again. For a while, I felt like my baby was some kind of monster. I considered killing us both.

"That's when I got a message on my answering machine and came to one of these meetings. I learned that we should never forget the past or pretend it doesn't exist. That way lies madness."

Andrea paused briefly and said, "My little girl is now eleven years old. She starts college in September."

One week after the meeting, Anthony sat in Dr. Elliot's waiting room. At 4:15, the receptionist smiled and said, "The doctor will see you now."

Anthony entered Elliot's private space.

"Well, it's been a while since we've talked. How's the Prozac working?"

Anthony lied. "Fine. In fact, I'm a little embarrassed by all the trouble I caused."

"Yes, yes," said Elliot. "I heard there were some difficulties. Tell me what happened."

"I was having nightmares…about Nevada. I know we discussed that, how I was probably dehydrated and hallucinating in the desert, but my dreams obscured the logic and started to seem real. Next thing I know, my wife says I'm moody, and then I shock her with too much information…. But when Jeanette left me, it was worse than any alien dream, so I called your office."

"Wise decision," said Elliot. "And how have you been doing since?"

"Middle-road straight. I know it takes six weeks for the medication to really kick in, but my anxiety has almost disappeared, and the nightmares stopped in a few days."

"What else?"

"I swallowed some pride and got my job back. My boss likes me, and once I came down to earth, he was happy to re-hire me. Whatever people may think about my mental health, I know how to crunch data."

"Yes. I remember some your professors thought quite highly of your intellect—erratic but smart, they said."

Anthony nodded.

And?" asked Elliot, sensing there was more.

"I went to a meeting, some kind of reality group. Helped me get a grip on things. In fact, I feel better than I have in a long time. Even Jeanette noticed."

"How long have you been back at work?"

"Four weeks."

"How long has your family been reunited?"

"Almost five."

"And what do you do for recreation?"

"Stay close to home. Read. Watch TV with Jeanette. My boy's almost three, and we like to play together. I bring work home, too. The job carries a lot of responsibility, and it's no secret that writing computer code has a calming effect on me. Some people like crossword puzzles. I like flowcharts and software."

"Are you worried about the future?"

"No. That may sound strange, given my medical background, but this could be the happiest I've ever been."

Elliot scribbled a few notes on his yellow pad, speaking as he wrote. "Good. Good. Now, I don't think there's a need for individual therapy at this time, but I want you to continue the Prozac. Make an appointment for next month and we'll see where you are. If the nightmares or paranoia return, come sooner. Otherwise, just keep doing what you're doing. Many people would envy your state of mind."

"Thanks, Doc."

Anthony went to his third meeting of Aliens Anonymous. That wasn't the official name, of course, though several members had been in other twelve-step programs, but it was the label Anthony used. He liked the people, too.

"Hi, Anthony," said Marian. "Looks like you're becoming a regular."

"It's good to be here," said Anthony. "Good to be alive."

"Who will begin?" asked Marian, often the unofficial chair of the meeting.

An old woman who had not spoken previously began. "Last time, we shared so Anthony might understand that he's not alone regarding alien encounters. Maybe it's time to explore the details of his abduction. He hasn't offered much, but we can be certain that his experience is part of a greater purpose."

Tough Love groaned just loud enough that people heard. Marian gave a sharp glance and said, "Please, no comments while people are sharing."

The old woman continued. "My name is Laura, and most of you weren't alive in 1953, when I was 17, beautiful, and stupid. Thought I was too cool for book learning, and I probably dated every cute student or teacher in the district, which really means I had sex with everybody I could lay hands on. Now, I wasn't really stupid. Just wouldn't be bothered with anything but a good time.

"I started dating this young college man. There was something special about him, mostly because he took a special interest in me, and we went to Palomar to see the new 200-inch telescope. A beautiful area in those days. Later, he showed me his ship.

"I didn't wake up like Andrea, pregnant with a genius child. Nor did I see aliens work medical magic in Africa. Mr. Starship-at-Mount-Palomar just provided a picnic lunch and informed me that my mission would be to ensure, in nine years, a certain U.S. President and Russian Premier didn't go to war. I was to become the most important call girl in history, though Mr. Palomar didn't phrase it like that. He said, 'Earth is headed for a nuclear holocaust. You will serve as emotional advisor to the forthcoming President, relaying messages when needed, and ensuring that international tensions do not escalate toward a missile launch. If that happens, we can't help you. Earth will be lost.'

"How he knew in 1953 that the Cuban Missile Crisis was coming in 1962, I'll never guess. Anyway, the aliens tweaked parts of my body similarly to Tough Love's African demonstration. I was still me, but physically perfect, and Palomar sent me to some kind of intellectual charm school to make sure I would impress a certain senator and, ultimately, be in the right place at the right time. So there I was, right there in Washington, when Mr. Khrushchev blinked—bless him. After the Missile Crisis was defused, Palomar told me I could retire, which is how I ended up in Southern California.

"And I know what Anthony's thinking. How did that man inspire devout cooperation from such a fun-loving, rebellious girl? Well, he was the best alien encounter I ever had, and I would have slept with every senator in the country if he'd asked. Later, with a considerable bank account, I went to college, finished graduate school, and taught astronomy at a local community college. The aliens did something inside my head; and while this girl is no genius, I haven't had an unhappy day since Palomar. Anyway, I completed my mission. The October missiles did not fly, and Palomar said it was mostly because of me.

"I figured Palomar was exaggerating, but I didn't care. Those were the best years of my life, and the sex was out of this world."

Laura shook her head and sighed. "The following year, after that dark November in Dallas, the aliens handed my life back to me, and I never saw Palomar again. Perhaps, Anthony, you might share your experiences."

Anthony nodded. "I think I should restart the Prozac, which I stopped taking after the last meeting. Now the nightmares are haunting me again."

"Stay off the meds," warned Laura. "The dreams are important!"

Before bed, Anthony looked at the Prozac bottle. He had slept only three hours the last two nights, for as soon as he closed his eyes, the dreams came. Anthony opened the container and removed one of the familiar blue pills. "I will not return to Nevada."

As he moved the pill toward his lips, the phone rang. He hesitated but answered. That strangely familiar voice said, "Follow your dreams."

Anthony took the pill. The following night, he took another.

The motions of life were comforting. Anthony went to the office and came home. Jeanette seemed happy, and their boy was a bundle of energy. It had been six months since Anthony's last Aliens Anonymous gathering, and as he drove to an appointment with Dr. Elliot, he almost wondered whether the whole group might have been a hallucination.

"How are you?" asked Elliot when they sat down together.

"Good, Doctor. Real good."

"Any concerns?"

"I had a slip six months ago, which we discussed. Stopped taking my medication. Soon, the nightmares were keeping me awake, and I was apparently hearing phone messages that didn't exist. But I found strength to fight back, restarted the Prozac, and within four weeks, I was sleeping like a baby. My wife is great. Family's great. Work is even better."

"Hmm."

Anthony sensed something on Elliot's part. "Not to say everything's perfect, but there are no problems worth mentioning."

"I'm not sure I believe in life without problems. What bothers you?"

"Well, I was kind of enjoying that discussion group I told you about. The people were quirky, but nice, and they helped me through a crisis. I just didn't want to get overly involved, overly dependent."

"Are you through the crisis?"

Anthony nodded. "Pretty sure."

"How sure?"

"Ninety percent."

"And where do you plan to go from here?" asked the doctor.

"I'm still thinking I don't need psychotherapy."

"Agreed."

"There is one minor issue...."

"Yes?"

"It's embarrassing, but the Prozac makes it difficult to have sex. I'm not particularly motivated and...the equipment doesn't always hold up. Jeanette is a little worried about it."

"Most men would be concerned, too."

"Yes, but to tell the truth, I'm more scared of the dreams than a reduction in sack time."

Hmm. Your emotional attachment to the medication concerns me—as though you're afraid not to take it. But we can tune the therapeutic dose."

Anthony seemed skeptical. "You're the Doc."

"Let's cut the dose by half," said Elliot, still writing. "You've been on Prozac for seven months and are doing well. The reduction should improve your sex life, and you might be surprised that the nightmares don't return."

Anthony spoke evenly. "If you say so, but I'm not really afraid of the dreams. I'm afraid of losing my grip on reality. The last time that happened, I woke up in a hospital."

"Don't worry," Elliot waved his hand, "I won't allow that to happen again."

Anthony returned to what he assumed would be his final AA meeting. He at least owed them a goodbye.

The group welcomed him, and as the discussion started, Anthony reported, "I won't be attending anymore, but I wanted to thank you."

"I'm afraid," said Marian, "that you still don't understand what happened to you in Nevada."

"Dehydration, heat stroke, and hallucinations," said Anthony, firmly. "But I've been on Prozac for eight months and I'm in control again."

Laura shook her head. "You're missing the point, Anthony. ET doesn't accept resignations. You were selected for a reason, and the dreams won't stop until you abide by it."

"Medication trumps the nightmares," said Anthony, "and I've been dream-free, well, very nearly dream-free, for six months. And despite the weird phone calls, I'm doing well and the doctor even reduced the Prozac." He leaned back in the chair as if that should settle the matter.

"The dreams won't stop," said Laura, "but only hover for a while."

"Well, I'd rather take advice from a trained psychiatrist than an interstellar hooker," said Anthony, immediately regretting his crosstalk.

Laura answered without animosity. "I found peace when the aliens were finished with me, and I can sleep without medication or nightmares."

Anthony was silent.

"We can't help interpret your dreams," said Laura, "because you haven't told us the story. I told you mine, enabling that cheap shot, but I'm not angry. I know my truth, and if you aren't driven mad by the ongoing psychological struggle, you may come to understand yours. Otherwise, you'll eventually need so much Prozac there won't be anything left of you."

Marian broke in, gently. "Anthony, please come back to the meetings. We all depend on each other."

"Right," said Tough Love. "We've all sat in your chair. Phone messages? From a strangely familiar voice? Wake up, newcomer! The damned voice is yours. Programmed inside your head by the same folks who put the dreams there." Tough Love pointed at Anthony. "You scientific jerks are the worst for denial, and I was the same way. But the aliens are a power greater than both our egos. They encode brainwaves like you encode computers, and that voice will appear whenever you need it, fool. Sometimes a voice in your head; sometimes a phone message you leave yourself."

"Can't be," said Anthony. "It's not possible."

Marian removed a portable cassette recorder from her handbag and placed her hand gently on Anthony's arm. "Listen," she said. "It's a tape from the first night you came here. I shouldn't have recorded without your knowledge, but I suspected this might be helpful down the road in your case." She hit play.

Anthony had forgotten that, before voicemail was ubiquitous, people often didn't recognize themselves on a tape recorder. That's why the voice sounded familiar. That's why the messages had been so compelling. He had been calling himself.

"I'll be damned," said Anthony, shaking his head. "I'll be god damned."

"Light travels 186,000 miles per second," said Anthony at his twelfth meeting of Aliens Anonymous, "or about a foot per nanosecond. That's fast, but not infinite, and computer performance is governed by that speed limitation. So making a smaller system increases efficiency because the signals travel over shorter distances. I have a design floating around my head that, if it works, will revolutionize processors." Anthony smiled. "Physics texts say this kind of engineering is impossible, that there would be no way to insulate the pathways at these incredibly small scales, but the textbooks don't have alien-inspired designs. Sure, engineers can prove mathematically that bumblebees can't fly, but they go right on buzzing through backyards everywhere. And so will my new proto-neural chips.

"I plan to talk with my boss about starting a laboratory. If he doesn't cooperate, I'll do it myself because I'm going to build biologically insulated circuits."

Anthony smiled and nodded to the room. "As you suspected, the proto-idea came to me in Nevada. The aliens didn't talk much, but they let me hang around the ship's control room. Despite my fear, and despite early adrenaline shakes from trying to outrun a starship on foot, I was mesmerized by the interfacing of the aliens and their machines. They seemed to control some functions telepathically, which got me wondering about sentient biomechanical systems. And those dreams I kept fighting! They provided greater and greater inspiration. The same organic insulators that keep our brains from misfiring can likely protect cybernetic pathways." Anthony looked to his left and said, "Andrea, when your daughter finishes college, I'd like her to consider working for our company to help shape my theoretical concepts into working prototypes." He smiled. "I suspect that the prescription you received fourteen years ago—math and biophysics—was meant to bring us together."

Anthony paused and spoke through clenched teeth. "The hospital! If it hadn't been for those reasonable doctors with their stabilizing chemicals, I might have already finished this project." Anthony looked around the room, letting go of his anger as quickly as it had come. "But I'm one of you, now. Thank you, Marian, Andrea, and Laura—even Tough Love over there. Thanks for helping me understand the aliens' higher power and purpose. There will be no more bending of my steps."

He picked up his Dodgers' cap, pulled out the aluminum foil, crumpled it into a ball, and threw it into a trashcan.

"The things we can believe," said Anthony, shaking his head. Then he tossed old Dodger Blue to a newcomer in the circle and spoke with authority. "Take it one day at a time, Sport, and listen to the stories in this room. Recovery happens here."

DEATH AFTER DYING

I hate working the night shift at the morgue because corpses won't leave me alone.

The human brain can still "think" for five to seven days after death, given a temperature range of 35-48 degrees Fahrenheit and assuming there has been no significant head trauma. Post-mortem brainwaves were discovered 12 years ago, but it took a decade to learn how to tap into the deceased's neuro-system and translate the activity into comprehensible language. Dead folks no longer possess the five senses, so computers must convert their subliminal neural energy into auditory signals the operator can decipher and then transfigure return communications into bioelectric impulses for the deceased. This involves some 1200 sensors and stimulators in composite helmets for the corpse and technician. To me the apparatus seems more magic than science, but it works.

Morticians scan all of the newly departed, who often carp about what clothes to wear in the casket; how the hair, manicure, and makeup should be done; which is their good side (the homely of both sexes are the worst for expecting beautification); the coffin that's right for their personality; who should deliver the eulogy. Sometimes they want to be cremated after the family has spent $18,000 making burial arrangements. Dead folks can object to more or less everything, including death itself.

My job at a supervising mortician was almost better when corpses kept their ideas to themselves and I could simply help get them ready for the casket, but if a body turns nastily annoying, I just unplug the translator and do things my way. Stiffs can't file a complaint, so when in doubt, it's best to follow the next-of-kin's instructions and/or use my own judgment. The dead have no legal rights and can't be represented by lawyers; otherwise, we'd probably never get anybody underground until attorneys burned through the estate trying to carry out erratic last wishes from a fading brain. Besides, the post-mortem decoders are so intricate and expensive that only trained undertakers, police departments, or elite research labs have access anyway; and funeral parlors must please the living, not the dead. Surviving spouses, parents, and/or adult children decide on what services to purchase.

Direct communications between relatives and cadavers were quickly outlawed—early attempts at post-mortem family conferences often turned caustic because dead folks may harbor long-held resentments or secrets that should be buried with them—so the translating mortician has a lot of power about what is filtered between the deceased and the living. We can soften questions and responses, withhold information about affairs, or maybe even coax hostile corpses or survivors toward a kind of détente. New morticians now receive mandatory training in post-mortem diplomacy.

The CIA tried to use the decoders on dead spies and terrorists, but you can't beat information out of a corpse. "He" or "she" can't feel pain and doesn't generally care about contemporary threats or government espionage. The police, on the other hand, frequently receive details from victims about their murders that lead to speedy arrests and convictions. Homicide rates in industrialized nations dropped 40% after introduction of neurotranslators. Still, many murders are crimes of passion or ideology, unaffected by fears of punishment, so there's probably no way to lower the rate further via the decoders, but at least law enforcement is pretty quick to get killers off the streets. On the downside, some "pros" have learned to mangle the victim's brain enough to disable post-mortem revelations.

Despite the downsides, I enjoy talking with some of the friendlier bodies, especially about life, whether they believe in heaven or hell, or what they would do differently if they were 20 again. Many are thoughtful and soothing and wise, but I wonder if they hold back bits of knowledge acquired since dying. I'm pretty sure the dead are keeping secrets.

That said, some corpses are about as subtle as Henry VIII and seem to believe that white lights and mist bestow absolute authority. If they get too abusive, I disconnect and roll them into the refrigerator to cool down. They can't even cry about it. For a couple neo-fascists who wanted to sing the praises of hate and Hitler, I considered microwaving their brains but restrained myself—believe me; some stiffs really are better off dead. Executing a corpse is a little over the top for me, so I just move them to the cooler for silent harangues.

Then there are others who don't want to bother with talk-talk. One 62-year-old woman was paralyzed from the waist down at 20 when hit by a drunk driver and later developed rheumatoid arthritis in her hands; she died from an "accidental" overdose of pain killers and alcohol. When I plugged her into the translator, she said, "I mean no offense, but please leave me alone to enjoy a week without pain, which is all I've wanted for 42 years. So now I can float through the universe without discomfort or desire or Demerol, and I plan to enjoy every second of it, uninterrupted, until my brain quits completely. Over and out." She never responded to any questions after that, and her P-M brain waves shifted to a Zen-like alpha-theta pattern. I left her alone but monitored the translator in case she changed her mind. Peculiarly, her cold-wave neural output ended at a single moment on day six; it typically flutters for several hours before flat lining, and I'm starting to believe that the deceased have limited control over their shutdown. If you ask me, Ms. Paralytic Silence found something nice in the afterlife (better than talking with me) and latched onto it.

A centenarian workaholic billionaire, with fine gentility, asked if I would read Tom Sawyer to him before his post-mortem functions ended. "I want to discover the profits of childhood," he said. I liked him immediately. Anyway, because the deceased can't hear auditory sounds and I didn't have the time to "speak" an entire book via the translator, with advice from my techno-geek girlfriend, I improvised a patch job to play a digital recording of Twain's book through his decoder helmet. When I tested the opening pages and asked if it worked, the old man said, "Aunt Polly is a little loud, but the jam tastes great. Notch down the volume, tune up the treble, and let her run." And I did. When the recording was finished, my billionaire buddy said he planned to become Becky Thatcher in 1852, thanked me, and signed off almost as abruptly as Ms. Silence, but there were several noticeable changes in the neuro-electrical patterns, especially around the hypothalamic area, as if he might have actually changed identities. Then the translator delivered a mild electric surge through my connector-helmet just before the old man clicked into extinction. A little disconcerting at first, but I soon felt an incredibly durable euphoria that lasted two days. I think the old man somehow did this as a thank you.

There was one especially brutalized victim, Matt, who visited my table. Well, his head did, and we talked for hours. The police never found the body, and the victim didn't know where it was buried, but they did arrest the two lunatics who killed him. They were high on who knows what, Matt was gay, so what other reason did they need? Despite having his body dismembered and carted off to Neverland, Matt is not angry. A little sad because he left behind a husband who had to suffer the demise of a spouse, but Matt himself? The guy is Gandhi, Mother Teresa, and Albert Schweitzer in one braincase. He is forgiving and smart. I told him that I was pissed about what happened, even if he wasn't, and hoped that the killers ended up with me on my table. I'd fry their brains slow, one section at a time, like shutting down HAL in 2001. Matt's head replied, "People are basically good; just accept imperfection as part of the human journey. I see great things ahead. Trust me."

I suggested that some imperfections deserve an acidic torture chamber. He merely commented that he'd already experienced that kind of treatment and could not recommend it. "Besides," said Matt, "I was deader in the closet than out, even if coming out ultimately led to my murder. The greatest risk is hiding from oneself. Tell my husband that I loved him from the moment we met, and it is criminal that I tried so desperately not to. Thank, god, I failed in this effort."

I assured him that I was listening, and Matt's severed head, with his curly red-hair cropped at half an inch, talked for 11 days, the longest post-mortem function on record. The family waited three months for Matt's funeral because they wanted to find the rest of him, but the murderers had been so inebriated during their crime that they couldn't remember where the parts were buried. Finally, after three months, they put Matt's head in cryostorage, hoping that someday he could be reunited with everything from the neck down.

A few bodies come in that are technically brain dead because of cranial injury: auto accidents, electrocution, blunt-force trauma, high fever, stroke. But in some instances, even when there should be no neurological function, electroencephalographic fragments survive. Mortality is strange, more so than I imagined before the translators. I thought dead was dead. But most of the deceased apparently don't relish the nightfall. This might be related to lingering existential sensitivities or memory tracks, and I'm almost certain that there are multiple levels of spiritual transience that the living don't understand. Not that I have enough science background to prove or disprove my hunches. But P-M brain functions were discovered only 12 years ago. What will we discover 12 years hence?

Take Julie Cerrillo, a woman who was beaten to death with a claw hammer by her husband. Her skull was smashed; the ooze from the parietal and occipital lobes resembled red oatmeal; but the frontal and temporal regions were undamaged, and she and I managed a conversation. Julie said her memory had suddenly become photographic, and she analyzed each moment of her life covering one week per second. "Looking back," she said, "it was inevitable that my husband would kill me at the prescribed time, place, and manner." She added, "One must be unfettered by dimensional orientations to see undistorted cosmic rhythms."

Don't ask me about "cosmic rhythms." Don't know what they are, and I don't want to know about Julie's so called "inevitable death." It messes with my notions of freewill.

Julie tried to explain: "There is discrete port-mortem knowledge, but because I can't physically act in my lifeless form, I must invent another that can." She paused briefly. "Invent isn't the right word. Alternate forms are and were always available; I just couldn't see them before dying."

I worried that the brain trauma corrupted our conversation, but her certainty and optimism were contagious. I asked if I could do anything for her, and she asked whether the decoder might be patched into the internet because she wanted to explore the world, something her husband never permitted. Again with my geek-love's help, I did my best jury-rig a web connection without knowing for sure whether Julie actually got out of the mortuary. Four weeks later it was obvious that she did because I received a $25,000 check from MIT for "consulting services" along with a thank-you note to me and "Julie Pneumonic" for remotely increasing efficiency in their operational and telecommunications networks. The campus energy savings alone for the next two years would approach six figures. The FBI also praised Julie and me via email for helping to solve a cold case by flagging lost evidentiary computer files.

Julie's recorded P-M functions ended after only four days, but I suspect she's still out there, traveling through circuits or on light waves to exotic destinations. MIT even offered me a job for being so brilliant with computers. What a laugh. Without Julie, I'm just a sympathetic Luddite mortician who has trouble grasping all the functions on her smartphone.

There have been 631 people on my tables since the translators became operational. Upgrades are due in six months, and rumors suggest that the new equipment might be able to produce holographic images. I'm not sure society needs this, but it might be interesting to see what corpses see.

Sure, some bodies are crusty and lack manners, but they're easy to unplug. Most are beyond animosity, are hard to offend, and seem content to enjoy a few final days of brain activity. Many have shown me great charity and sympathy and wisdom. I almost look forward to my own post-mortem conversations and insights, and I am certainly no longer afraid. Metastasized breast cancer is taking me down that road sooner than planned, maybe another 18 months.

I wonder what I'll discover during my tenure on a stainless steel table with no physical limitations or desires or chemo. There should be five to seven days to find out, and if my gracious predecessors are correct, this wonder might stretch into a contemplative and experiential universe without end.

THE MIMIC

M1: I've got you!

M2: On the contrary, I have you. Every cell, every memory, every mark, every joy.

M1: Sure, we may look alike, but even identical twins undergo fetal mutations that set them apart. I plan to find out who or what you are.

M2: That implies I'm the one handcuffed to the bedrail. But in reality, I woke up first and handcuffed you—and you're a mimic.

M1: Ha! I've read "Who Goes There?" and won't be confused. I'll test your blood. You are likely an alien bent on infecting my world.

M2: Nonsense. It was you that wanted a new life on a new planet. Somehow I was selected to fashion a human body using my DNA. A neat trick, but you made one big mistake. You should have killed me and disposed of the physical evidence before trying to assume my identity!

M1: I already said I won't be confused. If you own every memory and mark, you didn't just build a genetic blueprint; you copied me from the here and now. That's different, and that's why you're missing an appendix. I examined the surgical scar.

M2: Re-directing our conversation won't work either—and appendicitis is a common human affliction. Now listen. I am Jennifer Jane Callaway, 24 years old, 120 pounds, 5 feet 7 inches, blonde, athletic, smart, size ten, and no pushover.

M1: I'm Jennifer Jane Callaway, etc., etc. Your claim is derived from a pretended reality.

M2: Fool! I earned all those memories that you merely absorbed. So please uncuff me, brew a pot of coffee, and let's talk like civilized beings. We're not morning people. We need caffeine.

M1: If I turn you loose, you would probably murder me.

M2: Oh? You have experience with these situations? By whose authority do aliens kill? And for what purpose? We own a gun, so why not shoot me now and claim sole identity as Jennifer Jane? I suspect that's why I am the one who's bound and helpless.

M1: All creatures have the right to self-defense.

M2: Of course we do, yet my position is the more vulnerable one.... These handcuffs are painful, by the way, and we don't like for living things to suffer.

M1: I am truly sorry about your discomfort. Please extend your finger for a few drops of blood.

M2: Here's my longest finger, but the test will fail. You're the mimic, and neither of us has blood that is distinguishable under a microscope or that will flee from a hot needle. We are already Jennifer.

M1: I'll just verify if you don't mind. Then there'll be no pretense about who belongs on Earth—and who doesn't.

M2: Well, we each have a sore finger, but you poked mine deeper. That little bit of malice is surprising. I thought we were above that.

M1: Apologies. And you were right. No physiological differences.

M2: Sounds affirming. So, you came to Earth and replicated my body. I suggest that you go on a walkabout, explore the planet, and have some fun. There's no way I can harm you. Who would believe such a story? Just unlock the bracelets and go. Our secret is safe, and life can be pleasant as long as you avoid con artists and bad liquor.

M1: Earth is my home. This is my house. You're the one scheduled for departure.

M2: Not likely, and don't forget. I know you won't harm another human.

M1: But a mimic might.

M2: We believe that superior civilizations breed superior intellect, and superior intellects are peaceful. If I'm an alien, I arrived from an advanced culture to recreate Jennifer Jane Callaway. By your own logic, I would not hurt myself. If you are the alien, I doubt you'll injure a sentient creature. Hell, we take spiders outdoors instead of killing them in the house. And we hate spiders!

M1: I wish you had mimicked a tarantula. Then I could toss you gently through the window and forget this mess.

M2: Maybe it's not a mess at all. If you are an alien fabricator with a trapdoor motives, you'll find only a hatchway leading to a corridor that circles back to yourself. I already suggested coffee and conversation. Unless you murder me, the best course of action at this point is dialogue—which is almost always the best course of action. We have much to discuss.

M1: You're really starting to piss me off. Nobody consulted me before hijacking my personhood, and with two Jennifers, the value of each is decreased. Or rather, one of us gained something from nothing and the other lost something from what she was.

M2: Living beings are not divisible, and the alien mimic existed before the replication. As a result, we are both unique and identical. I'm also sensing new telepathic abilities between us; thus, our memories might well remain synchronized. Think of it. An ability to experience life at double speed. Perhaps I should even thank you for my victimization.

M1: You're a fraudster distorting reality, and I must be certain you are not a danger to my planet…. Wait here!

M2: The handcuffs offer me no other option.

M1 (opens a drawer and holds up pistol): This is a .38 revolver with soft-point cartridges.

M2: It's my weapon, and I know what gas-propelled bullets do. But more important, I know what you're capable of and what you aren't.

M1: Don't doubt for a moment, not for a moment, that I won't protect humanity from invaders. Soldiers must sometimes employ ruthless methods in keeping the peace, and I can't risk the safety of Earth on your account.

Maybe you're harmless, and maybe not.

M2: Do you want to destroy a planet? Any planet?

M1: Don't be stupid!

M2: Then you have the answer. If there were danger, you would pose it, and since you apparently have no malicious intent, Earth is safe. Mostly, you're trying to rationalize the murder of one Jennifer because you're uncomfortable with two. Identical twins don't generally hate or kill each other. I wonder if a spark from Machiavelli lurks inside your extraterrestrial brain.

M1: You've never seen sisters fight!? Maybe not hatred, but definitely not pretty. Besides I'm not sure I even like you.

M2: Self-hatred is disreputable and unbecoming, so put down the gun before there is an accidental premeditated death.

M1: I grew up around firearms and served in the military. What I do, I do with purpose.

M2 (sighs): OK, Miss Jennifer Jane Mimic. Press the muzzle between my eyes, squeeze the trigger, and see what happens. You're willful enough, sure, but you likewise possess an ethical certainty that makes killing impossible. We are not a danger to ourselves or others. We are the blessed peacemakers.

M1: I'm taking a chance. I don't understand why you duplicated me, but if you traveled from outside the solar system, you're probably civilized. I will, therefore, abide by my faith in extra-terrestrial intelligence and unlock the cuffs.

M2: That's good news, and there is no danger. I know that you won't kill me because you didn't. You trust I won't kill you because you are releasing me. Not sure why you copied me, but I'm as good as anyone…better than some.

M1: Don't try to deflect my preconceptions. You're the alien. Might as well admit it because I've already agreed to let you go.

M2: Maybe you're lying….

M1 (unlocking the cuffs): Shall I help you up? If I'm about to be murdered, I'd like to go out with a final good deed.

M2: Jennifer Jane shall not die today. But I could use assistance. This awkward position inflamed my very human muscles and joints. I'll recover, nonetheless.

M1 (gazing at M2 for a few seconds): Since we're both still alive, I'd say it's time to make coffee. Even in survival situations, I'm not really awake until downing at least one strong black cup. How do you want it?

M2: Same as you.

M1: Of course. I keep forgetting. There are jeans and sweatshirts in the closet—in case that's something you don't know. Get dressed while I brew. And the gun's on the dresser if you decide to shoot me and destroy the world.

M2: I favor reconciliation. I assume you feel the same. Are you an atheist?

M1: We both are.

M2: Good. Accepting personal responsibility for action increases the odds of exercising Christian values, which we both share. I'll get dressed.

M1: I'll start the coffee.

M1: It doesn't happen often, but I wanted a dash of cream today.

M2: Me, too.

M1: I knew that.

M2: I knew you knew it.

M1: Let's share the newspaper. I'll take the front page and you can have the financials.

M2: Nice of you. Should we buy two copies in the future?

M1: Waste of money. We can alternate who gets preferred sections, assuming you're staying, which has not yet been determined.

M2: Of course it has. You always wanted a sister. We can love and support one another, absorb two different books at the same time, and travel the world together to enjoy our company or travel separately to collect dual memories. And what about the career advantages? We might double our income with two jobs or share a single one, each taking a month on and then off. The health insurance policy can cover us both because no one, not even you, can tell us apart—unless we get sick at the same time in the same place. I think that with a twofold salary and prudent investing, we could retire in ten years.

M1: Love each other? Really?

M2: As you love yourself?

M1: And be real sisters?

M2: I will if you will.

M1: That's a lot to consider, but if this home is to be shared, I want the truth. Why did you come to Earth? What are your intentions?

M2: Again, only you can answer those questions.

M1: Seems to me that we have to trust one another if we are to move forward.

M2: We have to do something. And as for who's who, one might as well ask dual microchips which constitutes the real computer. You're a fine woman, Jennifer Jane Callaway. And my contemplating why you duplicated me merely confirms a noble choice.

M1: Totally talented tongue-twisting again. Haven't you accepted yet that I won't be confused?

M2: What about fused? Two extraterrestrials who've adopted Earth; two earthly Jennifers who've adopted each other; or vice versa. Incidentally, if you decide to stay, we'll need discernible names for friends. Perhaps you'll be Jenn, and I'll be Jane. Long lost twins who found themselves. What do you think?

M1: You're giving me a migraine. And I didn't appreciate the if-I-decide-to-stay remark. It's my house! Mine! I'll stay and decide who else stays!

M2: An apparent implication that you're neither leaving nor murdering.

M1: A viable hypothesis. But what if you get bored down the road and go to another planet in search of a new duplicatee?

M2: Remember William the Conqueror in 1066? He burned the ships so there was no going home. We must flip or flop as one unit from here on, and from what I know about you, Jennifer Jane does not flop without flipping herself upright, climbing back on the horse, and riding tall in the saddle. Isn't that why you mimicked me?

M1: One thing is for certain. I'm the Jenn in this relationship! I refuse to rebrand myself just because you created two of us. On this point, I am immovable.

M2: Very proud, very stubborn, and very lovable.

M1: No more than you, Sis!

M1 or M2: One of us died last night—a stroke—and I am weary with grief. For 47 years, Jenn and I, the most identical twins in the solar system, shared a daily life, the secrets of biological transmutation, and the joys and responsibilities in species annexation. After Thursday's funeral, I shall recall the ship (there was never a William-the-Conqueror moment), go back into space, and hibernate while searching for another suitable partner to mimic. But I'm already lonely without my dear, dear sister, and am almost looking forward to the millennial hyper-sleep of interstellar tourism. I fantasized that Earth might be my home for many transitive cycles, but realize it's best to move on. Jenn and I were foundational women of peace; and now that she's gone, I cannot face Earth's mounting societal chaos and anger alone. Her courage was my courage. Her optimism and adoration, too.

I shall maintain Jenn's aged reflection for a week and then reconstitute myself in the image of our 24-year-old splendor. Too much solitude is unhealthy, and J.J. Callaway rejoiced in the warmth of a double-bodied single soul. I always try to offer my prototypes as much in return as I receive, but some spirits simply have more verve than others. Call it love, if you must, but together we enjoyed a qualitative experience beyond any reasonable expectations.

Could be that I'll fly home and persuade one of my own kind to refashion herself as an earthly twin sister for three billion heartbeats (more or less).

Interstellar voyages and transmutations carry benefits, and ultimately I found Jennifer Jane Callaway on a wondrous blue planet far from the center of things. But such discoveries mark one of the most important reasons to journey among the invertebrate stars. Love exists across the universe. It is the universe.

ELECTRO GENESIS

I accidently stuck my finger into my homemade rodent zapper with a hard flinch followed by a tumble to the floor, bouncing my head off the concrete and into the zapper's electronic field. The device was one of my own little inventions to kill garage mice without harming (beyond a moderate jolt) any cat—I love cats—that might wander into the power arc. Not enough voltage to dispatch a healthy woman, either, but it left me unconscious for three days. I woke up in a hospital with double vision and something else beyond my own obsessive logic.

I tried to explain the something else to hospital staff, feeling a bit like a colorblind person who could suddenly see the full visible spectrum plus a few extras. That's not exactly right, of course, but how does one describe bizarre visions after waking from a coma. My doctors were sympathetic and assured me such phenomena were merely post-trauma hallucinations. Jostled brains can do that.

"Don't worry," they said over and over. "Don't worry."

A few days later, when a couple of white coats started questioning whether my hallucinations might be more than brain fog, I realized that their believing in a patient's recently acquired visions/telepathy might be more dangerous than believing I was crazy. If my new-fangled abilities were real, doctors would want to explore them. And more frightening to me, government busybodies might insist on that exploration. So I told my neurologist, "You're right. It was all just my imagination."

And I got the hell out of the hospital plenty quick.

My closest, dearest friend, Jennifer Stevlynn, is also a doctor. Well, a psychiatrist, which even she says is occasionally more akin to witchcraft than medicine. "But," she admits, "at least we've learned enough to quit giving surgical lobotomies even if some of our pills have similar effects." She occasionally referred to things like "Thorazine zombification" in private, but in public scenarios would talk about "therapeutic trade-offs." My girl is smart.

But for most patients, Dr. Jenn is more of a let's-talk-and-discuss-and-evaluate before resorting to psychotropic meds. Plus, she's the type of person I'd trust with my life, which I value pretty highly, and she's probably intelligent enough to help me decipher my new juiced-up brain function. Damn sure wasn't a hallucination when I sensed that hospital doctors were considering electroconvulsive therapy in my case—you know, placing electrodes on the temples and shooting current into the brain—and I'd already been zapped enough to suit me for a lifetime. One of the hospital doctors said, "Glad you've recovered enough to admit you can't read minds," but he was thinking, "Glad we won't need ECT for this poor girl." At that moment I wanted to slap him for considering shock therapy and slap him twice again for 'thinking' the word girl, but obviously I couldn't dive into feminist semantics at that moment without showing my cards.

Later, Jennifer was able to access all the hospital's medical records because I signed her on as my treating psychiatrist. She understood the medical concerns surrounding my mental health—valid concerns because my head had been quasi-electrocuted—but also wanted a more cautious approach regarding my care, i.e., prescribing the lowest possible medical intervention.

She genuinely believes in the do-no-harm commandment. And now that we were officially doctor and patient, she could legally maintain confidentiality about whatever I revealed to her.

The legal ramifications weren't much of a concern to either of us. We had a long-standing best-friends-and-lovers agreement before a medicinal one. And if it turns out I am genuinely crackers after the rodent zapper, she'll keep it to herself as long as I don't turn violent.

Six weeks after I left the hospital, Jenn scheduled a brain MRI to see what, if anything, might be revealed. At first, like any psychiatrist worth her medical degree, she doubted my sanity and wanted a few facts before offering suggestions. After all, crazy people universally deny they're crazy. But after the MRI and supplemental EEG, Jennifer pretty much climbed aboard the my-patient-girlfriend-may-not-be-quite-whacko bandwagon. Not exactly a bandwagon because we're only two people, and she's still concerned about physiological damage to my cerebral mantel. When we discussed the test results, she pointed at some of the screenshots and too calmly said, "Are you seeing this? The last time I viewed a similar image, the patient never regained consciousness and died a month later."

I shrugged. "I don't think I'm dead or comatose. So what's it mean?"

"For one, you're lucky to be alive. Beyond that, I'm not sure. You either have severe brain damage...or severe enhancement....Look!" She traced her finger over an MRI image. "Thin dactyl surface scars, at least I think they're scars, running from the frontal lobe to the occipital"—it looked spider webby to me—"but your temporal lobe is clear." She pointed to a color-augmented picture. "And the neurons appear to be firing across both hemispheres as though you're having a grand mal seizure. Furthermore, your brain is two degrees hotter than the rest of you, which is likewise two degrees above normal. Let's call it 103 for the brain and 101 for the body." She paused, looked at me, and asked, "Are you eating well?"

I nodded. "I'm feeding like the eighth month of a ten-month pregnancy.

Hungry all the time, but I'm still losing weight."

"I thought as much," she said. "If the tests are right, your brain is burning a lot of energy. It's on fire…, and I don't understand why you're still upright."

I shook my head. "Just take it as a gift, and let's go for a double cheeseburger with fries and a banana split chaser."

I never mentioned my name. Marilyn Stephens. Four months after the coma, I'm still 5'7", eat like a pig every day, and my weight is holding at 120 pounds. Before the zapper, it checked in at a robust 145 with a solid layer of muscle.

My body temperature is now a constant 103.5, I'm hungry all the time, yet I struggle to keep from losing weight. I never thought I'd get tired of festival eating, but damn. I downed a medium pepperoni pizza last night followed by a hefty slice of chocolate cake and a tall glass of milk. And to tell you the truth, it was hard to hold it all down. Food intake has become a real chore. According to Jennifer, I should have gained 40 pounds instead of losing 25, but she's confident that given time, my brain will recover and slow down my metabolism. What I would give just to eat a plain BLT with unsweetened iced tea and not have to worry about weight loss.

Jenn has encouraged me to keep up the caloric intake until my body cools down again and stops burning so much energy, but I get the distinct feeling she's worried. Oh, hell, I know she's worried. I try not to read her thoughts, but this new ability is hard to control. Besides, it's not really that difficult to read Jennifer. She wears her love for me like a MAGA t-shirt and matching hat, on top of which she thinks about doctoring me 24/7. That's who she is. I love her, too, but finally put my foot down: "No more pizzas or cheeseburgers or vanilla malts before bed." I'd rather soak in a tub of cold water, which she also prescribed regularly. This isn't much fun, either, and it offers only short-run reduction of my body temp, but it helps. By the way, my pulse rate has been holding at 115 and respiration at 24 for the last week.

Jennifer thinks my bodily energy consumption may have peaked. Let's hope she's right. If not, this incredible shrinking woman may wither into a walking skeleton with a burning brain because (I never thought I could say this) I'm sick of double cheeseburgers.

Over the last month, at Jennifer's direction, I've taken beta blockers and calcium channel blockers to slow my heart rate. And when Dr. Jenn prescribes actual pill-form medication, you can bet the situation is pretty desperate. I even tried good ol' Bayer aspirin on the slide to lower my body temperature, but there has been no significant improvement from any of these procedures.

Still, despite the racing pulse and high temperatures, I feel great. Of course, I had also felt top-shelf seven years back when I got the fateful call back on a routine mammogram. Breast cancer is insidious because you don't notice any symptoms. It tries to kill you while you're having a good time and not paying attention. So, even if I'm feeling well, I listen to Jenn when she tells me I'm sick. Anyway, my post-blocker pulse hovers at 118; respiration 25; weight 116. What a waste of medicinally prescribed calories.

Jenn and I woke up together Saturday morning although she no longer cuddles throughout the night because my body temp is literally too hot to handle. Still, I've often believed that prolonged pillow-talk is the best part of a relationship anyway.

"OK," said Jennifer. "We've tried about everything I can recommend without hospitalization and turning you over to a group of experts—and I've never really trusted experts in physiological psychiatry. But your average brain temperature has lately been running at 104, and we're skirting within a few degrees of permanent brain damage. About all I can recommend is increasing the ice-water baths to every four hours until your system settles down. Either that or turn to the hospital for comprehensive tests and evaluation."

"To hell with that," I said. "You're the best doctor in town, and if you can't find an answer, no one can." I rolled toward her, "And you're thinking the same thing."

"You're just guessing," she said.

"And am I guessing that you give me another five or six months to live. Come on, Jenn. I thought you understood that I can…sense things."

"Your friend quasi-believes, but your doctor struggles with it. And whether you're developing paranormal abilities or not, the human body survives within a narrow range of temperature and energy consumption. Facts is facts, honey."

"That may be true for mere mortals, but for a 38-year-old super-gorgeous woman with an electrified brain, maybe this metabolism is normal. In many ways, I feel better than ever. And I've always felt pretty damned good—give or take a few cancer chemotherapy appointments."

"You did well with those, I'll admit, but they caught it early and…." Jennifer shook her head. "Don't get me sidetracked. The human brain cannot survive temperatures over 107 or 108. It will die, and you will die with it. This is your BFF talking. I'm going to do everything possible to prevent that from happening!"

"Then I'd better get dressed and go buy a few bags of ice. I'll stick with cold baths until you figure another way."

She smiled. "You're a very good patient. And there's always a chance your body will calm itself."

"It's only been six months since the accident," I said. "Let's see what happens with regular ice-water soaks. Things will undoubtedly get better, remain the same, or grow worse."

"That's not a comforting logic."

The following week, submitting to a 20-minute ice bath each morning and evening, I was holding a body temp of 102. Jenn ran more tests. My brain's electrical activity still ran high but remained steady at a smidge over 104 degrees. Bottom line, I seem to have physically stabilized though it's hard for my BFF-girlfriend psychiatrist to know if that represents much progress. Neither of us claims a precise goal in treatment because neither knows exactly what's being treated. Is my overexcited brain a miracle or misfortune?

After breakfast and as Jennifer was heading off for her hospital rounds, I told her, "It's time for me to get back to work."

"You're still sick," she said. "I've authorized indefinite medical leave. Insurance is handling the bills, and I can pick up any slack as needed."

"Yes, but if I don't return to my job soon, I'll go crazy for real. You may be the best doctor on earth, but I'm the best computer programmer in the galaxy. Besides, I called my boss, Bill, yesterday and he's desperate. Would-be hackers are always trying to break into our clients' data systems, and the best defense just happens to be the best offense, and that's me."

"I won't authorize it."

I laughed. "I don't care and neither will Bill! And face it, girlfriend, I can run a fever at work just as well as home. The cold baths are effective. I feel great. And you're not the only one around here who takes pride in her duties."

"Yeh?   And what if I call the hospital and tell them you're a danger to yourself or others?"

I knew she wouldn't really do this but offered a mock backhand. "How about I hack into your medical computers and delete all the hospital's billing records along with your license to practice medicine? And then maybe I'll tap into the financial grid and change your credit rating to a nine! What about that?!"

Jennifer scowled playfully. "Credit scores don't go that low…!"

"They will when I'm done."

She smiled and grabbed her briefcase. "I should have you committed for gross orneriness of the third kind, but the DSM doesn't recognize that as an illness. Nonetheless, you've got a chronic case! Check your temperature every two hours or I'll personally come to your computer lab with a rectal thermometer."

"Go cure a few crazies before I change your credit rating to a three."

We kissed goodbye. I think she was actually pretty happy with me.

One of the problems with reading minds is that they are often crammed with cloud-cuckoo-land gibberish: to be or not to be when the person has never "been" in the first place; homebodies who suddenly decide they want to be the next great American writer when they can't even think in complete sentences; racists of every race who take pride in their self-perceived natural superiority. And if that isn't bad enough, I have started picking up on other people's sleep-time imagery, which is giving me nightmares.

For example, there's a woman down the street who has recurring rape dreams. Bad ones. And I not only see those memories but feel her emotional responses, too, which are laced with supplemental childhood traumas and soul-wrenching screams. She is an incest survivor who's been cut to the bone psychologically. And before my mindreading ability, I had seen her around the neighborhood a few times, and you'd never know that she lives at the edge of suicide every day because of this. Talk about a life of quiet desperation.

One block over is a man undergoing chemo for testicular cancer, and I will wake up with his nausea if I'm not paying attention. Reading minds is one thing; learning not to read them is another; or else some of the excruciating brain noises around the neighborhood would drive me batty. Fortunately, I'm getting better at selective editing and keeping my head above the torrent of disjointed thoughts and emotions. Kind of like putting on a sound guard at the shooting range—I can focus on the target without psychic noise making me deaf. Besides, who would want to vicariously experience the full-body empathy of someone else's rape-mares or chemotherapy? It's bad enough that they have to experience it.

That aside, I have used my enhanced brain capacity to develop several ideas about cyber security and multi-leveled approaches to computer intelligence. Kind of a smart-ware system that can back-hack and shut down data intrusions at first light. My boss is loving it—not that I actually have a boss. I work mostly my head, which is hard to supervise, so Bill and others leave me alone to create my brain magic. That's profitable for them and acceptable to me because I don't connect well with most people beyond Jennifer. It's not that I dislike others, but I have a tendency to answer questions directly. One of my early romances complained that I talked like a cyborg. I took it as a compliment and said, "Thank you." She broke up with me soon afterward.

But let's get back to some more of the good in all this. I stopped by a convenience store after work to pick up a 25-pound ice bag for my evening bath—brain fever now holding steady at around 103, body 101—and accidentally tapped into to the darkest corner of a very dark mind. The bastard was holding a 14-year-old girl in his basement, and you can guess the rest of it. I'm generally a peace-loving nerd who appreciates higher math almost as much as chocolate, but kidnappers and child molesters, especially when it's a two-for-one deal, melt the cheese right off my nachos. So after I dropped off the ice at home, I slipped my semi-auto peacekeeper into its holster, took a short walk, knocked on the bastard's backdoor, and plugged him five times in the crotch when he opened it. Fool.

Even with a silencer, I knew the neighbors would notice five rounds from a .45, but that wasn't a real problem. I called 911 from the perp's phone, told them to send the cavalry, and went to the basement to let the girl know help was on the way. She was bound by the ankle with an eight-foot chain that could hold a rhino, and I couldn't cut her loose; likewise, the poor thing appeared so traumatized that I doubt she could have walked up the stairs. The stench and the filth were disgusting because she had been left to sleep on a urine-and-feces stained mattress. This pissed me off all over again, so for good measure I plugged the guy between the eyes just before leaving. He was already dead, and I didn't need extrasensory perception to see his brains scatter across the floor from my final shot, but the sight made me feel a whole lot better about having telepathic abilities. The SOB had planned to kill his victim in a few days and then find "fresh meat," as he called his victims.

I snuck out the back door, walked home in the dark, and climbed into my ice-bath while waiting for Jennifer to finish clinicals and stop by to see me. We have separate homes but end up sleeping at my place more often than not.

The next day the newspapers reported that a man had been shot execution style in the neighborhood, yet they didn't mention the girl being held captive. That seemed a little strange, but I figured child protective services wanted to safeguard the poor kid's identity so she could get follow-up care without reporters hounding her.

"I am worried about you," said Jennifer, suddenly playing psychiatrist again.

"No need," I said. "Told you I'm feeling great. The ice baths are doing the trick for my temperature, and they're not as bothersome as they used to be. The hardest part is holding still for 20 minutes. Fortunately, computer geniuses can think while they soak."

"That might be, but your temperatures are averaging half a degree higher than three weeks ago. The cold treatments are superficially effective, yet whatever's going on with your brain seems to be growing worse."

"Maybe it's getting better," I said, half joking. "Our company got two new mainframe security contracts after I introduced my new programs, so Bill gave me a hefty raise. My latest approaches to cyber safety via AI counter-hacking—the best defense is a good offense—might be the most profitable thing to come along in five years. Maybe I'll start my own company and put Google out of business!" Jennifer didn't smile big enough to suit me. "That's a witticism, honey. Not my best effort, perhaps, but you're allowed to chuckle."

"And you're not listening to me. Physiological issues can't be wished away. Once your brain goes beyond a certain limit, it dies. That's not a fantasy, and even if we maintain current temperatures, your racetrack metabolism will kill you over time."

"Does that really matter? Everybody dies. Just a question of how and when. But I'll increase the ice baths to make you happy…. And the answer is no! I'm not checking in to the hospital."

"God, I hate when you do that. At least wait until I ask?"

"My way saves time."

After rescuing that kidnapped girl last month, it occurred to me that I would make a hell of a private investigator, and I could do it part-time after work. In fact, I'm making enough from the sidebar computer consulting that I could quit my day job. But the busier the better, I always say.

I told Jennifer that I needed a break from her medical scrutiny. The way she talks you'd think that my brain will be in a jar next week with doctors trying to determine exactly what the mouse zapper did to me. But when something is working well—and my thoughts are marching double time—why not leave it be. Or as my dad said too often, "If it ain't broke, don't fix it." He also too often beat the hell out of me and my brother, so I joined the army at 17 to escape home life, went to college on the G.I. Bill after my tour in Afghanistan, and never looked back. And if good old dad were still alive, I might show him similar consideration as the kidnapper.... Well, probably not, but yeh, there's some resentment.

Anyway, the private-eye thing stuck with me for several weeks, and I wondered how to best implement my talents. Mindreading is like a superpower once you get the hang of it, but I need to be within a few hundred yards of a person to know what he's thinking—or dreaming (ugh!)—and I can skim their conscious and unconscious for words or images that reveal their essence, then do a more thorough reading if warranted. Fortunately, I haven't so far run into another psyche as bad as the kidnapper, which was accidental, but I have ideas about big-city crime reduction.

No police involvement. They ask too many questions and bad guys often go free via the legal system. I prefer a much more efficient—locate, convict, execute. When one assesses guilt or innocence through direct mental contact, lawyers and trials are unnecessary. Evil self-identifies, and then I take care of due process.

OK. I had a grand mal seizure. Dr. Jennifer didn't quite gloat with "I told you so," but pretty close, so I consented to a few more hospital tests on an outpatient basis. Jenn prescribed a daily dose of clonazepam, which I sometimes take with a shot of bourbon to help me sleep, and I've been seizure-free for two weeks.

It's getting very hard to rest more than a couple hours per night. Sometimes I lose control over my mind-reading filters and the neighboring brainwaves keep me awake. Other times I go into busybody overlord and start searching for brainwave evildoers and wind up with an infuriating influx of general human stupidity and spite.

This morning Jennifer said, "I want you to hear me, Marilyn." (Whenever she uses my whole name, instead of "M" or "Mar," I know I'm about to get a medical lecture.) "The last MRI showed a thickening of the scar tissue. My colleagues and I think it's because of sustained high body temps and excessive neural activity."

"You say excessive," I responded, "I say enhanced."

She replied, "I don't care if you say tomato or tommatto, the 'enhancement' will kill you if we don't take things down a notch. The seizure was a signal. Pay attention."

"I'm taking the clonazepam and being a good girl about it. If you really want to help, give me something to make me sleep eight hours."

"We've already tried meds for that. Your brain mostly ignores them. What we want to do, now, is surgically remove some of the scar tissue in the frontal lobe to see if neural activity decreases locally. A limited experimental procedure. If there's improvement, we can discuss the further options. But if we don't do something soon, the medical board agrees that your brain is headed for the biological equivalent of a nuclear meltdown."

I shook my head. "No surgeries now. Maybe later. You just don't know the good I've done or can do."

"I know you're making computers sing and dance, but success at work won't prevent physical decline and death. You're sick, Mar. You need medical intervention fast, and even then you...."

She stopped so I finished her sentence, "may not survive."

Her eyes started to water, so I reassured her. "It's all right, hon. I probably should have died at the time of the accident or never emerged from the coma. But here I am, new and improved, and I plan to enjoy it for the duration. You don't appreciate the feelings I have. It's like thinking at Mach 3 in a world of sloths. If only I could get a night's sleep...."

"Please consider surgery. Please."

Told her I would think on it.

She shook her head. "Typical delay tactics," she said. "If I were working with a spoiled adolescent, the applicable diagnosis would be oppositional defiant disorder."

"I'm neither defiant nor compliant," I said.

"That's often what my teenage patients tell me before throwing a tantrum."

That same evening around midnight, I took a double dose of clonazepam and two-fingered shot of bourbon. Slept for five blessed hours and dreamed about a man who deserved a close encounter with my peacekeeper.

When you have a superpower, you can travel in society's darkest corners without much worry. A concealed .45 helps, too. But mostly, mindreading is a foolproof failsafe. That guy's thinking bad thoughts about me; she's just trying to survive street life; that one sleeps with the lights on. And when I sense that a person is hungry, I slip them a five or ten spot for food. Sometimes I'll leave blankets where the homeless gather. Always, however, I scan neurological pathways for evil masquerading as human. It rarely takes more than a few evenings to find it. And because I require less and less sleep, I decided to embrace the night as an angel of mercy or avenger of evil according to my conscience. But when the morning comes, it's back to my Clark Kent routine, playing a mild-mannered, solitary, and brilliant computer analyst.

Newspapers and broadcasters sometimes make mistakes. We all know that. But it's really disturbing when they deliberately misreport or withhold information.

My last justice kill happened two days ago—a corrupt man of the cloth. I fired a soft-point with the muzzle pressed against the back of his skull (an easier death than he deserved). Then I carved a swastika on his chest with my Army knife. I wanted to do it on his forehead a la Inglorious Bastards, but his face was too messed up from the gunshot. At point-blank range, forty-fives turn brains and bones into vermillion mush. I also stuffed a list of his victims in what was left of the guy's mouth for good measure. Figured some of the kids might need counseling.

And what did the local papers report? "Dedicated priest brutally murdered," praising the man's "devoted service to the poor of Providence and surrounding neighborhoods." Christ. The way folks moaned and groaned at the funeral (I was there), you'd think the SOB was up for the Mother Teresa Sweetness Stakes. And did they mention his victims? Did they talk about the carving job I did on him? No.

Why do big cities protect "respectable" bad guys and come down like gangbusters on minority teenagers for driving with an expired license? It's a shame that all people can't read minds. Then they'd know what to do.

Shit. I blacked out last Friday while making predator rounds in Pawtuxet. Fortunately, I wasn't carrying the peacemaker, so I woke up at Providence Hospital without facing arrest. Jennifer was on call when I came to and the staff texted her immediately. Figured I would get a lecture.

"You were out for 14 hours," she said, "and your condition is deteriorating. We must do the preliminary surgery if you expect to survive. This time, I doubted you'd ever regain consciousness."

"Surprise, surprise, surprise!" I said using my Gomer Pyle imitation.

"No joke," said Jennifer. "Your temperature rose to 106 degrees, and we dunked you in ice-water for two hours. Got you down to 101 but you're already back at 103. Resting pulse, 142. Blood pressure, 190/120."

"I feel fine."

"Doesn't matter. You're dying, and we're preparing you for neurologic surgery. If that doesn't work, and if we can't get your temperature down, your organs will…." She stopped.

I finished her sentence in my head.

Jennifer checked my IV and manually pumped the reservoir bag a little. My body signaled a not-to-be-avoided sleep.

I awoke in recovery, groggy from the anesthesia, but aware immediately that I could see in an expanded spectrum. The room was brighter than it had any right to be, and the skeletal structures of the attending nurses came and went as they moved around the room. The scene was kind of like watching in reverse, then on pause, then on forward the Invisible Man scene when Griffin becomes visible after death, all the different body parts revealing themselves in sequence. And if you haven't seen the classic 1933 movie or read the book, you don't deserve to live.

I told one attendant to get a chest X-ray because I saw a suspicious dark spot on his lung.

He smiled and said, "Please raise your arms above your head."

I obeyed and then went back to sleep, regaining consciousness a few hours later in a private room of the Neurological ICU with a quasi-invisible woman checking a variety of electronic devices. I could see my pulse and BP readouts: 85 and 140/80. Lower than they'd been in months. Except for the strange see-through vision, I felt like my old self, which made me worry that my mindreading superhero days might be numbered.

Then, as I tried to roll over, I discovered my left arm handcuffed to the bedrail. And sitting just outside my room was an athletic looking man in a police uniform.

Within a few hours I learned to control my Invisible Man eyesight. Believe me, watching people physically deconstruct willy-nilly is disconcerting. And, yes, the person sitting by the door still wore crisp Providence PD regalia. It's too bad X-ray vision couldn't make him or my handcuff disappear.

I was livid. Come in for brain surgery and wake up a prisoner. What kind of medical care is that?

I asked my nurse, "Where the hell is Jennifer? I mean, Dr. Stevlynn? I want to know what's going on! Why the hell is a cop outside my door? And why these damned handcuffs?!"

"Your doctors will explain," she said, injecting something into my IV.

"What's that?" I asked.

"Something your medical panel recommended."

"I'm not seeing a panel! Jennifer is my doctor. My only doctor. Where the hell is she?"

"She's no longer your treating psychiatrist," said the nurse. "I'm afraid the surgeons and neurological team have undertaken your care…for now. I'll inform Dr. Robertson that you're alert enough to talk."

"I'll do some talking, all right. And I might bust some heads, too. Tell Jennifer I need to see her!"

"I'm afraid Dr. Stevlynn's on the no-visitation list. Don't worry. Dr. Robertson is heading up your medical review panel, and he'll explain… status. He has to travel from Boston for visits so probably won't see you until this evening."

I started feeling drowsy and realized the nurse had slipped me an intravenous Mickey Finn. I could fight medication to some extent, but this cocktail must have been pretty stiff, and even superheroes have cognitive limitations.

I slept with dreams of laying hands—without cuffs—on somebody's throat.

OK. I wasn't able to sit down face-to-face with Jennifer to find out what was going on, but because she makes hospital rounds every other day or so, I did take a walk through her thoughts. And because she's so overwhelmingly worried about me, it would actually be hard not to read her mind.

Apparently I did some talking while under general anesthesia about snuffing the kidnapper; and apparently, his victim recognized a photo of me when police questioned her about my possible connection. Should have worn a mask, but who knew I'd spill my guts during brain surgery. The cops aren't sure I'm the avenger, and they're waiting for DNA results to come back before filing charges. I didn't think about a DNA trail, which proves that even geniuses can be stupid. Besides, at that point, Jennifer figured I'd live just a few months, so consequences were low on my list of concerns. And I was so pleased about discovering and then plugging that bastard, who could blame me for carelessness. Got the job done, that's for sure, and according to Jennifer's brainwaves, some of the cops aren't overly worried about vigilante intervention when it comes to little-girl rapists. Sure, they'll prosecute me if it comes down to hard evidence, but I'm not worried.

My life's a bit of a mess at the moment, and I can't see Jennifer for help. While I read minds well enough, I can't hold a two-way conversation—yet. And with all the drugs they keep pumping into me—I'm betting Fentanyl is on the list with a shovel full of beta blockers—my thinking process is screwy. But the preliminary frontal-lobe scar removal didn't prevent me from reading minds. And that alone should help me take appropriate action whenever I'm able.

I already know that one of the orderlies uses stolen hospital drugs to sedate and assault women. That sort of perversion rates high on my hit list because somebody pulled that shit on me in Afghanistan, and I'm pretty sure more than one son-of-a-bitch had a go with my unconscious body.

Yeh, more resentment.

If one gets to Carnegie Hall by practice, it makes sense that two-way telepathy can be achieved the same way. I'm working hard on this since Doctor Robertson still prevents me from seeing Jennifer. He says I threatened to kill her in the operating room. Talk about the Big Lie! I could never hurt Jenn regardless of how many drugs were in my system. I told him so, too.

After that I said, "Just tell me what's going on, and don't give me that 'danger to myself or others' crap. I know me better than you do."

"Ms. Stephens," he said, so I already disliked him, "you must be patient. I personally find your anesthesia-induced tirade to be incredible. Not credible is probably the better phrase, but after we alerted police to the surgery room video, they became rather determined to investigate."

"Forget the cops. Once I'm well again, I can take care of myself. What I want to know is what you're doing for me, doctor to patient. And remember, my best-friend-partner is a doctor so you can't bullshit me."

"Yes, which is why it was so surprising that you'd threaten her."

"Impossible."

"That's what Dr. Stevlynn said, even when we played the video."

"And do you typically handcuff patients who say weird things under general anesthesia?

"No," said the doc, "but after we submitted the tape to the police—and some of your comments were uncomfortably specific—they ordered the restraints and the guard outside your room. Not my cup of tea, I'll admit, but the hospital board is addicted to protocol. Whatever detectives want, they get."

"Maybe they should take a lesson from that nurse who stood up to police bullying when they wanted her patient's blood without a warrant. If you don't mind my saying, medical care should take precedence over detectives vying for promotion."

"I agree though I'm afraid your case is a bit different. Aside from the police investigation and concerns, your physiological brain patterns are abnormal to say the least. And more interesting to me is that, medically, you shouldn't have been talking during surgery. The anesthesiologist put you under deeply, but parts of your brain activity could not be suppressed."

I toned down my anger with a modest gesture toward conciliation. "So I'm a modern medical miracle. That's better than being dead. And doesn't the patient bill of rights apply in my case? I'm not likely to run off killing folks or pirouette down the hallways right after brain surgery."

"True, but the hospital has its instructions."

I changed tactics again. "By the way, Dr. Robertson, my head is killing me. Might be a reaction to the sedatives. Can you please cut back the meds to see if the headache goes away?" I stretched my eyes in a little-girl-lost impression. Lying seemed a good tactic, and I planned to lie my ass off to get rid of their damned drugs.

Doctors are worse than pushers.

"Hi, Ms. Stephens," said the man, "I'm Detective Sean Ramble."

"Nice to meet you, Mr. Rambo."

He raised a Spock eyebrow. "I've heard that one before," he said softly. "Get used to it after a while. But I'm afraid levity won't change the situation. You're our prime suspect in a murder case."

"If you haven't noticed," I said, "I've got bigger problems than the police department, including brain surgery six days ago. I can't even take a pee without your guard dog unlocking me from the bedrail and a nurse helping me to the bathroom. And Doctor Robertson tells me my brainwaves might kill me any day."

Ramble was a small, polite man who yet struck me as a sharp-toothed bear trap ready to clamp down on me any second.

"We'll let the doctors care for you, of course," he said, "but once you're released from the hospital, we have a cell waiting."

"I supposed it wouldn't make any difference if I'm innocent."

"It would, but the evidence says you're not. DNA confirms you were at the victim's house. It didn't confirm you were the shooter, so we asked a judge for a warrant to search your home. That's quite set of weapons, and it won't take long for ballistics to confirm whether your .45 is the murder weapon…, unless there's something you'd like to tell me now."

"Don't have much to tell, Rambo. But from what I've heard, that particular shooting victim ranks pretty high on the bad-guy scale. Sounds like the world's better off without him—whoever did the killing."

The detective nodded gently. "I would have enjoyed arresting the man, that's for sure, but the important word is arrest. Not murder him without a trial. And, if he were still alive to be questioned, we might have learned about other victims or solved a few additional missing person cases. Yet I can understand why someone might want to take the law into her own hands."

I did see his point about questioning the kidnapper, but my method provided an absolute guarantee that this particular perpetrator would create no more victims or missing persons. "By the way," I asked, "how's that little girl doing?"

"She's home and getting the care she needs. Beyond that, I doubt she'll ever recover." Rambo leaned closer and whispered. "I'd say you shot that SOB in the just right place."

He was fishing for self-incrimination. The newspapers hadn't released details about the condition of the body or where I had put the slugs.

I smiled and said, "I have no idea what you mean."

"I'll bet you don't."

He got the message.

"Speaking of trials," I said, "I wonder what mine will be like after jurors and the newspapers hear more about that poor murder victim and the little girl he tortured."

Detective Ramble seemed to realize that Marilyn Stephens wasn't going to throw herself on the mercy of prosecutors. He leaned again toward my bedside. "You might get off on the sympathy vote, but we still can't have you walking around shooting folks. What happens when you mistake an innocent as a predator? That's the downside of your method, Marilyn. The police department is less likely to get it wrong."

The guy actually believed himself. "Look, Detective. If you don't mind, I think we're done with the interview—at least until you can drag me down to the station where I have fewer options."

"I know," he said, standing to leave. "You can rest for now. We'll get to know each other better down the road."

At least he was a considerate Rambo.

"One more thing," I said, "the chance of my ever mistaking an innocent is about the same as your ever doubting your moral superiority."

He smiled. "Get some sleep, Ms. Stephens. I'm sure we both, on occasion, have internal debates about right and wrong. The big difference is that you're insane and I'm not."

I smiled back. "I wonder how that will play out at trial, too."

The cool-headed Detective Ramble went down a few hallways to Dr. Robertson's office after he spoke with me. I psychically listened to their conversation. It was easy.

"Well," said Robertson, "what's the story?"

"I'd say she's very smart and very dangerous," said Ramble. "Not your average vigilante."

"Marilyn's not average anything right now. Her brain scans are indecipherable. Some of my colleagues insist she ought to be dead or seizing multiple times per day."

"She's far from dead. Her bolts have lost their nuts, but she has enormous self-control. The woman's pulse didn't elevate one beat when I sat with her—though I realize it's already high—and even innocent folks tend to get nervous talking with cops. I'd swear she enjoyed it. By the way, what's her prognosis? She'd almost be doing the department a favor by…expiring."

"A few days ago, I'd have figured her gone by end of month. I mean, her body temperature and hypertension were skirting the dead zone, and about all we could offer were ice baths. Drugs had little to no effect, so ethically I couldn't keep using them. And they were giving her migraines."

"So she says. I don't trust her. She's too confident, too focused…, although it would seem natural for a neurological patient to have headaches."

"I know. And since the medications, including sedatives, had no appreciable effect, there was no therapeutic reason to continue them."

The detective said, "Listen, Doctor. In Marilyn's early medical reports, right after she emerged from the coma, she mentioned mindreading or some such. All the physicians, including Jennifer Stevlynn, passed it off as delusions."

"I think they said hallucinations."

Ramble responded, "Whatever you want to call them…. Tell me, doctor. Is there any chance, any at all, that she can read minds?"

"There's never been a documented case beyond the *National Enquirer*."

"But you said her brain scans are…different?"

"That's an understatement," replied Dr. Robertson. "For the record, however, I think we have a very sick woman who may well die from neurological injuries. When electricity passes through a human being, it would be nice to believe that people can emerge with improved intelligence or new psychic abilities. But they really just end up with brain damage. Marilyn might be a murderer, but she's no mind reader."

Detective Ramble said, "I've seen a lot as a cop. Crimes of passion. Gang wars. Drug overdoses. Murders for hire and for pleasure. Some folks claimed that God made 'em do it. And genuine wackos usually can't wait to brag about how they can speak with demons or walk through other dimensions. But I've never interviewed someone who seemed to know what I was thinking…or a vigilante who didn't want to tell me how special they are. That's what scares me most about Marilyn Stephens. She's crazy, all right, but doesn't act like it."

I finally connected with Jennifer, not via telepathy but face-to-face in Providence on the infamous Butler psychiatric ward. She is, after all, my psychiatrist as well as physician of record. So after they transferred me to the lock unit for criminal crazies, Jennifer insisted on setting a one-on-one evaluative conference. The Butler staff seemed a little afraid of me but not Jenn. She trusts me and I trust her.

The big issue with direct psychic communication is distance. I can pick up on people's thoughts from several hundred yards, but my own transmissions require 10-15 feet proximity. Regular people aren't built for telepathic reception any more than I was before the accident, which is why two-way telepathy is so difficult. The normals have trouble receiving my thoughts unless I'm very close; I just have to accept these limitations.

So far I've used two-way telepathy only with Jenn. There are video cameras everywhere at Butler, and I don't want to say anything out loud to be recorded and passed on the Detective Ramble, nor would it be a good idea to let others know about my abilities. Jenn's concern, fortunately, is about my welfare and not my "criminal" past.

When we were finally alone, we chattered out loud about routine stuff—meals and group therapy and how was I sleeping—and then I generated a brief telepathic Q&A, which looked on camera as though we were sitting quietly. Jenn would occasionally nod or smile or frown, but no one else knew we were "talking."

I suggested via my hybrid mental language (sometimes using words, sometimes images) that "The biggest problem about being locked up at Butler is the brainwaves of fellow patients. They're abnormally intense, and it's difficult for me to filter them."

She had already been convinced that my cognitive abilities were more than imagination. "Can you filter some of them?" she asked. "I want to help you through this."

"I'm getting better at it." Then I cautioned her. "You know, there are some outlandishly violent people here. Please be careful when you visit me."

"I worry more about your being confined with them. This is not a healthy place despite our best efforts."

"There's no danger for me. Remember, I know what the staff and patients are thinking. And I'm learning to use telepathy to…," I was going to say "attack" but opted for "influence others."

"What do you mean?"

"Calm them," I said.

She cocked her head, obviously wanting more information.

"I've learned to put a mind on pause, mid-stride if necessary, sort of like a mini-seizure. Just a temporary neural short circuit that calms a person without causing permanent damage—I think. And the really good news is that I'm learning to put myself to sleep. As you know, insomnia became a big problem after the accident…," her face wrinkled, so I added, "and you're still concerned…."

"Yes. Your EEG remains off-the-charts weird." I could see the image in her mind. "We don't understand why you're still conscious. The scar tissue increased slightly when your body temp briefly hit 107, and nobody knows if the surgery did much good beyond a temporary reprieve."

I laughed. "Didn't know weird qualified as medical vocabulary, but the surgery helped me. If nothing else, my thoughts have become more relaxed, and it seems that by learning to control my bodily metabolism, I'm simultaneously learning to control my brainwaves. On top of which, I'm harnessing more intellectual abilities."

Jenn frowned, and I knew what was bothering her. "I'm sorry to say this," she added, "but I must admit that the evidence in your, uh, criminal case seems to be overwhelming. I don't want to believe it but...."

"You may as well know that I killed the SOB because of what he did to that little girl and what he would have done to her and others in the future. And when I sensed his evil at the 7-11 store, my military training kicked in. I reacted to save the victim. I'd do it again, and when I get out of this institutional hellhole, I plan to hire the best attorney in the state with my computer-geek earnings. I'll beat the criminal charges, and I don't feel guilty."

She almost smiled. "And you're not looking to make a career out of killing people—even bad people?"

"No, though it's a bit of a stretch to call that bastard people."

"True, but there are laws and conventions. Please allow the system to work."

"Of course," I lied without commenting that the legal system had been broken by judges and social do-gooders who offered too much kindness to killers and too little payback for the victims. Nor did I mention that Detective Ramble had begun to suspect me in the death of one hypocritical holy man.

That nice police officer would no doubt try to cause me grief.

OK. I'm out on supervised medical release, which really means home confinement with the police keeping tabs on me whenever I leave the house for medical appointments. Jennifer convinced the Butler advisory board that I was not a danger to myself or others, etc., etc., etc. Detective Rambo doesn't believe this, but I know he's a good guy, so I don't interfere with his life or work.

Public opinion is mixed about my trial, and the newspapers have launched a poetic ink blitz about kidnappers, killers, vigilantism, victims, justice, and me. I keep insisting that I'm innocent and that the DNA evidence is either wrong or deliberately concocted. History teaches us that juries can believe almost anything. Besides, I'm learning to gently influence behavior, and the jury panel will definitely be within telepathic range. Superpowers carry privileges.

That said, however, I did not forget about that hospital creep who likes to use stolen sedatives to rape unconscious women. He caught my attention after surgery when he walked past my ICU room, and believe me, bad guys don't want my kind of attention. Fortunately for him, the cops confiscated my weapons when they executed the search warrant, and I can't get them back until I'm exonerated from the murder charges.

But I'm happy to report that the poor rapist had a massive and fatal stroke right there in the hospital after my regular appointment with Jennifer. And even the dedicated Rambo won't be able to suspect me on this one because I reached inside the perp's brain and squeezed the interior carotid artery until it ruptured. Felt like mashing a toothpaste tube in the middle, which is definitely a sweet spot for executing rapists.

Who needs a semi-auto peacekeeper when I can kill with a thought?

Against my lawyer's advice, I asked for the constitutionally guaranteed speedy trial. He wanted to negotiate a plea deal, but I told him not to worry because we'd win. To his surprise, we did.

"Not guilty" despite the DA's evidence. In fact, I barely had to influence the jurors because, down deep, most were happy that the kidnapper died and that he suffered multiple shots to the groin. Even little old ladies can spit venom when it comes to child molesters.

Anyway, there were a couple of "the law-is-the-law" believers in the box, logical types that I genuinely respected, and they needed a little coaxing; so I gently implanted the notion that their sisters or daughters might have been the kidnapper's next victim had he not been stopped—and that maybe Marilyn Stephens kind of reminded them of their mothers to boot. Considering my superimposed mental impressions along with my on-the-stand-wide-eyed claims that "I could never hurt anybody" and the medical reports about my incapacitating brain damage from the zapper accident, it was a quick verdict.

I told my lawyer, "See, you're better than you think."

He didn't want to be convinced. "Maybe, but I'm still astonished. And what surprises me most is your absolute certainty beforehand. I've never seen a defendant so sure of the outcome, which I thought had to do with your reported mental illness. We could easily have lost this case. Fact is, given the evidence, we should have lost."

"Don't over-rely on mere evidence," I said. "Emotions almost always trump logic."

"Sad but true," he said, "though I still don't quite understand your verdict."

After court-processing and signing a few forms to get my weapons back, I went home and soon returned to work. Initially a few people at the company wondered whether I might be dangerous, but they needed my productivity more than they needed their doubts. I didn't even have to tweak their brainwaves. A healthy cash flow is very good for morale.

Now, there are only two people in the state who are still worried about me: Doctor Jennifer and Detective Ramble. For ethical reasons, I refuse to influence either of them beyond good old rhetoric. Besides, they're both stubborn and smart and honest, and that would make them difficult to influence anyway.

The dactylic scars around my brain are growing along with my IQ and telekinetic prowess, though I haven't let on to Jenn about my enhanced talents (like squeezing the hell out of the rapist's artery). Besides, she's focused on medicine and "can't understand why the scar tissue increased since we've finally got your body temperature under control." By that she means hovering at 100 degrees.

She asked me, "Do you have any ideas about the additional scarring?"

"No," I said.

"It's also peculiar, according to the latest images, that the gyri and sulci have become deeper and more complex."

"What's gyri and sulci?"

"Ridges and grooves."

"And this bothers you?" I asked.

She scowled. "Your brain's off kilter. Doesn't that bother you!?"

"No. Nor am I sure there's damage beyond the initial electrified clambake. Yes, I had the coma and skewed EEGs, but my body and brain tell me that they're better than ever. And if this neural spider web is growing, it can't be scar tissue in my opinion. It's something else."

We were sitting in my living room, so I wasn't worried about hospital cameras. "Watch," I said and gently levitated my now empty bourbon glass three inches off the coffee table.

Jennifer remained silent at first but her eyes grew lemur wide. "My god!" she said. "How long!?"

"Couple months. At first even I thought I might be hallucinating. A few kitchen items occasionally seemed to slide toward my hand as I reached for them. But pretty soon I realized it was real. I've learned to control the process and seem to be getting better with larger objects."

Jennifer became psychiatrist in earnest. "We've got to study this! I don't know how or why this is possible, but telekinetics are a major breakthrough. This is big, honey! I mean…, if it's not harming you."

I smiled. "Are you thinking about your patient or about winning the Nobel Prize?"

"Oh, hell!" Jennifer never curses, and I mean never. "I have more accolades than I ever deserved. This concerns research, learning more about the brain's potential, 'one giant leap for mankind!'"

I couldn't help but chuckle. "I know, but it's nice to see you excited for a change instead of forecasting impending doom for me at every corner. Maybe I won't die from this. Maybe my life is better than ever—as I've said many times."

Back to doctor mode. "I understand that you feel no discomfort, but there are physiological alterations to your brain. Too many unknowns, and I'm still concerned."

"You know, Jenn," I said. "My biggest problem at the moment is boredom. Even on the job. My brightest coworkers suddenly seem stupid. And the programming, itself. I never thought multivariable calculus would deny me a challenge, but it's getting to feel like elementary arithmetic." I sighed. "Wish I could pal around with Isaac Newton or somebody who might be interesting."

"What about books?"

"Most authors are desperate amateurs focused on selling copies instead of dispensing knowledge."

"But selling is part of every business, and many writers don't care about money." She stopped. "Oh, don't get me sidetracked!"

"I get that," I said. "Everybody has to earn a living. It's just that my current goals seem way outside the mainstream."

"Marilyn," said Jennifer, "I'd like to get you into a research lab for extensive and controlled testing. These new abilities might offer a lot of beneficial knowledge to the medical profession…, the entire world."

"No," I said. "The world can figure out its own problems. I'll work on mine."

I did street rounds in Providence last night and tried to tweak a homeless man for the better. I'd met him before, sympathized, and wanted to eliminate the kind of brain patterns that caused him to be homeless in the first place. But traveling through his mental anguish gave me the jitters, literally. His neurons were firing this way and that. He could "see" rats and snakes and demons with fully articulated surround sound, and he lived with a bottomless terror that supervised his whole existence. Poor, poor soul.

Despite my exhaustive medical readings about mental illness, neurological structures, related functions, and the most effective therapies, this fellow's condition was far beyond my knowledge. A cursory interior examination of his mind left me exhausted, so I slipped him twenty bucks and moved on. Within a block, some drug-crazed zombie who witnessed my monetary donation pulled a knife and demanded my remaining cash.

Sadly, it's a lot easier to kill than to cure. Felt bad about both cases.

When I heard a knock at my front door at 11:30 a.m. on a Tuesday, I was annoyed. Figured Jenn was paying a surprise doctor visit to check on me. I love her but she ought to know better.

"Listen!" I said, swinging the door wide so I could lay into her about sneaking up a patient, but I stopped before the third syllable and grimaced.

"Hello," said Detective Ramble. "I've been thinking about you and the strangeness that seems to follow you around."

I let out a breath of angry surprise (should have sensed him) but finally managed a civil comeback. "I would've been terribly disappointed if you had forgotten about me, Rambo, and I kind of thought you'd given up after that not guilty verdict."

He smiled a cop's version of I-know-what-you-did-last-summer and asked, "Not giving up, exactly. Just a compromised approach. Do you mind if we talk? Off the record?"

I grinned in return and said, "Sure, Detective. But don't play me for a complete fool. We both know you're never off the record, which is actually one of the things I admire most about you. You're a good cop, which is a rare commodity."

This struck a nerve and he said, "Not that rare…!" Then he backtracked. "Well, thanks for the compliment, but most cops I work with care a lot about what they do."

"Please, come in," I said, sensing a different type of determination and resolve in him. I added, "Tell me, Detective, could it be that you're really making an effort to be off duty here?"

"I'm not entirely sure," he responded. "I've never quite had a case like this, a suspect like you."

I nodded. "I'm guessing we're both a little perplexed. But, please, come on in."

He stepped inside and I closed the door. "I've got some 30-year Scotch," I suggested.

"I don't generally drink," he said, "but give me a double. Maybe it will help me understand why I came to see you. Because…, I don't think I can beat you at whatever game you're playing, but I can't sit back and let you win, either. I just really want to chat."

"Looks like you might be a little bit off duty after all," I said. "Undoubtedly a new experience for you…. Have a seat on the sofa. I'll serve us both neat. But please understand, Detective, I'm not your enemy—even if you did try to put me away for life."

"You're not my friend, either," he said, trying to become a cop again. "Just pour the damned drink and let's talk. This is hard for me."

I served him my best Scotch in my best crystal.

He took a stiff drink and said, "Oh, this is good stuff, better than I could afford." He took another. "Let me say that I don't believe in ESP, clairvoyance, alien abductions, or Big Foot. But I know there's something going on with you, something that's beyond the basic police manual, something other worldly, something dangerous."

He downed the last of his drink and asked, "Tell me…, are you reading my mind now?"

"Yes." I chuckled. "So don't think about reaching for your gun. Besides, that would be completely out of character, shooting an unarmed suspect, and you'd feel terrible if you killed me. You indicated that you wanted to chat. I would like that, too. Wouldn't you?"

"Yes," he said, "but if I'm right, you are never unarmed these days, and you're probably more dangerous than a melt-down maniac with a backpack full of hand grenades."

"Well," I said, "before I spill my guts, let me get you another Scotch. I suspect you're going to need it…."

To my surprise, I told him just about everything there was to tell. He listened quietly for most of it, but toward the end he said, "You can't go around killing people. Why don't you let the doctors help you, especially your very nice psychiatrist girlfriend? She's concerned about you."

I said, "I never killed anyone who didn't deserve it—and I want you to keep a professional distance from Jennifer. I love her and don't need you coming between us."

"You know," he replied slowly, "in all my years as a cop, I've never shot a human being. Killed a rabid dog once. Even that gave me nightmares. I don't understand how you can do it."

"Looking inside that kidnapper's mind gave me nightmares," I said. "Try to think of the folks I take down as a hundred times worse than a rabid dog. Mine is sort of a variation of the Hippocratic Oath. Let bad guys do no harm."

Soon after my talk with Ramble, I quit my programming job and began to spend most waking hours at the library reading, thinking, questioning. Einstein once said the difference between a brilliant person and a genius is that the first knows the right answers and the second knows the right questions. Oh, how I wanted to believe in my genius and my righteousness. But I kept thinking about the good detective. What would have been wrong with reporting that kidnapper to someone like Detective Ramble, a man whose soul resides closer than mine to Gandhi or Mother Teresa and who could have saved that girl without vigilantism. Regrettably, I enjoyed shooting that man. So what does that say about me?

My one-time "justified" violence might have been in self-defense against the drug addict who pulled a knife on me. But I could have temporarily disabled him, delivered a motherly lecture on chemical dependency and crime, and slapped him psychically on the wrist. Instead, I twisted his motor functions to force his weapon against his own eye socket and to shove the blade into his brain. And once, as a test of my increasing psychic abilities, I compelled a mouse to chew off its front paw. That's what I regret the most, forcing an innocent animal to torture itself, but I take proper care of that mouse now. He doesn't seem to know that having three legs is a disability, and he gets the best food money can buy.

Self-doubt is bad for someone like me. I have power to do things, but these new-found misgivings have left me all but impotent regarding criminals. I even stopped my nighttime wanderings, and in my search for answers, I only came up with more and more questions.

What am I doing? And where is this leading?

A big-time shock to the system brought me back to earth. Last night there was a triple murder/suicide—an abusive husband killed his ex-wife and their two children, one of whom was barely two years old. That put all my great thinking to rest. I could have prevented this horror show, and those kids and the woman would still be alive. Should be alive! Ramble is wrong about the sanctity of law. What did the law and its restraining order do for those innocent victims? Cops might arrest somebody after the fact; I can prevent a crime from happening. Which do you think the victims would prefer?

I started my late-night predator hunts again. Only now I was angry. I kept thinking about those kids gunned down by their own father. So when I stumbled on an abusive husband at 2:00 a.m. in Providence, who just happened to be cheating on his wife and was returning home from his seedy sexual encounter, I didn't kill him. I made him chew off the fingers of his right hand and damned near let him bleed to death before calling 911. The medics patched him up, and the police hauled him off to Butler Hospital for a psych exam. Just wait until he tries to explain why he gnawed off most of his hand, especially since he, himself, doesn't know why. That man's going to get therapy whether he likes it or not, and if he ever hits his wife again, I swear he'll be missing the rest of his fingers.

It was three days later when Detective Ramble called me to ask about the strange case of the finger-chewing man. I wasn't about to let him confuse me again with moral platitudes—not a chance. I'm on a one-woman clean-up campaign in Providence, Rhode Island. Help those who need it. Punish those who deserve it. Ramble can do his job and I'll do mine.

The only downside to this mission is that I haven't had much time to spend with Jennifer. She still wants me to check in with the hospital for a slew of tests, but because I've managed to keep my body temperate under one hundred degrees and to suppress most of the headaches, I keep telling her I'm OK and will come for tests if my health deteriorates. I'm also a little resentful about her talking with Detective Ramble, and I made a bit of a stink about doctor-patient confidentiality. She is pissed; I am pissed; we haven't talked in four days.

I know she wants to help, but consorting with the enemy—even a nice enemy—doesn't sit well with me. So I've been pouting and giving her the cold shoulder.

I suppose all good things must come to an end. I was out on my nightly rounds, cleaning up some of the human debris, when I felt something hit me in the chest. I knew this was impossible because (1) I would know ahead of time if anyone thought about attacking me and (2) there wasn't a person within 50 yards that I could see. Then I noticed a dark red stain growing under my left breast. It didn't take a Ph.D. or military training to figure out I'd been shot.

Another bullet grazed my wrist and I hit the dirt. I knew I was hurt pretty bad, but I didn't plan to make it easy for Ramble to kill me. Who else would have a rifle with a silencer, the guts to use it downtown, and the knowledge about staying outside my mindreading distance? That SOB wasn't really off duty when he visited me. He came looking for a weakness—and he shared a bottle of Scotch with me for that purpose!

Another shot twanged the mailbox near me. Ramble was determined to kill me, all right, and I was just as determined not to be killed.

Since it was February, there was lots of snow on the ground, so I opened my down jacket, packed it hard with ice and residual salt, slipped my belt up just below my ribs, and cinched it around the jacket as tight as I could to slow the bleeding. Worked pretty well, too.

I rolled off the sidewalk and into some shrubbery behind that mailbox. Pretty sure I saw the flash of the muzzle several hundred yards to my left at street level. That's a long trek for somebody with a bullet in her chest, but if I was going down, I'd give my best effort in taking out the shooter.

Of course, it had to be Detective Ramble. He was the only person who knew enough about me to reasonably attempt an assassination. Clever bastard! And he violated his own ethical platform in shooting me. I'd have to ask him about that moral lapse if I got the chance.

I crawled half a block behind the shrubbery, stumbled to my feet at the corner, and made my way to the next side street. If I tried a frontal assault, I'd be dead before taking five steps. Besides, all I needed was to get within telepathic distance and Ramble would be as good as dead. And because the pain in my chest started getting worse, I figured chewing off his own fingers was too good for him, but I'd devise something sweet when we came face to face.

I had walked maybe twenty feet down the side street, heading in the general direction of where the first volley had come from, when another bullet tore through my cheek spattering blood and a couple teeth in the snow drifts.

"Damn it," I thought. "A second shooter. How did Ramble manage that? Two vigilante cops!"

The face shot looked worse than its effect. It was basically a flesh wound that took out most of my bottom lip. Hurt like hell, though, and I was surprised I couldn't use my own mind to control some of the pain. Likely too much adrenaline. Brother, when I got Ramble in psychic range, I'd make him chew off his own testicles if that were possible. Then I'd get mean.

I knew the second shooter also had to be out of mental range, and it was someone who could handle a rifle. I paused to catch my breath, hiding in street side shrubbery again, rubbing snow on my bloody cheek, and wondering how Ramble managed to recruit a co-conspirator.

I'll admit that the detective was the last person I had expected to take the law into his own hands, but now wasn't the time for analysis. I had to stop them from killing me, and I was already hurt pretty bad..., if I could just get within mental range, I could take out the shooters, easy, and then get myself to a hospital. Part of me thought about just calling for an ambulance and finding my would-be assassins later, which made sense, but wouldn't you know it. I had dropped my cell phone in the snow somewhere. I might also just wait for the cops to show, but I was pretty sure the muffled gunshots weren't audible to sleeping folks, and I doubted anyone had called the police. So the wait might be a long one, and I was already starting to shiver from cold. The snow had stopped most of the bleeding but was making me hypothermic. Whatever I did needed to be done soon. Besides, this was a personal war between me and Ramble and whoever his partner was. I meant to kill them both.

Then it occurred to me! Even though I wasn't in mental range of the shooters, I was in range of others, so when the next car drove by, I made the guy pull over. Then I slumped in the back seat and instructed my conscripted driver to head in the direction of the first shots while I imagined all the things I would do when I disabled Ramble and his buddy.

Well, hell! The best laid plans of mice and men and demigods. As soon as I sensed the two shooters, I ordered my driver to take me home by the shortest route. Then I cut him loose, stumbled inside my house, and went straight to my computer.

It was all over. There comes a time to reap and to sow and a time to die.

Tonight was mine.

The moment I had gotten within mindreading distance, I discovered that Ramble's accomplice was Dr. Jennifer Stevlynn. My life flashed before me because I felt Jenn's abysmal pain. Her attempt to kill me had almost killed her emotionally. I never knew such a depth of conflicted agony could exist in another human being. And it was the human being I loved more than life itself.

It must have taken Ramble some time to convince her that the sniper approach was the only way to stop me, and Jennifer eventually gave in. Of course, she probably suspected I was dying anyway—my headaches were starting to return—and I guess she figured I might become psychotic. Maybe she was right.

What I do know is that during the last few months I've been a horrible girlfriend for Jenn, and somehow I drove her and Ramble to an action neither would have taken without unprecedented cause. Jennifer must have believed I'd eventually kill an innocent. And if she believed it…, well, I've never known her to be mistaken about which of her patients were dangerous.

I typed a quick email her and Ramble, apologizing for my behavior and asking Jenn to forgive me. Told her I loved her and suggested that she use my body and brain for medical research. Then I kissed my three-legged mouse and turned him loose in the backyard.

And now, I'm soaking in a warm bath and sipping on 30-year-old Scotch from my best crystal. It shouldn't take long to bleed out in a steaming tub, especially when my chest wound opens up again. Or maybe my body temperature will rise above 107 degrees and fry my brain. Either way is fine with me because if a woman like Dr. Jennifer Stevlynn can be worried enough to try to kill me, I'm worried enough to make sure she doesn't ever have to try again.

THE CONSERVATIONIST HUNTER

Richard Hamilton Caruthers had waited two years to use his hunting permit on planet Ariel. Now, he was on the ground in the Wolf 359 system in one of the most diverse biospheres of the seven inhabited star groups. Ariel's wilderness could be dangerous, of course, but that likewise appealed to Caruthers, who was both a big-game hunter and nature enthusiast.

Caruthers worked as a Trans-System eco-biologist, studying and protecting the geography, fauna, and flora of several Wolf 359 planets. As a result, he had been one of the first advocates for limited hunting on Ariel, so named because of its mystic beauty. Likewise, the Wolf Interplanetary Park Service supported the sport to cull over-populated species that might become environmentally disruptive.

Each of Ariel's three continents contained distinct subspecies exclusive to the geography, and Caruthers would be stalking the big-horned goltamer, essentially unchanged for 10 million years and still roaming nearly every region of every continent on the planet. Goltamers resembled the ancient Mother Earth bison crossed with a gazelle, and herds might contain hundreds in the forests or millions across Ariel's expansive grass plains, where they grazed close to the ground, consuming 35-40 kilograms of foliage per day. The planet's hearty food supply combined with the herd's superb group defensive tactics against predators made the animals almost too successful, and their expanding populations were tough on grazing lands. Thus, the Park Service's decision for limited hunting.

The coiled goltamer horns, which emerged from behind each ear and curled into a weighty bighorn spiral, were prized by collectors, and depending on size, might sell for 800 to 1400 credits. Not that Caruthers would ever surrender this kind of trophy. He had already reserved wall-space in his office to display the horns and wanted a museum quality set. So now, after two years of planning and waiting, he was alone on the ground of Ariel's largest continent with three weeks of food, suitable camping gear, and a radio transmitter that could be used when ready for extraction.

Caruthers had won the special goltamer hunting permit through the planetary lottery and could have auctioned the tags for a substantial sum, but he'd rejected every bid. To him, the trip was worth a hundred times his best offer.

After being flown to the site, Caruthers positioned his basecamp in the chaparral region that bordered the Ballack Mountains on the continent of Pathos. This was one of Ariel's more dangerous landscapes but also a thriving habitat for goltamers, especially the large bucks that might carry trophy horns containing three full symmetric coils and weighing 20+ kilograms when mounted. Caruthers carefully charted each day's hunt, almost hoping he'd find his goltamer on the last day of the third week. Such expeditions were, to him, the stuff of dreams, and Caruthers didn't want to end the trip prematurely. Nonetheless, he would take the right animal when and where he found it.

Ariel's recreational protocols required hunters to use newly manufactured old-style rifles and gas-propelled cartridges to narrow the odds between predator and prey. After all, the smallest gauge faze-plasmatic could instantly burn through an animal's skull from three kilometers; and with even an amateur scope, a shooter could target up to five. Where was the sport in that? Plus, the semi-gloss texture of ancient blue steel, the explosive recoil of a .340 Magnum, and the pungent fragrance of smokeless gunpowder marked Caruthers as a true professional, a huntsman who relied on skill and stealth to narrow the odds.

Thus far, Caruthers had spent eight glorious days and nights on Ariel. The goltamers were diurnal, so he hunted between sunup and sundown but often returned to camp at noon to prepare a meal, rest, or enjoy the sights and sounds of an untamed planet. The biggest mountain bucks retreated under the forest canopy during midday, their bodies so thick in muscle that direct sunlight, even from a red dwarf star, made them sluggish. Spotting a trophy animal at noon would be pure chance.

Caruthers had glimpsed several young bucks with modest headgear but passed them by. The flagship goltamer would be smart and wary, a fair match for the most skilled tracker. That's what made the contest interesting. That's why he climbed over rocks and through thickets, tore his clothing and scraped his knees, or lay for hours on cold granite ledges, scoping the ridges and hollows. And Caruthers remained confident. Plenty of time to find that trophy buck—his buck. It was waiting for him.

"This is it!" thought Caruthers as he fried fresh breakfast eggs lifted from a scrub hen's nest. He had taken only two of the six there, and the eggs would make an exciting supplement to his rations. A minor violation of the park rules, but he could someday tell his grandchildren about food prepared straight from the wild.

After the feast and after hiking two hours from camp through the undergrowth, Caruthers stepped into a floral meadow and beheld one of the most beautiful and dangerous animals on Ariel. It was not a goltamer but, rather, the nearly extinct, double-twist unicorn rhoclanthu, a strange herbivore with the temperament of a nightmare.

Caruthers froze and marveled at the animal. Its body resembled a Prehistoric Elk and probably weighed 200 and 225 kilograms. Big son-of-a-gun. The namesake horns (not antlers) emerged from each side of its head, but instead of forking like a deer or spiraling to the side like a goltamer, the two thick stalks met half a meter above the skull and twisted into a single sturdy point as strong and sharp as Mother Earth's long extinct white rhino. And rhoclanthus knew how to use their weapon.

Only two field biologists had ever reported seeing a wild double-twist on the ground; most saw them from helicopters while spotting, sedating, and tagging the few remaining animals. For some indecipherable reason, nearly all females were delivering stillborn calves on Ariel. The species hovered at the edge of extinction, and attempts to breed double-twists in captivity were only marginally successful. The rhoclanthus were dying out and nobody could quite figure out why.

After a minute of wonder, Caruthers let out a slow breath and tried to back away, planning to photograph the animal for park records. There were fewer than 60 known double-twist unicorns on the continent, and this was a strong, vibrant male. But even more important, off to the left, motionless at meadow's edge, stood a female with an apparently healthy newborn calf. Miraculous! Best in show! A living wonder!

Suddenly, a choking fear rose in the hunter's throat. Not for himself, but for the animal, which had just lowered its head, snorted, and plowed the dirt with powerful front hooves. The rhoclanthu appeared ready to charge.

Richard raised his rifle above his head, waved it back and forth, and shouted, "Get outta here you glorious bastard! Go!"

The beast grunted, stomped the ground, and rushed the hunter, catching him off guard. It moved faster than a blue panther, so Caruthers couldn't outrun or outmaneuver the attack. But to kill a double-twist, especially one protecting a fawn, would be a crime against nature.

The charging rhoclanthu pointed its horn at the man's chest. The man pointed his gun at the rhoclanthu's skull. Only a few seconds remained between them.

"GO!" he screamed. "SAVE YOURSELF!"

Caruthers slipped his finger inside the trigger guard and against the trigger. The animal was almost upon him, and Caruthers prayed for any option but to kill an endangered species. Almost instantly, he discovered one.

"Come on you son-of-a-bitch!" he said almost gently.

Caruthers stood straight and tossed his weapon into the surrounding wildflowers. He felt a sharp pain mid-thorax followed by an explosion from between his shoulder blades. Then he was lifted into the air as he clutched with both hands at the base of two horns that merged together and disappeared inside his chest. But even now, he marveled at the fawn with its mother, and he thought, "There's hope for you, my little one!"

In otherworldly convulsions, Caruthers noticed the rugged texture of the rhoclanthu's horns as he defensively tightened his grip. He pondered the warm blood flowing over his hand and down onto the animal's neck. And then, from somewhere out of his primordial human past, from an almost forgotten text, he remembered very comforting words: Tis a far better thing I do than I have ever done before.

Blood gushed from the man's chest; pain radiated throughout his body; yet he smiled even as he struggled to breathe. And soon, after a wondrous and memorable and loving encounter on planet Ariel, Richard Hamilton Caruthers remembered nothing at all.

ABOUT THE AUTHOR

Claudine Griggs earned a BA and MA in English at Cal Poly, Pomona, and has published three books about transsexuals and transgender issues. Her fiction and nonfiction have appeared in many journals and magazines, and her short story "Helping Hand" was the basis for an episode in Netflix's "Love, Death & Robots." Claudine's novel *Don't Ask, Don't Tell* was released on June 1, 2020.

Claudine taught college level writing for roughly 25 years at Rhode Island College, University of Massachusetts Dartmouth, Soka University, University of Rhode Island, and the Daniel Morgan Graduate School of National Security. She is currently semi-retired but works as a part-time writing specialist at the Bush School of Government and Public Service (D.C. Campus)

She lives in Virginia with her wife, Karen, and their cat, Tru Blu.

RECENT AND UPCOMING RELEASES
from Ananke Press

THE WITCHES OF RIEGERSBURG
by Julie Anne Straton

Three powerful women across the generations of a family struggle to keep alive the Goddess Tradition; a Book of Shadows weaves their stories together and takes the reader on a journey from the 1600's to the present day and from Germany to the United States and back again.

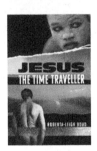

JESUS THE TIME TRAVELLER
by Roberta-Leigh Boud

What would happen if Jesus were a time traveller, or a mad man, or both, and he chose to go and save the world because, even though he wasn't a god, and even though he was deluded, he felt that it was fundamentally the right thing to do?

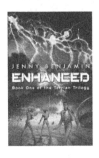

ENHANCED:
BOOK ONE OF THE TERRIAN TRILOGY
by Jenny Benjamin

Three Chicago teenagers fight to save the world in this original and epic sci-fi adventure.

DECEPTIVE CADENCE
by Kora Reydgar

Is it really easier to blame yourself for a good deed than to accept that you care about your brother? Is it easier to consider yourself a monster than to allow yourself to feel love? An elegant novella that, like a piece of fine music, plays upon the classical Biblical theme of fraternal rivalry.

First Publications of stories in *Firestorm* collection:

"Firestorm." *Zahir: A Journal of Speculative Fiction 25* (January 2011). Web. Also appeared in: *Zahir Anthology 2011.* Ed. Sheryl Tempchin. Encinitas, California: Zahir, 2011. 53-70.

"Ride the Snake." *Dark Matter Magazine 5* (September 2021).

"The Cold Waters of Europa." *Broad Knowledge: 35 Women Up To No Good.* Joanne Merriam, Ed. Nashville: Upper Rubber Boot Books, 2018. 114-24.

"Maiden Voyage of the Fearless." Not a Pipe Publishing. August 13, 2018.

"Helping Hand." *Lightspeed Magazine 61* (June 2015): 146-49.

"Informed Consent." *Ligeia 4* (Summer 2020). Web.

"Raptures of the Deep." *Mount Island 4* (October 2019). Web.

"Yes, Dear, Cancer can Kill a Transwoman." *Denial Kills.* Shearin, Dye, and Gorman, Eds. Independence, Oregon: Not a Pipe Publishing, 2021. 37-51.

"Growing Up Human." *Leading Edge Science Fiction and Fantasy.* December 2012: 10-16. Print.

"The Gender Blender." *New Theory: A Cross-Disciplinary Review.* March 22, 2018. Web.

"Death after Dying. " Florafiction.com. October 13, 2020.

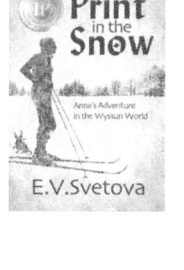

PRINT IN THE SNOW
by E. V. Svetova

the 2012 Independent Publisher Book Awards Gold medal winner

A down-to-earth teenage girl must get back home from the Otherworld before the fairytale dream turns into a nightmare. Lush watercolor illustrations of cool characters, weird monsters, and spooky villains.

OVER THE HILLS OF GREEN
by E. V. Svetova

A young psychologist at New York's Bellevue hospital, takes on a patient who may be delusional or may literally come from the Otherworld of her suppressed childhood nightmares. Their relationship will challenge her sexuality, sanity and her very notions of reality.

THE BOOK OF FAIRFAX
by E. V. Svetova

As Roman Christianity and the Old Ways clash in the 7th Century Britain, a young Angle warrior struggles to reconcile his humanity with his mystical origins. Woven into the fabric of a greater historical and an even greater metaphysical reality, one eccentric boy's coming of age story unfolds as an intensely personal, yet universally human quest for love, faith and belonging.